REID'S PLAN OF CENTRAL NEWCASTLE UPON TYNE

Scale: Six Inches to a Mile.

ARMSTRONG PARK

HEATON PARK

RAILWAY LINE TO WHITLEY BAY

THE GREAT NORTH ROAD - THE WAY TO HOLY ISLAND

THE NORTH EAST COAST EXHIBITION

DR. MALONE'S OFFICE

FENWICK'S DEPARTMENT STORE

PILGRIM ST POLICE STA

EXHIBITION PARK

ROYAL CENTRAL STATION HOTEL

UNCLE BOB'S HOUSE

TOWN MOOR

CASTLE LEAZES

LEAZES PARK

EMERSON CHAMBERS - JENNINGS AND JENNINGS

WALLACE ENQUIRY AGENCY & LEVINE COSTUMES

NEWCASTLE RAILWAY STATION

WEST ROAD LEADING TO LEMINGTON AND ELLIE FENDER'S HOUSE

D0531566

REFERENCES TO RED NUMBERS ON PLAN

(Public Buildings, etc.)

Also by Fiona Veitch Smith

The Poppy Denby Investigates series

THE PICTURE HOUSE MURDERS

FIONA VEITCH SMITH

embla
books

First published in Great Britain in 2023 by

Bonnier Books UK Limited
4th Floor, Victoria House, Bloomsbury Square, London, WC1B 4DA
Owned by Bonnier Books
Sveavägen 56, Stockholm, Sweden

A CIP catalogue record for this book is available from the British Library.

ISBN: 9781471415708

This book is typeset using Atomik ePublisher

Embla Books is an imprint of Bonnier Books UK
www.bonnierbooks.co.uk

For Gill
Remembering our Kalk Bay Writers' Stripe

Prologue

The woman in the cage swung out over the audience, enthralling them with her bird-like song. Back and forth she swung; her exquisite face, framed by a headdress of feathers, was the visage of an untouchable goddess, while her shapely legs tempted every man and woman in the theatre below. On a nearby balcony, only two men seemed immune to the Canary's charms: the gentleman detective Philo Vance, and his client, the father of a young man who had fallen victim to the showgirl's seductive blackmail.

On the other side of the silver screen, through a haze of cigarette smoke, the whirr of the projector was not quite drowned out by the dramatic music accompanying the Canary on her swing and then, when Philo Vance – played by the debonair William Powell – uttered his very first words, the cinema audience gasped and burst into appreciative applause.

Clara Vale, a dark-haired woman of around thirty, had what some would call an air of aloofness (but others, more discerning, a quiet watchfulness), smiled to herself; she too was thrilled to attend her first 'talkie'. To hear William Powell's dulcet tones made him even more attractive. Clara wondered what the Canary – the talented Louise Brooks, whom she had previously only seen in silent films – would sound like. The first full talkie, *Lights of New York*, had been released the previous year, but it had taken time for picture houses to upgrade their facilities to show them – even here in London.

Now here she was, finally, surrounded by men in tuxedos and women in furs, hearing actors speak words to accompany their actions, and with a built-in soundtrack rather than a live piano. It was intoxicating. However, once Clara got over the euphoria of the experience, she settled down to enjoy the flick, and to engage her little grey cells, as Mrs Christie's fictional detective Hercule Poirot put it, to work out who killed the Canary.

Clara was on the edge of her seat when Vance announced that there were fingerprints on the inside of a closet door, in the room where the Canary was murdered, and that the New York police should 'dust them'. But then she slumped further and further back as Vance failed to follow through on the scientific method. Yes, the fingerprints were eventually matched to a witness with a criminal record, but he, it turned out, wasn't the murderer. The murderer, one of four possible suspects who had reason to throttle the scheming Canary, could easily have been identified much earlier if fingerprints were taken of everyone. Why on earth hadn't Vance done that? And why, Clara asked herself, did Vance not follow through on the voice on the gramophone recording that was apparently a man pretending to be a woman? Scientifically, it could have been proven if the recording was slowed down. Even the greenest of science undergraduates knew that the frequency of a man's voice differed from that of a woman (85–155 Hz, compared to 165–255 Hz) and that this could be evidenced graphically.

Clara was still muttering to herself as the final credits came up. She applauded with the rest of the audience – genuinely appreciating the technological wizardry that had brought images and sound together – but she was disappointed with the plotting. As she gathered her cloche hat, gloves and coat from the cloakroom, she wondered if one of the fictional lady detectives she knew would have done a better job. Not that there were many . . . Patricia Wentworth's Miss Silver? Baroness Orczy's Lady Molly? Or Mrs Christie's Miss Marple, from those magazine stories, who – it was rumoured – was about to make her novel debut . . .

Perhaps. Perhaps not. Clara smiled to herself as she waited for a taxi – the only woman there, it seemed, unaccompanied by a man – and dared to believe *she* would have done a better job. It was simply logic, wasn't it?

Chapter 1

Friday 16th August 1929

The Hotel Russell on Russell Square was a monstrous red terracotta affair of arches, towers and domes. The main entrance was guarded by life-sized statues of the four British queens – Elizabeth, Anne, Mary and Victoria – after whom the hotel's palatial suites were named. The foyer was dominated by a Pyrenean marble staircase, and the dining room – which led to an indoor sunken garden and solarium – had been devised by the same interior designer who had worked on the *Titanic*.

Clara and her mother, Vanessa, were having breakfast in the sunken garden. They had already twice moved table as Vanessa had complained about the heat of the sun.

'We'll turn into prunes if we stay here much longer!' she had declared, imperiously.

'I'm sorry, Mrs Vale, we'll find you a table in the shade,' said the maître d', snapping his fingers to a waiter.

'That's *Lady* Vale,' corrected Vanessa, loud enough for the other patrons to hear. At which the maître d' made profuse apologies.

Clara rolled her eyes. Her banker father, Randolph Vale, had only recently received a letter from the palace informing him that the king was bestowing upon him a knighthood. He had not yet received the honour, but Vanessa had already had all their stationery redone.

'Don't worry,' said Clara to the maître d', after they were repositioned behind an elephant fern, 'I'm still a miss.'

4

Vanessa glared at her from under the brim of her ostrich feather hat, then pursed her lips. 'What have you done with your hair?'

Clara shook out her bobbed hair – inspired by the actress Louise Brooks' fashionable crop – and held her mother's gaze from under the blunt, black fringe.

'I've had it bobbed. Do you like it?'

'It makes you look like a boy,' said Vanessa with a dismissive waft of the hand.

'Well thank you, Mother. Complimentary as ever.'

Vanessa shook her head in an approximation of sympathy. 'I'm sorry, my darling, but you only have yourself to blame.'

'For what?' snapped Clara, challenging her mother to spell out what they both knew she would say anyway.

'Your lack of prospects. You've had every opportunity money could buy. Just like your sister. And look how well she's done, bagging herself a viscount. But you choose to present yourself like *that*?'

Clara started to drum her fingers on the table She would not allow herself to get worked up. Not before she'd had a chance to discuss something very important with her mother. She paused while the waiter poured them a second cup of tea, then she withdrew a letter from her handbag.

'Mother, I have received a letter from a solicitor in Newcastle.'

'You have?' asked Vanessa, as she gave a polite nod to a well-to-do elderly lady and her companion at a nearby table. 'There's the Duchess of Colchester. I do believe she may have recognised me. We were at the same shooting party last autumn, if you recall, and she mentioned that—'

'Mother!' snapped Clara. 'I'm trying to talk to you about something important.'

It was Vanessa's turn to roll her eyes. 'What is it, dear?'

'It's this letter I've received from Newcastle. Uncle Bob is dead! And the solicitor tells me that he has already written to you – three weeks ago. Why didn't you tell me?'

Vanessa paled behind her artificially rouged cheeks. 'I – well – I – I hadn't got around to it. I was waiting for the right time.'

'The right time?' hissed Clara, struggling to keep her temper in check. 'When would be the right time? I saw you last week at that bridge evening and you didn't mention it then. Nor today. Granted, it was I who invited you here, but you could have taken the opportunity to tell me my uncle had died!'

Vanessa looked to left and right then leaned across the table and lowered her voice. 'Do keep your voice down, dear, you're making a scene.'

'I am *not* making a scene!' said Clara, knowing she very much was.

Vanessa nodded and smiled at the Duchess of Colchester's companion, who glanced over at their table. 'Yes, you are,' she said through a fixed smile. 'And if you want me to entertain your histrionics any further, you will moderate your tone.'

Clara took a deep, calming breath. 'All right,' she said, finally.

Her mother nodded her approval. 'Good. So, as I was saying, I was waiting for the right time. You haven't seen Bob for years, not since you were a child, so frankly, I wasn't sure how well you'd remember him.'

Clara blinked with incredulity. 'I remember him very well, thank you. He used to come to our holiday house.'

'When you were a child . . . and now you're over thirty.'

'I'm not *over* thirty. I have just turned thirty. But that's by the by. I was fifteen the last time I saw Uncle Bob in Cornwall. And after that we kept up a correspondence and occasionally met. You knew this, Mother. I told you.'

'Did you?' she asked, vaguely, nodding to a splendidly dressed couple as they passed by.

'*Yes I did!* And he also came to my graduation ceremony at Oxford.' Clara was getting herself worked up again. 'Not that *you'd* remember *that.*'

Vanessa threw up her hands in despair, forgetting – for a split second – the social gatekeepers who were eavesdropping on their conversation. 'Oh, for heaven's sake, girl! When are you going to let that go? You know I wasn't able to attend because it was your sister's coming-out ball that weekend. And if anyone should feel slighted, it's Laura. Her only sister wasn't even there to see her presented to society. She was inconsolable for weeks!'

Clara snorted with disbelief. 'Oh, I doubt that. So,' she said, reining herself in again, 'did you go to his funeral?'

'Whose?'

'Bob's! Your only brother. Did you go to Bob's funeral?'

Vanessa paled again, and this time swallowed hard. After a few moments, and in remarkably measured tones, she replied: 'No, dear, I did not. It would have been hypocritical of me to do so. We never got on, as you know. We had completely different approaches to life. I never approved of his and he never approved of mine. On top of that, he blamed me for not doing enough to help with your grandparents when they were infirm. Unfairly so, and everybody knows it. What could I do? I was here, he was there. Newcastle is not just a hop, skip and a jump away, you know.'

'So, you didn't go to the funeral?'

'No, Bob wouldn't have wanted me to. And besides, we were having the drawing room redecorated that week.'

That was the last straw. Clara stood up and threw down her napkin. 'Thank you, Mother, for finally telling me the truth. Now, if you'll excuse me, I am going to be late for work.'

Vanessa flashed a look across to the Duchess of Colchester's table and lowered her voice again.

'Please don't embarrass me like this, Clara. People will think you actually *have* to work.'

'I *do* have to work, Mother,' she said, as if on stage at the London Palladium. 'That is, if I want to pay my own way.' And with that, she left her mother to finish her crumpet and mop up any social disaster she'd left in her wake.

Outside the Hotel Russell, in the bright morning sun, Clara calmed herself as she walked briskly from Russell Square to Bloomsbury Library, making a point of greeting the regulars on her route. There was the security guard at the British Museum, the street sweeper on Great Russell Street, the lad who cleaned up the horse droppings, and the manager of the tobacconist on the corner, muttering under his breath as the metal shutter creaked and groaned as he wound the crank.

'You should give that some oil, Mr Barnes,' she said.

'Morning, Miss Vale. You're right, I should. I'll have to pick some up at the ironmonger's.'

'I can lend you some. I'll drop it off after work.'

'That's very kind of you, Miss Vale,' he said, nodding his appreciation.

'You're most welcome.' Clara smiled then carried on, feeling calmer with every step further away from her mother. She waited to cross the road as horses and carts jigged for space with motor vehicles and omnibuses in the London traffic, then hurried on her way. She absolutely couldn't be late.

She had been working at the library for nearly two years. It was a small building, nowhere near as grand or well stocked as the British Library housed in the museum, but it served the ordinary folk of the borough with light novels, non-fiction and a small collection of newspapers and periodicals. Clara wished she worked at the grand British Library, with its astounding array of books and manuscripts, both ancient and modern, and in particular the science section. She became almost giddy when she thought of the original texts by Newton, Faraday and Babbage.

She had once applied for a job there but had not been successful. She had not been successful in most jobs she'd applied for since graduating with a degree in Chemistry – something her mother repeatedly reminded her of, asking why she couldn't just live off the annual allowance her father gave her. Like any sensible girl would.

Well, Clara was not a 'sensible girl'. At least not in the way her parents wanted her to be. So, she continued to try to find suitable employment for a university graduate educated in the sciences, determined to make her own way in the world. As she had been in the very first intake of female undergraduates in 1920 who would be permitted to earn a degree at the end of their studies, she felt she had a responsibility not just to herself, but also to the whole of female academia. However, outside the stimulating and supportive environment of the women's colleges of Oxford, including her own, Somerville, the rest of the world wasn't quite as impressed by a lady with letters after her name. The most recent rejection was a chemist on Tottenham Court Road, who said they would prefer a man. And that wasn't the first job she'd been turned down for because of her sex. Clara sighed. She was getting upset just thinking about it, so she tried to put it out of her mind.

However, as her Mary Jane heels clicked along the pavement past the British Museum, she could not put Uncle Bob out of her mind or her heart. Her mother was right, Vanessa and Bob had never got on – they were chalk and cheese. But Clara's father, the soon-to-be Sir Randolph, had attempted to patch things up between the siblings over the years and would occasionally invite Bob to stay with them at their town house in Kensington, their country manor on the outskirts of Henley-on-Thames, or their beach cottage in Cornwall. Clara always looked forward to Uncle Bob's visits. He had a million and one stories to tell her and her brother and sister. Although not formally educated beyond secondary school, Uncle Bob was exceptionally well read, and could speak on nearly any subject. Clara, who was dubbed a disappointingly 'bookish girl' by her parents, found in her uncle a kindred spirit.

Clara had not seen Bob in person since she had been awarded her degree seven years earlier, in that magnificent ceremony in the Sheldonian Theatre, where he was the only member of her family to see her receive her honour. After that, life had somehow got in the way. Life and her shame at not getting the job in science she always expected she would. The uncle and niece continued to correspond, but the gaps between the letters had become longer and longer. She didn't want to disappoint him with yet another tale of rejection.

From his side, he told her of his various travels – which Clara imagined were a little like those of Phileas Fogg in *Around the World in Eighty Days* – but spoke very little of his life in Newcastle, other than to say he did 'criminolegal' work, sometimes for a local solicitor. What that work consisted of, he never really explained. Instead, he shared his views on this or that scientific advancement and asked Clara for her views in return.

And now he was dead. Clara so wished she could have rolled back the last seven years. That she could have taken him up on his invitation to visit him in Newcastle. Or to accompany him on one of his foreign travels. Or even to have just replied to his letters more often. She was furious with her mother for not getting around to telling her – and that no one from the family had been there for the funeral. *They were having the drawing room redecorated that week?* Clara was utterly ashamed. And now, to rub salt in the wound, here was a letter saying she had been named in her uncle's will.

Dear Uncle Bob, reaching out to her once again. She would finally go to Newcastle and see where he had lived and worked. But she wouldn't mention it to her parents. She wasn't expecting to receive much in the will, but that didn't matter. She would do her best to pay her respects. It was the least she could do now.

Finally, she reached Bloomsbury Library, with five minutes to spare before the start of her shift. She sighed inwardly as she hung her hat and coat up in the staff cloakroom. Despite what she'd just said to her mother about wanting and needing to work, she had to admit she was bored here. She was bored with the limited collection of books and bored with the chit-chat she was expected to engage in with the regulars. Clara would far rather work in the back room, cataloguing and indexing. But that job was for senior librarians only – in this case a very senior one called Mr Rose. Mr Rose should have retired five years ago, but he refused to budge.

Now Clara needed him to budge on something else. She wanted to take some time off work. She found Mr Rose reading through the morning papers before she would be expected to put them out for the public. It took her a while to get the old fellow's attention, but when she did, she told him that her uncle had died and she needed some time off to help settle his estate.

Mr Rose stared at her over his spectacles. 'How much time?'

'A week? Perhaps ten days?'

He snorted irritably. 'I can give you five.'

Clara assured him she'd be back in plenty of time: a quick trip there and a quick trip back. He would barely know she'd been gone at all.

Chapter 2

Newcastle upon Tyne, Monday 19th August 1929

Her legs were lithe and long, draped at an anatomically dubious angle. The burnished orange of her bathing suit, cinched just above the knees, offset her lightly tanned arms and calves, while her impossibly white smile was framed by a cloche sun hat, casting not a shadow on her flawless face. Below the woman, who was perched on the wall of a seaside promenade, were the tiny figures of beach revellers, playing games or walking hand in hand past candy-striped tents, while children in knickerbockers and bold young men in bathing vests braved the cold North Sea.

'Next stop Newcastle upon Tyne, ladies and gentlemen. Please gather your belongings.'

Clara nodded her thanks to the train guard, then turned her attention back to the smiling young woman in the LNER poster. As she buttoned up her fur-trimmed coat, she wondered how far Whitley Bay was from Newcastle upon Tyne. Not that Clara had packed a bathing suit, of course, but that could be remedied.

'Are you going to the exhibition?' asked a lady in the next booth as her husband folded his newspaper and straightened his fedora hat.

'The exhibition?' asked Clara.

The woman smiled and pointed to another poster on the opposite side of the carriage. 'Yes, the North East Coast Exhibition. That's where we're going.'

'In Whitley Bay?' asked Clara, hopefully.

'No,' said the woman. 'In the Toon.'

Clara had no idea where the *Toon* was. But she smiled anyway.

The Flying Scotsman was crossing a river and gasps went around the carriage at first sight of the newly built Tyne Bridge, like the top half of a giant iron wheel, silhouetted against the August sky. Through the spokes Clara could see the higgledy-piggledy buildings of the northern city, and she wondered if she'd be able to find her way around.

'So, you're not here for the exhibition?' asked the woman.

'No,' said Clara, 'I'm here on family business.'

Clara was very relieved to learn that the Royal Central Station Hotel had not been misnamed and was, literally, a few dozen steps from the classically pillared entrance of Newcastle Central Station. Not like the Central Hotel in Paris where she'd once stayed, which turned out to be nowhere near the centre and was barely a hotel – but at least it had been in Paris. She had put that down to her poor grasp of French when she made the booking, and the spurning of her mother's suggestion that she really ought to have consulted the Bradshaw.

She was greeted by a liveried doorman in top hat and tails at the bottom of a short flight of marble steps, who carried her suitcase up and into the hotel. The foyer was all faience tiles and wood panelling, but a spectacular mosaic floor with fleur-de-lis motifs and an impressive atrium towering six floors above a magnificent chandelier gave a light, modern feel to an otherwise traditional Victorian hotel. Clara nodded in approval, thanked and tipped the doorman, then turned her attention to the receptionist.

'Will Mr Vale be joining you shortly?' he asked, after taking her name and checking against his booking list.

'It's *Miss* Vale. Miss Clara Vale. And no. No one will be joining me.'

The mutton-chopped gent – who appeared not to have been updated in the last twenty years – cleared his throat.

'Very well, *Miss* Vale, I have your reservation right here.' He busied himself getting her a key, then asked: 'May I ask if you were named after the village?'

'The village?'

'Clara Vale.'

'I had no idea there was a village of that name.'

'Indeed there is, miss. Just south of the river. Not far from here.'

'Well, how very interesting,' said Clara as the receptionist instructed a bell boy to take Miss Vale to room 310. On the way up in the lift the boy also asked if she were there for the exhibition. Again, she said no. But apparently almost all of the other guests in the nearly full hotel were – 'some of 'em has come from foreign lands', the lad informed her. Clara informed him that she'd only come from as far as London.

As Clara unpacked in the well-appointed bedroom – with a view of the densely packed rooftops of the city – she decided that once she'd finished her business at the solicitor's she would have to visit this exhibition or she'd never get any peace. And as for being named after a village, she'd have to ask her mother about that!

Tuesday 20th August 1929

The next morning, after a hearty North East breakfast, including black pudding and scrambled eggs, Clara followed the directions of the hotel receptionist into the centre of Newcastle. She could have caught the tram that ran past the hotel, but she worried that she would not know exactly where to get off and miss her stop. So, instead, wearing a pair of sensible walking shoes, she headed along Neville Street, past a memorial to George Stephenson – of the steam engine fame – then along Collingwood Street, with something called the Literary and Philosophical Society on her right. She was surprised that a city like Newcastle, famed for its industry and working-class image, would have something like a 'literary and philosophical society'. But a lot was already surprising her about the city. Yes, there was a grim layer of coal dust over everything, but that was no worse (and perhaps a lot better) than the foul sulphuric smog that would settle over London from time to time. And the buildings, in beautiful honey-coloured Georgian stone, were as lovely as any in the capital.

She turned left into Grey Street and took a steep climb up a cobbled, curved street, hemmed on both sides by more Georgian architecture. It was a Tuesday morning, and the pavements were awash with gentlemen in dark suits, carrying newspapers under their arms and with bowler hats on their heads, marching to work in offices. Women, neatly but not poshly dressed in summer frocks, were out and about to do their shopping. Or perhaps, Clara thought, the younger ones, wearing Chanel-inspired two-pieces, might be going to work in the shops. The shops were a mixture of more well-to-do storefronts with mannequins in windows and pavement stalls with striped awnings, where Geordie men in flat caps called out to passers-by: 'Two for a shillin'! Howay, pet, they's fresh I swear ya!' Or at least that's what Clara thought they said. The dialect sounded almost foreign to her ears.

As instructed, she kept her eye open for the Grecian columns of the Theatre Royal on her right and the Victorian mosaic masterpiece of the Royal Arcade on her left. Carrying on up the hill, with the towering pillar of the Earl Grey monument as her marker – he of the tea fame – she looked to 'eleven o'clock' and found Emerson Chambers, an extravagant Edwardian fusion of baroque and art nouveau, towering six floors above Blackett Street. Clara stood for a moment and took it all in. It truly was an architectural extravaganza with its pillars and intricate mouldings. The ostentatious clock on the roof wouldn't have looked out of place in Zurich, she thought.

The concierge at the hotel had told her the basement housed the high-class Emerson's restaurant – a dining option for one of her evenings out, perhaps – complete with its own orchestra. While the ground floor housed a photography supply shop and studio, offering portrait sittings for five shillings.

She checked the letter she'd been sent by Uncle Bob's solicitors – Jennings & Jennings – and noted that their office was on the third floor. Ten minutes later she was sitting in a comfortable chair in their office drinking a well-brewed cup of Earl Grey tea. Barnaby Jennings, her Uncle Bob's solicitor, smiled beneficently at her across his solid mahogany desk. His half-moon glasses and full grey beard reminded her of old King Edward who had been on the throne when she was a young girl.

'Well, Miss Vale, I can certainly see the family resemblance. You have the same dark hair and dark eyes as your mother – and her pale complexion.'

'You knew my mother?'

Jennings interlaced his fingers over his full belly and twirled his watch chain with his thumb.

'I did. We were at the same infant school, believe it or not!'

'Goodness me!'

Jennings smiled. 'And she grew up to be a fine young woman. No wonder your father snaffled her. I believe they met in Harrogate, when both families were taking the waters. And within a matter of weeks he had whisked her off to London to be his bride. London's gain was very much Newcastle's loss,' said the solicitor wistfully.

'That's the story we heard growing up, too,' said Clara, suppressing the desire to correct the gentleman's rose-tinted impression of her mother. If anyone had snaffled anyone it was her mother who had set her sights on the eligible and wealthy banker, Randolph Vale, in the heady atmosphere of the Yorkshire hot springs. Vanessa had been very open about it to her daughters when coaching them on how to attract a suitable beau – a lesson that Clara's younger sister Laura had taken to heart and successfully implemented when she 'snaffled' her eligible young stockbroker husband on a holiday in Leamington Spa. And to put the cherry on the cake, he was the son of a viscount, too!

Clara had yet to do any snaffling and frankly was not in the least bit interested. At thirty years old she was already being referred to as the maiden aunt by Laura's growing brood of future little stockbrokers. While her brother, Antony, treated her as a dull curiosity when he introduced her to his friends and colleagues as his 'spinster sister – you know, the suffragette type'.

'So,' said Mr Jennings, 'how is your mother? Better after her illness?'

'Her illness?'

'Yes, that dreadful influenza that prevented her from coming to your uncle's funeral. I expect you had it too. Frightfully contagious, I believe.'

'Yes, frightfully.' Neither Vanessa Vale nor any of the Vale household – servants or family – had had influenza in the last six months. 'She is much better, thank you. And of course, feels awful that she wasn't able to come to Uncle Bob's funeral. As do we all.'

'I quite understand,' said Mr Jennings, kindly.

Clara felt terrible about lying to the good-hearted solicitor and quietly cursed her mother for putting her in this position.

'I never did quite understand Bob's animosity towards Vanessa. She always seemed like a perfectly lovely young lady to me. Sibling rivalry, I suppose. But I deeply regretted that they had never been able to lay aside their bad blood over the years. However, I suppose Bob's offer to you goes some way to healing that rift. Which brings me to the business of the day . . .'

Finally, thought Clara, who was wondering how much longer she would have to keep up the pretence of her 'lovely mother' who had been too ill to attend her only brother's funeral.

'As I explained in my letter, your Uncle Bob named you in his will. You are the main beneficiary, although he has also left some small endowments to various charities and a monetary gift to his housekeeper. None of that need concern you and I can assure you that it is only a small portion of his estate.'

She smiled, nodding her understanding. 'Did Uncle Bob work for you, Mr Jennings?'

Mr Jennings gave her a curious look. 'You don't know what your uncle did for a living?'

'I believe he worked with a solicitor as some kind of paralegal. He called it "criminolegal" work. I'm not sure what that entailed. Some kind of clerical job?'

Mr Jennings shook his head. 'Oh no, Miss Vale, you are misinformed. Bob Wallace sometimes did work *with* me, not for me, on a contractual basis, a very well-paid contractual basis, I might add. He provided professional services as an enquiry agent. But I was only one of his clients.'

'An *enquiry* agent?' Clara was dumbfounded. 'You mean, Uncle Bob was a private detective?'

Mr Jennings chuckled. 'Indeed, he was. And a very experienced one too. I thought you knew.'

Clara shook her head. 'It's the first I've heard of it! Mr Jennings, what exactly has Uncle Bob left me?'

Mr Jennings opened a file, adjusted his spectacles, cleared his throat and read: '*In the event of my demise, I Robert Wendell Wallace, being of sound mind, on this thirteenth day of June in the year of our Lord 1929, leave my house at 22 St Thomas' Crescent, Newcastle upon Tyne, with all of its contents, and the remainder of my personal assets (after payment of bequests to the below-mentioned beneficiaries)* – those are the charities and small bequests I mentioned, Miss Vale – now where was I? Ah yes . . . *the remainder of my personal assets, including the business known as Wallace Enquiry Agency, registered at 41b Percy Street, Newcastle upon Tyne.*'

Clara felt suddenly and inexplicably faint. She blinked a few times and took a deep breath until her equilibrium returned. 'I – I – I've inherited a *detective* agency?'

Mr Jennings' eyes twinkled behind his half-moon glasses. 'You have indeed, Miss Vale. And I believe this letter, which your uncle asked me to give to you at the reading of the will, will explain to you why he decided you were the best person to inherit it.'

He passed across a sealed envelope with Clara's name inscribed in an energetic hand.

Clara, her hands now shaking, took the envelope from him.

'Well, I'd better have a read then.'

Chapter 3

My dearest niece,

If you are reading this, it will be because I have died. As I write, I have no intention of leaving this world before my time – and have no plans to do so – but time is not our own to make. I have been unwell these last few months; the doctor says it is my heart. However, he says that if I look after myself I could still live a good long time. On the off-chance that he's wrong (like the time he told me treatment for my ingrown toenail would not hurt a bit), I am writing this letter and updating my will with Jennings & Jennings. You will no doubt have met Barnaby Jennings if you are reading this letter. Be assured he is a good man, a good solicitor and a good friend. If he can help you in any way – beyond the scope of this will – he will do so; do not be afraid to ask.

But I digress. So now, dear Clara, we both know I am dead. I hope you enjoyed the tea and cakes Mrs Hobson put on at my funeral. That is my housekeeper, and I hope you find a way to either keep her in employment or secure another position for her. If you are unable to do so, I trust that Jennings will take it upon himself.

By now I expect you will have heard that I am leaving my house and business to you. Why? You may rightly ask. Well, as you know, I never married, and my sister and her children are my only family. I could have left all to charity, but something in me cried out for someone of my own flesh and blood to carry my memory forward. My sister would not be an option. You know she and I have never got on (did she dislike the cakes as much as I expected her to? She never did like lemon drizzle), so that leaves you, Antony and Laura.

To be brief, as by now I'm probably cold in the grave and you are wishing I would just hurry up and get on with it, your brother is feckless and your sister inane. He is only interested in making money to spend on gambling and frivolity; she only in as much as it will buy her a fancy house and frocks. But you, dear Clara, are cut from a different cloth. I like to think that some of my blood flows in your veins.

How do I know this? Well, remember that week together back in '15 at your parents' summer cottage in Cornwall (although how a six-bedroomed house could be called a 'cottage' I have no idea)? I was greatly impressed with you. I loved the talks and walks we had along the cliffs. I delighted in your questions and your answers. You were curious about everything from the stars in the sky to the ants at our feet. You had thoughts too about the dreadful war, and why we were allowing our young men to be sent like lambs to the slaughter. And you spoke to me about the books you had been reading: from Darwin to Planck! And Jules Verne and Conan Doyle. It was such an eclectic mix for a girl of your age.

I looked forward thereafter to the occasional invitations from your father to visit you all in either London or Cornwall. He hoped your mother and I would settle our differences; I hoped to spend more time with you. And I enjoyed every minute we spent together – though alas, they were too few.

I followed your school career with interest and was delighted with every letter you wrote me. I was sorry that the letters tailed off as you got older, but I expected you didn't have much time to write to your old uncle when you were an Oxford undergraduate. Who would have thought that a child of my sister would ever have gone up *to Oxford! And to read science! Such a brave choice for a young woman. Attending your degree ceremony was one of the proudest moments of my life. I still remember how magnificent you looked in your cap and gown, alongside those other most esteemed ladies. And the splendid tea we had afterwards in the gardens of the Radcliffe Camera.*

I was, however, saddened to hear how you struggled to find long-term employment after graduation. All those laboratories that turned you down! Then that boarding school for girls that discontinued its science programme. Then that school for boys and girls that would not hire you when they heard you were a woman. And didn't you have a short-lived stint as an assistant in a chemist shop? I wonder why that didn't continue? The last I heard you were working in a library. Such a waste of your talents! But I was still heartened to hear that you were at least trying to make a living on your own, and not depending solely on a stipend from your family (although your father can more than afford it). You are now thirty years of age – and still unmarried – which suggests to me you are not waiting for a husband to support you.

However, again, I digress. You may be wondering what on earth you will do with a detective agency, but I think that if anyone can make a go of it you can. Being a detective requires an enquiring mind – which you have in abundance – and someone who is best suited to working alone. I believe you are that person. And, as you will soon find out if you take on this challenge, your scientific training will be most helpful too. If you do not agree with my assessment, or do not wish to take on the challenge, then you may sell the agency – and the house, if you will – and use the money to further your prospects in whatever way you choose. But I do ask you to give it some serious thought.

As I said at the opening of this missive, Barnaby Jennings will help you in any way he can.

So now, my dear, I wish you well in your future

endeavours. I know it will annoy your mother, and that
gives me no end of delight. I jest (but only a little).
    Your distant, but no less loving, uncle
    Robert Wallace (Uncle Bob)

Clara's hands were still shaking as she refolded the letter and put it carefully back into its envelope. She looked up into the curious eyes of Barnaby Jennings.

'Do you know what is in this letter, Mr Jennings?'

'I do. Your uncle let me read it before he sealed it and gave it to me for safekeeping with his will.'

Clara nodded, her thoughts rushing back to those Cornish cliffs and the kind, funny uncle she had once known. He had been so full of life.

'Did he suffer much in his last days? With his heart?'

Jennings shook his head. 'Not much, no. He got tired easily, but I don't think he was in much pain. It was a mercy, too, that he died quietly in his sleep. But I wrote all this in my letter to your mother. Didn't she tell you?'

Clara shook her head, all effort to keep up the pretence to shore up Jennings' rose-tinted memories of her mother gone.

'No,' she said, her voice quivering on the verge of tears. However, she was not a woman who wept easily, and she brought her emotions back under control.

If Jennings was shocked at her admission that Vanessa Vale had not told Clara about her uncle's state of health and his death, he hid it behind a polite, professional mask.

'So, what are you going to do, Miss Vale? Are you going to take on the agency? I told your uncle it was a strange bequest to give to a young woman – and perhaps more of a curse than a blessing – but he seemed sure you would embrace it. Was he wrong? Or am I?'

Clara shrugged. 'I honestly can't tell you, Mr Jennings. I think I'll need a bit of time to think it all through.'

'I understand. But if you decide to sell it – which, if I'm frank, might be the best option, despite your uncle's romantic notions of you becoming a lady sleuth – I will be able to help you with that. Do not fear. Or you might want to sell the agency but keep the house. But of course, you can sell them both if you so choose. As you'll see, it's a lovely property, in a handsome part of town, and you should get a good price for it. Are you in Newcastle long?'

Clara blinked her dark brown eyes, trying to take in all the solicitor was telling her. She would definitely need more time to think everything through. 'I am to travel back on Friday morning, Mr Jennings. So I have three more full days. Might you be able to show me Uncle Bob's office? And, of course, the house.'

'Of course,' said Jennings. He checked his pocket watch. 'We can go now if you like.'

Uncle Bob's office was only a five-minute walk from Emerson Chambers. They passed a war memorial in the middle of a formal park, in the centre of a genteel commercial and residential square, then headed along Barrack Road.

'I have been very impressed with Newcastle, so far,' said Clara, making small talk, as Jennings raised his hat and nodded his greetings to people left and right.

'It's a lovely city,' said Mr Jennings. 'With very friendly folk. I'm surprised anyone would want to live elsewhere.'

'I'm surprised how well-to-do it is. Down south we've heard that there is extreme poverty here.'

'There is, Miss Vale. Like any city. And you won't have to go far from here to see it. But the same can be said for Bristol, or Manchester, or London . . .'

'That's very true,' said Clara as they turned right into Percy Street, a busy shopping concourse with pubs and a picture house jostling for space with grocery stores and tea rooms. A tramline ran down the middle, with a road for free-moving traffic – horse-drawn and motorised – on either side. Jennings stopped outside a costume shop at the corner of Percy Street and the steeply rising Leazes Park Road. At the crest of the hill, Clara glimpsed what she thought might be the wooden edifice of a football stand.

'Here we are,' said Jennings and took a key out of his pocket.

Clara, taken aback, looked into the window of the costumier

(called Levine's Costumes according to the sign), which showcased pirate outfits and Roman togas, and said: 'My uncle worked *here*? Was he one of those detectives in disguise?'

Jennings chuckled. 'No. His office is above the shop.' Jennings ushered Clara around the corner from the shop entrance to an unassuming wooden door. There was a discreet plaque on the wall which read: *Wallace Enquiry Agency*.

'Did he own the building?'

'No,' said Jennings. 'He rented the office space from the people who own the costume shop. I have kept up payments from his estate. The business is separate from the lease, so if you decide to take over the agency you don't have to stay here. And of course, if you sell it, the new buyer can set up office wheresoever he chooses. Best you decide soon though, to save you on the rent money.'

Mr Jennings pushed open the door to reveal a narrow staircase. 'After you, Miss Vale.'

Clara climbed the stairs, asking as she went: 'So what exactly does the business consist of? If I'm to sell, what exactly would I be selling, if not the office space?'

'You'll be selling your uncle's contact book, his open cases and capital assets. He does not have full-time employees, but he does have a number of agents on his books that he employs from time to time. Legally, you're not obliged to keep them on, as they were paid cash in hand for each job. We will, however, have to check whether there are any debts outstanding. My son – whom I'll arrange for you to meet tomorrow – is currently going through the books with your uncle's accountant, so we don't yet have a final value on the business. The house, on the other hand, is far more straightforward. I believe you could get two thousand pounds for it.'

'Goodness me! That much?'

'I believe that's what houses on St Thomas' Crescent are selling for these days, yes.'

Clara had reached the top of the stairs and pushed open the door. It opened into a reasonably well-lit room, about twenty feet square, with a door leading off the back. It was furnished like any ordinary office: a desk, chairs, filing cabinets and bookcases. There was a gooseneck telephone on the desk and a black cast-iron Underwood typewriter on the desk. Through the doorway at the back, she glimpsed a lavatory and basin separated from a small kitchenette.

Jennings followed her gaze. 'Yes, there are indoor ablutions. Which pushes the rental up.'

'A price worth paying to spend a penny,' she observed drily.

'Quite,' said Jennings, with a twinkle of humour.

Clara stood in the middle of the room and did a slow 360-degree turn. Then she turned to Mr Jennings. 'I don't really know what to say. I mean, where do I start? Do I sell? Do I keep it? If I keep it, how do I run it? What do I even *do* as an enquiry agent?'

Jennings smiled, sympathetically. 'I know, it's a lot to take in. And my advice would be to sell the agency. But take your time and think about it for a while. As for what you actually do here, I can perhaps set up a meeting with one of your uncle's regular agents. He can give you a better idea of the day-to-day running of the business. Would you like me to do that?'

'Oh yes please,' said Clara, with immense relief. 'I should be most grateful if you could.'

Chapter 4

To Clara's surprise, Mr Jennings was able to track down one of Uncle Bob's agents in a very short space of time. He called his office – using Uncle Bob's telephone – and asked his secretary to look in the Lady Loughborough file to find the phone number of one Jack Danskin. Within five minutes he had Danskin on the blower and asked him if he was able to pop down to 'Old Bob Wallace's office'. It seemed that Danskin could.

As Jennings and Clara waited for the agent to arrive, the solicitor explained that the Lady Loughborough case was one of Uncle Bob's recent jobs: a divorce where Danskin had been used to gather evidence on Lady Loughborough's philandering husband. 'So you see, Miss Vale, why running an enquiry agency might not be the most suitable occupation for a polite young lady of social standing.'

Clara gave Jennings a polite, non-committal nod, biting back a retort that she was not that young, nor, in her more unguarded moments, particularly polite. And as for social standing, well, she'd shunned that by refusing to play the 'let's catch a husband' game and insisting on getting a job and working for a living instead of leeching off her father's considerable assets. She was certainly not, and never would be, *Lady Clara*. Clara sat down at her uncle's desk and ran a finger over the oak surface, drawing a line in a light layer of dust. It had been around six weeks since he had died, and it seemed that the office had been shut up since then. She looked over her shoulder at the filing cabinet and said: 'I should imagine Uncle Bob has a Lady Loughborough file of his own.'

Jennings nodded. 'I should imagine he has. Had. I should imagine he had.'

Clara felt a surge of curiosity and desperately wanted to open the filing cabinet. She drummed her fingers against the desk, wishing Jennings would leave so she could snoop in peace. Then she berated herself. The kindly solicitor was just looking out for what he considered her best interests. He wasn't to know – only having met her for the first time less than two hours ago – that he had perhaps misjudged her. Had he misjudged her? Or had her uncle?

Clara gave herself an inner shake. Just a short while ago she had been standing in the middle of the office, feeling like a small girl, completely out of her depth, asking: what am I to do with this place? But something had happened when she heard the phrase 'the Lady Loughborough case'. Something had stirred in her. The same thing that had stirred in her when she watched *The Canary Murder Case* last week. Call it scientific curiosity if you will – the same curiosity that compelled her first at school, and then at university to conduct experiments in chemistry and physics. The questions 'I wonder what would happen if . . .' or 'I wonder why that happens the way it does . . .' were never far from her mind. Then she thought back to a walk with her uncle on the cliffs of Cornwall where she asked the very same type of questions. 'Uncle Bob, do you ever wonder why . . . ?' And the Sherlock Holmes stories she and Uncle Bob delighted in recounting to one another. Holmes was scientifically minded, as she was, and like her he didn't give two hoots for social standing.

But Sherlock Holmes was a fictional detective. And *The Canary Murder Case* was just a moving picture. This was the real world. Of filing cabinets and ledgers and a job at a library back in London that she would lose if she didn't return there next week.

There was a knock at the door, jolting her out of her reverie. 'Come in!' she called, startling Barnaby Jennings with her proprietorial tone.

The door opened to reveal a dark-haired man in his mid-thirties, sporting a trim moustache and the suggestion of an afternoon shadow on a square jaw. He wore a reasonably well-cut suit and tie that put him above the level of artisan or shopkeeper, but below that of the professional classes – as did his fedora hat, which was wearing a little thinly around the rim. Clara immediately chastised herself for applying her mother's method of pigeonholing people and stood to greet the gentleman.

Jennings had already intercepted him and was shaking his hand. 'Thanks for coming at such short notice, Danskin. May I introduce Miss Clara Vale, Bob Wallace's niece. Miss Vale has very kindly come up from London to help settle her uncle's estate.'

'I'm pleased to meet you, Miss Vale. How do you do. Please accept my condolences on the passing of your uncle. He was a good man.' His voice, Clara noted, matched his suit. Clearly North Eastern, but more easily understood than the colourful Geordie dialect she'd heard shouted from the barrow boys and grocers on her way up Grey Street.

Clara nodded her thanks. 'How do you do. Thank you, Mr Danskin, my uncle will be sorely missed. And thank you too for coming.' Clara was aware of Jennings hovering, like a worried mother bird, waiting to chirp back into the conversation, so she cut in before he could start.

'Mr Jennings here tells me you were one of my uncle's agents. I was wondering if you might talk me through exactly what goes on at a detective agency.'

'Er yes, Danskin, that's exactly why I asked you here. Miss Vale is curious about what her uncle did. Quite understandable, a niece wanting to know more about her uncle's life, wouldn't you say?'

Well, thought Clara, *that's not exactly why I want to know . . .* but before she could vocalise her thoughts the telephone rang, startling them all.

'Bob wanting to have a word?' quipped Danskin, raising one of his dark brows.

Clara bit back a giggle.

Jennings gave a nervous laugh. 'Shall I get it?'

'No, I will,' said Clara, turning on her heel and picking up the receiver.

'Er, hello,' she said. 'Er, Wallace Enquiry Agency. How may I help you?'

Clara looked across at the two men. Jennings clutched his worried hands, apparently startled at her boldness. While Danskin gave a rakish grin, clearly amused.

'Oh, hello. Is that Miss Vale? It's Mr Jennings' secretary here. Is he still there?'

'He is. Do you wish to speak with him?'

'No, that's not necessary. But can you please ask him to come back to the office immediately. Tell him it's the Balshard brief. And I'm afraid it's urgent.' The line was muffled for a moment, as if a hand had been placed over the mouthpiece. Then Clara heard: 'Of course, Mr Balshard. I understand, Mr Balshard. Mr Jennings is on his way.' The secretary spoke directly to Clara in an anxious whisper: 'Please, Miss Vale, tell him it's urgent.' Then she rang off.

Clara hooked the earpiece on its cradle and turned to Jennings. 'It was your secretary, Mr Jennings. She asked you to come back to the office, please. She said to tell you it's the Balshard brief, and it's urgent.'

Jennings visibly paled. 'Balshard? Oh heavens, I'd better get back. So . . .' he looked first to Danskin then to Clara '. . . we'd better leave this meeting for another time. Is that all right?'

'No need for that,' said Danskin, removing his hat and hanging it on a coat stand, 'I think Miss Vale and I can handle this on our own. If that's all right with you, Miss Vale?'

She was slightly taken aback by his presumption, but then realised that Danskin had just voiced exactly what she was about to say.

'Yes, Mr Danskin, that is perfectly all right. My time in Newcastle is short. Don't worry, Mr Jennings, if you leave the key, I'll lock up. And,' she said, softening her tone with a smile towards the kindly but worrisome solicitor, 'good luck with Balshard.'

Jennings clutched his hands again, but then eventually nodded and hurried off.

Danskin and Clara were left alone, standing in the middle of Uncle Bob's office. Without the hat, thought Clara, the agent bore a striking resemblance to the actor Ronald Colman, whom she'd recently seen in the silent picture *Beau Geste*. And, she believed, was starring in a talkie version of *Bulldog Drummond*. Yet another fictional detective . . .

'So . . .' said Danskin.

'So . . .' said Clara. She gestured to the two chairs on either side of the desk. 'I suppose I should sit here,' she said, slipping behind the desk to the chair she'd recently vacated.

'That's where your Uncle Bob sat,' said Danskin, with a sad smile. 'I meant what I said, Miss Vale, your uncle was a top bloke.'

'Thank you, Mr Danskin, please take a seat. Now, I'm not sure if you've heard, but my uncle has left the agency to me. It's up to me whether I keep it or sell it, but I would like to find out a bit more about it before I make my decision. Mr Jennings doesn't think I should keep it on, but my Uncle Bob seemed to think it might be something suited to me. And he knew me a bit better than Mr Jennings. But I confess, I'm not yet sure which of them is right. So, can you tell me what you did for Bob and what running a business like this might entail?'

Danskin leaned back, unbuttoned his jacket and relaxed into the chair. His expression was measured and thoughtful although, annoyingly, his eyes did fleetingly glance over her body before he spoke. 'Well, Miss Vale, as I know you even less than Jennings does, I will not hazard a guess as to your suitability for the role. You are of course a woman . . .'

'And there are no lady detectives?' snapped Clara.

Danskin shrugged. 'Well, there are, but they're not as common as men. And there's a reason for that—'

'What about the infamous Maud West? She's been running an agency in London for years.'

'Aye, she has, and she's a cracking sleuth by all accounts, but . . . well, there's no lady who owns an agency in these parts. That's all I'm saying. That'll be a first for the Toon.'

Clara gave him a measured look. 'Let's cut to the chase, Mr Danskin. Are you saying I could not take over my uncle's business just because I'm a woman?'

'Oh I'm not saying that . . .'

'Good. I'm glad we've cleared that up. So you wouldn't mind if I became your employer?'

Danskin threw back his head and laughed. 'Oh, you wouldn't be my employer, Miss Vale. Jack Danskin is his own man. But I might consider providing my services to you if you continued to pay at the same rate as your uncle.'

Clara nodded, glad they'd reached some kind of understanding. 'I'm sure that could be arranged, Mr Danskin. But first, could you give me a brief summary of what the agency does and how Uncle Bob went about it?'

Danskin ran his thumb over his chin, taking a while to compose his answer. 'Well – as the name says – we make enquiries. Clients pay the agent to make enquiries, to find out information that they might not easily be able to find otherwise. Or to provide evidence of someone's guilt or innocence of something.'

'Such as?'

'Such as whether a husband or wife is guilty of having an affair. We get a lot of that. We collect evidence to be used in divorce proceedings, to prove one party has been unfaithful.'

Clara's brows furrowed. 'And how do you get that evidence? By spying on them?'

Danskin shrugged. 'That's one way. Otherwise we pay people at certain establishments to pass on information about who has been there and when. A couple signing in for a weekend away, for instance. A waiter who has served a couple, and so forth.' Danskin looked directly at Clara. 'If this shocks you, Miss Vale, then I suggest you call it a day, because that's the bread and butter of any agency.'

Clara consciously unfurrowed her brows. She was no innocent. She had known of enough people who had been divorced – or had read about it in the papers – to know what went on. No, she wasn't shocked, but she was a little underwhelmed. It was hardly Sherlock Holmes. Or Philo Vance.

'No, not shocked at all. I am aware of such things. You say this is the bread and butter, but what else?'

Danskin grinned, managing to look charming and rakish at the same time. Clara was beginning to think the handsome agent cultivated that look.

'Well, there is also work in some of the larger department stores and higher-class retail outfits. Bob has a few ladies on his books who do in-store security, on the lookout for shoplifters. The thieves are usually women, so women detectives are needed. They work at the shop undercover, pretending to be customers. There's a fair bit of that. The same women sometimes get placed at big houses too – posing as housemaids – if there's pilfering suspected among the staff.'

'So Bob employed women detectives?'

'Aye,' said Danskin, nodding towards the filing cabinet behind her. 'He kept all the agents' files in there.'

Clara was itching to get into the files.

'And what, Mr Danskin, did Bob hire you to do?'

'Ah, I helped Bob with more specialised work, usually passed on to him by Mr Jennings. Tracking down the beneficiaries of estates, for instance.' The rakish grin again. 'If you hadn't been found so easily, I might have been on your scent now too.'

Clara felt a little flush creep up her neck. She cleared her throat. 'Anything else?'

Danskin nodded. 'Bribery, blackmail, abductions. They're not as common, but Bob and I worked on a few such cases. Oh, and a couple of murders.'

'Goodness!' said Clara, trying to appear nonchalant. 'Really?'

'Yes,' said Danskin, beating her in the nonchalance stakes. 'But just a couple. One was an inheritance case where it was assumed a fellow had died in an accident. Bob was hired by an insurance company to investigate the circumstances before paying out to the heir. But Bob discovered that it was in fact the heir who had killed his relative, making it look like an accident. It was all over the papers. I'm surprised you didn't read about it.'

Clara shook her head. 'So am I. Perhaps it didn't make it down to London.' She leaned forward in her chair. 'Anything else?'

'Yes. There was a poisoning case last year. The wife was arrested for it, but, fortunately, the wife's lover had a lot of money and could afford to hire Bob. We were able to prove that it was in fact the husband's lover who had done it, when he refused to get a divorce.'

Clara blinked rapidly. This was all proving to be rather sordid. Sordid . . . and exciting. 'But those are the rare cases, are they? The bulk of them are what you describe as "bread 'n' butter".'

'Aye, Miss Vale.' He nodded. 'In all seriousness, you need to think about this very carefully. Yes, there are a few exciting cases, but it's mainly drudge work. And most of it is dealing with either very nasty or very sad people. Bob seemed to think you're up for it though. And Bob was a very good judge of character. But I'll leave it for you to decide.'

He stood up. Clara stood too. 'Thank you, Mr Danskin. You have given me a lot of food for thought. And I do appreciate your time.'

Danskin plucked his hat from the coat stand and tipped it to Clara before putting it on his head. 'You're very welcome, Miss Vale. Do let me know if I can be of any further help. As I said, if you pay as fair as Bob, I'll be willing to give you a chance. I can't promise others will, though. And there's other agencies in town.'

'Really?'

'Oh, yes. You'll have competition if you decide to stay. But Bob always paid more than them. However, for some agents on the books, that won't be the only deciding factor.'

'What do you mean?'

'You being a woman, of course.' He grinned. 'Not everyone is as forward-thinking as yer Uncle Bob.'

Chapter 5

Uncle Bob's files were beckoning. The filing cabinet was locked, but Clara found the key on the bunch Barnaby Jennings had left with her. She opened the cabinet and was pleased to see that everything seemed neatly sorted into alphabetical order. As a librarian – and a scientist – she appreciated the efficiency of it. She wondered where she would find information on the agents who worked for her uncle. 'A' for agent or perhaps 'E' for employee? She searched both sections and couldn't find anything that seemed to fit the bill.

Under 'A' there was a thick file entitled 'Armstrongs' and a quick flick through suggested it was work done involving the big armaments factory of that name in Gateshead. It appeared as if there had been theft of weaponry components and bullets. *Goodness me*, thought Clara, *that's a cut above a divorce case*. It detailed how an agent called Johnson had been sent in undercover as a machinist and had eventually tracked down the culprit, to the satisfaction of the client and full payment of the bill.

Clara was taken aback by the size of the bill – far more than she would earn in a year at the library. She wondered what the meeting with Jennings' son and the accountant tomorrow would reveal about the value of her uncle's estate. That and the two-thousand-pound house – which she still had to see – suggested she might be in for more than she had expected. She'd come up to Newcastle more out of respect for her uncle than with a genuine expectation that she would inherit anything of substance. Could this actually be a viable business? Could she seriously take it on? Could she honestly see herself tracking down bullet thieves and poisoners? She still didn't know, but she had to admit that she hadn't been this excited about a new opportunity since that first day at Oxford University, nearly a decade ago now. *Yes*, she reminded herself, ruefully, *and look how that turned out. Don't get your hopes up too high, old girl.*

Clara sighed and flicked to the 'J' section to see if she could find Johnson. Yes, there was a file there with that name. She was just about to open it when there was a knock at the door. She went across and opened it and was slightly disappointed to see Barnaby Jennings, all red-cheeked and mutton-chopped. 'Mr Jennings!'

'Miss Vale! So glad you're still here. Dreadfully sorry I had to rush off like that, but Mr Balshard is a long-standing client who can be – ah – a little demanding.'

Clara smiled reassuringly. 'That's all right, Mr Jennings. Mr Danskin and I had a good talk, and he has helped me understand a bit more about how the business works.'

'Ah, well, yes, good. I hope he behaved himself?'

Clara suppressed a smile. 'Of course.'

'Well, I'm glad to hear it. He has, well, let's say he has a bit of a reputation with the ladies, and in ordinary circumstances I would never have left you alone with him, but well – er – these were not ordinary circumstances. I hope you understand?'

Clara nodded and resisted the urge to pat the earnest gentleman on the shoulder. 'Of course I do. Not to worry, Mr Jennings, Mr Danskin was the perfect gentleman.'

'Ah, well, yes, good.' Jennings cleared his throat. 'So, are you ready to view the St Thomas' Crescent house? It's just around the corner.'

Clara's interest was piqued again. 'Oh yes please! I should love to.'

St Thomas' Crescent was only two minutes' walk away from the hustle and bustle of Percy Street, but it seemed as though it was another world. The crescent of Georgian terraces curved gracefully up to the edge of leafy Leazes Park with its tennis courts, bowling greens, bandstand, croquet lawns and artificial lake, home to ducks and swans. Opposite the park, Mr Jennings told her, was the Royal

Victoria Infirmary and just further down the street, Armstrong College and beyond that the Hancock Museum.

Jennings took Clara to the door of a three-storey town house, near the top of the crescent. All the houses uniformly presented a brown brick façade, black-painted front doors, tall sash windows with white trim and grey slate roofs. Each house was fronted by a postage stamp garden behind black wrought-iron railings. There was something calming and peaceful in the uniformity, and Clara's first impression was that this was somewhere she would enjoy living. Jennings took out a separate bunch of keys to the office ones – which Clara now had in her handbag – and opened the door. The house exhaled its stale air into the face of its new visitors.

'It's been shut up for a while,' Jennings observed.

'What about the housekeeper, Mrs Hudson?'

'Mrs Hobson. She was never a live-in. She came in each day. I gave her three months' wages to tide her over, but as your uncle says, you'll have to decide whether you keep her on.'

Clara's heart sank as Jennings led her through the house. The order and efficiency that had characterised the office was not evident in Uncle Bob's home and every surface and corner was filled with artefacts and ornaments. Jennings noted her discomfort. 'Your uncle was a great collector. He travelled the world and brought back keepsakes from every continent. He went on digs to Egypt and the Levant. He spent time in Indochina, and he told me he once travelled up the Amazon River in a canoe! In fact, he continued travelling abroad on short trips to archaeological digs and such at least once every couple of years, until quite recently. And this, I'm afraid,' he said, gesturing to the clutter, 'is the result.'

Yes, Uncle Bob had told Clara some of those stories when she was younger, but they were served in small, bite-sized chunks. What faced her now was a banquet of Roman proportions – far too much to digest. But – *good gracious, is that a shrunken head?* – if she could get her anxiety about the chaos under control, she would be very interested to see what curiosities her relative had amassed over the years. 'The housekeeper didn't seem to do much cleaning,' she observed.

Jennings nodded in sympathy. 'It was not for want of trying, I can tell you. But Bob wouldn't let her move anything. She kept the kitchen spick and span though. That was her domain. And the bathroom too – if I recall – although the water closet is outside. You might want to have that changed if you decide to stay. Or even sell. It will add value to the property and there should be enough in the estate to cover the renovation quite easily.'

'Yes,' said Clara, 'an inside lavatory is essential. I assume the house has hot water?'

'Oh yes, inside plumbing and all the modern conveniences in the kitchen – Mrs Hobson insisted – but she never quite managed to get him to modernise the ablutions. He spent most of his time here in his laboratory, so for him it was just as easy to step out from there than to walk up three flights of stairs to the bathroom.'

'He had a *laboratory*?' asked Clara, wondering where on earth he found space for it and why no one had mentioned it before.

'Oh yes, but no one else was allowed down there. I've never seen it myself. It's in the basement. Would you like to see it?'

'I should love to!'

Jennings led Clara through the kitchen (which, as promised, was in perfect order) to a door beside the larder. En route, he pointed to the outside lavatory through the kitchen window. The door to the basement was locked and it took him a while to find the correct key on the bunch. He tried a few keys more than once and Clara was itching to snatch them from him and do it herself. But she restrained herself, only allowing an impatient tap of her toe on the slate tile floor. Eventually the door was opened, an electric light cord was pulled, and a short flight of stone steps was revealed.

Clara sniffed the air and was thrilled to catch a miasma of chemical odours.

'What did Bob do down here?' Clara asked as they descended the stairs.

'He called it "criminalistic science" or just "criminalistics". It's a scientific way of forensically examining evidence. I think he was just an enthusiastic amateur, really. But he did manage to identify the poison that killed someone a year or two back.'

'Ah yes, Mr Danskin mentioned something about that. Goodness me, I had no idea Uncle Bob used science in his work.'

'That and photography,' said Jennings as he pushed open a door to reveal a small but pleasingly tidy laboratory, complete with microscope, a Bunsen burner, a rack of clean test tubes and a shelf of variously sized beakers. There was also a kitchen dresser lined with neatly labelled chemical bottles and jars. Jennings nodded to another door on the far side. 'I think that must be the darkroom over there. Bob told me he partitioned off part of his laboratory for his photography.'

Clara was itching to have a sniff around, but Mr Jennings was already heading back towards the steps. She was disappointed, but, she realised, if she got the house keys from Jennings – and why shouldn't she, they were now legally hers – she could have a look around at her leisure later.

But as she left, one thing caught her eye. There was a sample tray on the bench beside the microscope, and in it a piece of wood. Beside it on a notepad was a chemical formula; she didn't have time to look properly, as Jennings was already halfway up the stairs, but it looked like the composition of kerosene. *How interesting*, thought Clara, *how very interesting*.

Mr Jennings locked up the St Thomas' Crescent house and was just about to pocket the keys when Clara thrust out her hand.

'Perhaps I should take those now.'

'Oh? Have you decided to accept your uncle's inheritance?'

'Well, I haven't decided not to. I think I should take a bit more time to think about it all. As you've said already, I can sell if I want to. But it's too early to tell yet. And I think I would like to come here again and spend some time going through Uncle Bob's things. There was a lot to take in on such a short visit, don't you think?'

Jennings looked mildly chastised and nodded. 'Yes, you're quite correct, Miss Vale. My apologies for rushing you. It's just that I have another client to meet this afternoon.'

Clara gave an appreciative nod. 'That's quite understandable, Mr Jennings. And I don't want to keep you any longer. If you don't mind, I'm going to have a spot of lunch then I might come back here on my own. Would you have any objections to that?'

'Of course not. Shall I direct you to a decent eatery?'

'Oh yes please,' said Clara. 'I'm famished.'

Chapter 6

Clara was feeling much better after eating a delicious meal of steak and kidney pudding and mashed potato at the Fenwick's Terrace tea room, accompanied – charmingly – by a luncheon string quartet. Fenwick's was a department store, not unlike Bainbridge's or Selfridges on London's Oxford Street. There was a Fenwick's in London, too – on Bond Street, if Clara recalled – but it was not as expansive as this northern emporium of shopping delights. Not that Clara was much of a shopper, but she recognised quality when she saw it. Her mother and sister would love it. In fact, she now recalled her mother mentioning that she used to shop there as a young woman before meeting Clara's father and moving to London.

What Clara did buy, however, was a swimsuit. The poster of Whitley Bay on the train had piqued her interest. As she had to go back to London on Friday, if she could get her business done with the solicitor tomorrow, she could, perhaps, head to the coast on Thursday. Clara loved to swim, although she imagined the North Sea would be a tad cooler than the waters in Cornwall.

With her swimsuit packed in a beribboned box under her arm, Clara stepped onto busy Northumberland Street, took her bearings and turned left, back up to Percy Street. Five minutes later she was outside the costumier. She considered popping in to introduce herself, as they were her uncle's downstairs neighbours – and owners of the building – but she stopped when she saw a woman writing a note and posting it through the letter box of Wallace Enquiry Agency.

'Good afternoon,' said Clara. 'May I help you?'

Startled, the woman turned to see who had spoken to her. She was around forty and dressed all in black, her face pale with dark rings under her eyes. 'Oh, good afternoon. I was just leaving a note for Miss Wallace. Are you Miss Wallace?'

'I'm Miss Vale. Is it Mr Wallace you are looking for? I'm afraid he has passed away.'

The woman shook her head, confusion fleeting across her face. 'No, no. I know he's passed. It's his niece I'm looking for. I was told she'd just been to the office. Are you she?'

'I am,' said Clara. 'But my name is Vale. Miss Clara Vale. Erm, how did you know I was here?'

'Miss Levine rang me.'

'And who is Miss Levine?'

'Oh, sorry, haven't you met her? She runs the costume shop. With her brother. Juju and Jonny Levine. They own the building and were your uncle's landlords.'

Clara peered through the window of the costumier and saw a woman waving. Clara waved tentatively back. Juju Levine, she assumed. 'No, I was actually just about to pop in to say hello when I saw you leaving the note.'

The door to the costumier opened with a cheerful ring of a bell and a woman in her fifties, wearing a colourful blouse covered in appliqued butterflies, flitted out.

'Aha! What splendid timing! Hello! I assume you're Clara. Your uncle spoke so much about you. I'm Juju. Juju Levine.' She thrust out her hand with a pin cushion strapped to her wrist.

Clara took the hand, pleased by the warm, firm grasp. 'How do you do, Juju? What an unusual name!'

'Oh, it's really Judith. But I've always been called Juju. But enough about me. I'm glad Alice has caught you. I'll leave you two ladies to talk. But do drop by for a cup of tea when you're finished, or . . .' she winked '. . . something stronger if we're past the yardarm.' And then she fluttered back into her shop, leaving Clara and the woman in black on the doorstep.

'I'm sorry, we haven't been properly introduced. Alice, is it?'

The woman reached out a tentative hand. 'My apologies. How do you do? Yes, I'm Alice Whittaker. Mrs James Whittaker, actually.

My husband also passed quite recently. I'm one of your uncle's clients.'

'How do you do, Mrs Whittaker. And please accept my condolences regarding your husband. I'm not sure how I can help you, but perhaps we should go upstairs and have a chat.'

'Thank you, Miss Vale. I should appreciate that very much.'

Clara dug out the keys from her handbag and opened the door.

A few minutes later, the two women had removed their hats, coats and gloves and were seated on either side of Bob Wallace's desk.

'Well,' said Clara, pushing the heavy cast-iron typewriter to one side and folding her hands in front of her. 'How may I help you?'

Mrs Whittaker cleared her throat. 'I know you have just arrived and haven't had time to familiarise yourself with your uncle's cases, but I just wanted to ask that when you do, you perhaps look at my case first. For obvious reasons, with your uncle's passing, my case has gone on hold. But it's been over six weeks now, and things are not getting better for me. I need this to be sorted soon. I need the insurance money. I have three children and I'm struggling to pay the rent and the bank are foreclosing on a loan my husband took out before he died and I might lose what's left of the family business, too.'

Clara blinked a few times, taking this all in. 'Well, Mrs Whittaker, I'm not sure what to say. As you've already pointed out, I've only just arrived . . .'

'I understand that, and I don't want to rush you, but I hope that as soon as you start work you will put my case first.'

'I – well – I'm not sure whether I *will* be working here. Today is the first time I have even heard that my uncle ran an enquiry agency. And that he's left it to me in his will. I came up here expecting to inherit a few hundred pounds and perhaps a stamp collection, at best. Not a business.'

Mrs Whittaker's pale face slackened in disappointment. 'You're not taking over from your uncle? Then who will? When will all the cases he was working on be opened again? When will my case be opened? When will – when will – oh—' And then she started to cry.

Clara froze. She had absolutely no idea what to do. She wasn't an emotionally demonstrative person herself and hadn't a clue how to handle this. What would her uncle have done? What would anyone do?

'I – well – here,' she said, fishing a handkerchief out of her handbag and passing it across the desk. 'I'm sorry you're so upset. But I'm not sure what I can do. This has all come out of the blue. My uncle left the agency to me, yes, but he hadn't discussed it with me first. I think I have two choices. Or three, I suppose. I can sell the agency to someone else. Or I can hire someone to run it for me. Or – well – I could do what my uncle wanted and take it on. But I've literally just arrived. I haven't had time to decide. I'm sorry, Mrs Whittaker, I need a bit more time.'

Mrs Whittaker dabbed at her eyes and sniffed. 'Yes, yes, I understand that. And I'm sorry. It's just that I'm so desperate.'

Clara nodded. 'No need to apologise. I understand. Isn't there another agent who can help you? I've been told there are other enquiry agencies in town. Or detective agencies, as I believe they're sometimes known. Is that correct?'

The widow nodded. 'Yes, there are. But I've tried them all. Bob Wallace was the only one who would take my case. The rest have already turned me down.'

'And why is that?' asked Clara, curiously.

Mrs Whittaker let out a long, painful sigh. 'Because your uncle was the only one who wasn't in the pocket of the insurers. He was the only one brave enough to stand up to them. I – well – I was hoping you would be too. I'm sorry, Miss Vale, it was silly of me. And I've taken enough of your time.'

She put Clara's handkerchief on the desk and stood. 'I'll see myself out.'

But as she turned, Clara felt something stir in her: curiosity. If this woman left now she might never find out why her uncle was brave enough to stand up to the insurers. And she might never know why he thought she might be brave enough too. No one in her family had ever had any faith in her. Except him. Could she possibly live up to it? There was only one way to find out.

'Please, Mrs Whittaker, don't go. Let me see if I can help. Perhaps I can temporarily hire someone to continue with your case. Or perhaps I can do something myself. But you'll have to tell me all about it first. Can you do that?'

A flash of hope momentarily lit the widow's eyes. 'Yes, I can do that. If it'll help. Where should I start?'

Clara took her notebook from her handbag and unscrewed a fountain pen. 'The beginning, I suppose. That would be the logical place, don't you think?'

Chapter 7

Clara and Alice went through a pot and a half of tea in the telling of the tale. Alice's husband, Jimmy, and his brother, Richard, owned two small picture houses in the seaside villages of Whitley Bay and Tynemouth: the Paradise and the Carousel. Jimmy and Alice ran the Paradise and Richard the Carousel. Jimmy had shares in the Carousel, having helped finance his younger brother to buy what had previously been a variety hall theatre and to convert it into a cinema. Both picture houses were doing well, until the talkies came. Neither the Paradise nor the Carousel could show talkies, so Jimmy took out a loan from the bank to buy two new talkie projectors that had to be imported from America – which were still on their way – and to fit out the buildings with sound systems.

'We wouldn't have needed to convert so quickly if the Majestic hadn't opened,' explained Alice.

'The Majestic?'

'Aye, the big new cinema at the Spanish City in Whitley Bay – they call it a pleasure palace. It can seat a thousand, and we can only take two hundred, tops. And they're fully equipped for talkies. We were beginning to lose business. Jimmy and Rich both put everything they had into buying the new projectors.' She gave a bitter twist of her mouth. 'Jimmy more than Rich – but that was always the case.'

Then Alice paused and let out a tired sigh. 'With the new projectors we would have been all right, Miss Vale, if it hadn't been for the fire.'

Clara leaned forward, sensing they were approaching the climax of Alice's story and the reason Wallace Enquiry Agency had been involved. 'Tell me about it.'

'Well, it was the Thursday before the May Day weekend. We were going to be showing *Joan of Arc* in Tynemouth and *The Fall of the House of Usher* in Whitley Bay. Both silent.'

'Both wonderful pictures,' said Clara encouragingly. 'I've seen them.'

'Aye, they are. They were last year's releases, but like I said, we can't show the talkies yet. We would show one at one picture house, then switch them round. We were due for a big audience on the Friday night for the beginning of the holiday weekend. But just after midnight on the Thursday Jimmy got a telephone call from his brother to say the Carousel was on fire. By the time Jimmy got to Tynemouth – I stayed with the children – the fire engine was there but it was too late, the fire was too far gone.'

'Oh I'm so sorry,' said Clara. 'Was anyone hurt?' she asked, fearing the answer as she noted Alice's mourning attire.

Alice shook her head. 'Fortunately not. There was no one there. But we lost the building and everything in it.'

Clara let out a sigh. 'I'm so sorry you lost everything. But so glad no one was hurt. And at least you were insured.'

Alice nodded, her mouth set in a hard pout. 'Aye, we were. With Balshard Insurance. But they wouldn't pay out. The investigation was done and dusted within two weeks and it was declared that we had not met proper fire safety standards. Which was absolute nonsense. But that's what the fire inspector said. And that's what Balshard's investigation – if you could call it that – decided too.'

Clara leaned in. 'Tell me a bit more about this insurance company.'

'It's owned by Humphrey Balshard. He's a bigwig around these parts. It's the biggest insurance company in the area and—' she smirked '—he's recently opened a string of picture houses too – all called the Majestic. Including the one I just told you about in Whitley Bay.'

Clara's eyes opened wide. 'I see!'

'Exactly,' said Alice. 'And that's why I said your uncle took on the case, because he was the only one not in the pocket of the insurers. You see, Jimmy and Rich were both convinced that it was arson. They'd found a window that had been jimmied open – and Rich swore it had been shut when he locked up after the last show. But the fire inspector, the police and the insurers all say it was just forced open by the heat.'

'Was the glass shattered?' asked Clara.

'No, it wasn't.'

Clara nodded, making a note to check the scientific plausibility of heat forcing a window to open but not shattering the glass. She looked back up at Alice. 'How did the fire inspector say it was started?'

'Faulty wiring. But we don't believe that's true. We had all the electrics checked just the month before. Jimmy gave your uncle a copy of the certificate. It should be in the file.'

'I see. But the fire inspector and the insurance company wouldn't take that as proof?'

Alice shook her head, barely containing her anger.

'Why not?'

'They said that we had left something plugged in, in the projection room, and that Rich hadn't put the nitrate film in the metal chest it should be kept in for fire safety. When the inspector checked, the chest was open and there was evidence of film reels on the floor. They said Rich had forgot to put them away and that's what caused the fire to spread. But Rich – whatever other issues I have with him – is not a liar. And if he said he put them away, he put them away.'

Clara continued making notes then asked: 'So you, your husband and his brother, all think that someone came in the window, opened the chest and scattered reels on the floor?'

'Aye, we do. We always packed the reels in that metal storage chest in the projection room. Always. I don't know if you know this, Miss Vale, but nitrate is very flammable – that means it can catch alight easily. It's caused fires before in other picture houses, so we took every precaution with it.'

Oh, Clara knew, but she didn't want to interrupt the flow of the conversation by regaling Mrs Whittaker with her scientific pedigree. But what she did want to ask, and was frightened to hear the answer to, was how Alice's husband had died.

'So my uncle was helping you – and your late husband – prove that it was indeed arson?'

'That's correct.'

Clara paused for a moment, hoping that Alice would voluntarily talk about her husband's demise, but nothing was said. Clara couldn't skirt around it much longer.

'Forgive me, Mrs Whittaker, but I need to ask. You said no one was killed in the fire. However, you said you were recently widowed. And if the fire happened in May . . .'

Alice's sea-green eyes welled up. 'Aye,' she said, her voice thick with unshed tears. 'Well, first of all we lost Rich.'

Clara's hand slapped to her mouth.

'Oh no, not like that, Miss Vale. He's just gone to Hollywood. When Balshard turned down the insurance claim he had no business left. He's a young man, a bachelor. He's always wanted to make pictures, not just show them. He was inspired by Stan Laurel – you know the actor from the Laurel and Hardy films – who used to live in these parts. He went to school in Tynemouth, did Stan. So Rich decided he might as well up and leave and follow Stan to Hollywood as there was nowt left for him here.' Her mouth twisted into the now familiar bitter pout. 'Well, nowt but debt, which he was happy to leave my Jimmy with.'

Clara nodded in sympathy. She too had a profligate brother, so she could understand. 'What happened then?' she prompted.

'Well, me and Jimmy decided we were not going to take it lying down. We still had a business here. The Paradise was – and is – still a going concern. But with our income gone from the Carousel, and the loan we'd taken out from the bank to buy the new projectors partly underwritten by that – we needed to overturn the decision of the insurance company. We needed – and still need – the money. We've got three children. It wasn't that easy for us to just do a moonlight flit to Hollywood! So that's when we hired your uncle. That was . . .' she did a quick finger calculation '. . . early June. Aye, that's right, the first of June. Your uncle made some good progress on the case, but then, by the end of the month he started to turn a bit poorly. He said it was his heart and he'd have to ease off a bit – doctor's orders. But he was still investigating and told us he thought we definitely had cause to think it was arson. He said he needed a few more weeks to complete his investigation. But then . . . well, you know what happened then, Miss Vale. It wasn't long after that that your uncle passed in his sleep. And I'm very sorry for it. He was a very kind man. But it also meant that our case was put on hold.'

Clara nodded. 'Yes, I understand that must have been a big blow for you. So, what did you . . . and your husband . . . do then?'

Alice slumped back in her chair, her hands clutching and unclutching the handkerchief. 'Well, Miss Vale, that's when I lost him. When I lost my Jimmy. He heard about your uncle passing and came to try to see who was going to be taking over from him. If the business was to be sold or something. Juju Levine, downstairs, told him who Bob's solicitor was. He went to see them – Jennings, I think – but they couldn't tell him much. They said there was a will, but it wouldn't be read for another month as they still had the funeral and everything to sort before then. So, they asked Jimmy to come back in six weeks' time.

'Well, there was nowt he could do, was there? Nowt but wait. But he was so upset about it all that . . . well, Miss Vale, that's when he had his accident. The police think that he was so distracted after his meeting with the solicitor that he wasn't looking where he was going. And he stepped out in front of a tram . . . he . . .' Alice's tears were now flowing freely.

'That's all right, Mrs Whittaker, you don't have to continue.'

Alice nodded, wiping at her cheeks with the handkerchief. 'The coroner says he was killed instantly. He didn't suffer. So that's a grace.'

Clara slowly screwed the lid back onto the fountain pen. She had absolutely no idea what to say. What did one say to a woman who had experienced such tragedy?

'So,' said Alice, eventually, saving Clara from thinking up something, 'you'll reopen the case, Miss Vale?'

Clara's heart sank. What could she say? *The truth*, she thought, *that's the best thing to do.*

'I'm sorry, Mrs Whittaker, but I am still not able to tell you that yet. As I said earlier, I have only discovered my uncle left me his business today. It's a lot to take in. I have absolutely no experience running a detective agency, so I don't think I would even be the best person to help you. But I said I'd try to help, and I will. I'll make enquiries – I've just met someone who I think could advise me – and see if there is someone I could pass the case on to. But I'm afraid I can't give you an answer today.'

Alice composed herself and folded the handkerchief into a neat square. 'I understand, and thank you for taking the time to hear me out. Will you be staying in Newcastle a while?'

'I'll be heading back to London on Friday.'

Alice's shoulders slumped. 'Oh. I was hoping you might come to the Paradise and I could take you to the ruins of the Carousel so you could see for yourself.'

Clara looked at the sad woman in front of her. Did she really think she, Clara Vale, could do anything to help? How desperate would she have to be to think that? *Desperate*, thought Clara, *very desperate*. So, before she could stop herself, she said: 'Well, I had been thinking about taking a trip down to Whitley Bay . . .'

Alice sat bolt upright, her face alight with hope. 'Oh, Miss Vale! Will you, will you really?'

Clara nodded decisively. 'I will. I'll come and see it. But I don't know what I'm going to do yet. About the business. And that means your case too. But I will come.'

'Miss Vale, it's all I can ask. Thank you. There's a show on Thursday afternoon. A special matinee for the school holidays. It'll be finished by four. If you come then, I'll take you over to Tynemouth. Or, you could come earlier and see the flick, if you like. It's *The Circus* with Charlie Chaplin. It's up to you. Here's the address.'

Chapter 8

Clara lay on her bed at the Royal Central Station Hotel, her naked body wrapped in a towel. She'd just had a bath in the en suite. It had cost her extra for the luxury of her own bathroom, but Newcastle prices were a fair bit cheaper than London, so it was not such a hit to the pocket. Not that she would have to worry about such things if she accepted the allowance from her father. But she didn't, and that was that. However, as a poorly paid librarian it was hard to turn her back on it, despite the entangling strings. But now – thanks to Uncle Bob – it looked like she might finally be able to cut herself loose once and for all. A two-thousand-pound house and a going business – value still to be determined. The house alone, even if she sold it, would put her in a very good place financially. She sat up, propping herself up on a pile of pillows, and started massaging the courtesy Ponds cold cream into her feet and legs.

But what about the business? What was she to do? She was very curious to know what the accountant had to say about its worth. She was to meet him – along with Mr Jennings' son – at ten o'clock tomorrow. If she were to sell it, how much would she get for it? And who would she sell it to? And who would deal with the whole thing? She had only intended to stay in Newcastle for a few days and was due back at work in London on Monday. She had a return train ticket booked for Friday and could extend it to Saturday or Sunday. But in terms of office days, that only gave her three more days – hardly time to initiate and conclude a business deal. Particularly as she'd already committed to spending Thursday afternoon in Whitley Bay. No, she would have to appoint an agent to deal with it all in her stead. Mr Jennings had intimated that he would be willing to undertake that task.

But while that was all being worked out, who would take care of any ongoing clients? Alice Whittaker's sad tale had opened Clara's eyes to the fact that the files in Uncle Bob's cabinet represented real people whose lives had been put on hold. Did she have a responsibility to them? Was there someone she could pass the cases on to, or would they need to be part of the sale to a new owner? But that could take months to sort out. In the meantime, what would happen to Mrs Whittaker and her children?

Clara screwed the lid on the jar of cold cream and put it on the bedside table, next to a small pile of files. She had brought them back from the office to read this evening, after supper. Topmost was the Whittaker file. The other files were a random selection of other clients that at first glance did not appear to be closed cases. Clara still had to figure out Uncle Bob's system, but she had noticed that a copy of a bill was pinned to the inside of each file. 'Paid in Full' was written in red ink on some of the bills, but not on others. She assumed the ones without it were still open cases. Either that or they just hadn't been paid.

Mrs Whittaker's file had a running tally of expenses, so far amounting to seventy pounds. That was a lot of money for a widow with already substantial debts. Clara bit her lip and sighed. Mrs Whittaker's plight really tugged at her heartstrings. And, if she were honest, it also teased her mind. There were a number of lines of enquiry – some scientific – that she would like to follow up if she were to take on the case. But how could she, with only a couple of days to spare? Not to mention not having the first idea of how to actually conduct an investigation. However, she had promised Mrs Whittaker she would see what she could do in the short time she had. Even if that just meant finding another investigator to pick up the case.

She planned to telephone Jack Danskin in the morning and ask him to meet her at the office. He was the only investigator she knew, and she would ask his advice on how to proceed. Perhaps he could be persuaded to take it on himself. Mrs Whittaker had told her that her uncle had worked on the case alone and hadn't got any of his other agents involved.

Clara was tempted to start reading the Whittaker file now, but a glance at the bedside clock told her that she needed to get dressed for dinner. She had a table booked downstairs.

Half an hour later Clara stepped out of the elevator and into the hotel foyer. Her straight, raven-coloured hair with its fresh bob and blunt fringe hovered just above her slick black eyebrows. What she hadn't told her mother at breakfast a few days ago in London, was that she'd been reluctantly talked into the fashionable cut by her hairdresser, who thought it made her look like Louise Brooks. The hairdresser assured her it would require less maintenance than her longer tresses that always needed to be pinned up. However, Clara realised, as her dark locks had fallen to the floor, that it would be sending her back to the salon more often to keep it neatly trimmed – and that could prove expensive, particularly as she was not on the Hollywood salary of Miss Brooks!

Her hair, coupled with the dress she was sporting – a claret-coloured Charles Worth cocktail gown with brown velvet trim on the hem and shoulder straps, and gold embroidered gardenias running down one side – made her appear far more fashionable than she normally was. The dress was a cast-off from her sister. From the 1927 Worth collection, it was apparently now far too 'last season' for the stylish Viscountess Laura Simpkins (née Miss Vale). Clara, though, suspected it was more to do with the extra weight her sister had failed to shift after popping out the latest little Simpkins. Either way, Clara was happy to accept the cast-off.

Her shoes – an old but well-maintained pair of pumps with gold brocade over brown velvet and three-inch Louis heels – were rarely worn. Since leaving Oxford seven years previously, Clara had not had many opportunities to dress up for dinner (other than the interminable affairs at her parents' houses, and the trip to Paris a couple of years ago), so she did not glide across the mosaic floor like a bright young thing on the way to Zoots Jazz Club. Within two or three steps she wished she hadn't bothered. She was, after all, a thirty-year-old woman dining alone. Who was she to impress? And God forbid anyone thought she was trying to. She was just about to turn around and head back upstairs to change into something less showy, when she recognised a man striding towards the cocktail lounge. The man – wearing a tuxedo and white bow tie – recognised her at the same time and greeted her with an appreciative smile and a raised eyebrow.

'Well, good evening, Miss Vale. May I say how lovely you look this evening?'

Clara nodded in return. 'Thank you, Mr Danskin. And a good evening to you too.'

'Are you meeting someone?'

'I wasn't planning on it.'

'That's a pity.' His brown eyes twinkled as he gave her his best Ronald Colman-esque smile. Clara imagined for a fleeting moment they were in the latest Bulldog Drummond flick.

She gave herself an internal shake and in a matter-of-fact voice said: 'I don't always dress like this and probably shouldn't have tonight. But I packed in a hurry and my supply of evening wear is limited. And to seriously answer your first question, no, I am dining alone.'

'Then perhaps I can change your mind.'

'About?'

'Dining alone. Would you care to join me for dinner?'

'You have a table booked here, Mr Danskin? My, that is a coincidence,' said Clara, sarcastically.

He grinned. 'I don't, but I can soon remedy that. Will you join me?'

Ordinarily, Clara did not like being steamrollered into decisions. And she certainly didn't take well to flirtatious men – although, she had to admit, it had been a long time since a man had flirted with her. However, she *had* been planning on speaking to Jack Danskin tomorrow anyway. What would be the harm in bringing the meeting forward? So yes, she would have dinner with him. In a professional capacity. And she would make sure he knew that that's all it was.

'All right, I will. I was going to give you a ring in the morning anyway. This will save me the time – as long as we can talk shop.'

Danskin cocked his head to the side and said, playfully: 'Of course! What else could we possibly talk about?'

Clara pursed her lips. 'I'm serious, Mr Danskin. This will be a professional conversation. As long as you agree to that, then you may join me. I already have a table booked. I shall inform the maître d' to set it for two.'

Ten minutes later, they were seated at a corner table furthest from the bandstand, at Clara's request. The menus were consulted and hors d'oeuvres ordered: goose liver pâté on toast for Danskin and a crab cocktail salad for Clara.

'Well, Mr Danskin,' said Clara as she speared some crab and lettuce with her fork, 'do you often drink in this hotel – alone – on a Tuesday evening?'

Danskin smeared a dollop of pâté on a finger of toast. 'Not often.'

'And it was just coincidence that you did so this evening?'

Danskin grinned. 'No, not a coincidence. I was hoping to see you. I won't beat around the bush.'

'No, best not. Why did you want to see me?'

'Because, Miss Vale, I've been giving our conversation earlier today some thought. You know when I said I would not be prepared to be employed by you, but would be prepared to continue working on the same basis I did with your Uncle Bob? On reflection I've realised that that's not entirely true.'

'Oh?'

'Yes. I think, in reality, I'm ready for a change.'

'So, you do want to be formally employed then?'

Danskin grinned. 'Not on your nelly, as me granny would say. No, Jack Danskin is his own man. But I'm thinking that maybe it's time to settle down a bit.'

'Are you married, Mr Danskin?'

'I'm not, but I am at that time of life when I need to start thinking about it.' Danskin's dark brown eyes held Clara's for a while longer than they should have.

Alarm bells went off in Clara's head. 'Pardon me, Mr Danskin, but are you *proposing* to me?'

This was not the first time Clara had received a proposal and she'd worked hard to push that previous encounter out of her mind. But suddenly all the memories came flooding back. The awkward fumbling in an Oxford flat after one too many drinks at a dinner party. The messy, sweaty few minutes of intimacy, which was over before it had barely begun. The embarrassed gathering of clothing the next morning, and then the mortified young man apologising for letting everything get out of hand, followed by an excruciatingly worded proposal, and, finally, his blatant relief when she said no.

Danskin threw back his head and laughed, drawing curious glances from the other diners. 'Would that be so unpleasant if I were?'

Clara put down her fork and pursed her lips. 'I think it would be very presumptuous of you. We've barely met. Perhaps we should call this "meeting" to an end.' Clara sat up straight and turned to signal the maître d'.

Danskin raised his hands placatingly. 'Hold your horses, Miss Vale. I'm not proposing. Not marriage, anyway. But I am proposing a business relationship.'

Clara held up her hand and shook her head to indicate to the maître d' that he was no longer needed. 'And what exactly do you have in mind?'

'I propose buying half of Wallace Enquiry Agency.'

'Why only half?'

'Because I have no desire to handle the administration. I would be the active partner and you . . .' he grinned '. . . the passive one.'

The double entendre was not lost on Clara, but she chose to ignore it. 'And what would be the division of labour between these partners?'

Danskin held a piece of toast between thumb and forefinger and paused before popping it in his mouth. 'I will do the investigating and you will manage the office.'

'Oh, will I now?'

Clara waited, her annoyance rising, as Danskin chewed. Then, finally, he said: 'That's my proposal. I enjoy the investigative work. It's what I'm good at. And I don't want to get bogged down in administration. You, on the other hand, know nothing about investigative work.'

'A few hours ago you were suggesting I might be able to be an investigator. You agreed with me that other ladies had done so.'

'I did and they have. But it will take you time to learn. I could, of course, teach you. But while I do, you could manage the office.'

'What makes you think I have the skills to be an administrator?'

He shrugged. 'Well, if you don't, and you don't know how to investigate, then perhaps you should sell the business. I might be persuaded to buy the whole thing and then hire an administrator. But that would not really be respecting Bob's wishes. He wanted to hand the business over to you. And, as I said before, I had a lot of respect for Bob and his instincts. This partnership offer would be a way of doing that.'

Clara mulled this over for a moment. It was certainly an interesting offer. But, frankly, if she wanted to work as an administrator there were plenty of office jobs available to women in London. It was not something she had ever desired to do. Eventually she said: 'Thank you for the offer, Mr Danskin, but I think I will decline. I have not yet decided if I will keep the business, but if I do, I would want to do more than just totting up accounts and answering telephones. Also, forgive me, but I don't know you from Adam, and entering into a fifty-fifty business relationship with a near stranger would not be the wisest thing to do. I will, however, consider your offer to buy the business outright. I have a meeting tomorrow with Uncle Bob's accountant; after that I'll have a better idea of its value and what I might ask for it. Is that acceptable to you?'

Danskin smiled. 'I can wait until tomorrow. Now, are we ready to order the entrée?'

With the next course ordered (a breast of guinea fowl for Clara, pork chops for Danskin) Clara finally broached the subject of Alice Whittaker, explaining how the widow had come to the office earlier in the afternoon. 'So, even if I don't keep the business, I would still like to help her. Would you be willing to take on the case?'

Danskin let out a sigh, his face expressing regret. 'Unfortunately, Miss Vale, I would not be able to do so. You see, there would be a conflict of interest. I told you I do work for other people, and – as it turns out – I was recently employed by Balshard Insurance, to investigate the fire at the Carousel Picture House. I was just one of a team of investigators, and I didn't have a large role to play, but it would be enough to disqualify me from taking on Mrs Whittaker's case.'

'How so?'

'Because, firstly, my work for Balshard is confidential and I had to sign an agreement not to divulge any information I unearthed in the case to a third party. And secondly . . .' he paused, contemplating the right words '. . . secondly, I'm afraid all of the evidence *did* point to Richard Whittaker not packing the reels away properly – and that there was faulty wiring.'

'What evidence is that?'

Danskin shrugged, ruefully. 'That's what I can't tell you. But it was submitted to both the insurer and the fire department. I'm sorry, Miss Vale, but while I'm aware that Mrs Whittaker thinks differently, her brother-in-law was responsible for that fire. She is a woman overwrought with grief. The death of her husband – so soon after the fire – was a tragedy, and that's clouding her thinking. But the rest of us, with cooler minds, need to see this for what it is. Giving her false hope will not help anyone.'

Clara sipped her glass of wine as she listened to Danskin's explanation. And her heart sank. Poor Mrs Whittaker. But . . . a thought suddenly occurred to her. 'All right, I hear what you're saying. And I understand your position. However, why then did my Uncle Bob take on the case?'

Danskin's rueful expression deepened. 'I honestly don't know, Miss Vale. And I don't want to speak ill of the dead. As you know, I respected Bob Wallace immensely, but . . .'

'But what?'

'But your uncle was not in the best of health in the months

before he died. And, well, perhaps that affected his judgement. He was acting erratically, quite out of character for him. I was most concerned.'

'You're saying my uncle was losing his marbles?' asked Clara, incredulously.

Danskin shrugged again. 'Unfortunately, Miss Vale, I am.'

Chapter 9

It had been a long, tiring day. It was only nine o'clock and the hotel dance band was still playing with gusto – a feisty foxtrot for the guests to kick up their heels – yet Clara was already in bed. She had begged off pudding and after-dinner drinks and had left Danskin to fend for himself. If he had any notions that the meal was anything more than a business meeting then Clara's abrupt withdrawal, after she'd finished the last of the guinea fowl, put paid to that. She had instead ordered coffee to her room – a pot for one – and was now finishing off the last of the brew. She ordinarily wouldn't drink coffee so late, but she wanted to stay awake a little longer to look at the Whittaker file.

What Danskin had told her about her uncle's failing judgement during the last months of his illness troubled her. Mr Jennings had not mentioned that to her. If Uncle Bob had indeed not been of sound mind, where did that leave the will? She laid aside the file and took out the letter he had written to her.

My dearest niece,
*   If you are reading this, it will be because I have died.*
As I write, I have no intention of leaving this world before
my time – and have no plans to do so – but time is not our
own to make. I have been unwell these last few months; the
doctor says it is my heart. However, he says that if I look
after myself I could still live a good long time . . .

It was dated 21st June 1929. That was seven weeks after the fire at the Carousel Picture House and just three weeks before Uncle Bob died. She reread the letter. He certainly didn't sound confused, and Mr Jennings would surely not have taken the letter as an addendum to the will if he had considered him to be. But, if what Danskin said was true, then surely he would have been showing signs of the confusion by this time . . . *if* what he said was true . . . but why would he lie about something like that? Unless it was to cast doubt on Uncle Bob's investigation into the Carousel Picture House fire.

With a notebook and pen to hand, Clara picked up the file and opened it. She skimmed through the contents and noted there was a series of photographs of different parts of the picture house: the shreds of the burned screen, the fire-ravaged auditorium, a fire bucket, the gutted projection room with what looked like the remains of circular tins – the film reel canisters? – the charred window frame with the intact glass. If there were any signs of jimmying on the lock they would be hard to see after the fire damage.

Then there were copies of reports from the fire chief and the insurance company. She noted the final report was dated only four weeks after the fire. Was it normal to wrap up an investigation that quickly? Clara had no idea, but it did feel rushed. Unless, in what were open-and-shut cases, it was done quickly. And from what the series of reports said, it was – as Jack Danskin had told her – clear the authorities believed it to be so. According to all of them, Richard Whittaker had left out film canisters and a desk lamp had been left plugged in in the projection room, leading to overheating and the plug catching alight. This had spread to the film canisters, some of which weren't even properly closed, never mind put in the fireproof chest.

Uncle Bob's notes included the comments: *When was lamp plugged in? How could window have opened from fire but glass not shattered? NB: lock charred, but not warped.*

All very good questions, Uncle Bob, thought Clara. And then, there was one further note: chemical formula $C_{12}H_{26}$–$C_{15}H_{32}$ circled with a large question mark next to it, and the comment '*why not noted in reports?*'

Kerosene, thought Clara. Now where had she seen that before? And then she remembered: it was in Uncle Bob's basement laboratory. He'd made a note of it there, next to a sample near the microscope.

What criminalistic science had he been up to? A thrill of excitement ran through her like an electric current. Perhaps Uncle Bob knew exactly what he was doing when he left his business to her in the will. He knew she was a scientist. He knew that she, unlike most other detectives, would be able to continue with the scientific investigations. In fact, he had said that her scientific training would prove useful. So why then hadn't he mentioned the laboratory and that aspect of his work in the letter to her? She contemplated getting up then and there and going to Uncle Bob's house, but it was now after eleven o'clock and time to call it a night.

However, Clara struggled to sleep. A combination of the later-than-usual caffeine and the unexplained threads of the investigation spinning a web in her mind, meant that it was well after midnight before she finally dropped off. And when she did it was to be embraced by dreams of the woman from the poster on the train, welcoming her to Whitley Bay – she with the impossibly long legs and white smile, wearing an orange bathing suit and cloche hat, and waving to her from a beachside promenade. The woman morphed into the Canary swinging backwards and forwards on a swing over the auditorium of the Carousel Picture House, engulfed in flames. And then, suddenly, Clara herself was on the swing going faster and faster, mere inches above a sea of fire. And all the while, from a balcony, Jack Danskin, with a hand-held movie camera, filmed the whole thing.

Chapter 10

The next morning, at ten o'clock, Clara presented herself at the offices of Jennings & Jennings. It was turning out to be a hot August day and her Coco Chanel tweed suit – with collarless box jacket and slimline skirt – was already proving to be too warm. But she did not feel that she could take off her jacket for such an important meeting. It was imperative that she give the impression of being professional and in control. She felt that last night, with Jack Danskin, her frivolous attire had given the wrong impression and she had let her guard down too much. She was concerned that so far both the men she had met in regard to her uncle's will – Danskin and Barnaby Jennings – had the impression that she would probably be selling the business. However, after her time perusing the Whittaker file last night and her growing belief that Uncle Bob really did think she had what it took to be a good detective, the idea that she might stay on to run Wallace Enquiry Agency was beginning to take root.

Why shouldn't she? What did she have to lose? Yes, she had a flat and a job in London, but she was not happy working at the library, and hadn't been since she started. It was certainly better than teaching, which she hated, but neither job required research and investigation. As a science student she had loved those aspects of her course and what she really wanted was to work in a laboratory. But in the seven years since graduation, she had been unable to secure any work in the field. She had been to plenty of interviews, but each time a man had been given the role over her, even though, she suspected, in some cases they weren't as qualified as she.

But now, here she was, being offered her own laboratory and opportunity to put her research and investigation skills to good use. Granted, it was all a very amateurish affair – scientifically – but it was still *hers*. She could own her own business, run her own affairs, dabble in science . . . and she would have a lovely house to live in too. To top it all, she would not have to be financially tied to her parents again. It was 1929. She was a modern, educated woman. She was able to vote. She was able to work. She was able to own her own business. Clara straightened her shoulders, feeling the sun on her back through the tweed jacket, and stepped into Emerson Chambers.

'What do you mean, I will need my father's signature?'

The two gentlemen looked at one another awkwardly. Roger Jennings, a man in his mid- to late thirties, was a younger, clean-shaven version of his father, although he did not appear quite as convivial. There was a tough edge to Roger Jennings, but, in his line of work, Clara decided that was not a bad thing. She wondered if Jennings Snr was a bit too much of a walkover and that it was left to his son to make the hard business decisions. The other man – the accountant, Andrew Ridpath – was also in his mid-thirties, handsome with wavy auburn hair, tamed with brilliantine, and a neat little moustache. Ridpath cleared his throat and said, apologetically: 'I'm very sorry, Miss Vale, but the bank will require your father's signature in order to transfer your uncle's accounts into your name. Despite the enlightened times we live in, you will understand that most banks will not allow a woman to hold an account in her own name. If you were married, it would have been possible for you to become a secondary account holder to your husband, but as you are not, you cannot have an account unless your father – or another male relative – attests to your competence in matters financial.'

Clara sat back in her chair, uncomfortably hot and now with the wind well and truly knocked out of her sails. 'So, I cannot inherit my uncle's estate unless my father gives his permission? That's, well, that's ridiculous!'

Roger Jennings shook his head. 'No, Miss Vale, that is not quite right. You can inherit the estate – the house, the business and the residual liquid assets are yours, with or without your father's permission – however, you will not be able to gain access to the bank accounts without it. And that's where the bulk of your uncle's money is kept. Is that correct, Ridpath?'

The accountant nodded. 'It is. Although there are a few hundred pounds in cash in the safe at the office. Your uncle liked to keep cash on hand for various expenses in the middle of an investigation. But apart from that, the rest of the capital – amounting to £10,000 – is in Lloyds Bank on Grey Street.'

Clara caught her breath. 'Ten thousand pounds? That much?'

'Yes, that much. And there are a further five thousand pounds in stocks and shares. Those will also be transferred into your name, but redeeming them, or accessing any dividends, will again require the transfer of your uncle's bank account into your name. Do you think it will be a problem for your father to sign a letter to that effect?' Ridpath looked at Clara in anticipation.

Clara had to consciously prevent herself from slumping. Yes, that would be a problem. Clara's father did not approve of women working and didn't see why she couldn't live on the stipend he offered her. He had, with much reluctance, given permission for her to study at Oxford, but he had done so, mainly, because his wife had suggested that Clara might meet her future husband there, and as everyone knew, the aristocracy all sent their sons to Oxford or Cambridge. The Vales were *nouveau riche* and did not often get invited to social gatherings of blue bloods. This smarted. So, when the daughter of an acquaintance of Clara's mother met and married an earl when she was reading English Literature at Oxford, Vanessa Vale got it into her head that Clara too might do as well. She convinced her husband to agree to pay for Clara's studies. Science, of course, was not Vanessa's subject of choice for her daughter, but when Clara refused to go up to the university unless she could read science, her parents grudgingly agreed. However, despite passing her 'schools' with distinction, she turned out to be a great disappointment to her parents, graduating without acquiring a husband.

Seven years later, and she was still a disappointment to them.

She sighed. '*Must* it be my father who signs? We're not on the best of terms. Isn't it sufficient that my uncle considered me competent enough to leave his business to? Can't you present the bank with the letter he wrote to me?'

The accountant nodded, thoughtfully. 'It might, but it might not. And I fear it most likely will not.' He smiled ruefully. 'I'm afraid men in the financial profession are sticklers for procedure and bureaucracy. The correct form, the correct signature . . . this might be too out of the ordinary for them. But that's not all. I believe your father himself is a banker. And the fact that he might be unwilling to sign an endorsement for his daughter might very well ring alarm bells. No doubt false alarms, I might add, but alarm bells nonetheless. So yes, you will need your father or another male relative – who is still alive – to endorse you.'

Clara lost the battle to stop herself slumping. 'Oh,' she said in a quiet voice. The triumph she'd felt walking into Emerson Chambers only half an hour ago had all but gone. But then, suddenly, the despondency was replaced by rage. This was *her* inheritance. This would be *her* business. How dare those bankers – those *men* – try to stop her. If it were her brother, Antony, who was inheriting it would not be a problem – and he was positively profligate with money – but *she* was the one who needed her father's endorsement, she who had always been frugal with money and carefully ran her own affairs. *Hang on . . . Antony . . .*

She looked up. 'Did you say that it could be another male relative who could endorse me?'

Ridpath nodded. 'I did. But he needs to be alive. It couldn't be your uncle.'

Clara shook her head. 'No, I wasn't thinking of him. I was thinking of my brother.'

'Is he over the age of twenty-five?'

'He's thirty-two.'

Ridpath looked at Roger Jennings. 'What do you think, Jennings?'

Jennings tapped his forefinger to his lips. 'I don't see why not. Might you check with the bank first to see if they'll accept it?'

'I can do that right now.' He asked to use Jennings' stylish marble and brass telephone and within a few minutes connected with the operator and asked to be put through to the bank manager. After a few minutes of quiet conversation he put down the receiver, grinning. 'Good news, Miss Vale. The bank will accept an endorsement from your brother. The truth is, it's not in their interest to keep this thing dragging out. The accounts are currently frozen. As soon as the business starts running again, the accounts will become active. Active accounts are profitable accounts. So, can you get that endorsement from your brother?'

Clara's mind was ticking over. 'I think so, but I'll need some cash. How much did you say was in Uncle Bob's safe?'

'Four hundred pounds.'

'Can I have two hundred of it? And can it be deposited into my brother's bank account?'

Ridpath nodded. 'I think that can be arranged. But let me clarify something here, are you proposing to *pay* your brother to endorse you?'

Clara smiled. 'I am. Two hundred pounds to secure ten thousand pounds is a reasonable investment, wouldn't you say?'

Ridpath and Jennings looked at each other and both nodded. 'I would say so,' said the accountant.

'Good,' said Clara, leaning forward. 'May I borrow your telephone, Mr Jennings? And may I have some privacy?'

A quarter of an hour later, Clara put down the telephone and let out a sigh of relief. She called the men back into the office. 'Well, he's agreed. He'll write the letter today and it should get here tomorrow or Friday. But he wants to make sure the money is in his account first. Can we arrange that today, Mr Ridpath?'

'We can, if you give me his account details.'

Clara had written these down and passed them to Ridpath. 'So,' she said, engaging both men. 'Is there anything else I need to do to claim my inheritance?'

Jennings nodded. 'I have some papers for you to sign.'

'Do we need to wait until I get the letter from my brother?'

'No need for that. As I said, the inheritance is yours. The only complication was accessing the bank account. Which is why I invited

Ridpath here to the meeting. That, and to witness your signature.'
Jennings opened a file and passed over a sheet of paper.

'That is a statement of the value of your assets and liabilities as
drawn up by Mr Ridpath. As you'll see, the business, taking into
account monies owed and due, is worth fifteen hundred pounds,
and if you were to sell it, that would be the asking price. I think my
father has already mentioned to you that we would be willing to
facilitate any sale.'

Clara nodded, her eyes ranging over the figures. Fifteen hundred
pounds. That was the least valuable component of the inheritance. She
could sell the business and still have ten thousand pounds in savings,
five thousand pounds in stocks and shares and a two-thousand-pound
house. Should she mention that Jack Danskin was a potential buyer?

No, she thought, *not yet*. Keeping the business was still very
much an option. And why muddy the waters any further? She'd
get the bank account sorted first, then deal with the rest. *Thank
God for Antony and his gambling debts.*

Chapter 11

Clara exited Emerson Chambers into the hot sun of Newcastle city centre, accompanied by Andrew Ridpath. The accountant had offered to take her to Uncle Bob's office to collect the cash for Antony. They had just spent half an hour going through the finer details of Uncle Bob's accounts. Roger Jennings had excused himself from that, having to leave for a meeting elsewhere in town, but had allowed Ridpath and Clara to use his office.

Now here they were, walking together along Blackett Street. They passed clothing boutiques in Eldon Square with mannequins sporting light floral frocks. Clara could feel the sweat pooling at the base of her back. Although she wore a light blouse under her jacket, she dared not take it off. No longer because of fear of not appearing professional enough, but because she expected she would not smell that pleasant. She wished she could pop back to the hotel to change, but decided it would be best to conclude the business with Mr Ridpath first.

Ridpath made polite small talk as they walked, matching his stride to hers. He was not, physically, what Clara conventionally thought an accountant should look like. He was tall and athletic, and she imagined he might do well playing tennis. He, like Jennings Snr, greeted people they passed with a polite nod and a warm smile, occasionally raising his hat, but she never felt for a moment that his attention was on anyone other than her.

'Is this your first visit to Newcastle, Miss Vale?'

'It is. Although my mother was born here we never visited as a family. The times I saw Uncle Bob he came down to us. Did you know my uncle well?'

'Reasonably well. I've been his accountant for ten years.'

'So you know where all the skeletons are then,' she said, in a tone that surprised her in its playfulness. There was something about Andrew Ridpath that made her relax, despite her personal hygiene worries.

He laughed. 'Spoken like a true detective, Miss Vale!'

She turned to him and caught his gaze. 'You're joking, I know, but in all seriousness, that's the real issue here. Will I make a good detective? Should I keep the business or sell it?'

'Why do you have to decide that now?'

'Well, because that's what I'm here for. To receive my inheritance. And that includes the business.'

Ridpath gestured for Clara to turn right onto Percy Street. 'But the business is only eight per cent of the total inheritance.'

Clara considered the figures for a moment, doing a quick calculation. 'It is, on paper, but in terms of worry, it's the majority portion. It was the business that was at the core of Uncle Bob's concern when he named me his heir. And, in terms of responsibility, it's my biggest worry.'

Ridpath stopped and turned to Clara. 'I'm sorry to hear that it's a worry. Why do you say that?'

Quite. Why did she say that? She gathered her thoughts as they waited for a tram to pass, mindful not to be distracted as poor Jimmy Whittaker was, then said: 'Because I think my decision about whether or not to move to Newcastle – to leave my job and my life in London behind – hinges on it. This is not just an inheritance and a financial nest egg, but a potential turning point in my life. And that's hard to quantify in percentages.'

Ridpath nodded and then gently touched Clara's elbow to guide her across the road and the tram track, careful too to avoid piles of horse droppings. On the other side he said: 'I'm just a humble accountant, Miss Vale, and I find comfort in assigning values to things, but I know too that money is not the only thing of worth.' He grinned suddenly, his green eyes lighting up under the shadow of his hat. 'But don't tell my clients that.'

Clara chuckled. 'I won't. But you're right – it's not just a question of money. That's why it's harder to make a decision about it, and calculations cannot be made the same way. I understand calculations too; I'm a scientist by training. But this is different.'

'Is it?' he said, carrying on up Percy Street towards the office. 'Isn't it just a matter of replacing the values on the profit and loss statement with things other than pounds and pence? Things like happiness, satisfaction, security, family responsibility, and so on.'

Clara stopped walking. 'Now that makes sense. So, what would I put in the profit column?'

Ridpath looked down at her. 'Well, that's up to you. But the first question I would ask myself if I were in your shoes is, do I actually want to be a detective? And what then would be the pros and cons of pursuing that path.'

'And whether I have the skills to do so. Or if not, where I lack, can I buy those skills in?'

'It sounds like you've already been thinking along these lines.'

'I have. I must say it hit me like a bolt from the blue yesterday when I heard Uncle Bob was leaving me a detective agency, but I've been doing a lot of thinking about it in the last twenty-four hours. Mostly I've been thinking about what he saw in me to make him believe I'd be good at this. But . . . on top of that, I had a visit from one of Uncle Bob's clients yesterday, and I've started to look into the case—'

Before she could finish a woman waved frantically to them from the doorway of the costumier. Juju Levine, Clara realised.

'Oh, Miss Vale! I'm so glad you're here. I wasn't sure how to get hold of you. But, oh my, I'm not sure how to tell you this, but there's been a break-in in the office upstairs.'

'Good gracious! What happened? This is Mr Ridpath, by the way.'

Juju nodded to Ridpath. 'Yes, we've met. Oh, Miss Vale, Mr Ridpath, I heard someone moving around upstairs and I assumed it was you. So I went up to ask if you wanted a cup of tea – it'll be lovely to get to know you more, you see – but as I opened the door of the office, someone barged past me and pushed me to the floor and ran down the stairs!'

Clara assessed the woman, quickly, from head to toe. 'Are you all right? Are you hurt?'

'No, no,' said Juju, who although not injured was clearly panicked, 'but he did give me a fright.'

'Did you see who it was?' asked Ridpath. 'And have you called the police?'

'No, I didn't see. It was all so quick. It was a man; that's all I could tell. Youngish – I suppose – but I couldn't swear to it. Dark blue overcoat, possibly, but that's not much help. Oh, I'm so sorry, Miss Vale! By the time I'd gathered myself and run down the stairs, he was gone. I was just about to call the police when you arrived.'

'Stay here,' said Ridpath, and approached the door to Wallace Enquiry Agency.

Clara ignored him and followed, as did Juju.

'The door hasn't been forced. So someone used a key. Who has keys?'

'I have no idea,' said Clara. 'Mr Jennings gave me keys, but I don't know who else has them. Best I have the locks changed.'

'Best you do. I can recommend a locksmith.'

The three of them ascended the stairs: Ridpath, Clara then Juju. Ridpath again asked them to stay where they were until he had checked that there was no one else there. This time Clara and Juju waited. A moment later he returned after having checked the toilet and kitchenette behind the office. 'All clear.'

Clara looked around, taking in files strewn across the desk and the floor. The filing cabinet drawers were open, but she had no idea what had been taken. Then a thought struck her: 'The safe! Where's the safe? Has he taken the money for Antony?'

Ridpath opened what appeared to be a cloakroom cupboard and got down on his knees. Clara peered over him and saw a metal safe on the floor at the back.

'It's not open, but it might have been. Let's see.'

'Hold on a moment,' said Clara, and strode across the office floor and shut the door at the top of the stairs, bolting it from the inside. 'Just in case he comes back,' said Clara to a pale-faced Juju.

'I'll need the combination,' said Ridpath.

'Hang on, I'll get it.' Clara opened the document file that Jennings Jnr had given her when she signed her acceptance of the inheritance. The combination was listed in there.

'What is it?' asked Ridpath.

'Here, let me,' said Clara, indicating that Ridpath should come out of the cupboard and let her in. She had no reason to distrust the accountant, but she had no reason to trust him either. He politely acquiesced.

Clara noted that the safe was similar to the one her father used, and after a quick appraisal of how the locking mechanism worked, dialled the six-digit number and opened the safe.

Inside there were some more files, a petty cash money box and a revolver. She was startled when she saw the weapon but that was not her main concern for now. The petty cash box was locked. She checked her bunch of keys and found a couple of small ones that might fit. The second one did the trick. She opened the box and was relieved to discover that there was a hefty wadge of high-denomination banknotes. She didn't count it, but it could easily amount to hundreds of pounds. She let out a sigh of relief. 'It doesn't look as if he's been in here.'

She took out the money box and relocked the safe, reminding herself that she would still need to reset the combination.

Ridpath helped Clara to her feet as she held the box under one arm.

'So,' said the accountant, 'for now, it looks like he either didn't find the money or Miss Levine here interrupted him before he could do so.'

'Or,' said Clara, taking in the strewn files, 'he wasn't after the money at all.'

'Do you really think so? What else might he have taken?' asked Ridpath.

'I don't know, but my bet will be a file. Miss Levine, did you see him holding anything as he pushed past you?'

'Please, call me Juju. And I'm sorry, I didn't see. I was face down on the floor and he was gone by the time I looked up.'

Clara was frustrated that the only witness was not a particularly observant one, but she gave Juju an understanding nod. Then she approached the filing cabinet. There were four drawers. The top drawer, A–F, wasn't open, the next two were partially open, and the bottom drawer, S–Z, was fully open and its contents scattered.

'It looks like he was searching this drawer. Might he have been looking for something alphabetically?'

'Are you suggesting he was looking for a specific file, as in a specific case of your uncle's?' asked Ridpath.

'It's possible,' said Clara, noting that W for Whittaker would have been in the bottom drawer, if the file was not in her hotel room. 'But I won't be able to tell until I know exactly which files should have been there. Do you know if my uncle kept a list of his cases in a separate register?'

'He probably did, but I'm not sure where he kept it.'

'I can help you look for it,' offered Juju. 'And to tidy up. I'll just have to let Jonny know what's going on so he can watch the shop.'

Ridpath looked at his watch. 'Unfortunately, Miss Vale, I won't be able to help you with that. If you still want to get to the bank this afternoon, we'll have to go quickly. And I'll have to arrange that locksmith. And the police . . . we'll have to report a break-in.'

'But it wasn't a break-in,' said Clara. 'Someone let themselves in. Will the police consider it a crime?'

'We should probably still report it,' said Ridpath.

'All right,' said Clara. 'Let's divide up the jobs. Do you need me at the bank?'

'Not really. You've given me your brother's account details. I'll transfer the money from my business account to his, then reimburse myself from the cash here. And there's a locksmith not far away; I'll drop in on my way down to the bank and ask him to come here.' He looked concerned. 'Will you be all right on your own?'

'I will, thank you,' said Clara, remembering the revolver in the safe. 'Juju here has said she'll help me. And I'll ring the police and they should be here soon, too – one should hope.'

'All right then. If the police need a statement from me let them know I'll come into the station later to give it. Give them my name and telephone number and they can give my office a ring.' He handed

Clara his card. She handed him the petty cash box, which he slipped into his briefcase.

Ridpath waited until Clara had telephoned the police and was assured that someone would be around in half an hour before he and Juju withdrew.

'I'll be back in a tick!' said Juju, skipping down the stairs like a woman half her age.

'And I'll be back . . . when? Where shall I meet you?'

'Do you need to meet me?'

'Well, I suppose I should confirm to you that the money has been transferred. Where are you staying?'

'The Royal Central Station Hotel.'

'All right, I'll give them a ring and leave a message for you.'

Ridpath raised his hat and left as Juju was trotting back up the stairs, carrying a jug of milk. Clara let her in then shut and bolted the door.

Chapter 12

Juju Levine was as colourful and chatty as a parrot. Far chattier than Clara was comfortable with, but she soon realised that the costume designer was one of her best bets at having a glimpse into the life of her uncle. But first, as the two women gathered up the scattered files, she got a potted history of the life of Juju and her twin brother Jonny (whom Clara had yet to meet). Their father came to Newcastle from Poland in the 1860s. He set up a tailoring shop in the Grainger Market and soon met and married a young actress and singer who trod the boards of the variety halls in the North East. She wasn't Jewish but converted, and the twins were both raised as part of the Leazes Park Road Synagogue. After they were born, their mother retired from the stage and joined her husband in the tailoring shop, specialising in making costumes for the theatres and variety halls in the city. By the time Juju and Jonny inherited the business, it had lost its tailoring wing and was solely a costumier. With the vogue for fancy-dress parties, the twins expanded that part of the business and opened the shop on Percy Street.

'So we've been in this building fifteen years. We first rented this office to your uncle around ten years ago, and he's been the perfect tenant – and also a good friend. He even became one of our customers, as he sometimes needed outfits and disguises for his cases. Either for himself or his agents.'

'Oh, how interesting! What kind of disguises?' Clara leaned forward, intrigued.

'Nothing too complicated. Wigs, moustaches and such. If he was following someone for a few weeks to gather information, he liked to change his appearance so he wasn't as easily spotted. Aha!' said Juju. 'I think this might be what we are looking for.' She dug out a black leather book from the top drawer of the filing cabinet and passed it to Clara.

Clara opened it and sure enough there was an alphabetical listing of cases with the date each file was opened and closed. She flicked to W. Yes, there was Whittaker, opened 1st June 1929, with no date under 'closed'.

'This is just what we need! Thank you, Juju. But it will require a fair bit of work to go through this lot and see what's here and what isn't. By the way, you seemed to know Mrs Whittaker, yesterday.'

Juju, without asking, walked into the kitchenette and started boiling the kettle. 'I do,' she said, over her shoulder. 'I telephoned her to tell her you were here. The poor, poor woman, losing her husband like that, and that thankless brother-in-law flitting off to Hollywood instead of staying to help. Bob did a good thing taking on their case. But he always had a soft spot for the underdogs. Now poor Alice is up to her neck in debt – and through no fault of her own!'

'How was she to pay Bob then?'

'Oh, he would have agreed to get paid when the insurance paid out.'

'And if it didn't?'

Juju smiled sadly. 'Then he wouldn't get paid. He knew that, but took the case on anyway. He was a good man, your uncle, and I'm very sad that he's gone.' Juju sniffed and wiped a tear from her eye.

Clara was touched. 'Juju, how poorly did my uncle get before he died? Was he in bed at home? In hospital?'

Juju shook her head. 'No, he worked right up to the day before he died. We knew he wasn't that well. He didn't have the energy he used to; he had lost some weight. But no one who knew him thought his death was imminent. He had a weak heart though, and that in the end is what got him. You should speak to his doctor. I can give you his details.'

'That will be helpful, thank you. So, you didn't see much change in him, other than him lacking energy.'

'Not really, no.'

'How about mental change? Did he seem to still have all his faculties?'

Juju laughed. 'Your uncle? Oh yes! He was still as sharp as a tack. And funny, Bob was so very funny.' She wiped at her eyes again. 'Sugar?'

'Yes please, if there is any.'

'Oh, there is. Your uncle had a sweet tooth. He would always be bringing in cakes that his housekeeper had made.'

'Mrs Hudson, is it? Like in Sherlock Holmes?'

'No, Hobson. Funny bird, that.'

'Oh? Why's that? From the letter Uncle Bob wrote I got the impression he was very fond of her.'

'He was,' said Juju, carrying two cups of tea out of the kitchenette without saucers. 'But, and it's not really my place to say so, but I think she hoped he would be fond of her in a different sort of way.'

'Meaning . . . ?' prompted Clara then took a sip of her tea.

'Meaning . . . well, I'm not sure how well you really knew your uncle.'

'Not that well, to be honest. Not in recent years, anyway.'

'I thought as much. But he obviously loved and trusted you enough to pass on his whole life to you. So I think you should know what his whole life was. Because you might find out from someone else. Someone like Mrs Hobson, who might put her own slant on it.'

Clara put down the cup on the desk. She didn't like all this beating around the bush. 'What are you saying, Juju? Spit it out,' she said frankly.

Juju put down her own cup and took Clara's hands. Clara forced herself not to pull away. Unexpected physical contact always made her uncomfortable.

'I have a feeling, Clara, that you are not very shockable. And that's just as well. Because, you see, Mrs Hobson, the housekeeper, is a widow. Your uncle was a bachelor. She made it very clear that she hoped he would marry her. She is in her forties. He was in his early sixties. She carried a torch for him. Even though he made it clear that he was not interested in marriage. She still kept on hoping.'

'Well, that's not so shocking. Is that all?' said Clara, relieved.

'No, that's not all. You see, the reason your uncle was not interested in marrying Mrs Hobson, or anyone, was that he was not interested in women. Not romantically.'

Clara suddenly realised what Juju was trying to say. 'Are you trying to tell me my uncle is – was – a homosexual?'

Juju nodded seriously. 'I am. I don't think anyone else knew. But he told me and my brother because, well, let's just say my brother is of a similar disposition. They were just ordinary friends, not "special" friends, if you know what I mean. In fact, I don't think your uncle had a "special friend". If he did, he didn't tell me or Jonny. But I think Mrs Hobson suspected that Bob and Jonny were more than they were – and she got herself worked up about it. So, when you meet her, be careful. That's all I'm saying.'

'I will, thank you. And thank you for telling me about Uncle Bob. I honestly don't know if my mother knew. If she did, she never said. They never got on.'

'So I heard. But he spoke about you a lot. He even showed me some of the letters you wrote to him. He kept them all, you know. He was so proud of you, going to university and reading science. He always saw that as proof that you took after him.'

'Yes, it seems that I might have.' Clara had a pang of guilt that she had not kept up a correspondence with her uncle in recent years. And a deep sense of sadness crept up on her for the man she could have known so much better.

Clara's thoughts were interrupted by a knock on the door. 'Locksmith!'

Then another voice. 'And the police!'

Chapter 13

Clara was relieved to finally have a chance to change out of her tweed suit. It was almost five o'clock and she had sponged herself down in her en suite bathroom and changed into a summer frock of sky-blue rayon with a dropped waist and white cotton trim.

She crossed the hotel foyer from the lift and asked for a parcel wrapped in newspaper to be placed in the hotel safe. It was the Whittaker file. Although she had not yet had a chance to go through Uncle Bob's file catalogue in detail, she had a sneaking suspicion that this was what the intruder at the office might have been looking for. So, she was not going to take any chances. The locks on the office door had been changed – and she alone now had the key – and the file and notes she'd taken from the office were now under tight security. The last thing she wanted was for her hotel room to be ransacked when she was out, but if it were, she felt confident that the intruder would find nothing.

Her meeting with the police constable had proven fruitless. Juju Levine, despite being a delightful person, was an imprecise witness, and Clara herself could not tell the constable for certain that anything was missing – which, she realised, didn't reflect too well on her either! She could tell him that the money in the safe had not been taken, but that was a notch up on the intruder's scorecard, not against him. The constable was also keen to point out (as Clara had expected) that there had not actually been a break-in and that as her uncle's estate was currently in transition, a number of people had keys. How did Clara know that the person who had come to the office had not had a legitimate reason to be there?

'Then why did he push Miss Levine to the ground?' Clara had asked.

'Perhaps he was in a hurry and accidentally knocked her over without realising?'

'And left her on her knees?' she asked, scornfully.

'Well, that wasn't very gallant, Miss Vale, I'll give you that, but unfortunately rudeness is not illegal. Were you hurt, Miss Levine?'

'I was not, Constable.'

'Well then, I'm afraid, ladies, there's not much more I can do here. Your locks are changed, and hopefully that's the last you'll see of this fellow.' He had snapped his notebook shut having, Clara noted, sullied a page.

As Clara was handing in the file at the hotel reception, asking for it to be put in the safe, there was a telephone call for her. It was Andrew Ridpath. She was ushered into an office and given some privacy for her conversation. After pleasantries she asked: 'Did it go all right at the bank?'

'It did. The money should be in your brother's account by next Monday.'

'Monday? I thought it would be tomorrow.'

'Unfortunately not. Is Monday a problem?'

'I was hoping he'd send the letter immediately to arrive by first-class post so we can get the bank account sorted. I'm only here for a few days.'

Ridpath's voice was filled with sympathy. 'I'm sorry, Miss Vale. Even if it arrived tomorrow, it will take until at least the end of next week to be sorted.'

'Really?'

'Really. I'm sorry. These things, involving probate, take time. And of course, with you being a woman, it's not a regular transfer. It will require meetings and board approval.'

Clara gave a deep sigh. It had already been niggling at her – the idea that she might have to extend her stay and risk the wrath of Mr Rose at the library – but up until now it had not quite crystallised. When she had arrived here on Monday evening, she had anticipated a visit to the solicitor's office on Tuesday, to hear that she'd inherited perhaps £100 or so and maybe a stamp collection, to spend a few days here then to return to London before the weekend. She had come more out of respect for her uncle – and regret that no one from the family had attended the funeral – than any expectation that she would be receiving a life-changing amount of money. And a house. And a laboratory. And a detection business. And now, very possibly, she was going to be taking on one of her uncle's open cases. Goodness, if she was the type to take a giddy turn, then now was the time. But she wasn't. Instead, she made up her mind and said: 'I shall cancel my train ticket for Friday then, and ask for an open return. I'll let the library know I shall be taking next week off too. I'll send them a telegram.'

'Will they be happy to give you the time off?'

No, Mr Rose would not be happy. Not one little bit. But it was a chance Clara was prepared to take.

'We'll just have to see,' she replied, then said goodbye. She wrote out the telegram, handed it in at reception, then took herself to the hotel terrace for a cool glass of lemonade.

Under the sparkling lights of its spectacular chandelier, the lobby of the Royal Central Station Hotel was abuzz with guests on their way to or from dinner, the bar or the billiards room. Clara was dressed again for dinner, this time not worrying if anyone thought her over- or under-presented. She was informed her table was not yet ready, so she decided to wait in the cocktail lounge with a frosted glass of Bee's Knees. The chilled gin, lemon and honey hit the right spot and Clara leaned back in her chair, closed her eyes and waited for the stress of the day to unwind. And what a day it had been.

Ten thousand pounds! And a further five thousand more in shares. Who would have thought? Once she had the letter from her brother she would be an independently wealthy woman. Granted, she wasn't about to make it onto any rich list, but it was a very nice nest egg. Very nice indeed. The fact was, if she managed the money carefully, she might never have to work again. Particularly if she were to live rent-free in the St Thomas' Crescent house. Or if she wasn't going to live in Newcastle, she could rent it or sell it. Mr Jennings the solicitor hadn't mentioned renting as an option, but it certainly was. It would bring in a tidy little income so she might not even have to touch her capital.

However, all of that paled in light of the break-in at the office. Could it really be connected to the Whittaker case? Well, she had ten days or so to prove it. She was booked into the hotel until Friday morning; thereafter she could extend her booking (she could now certainly afford to), or she could move into Uncle Bob's house. Now that was a tempting idea. She couldn't wait to have a sniff around his laboratory. She had hoped to get there today, but everything else that had happened had crowded it out. Perhaps tomorrow . . . What was she going to do tomorrow?

Well of course, there was the trip to Whitley Bay. She had decided that she would indeed go to the Chaplin flick and then meet Mrs Whittaker afterwards. She thought for a moment about asking Andrew Ridpath to accompany her but decided that she didn't want to be too reliant on him. She needed to find out whether she could cut the mustard as an investigator on her own, not as someone's sidekick.

She was startled from her reverie by a male voice. 'Good evening, Miss Vale, sorry to interrupt your forty winks.'

She opened her eyes to see the tall figure of Jack Danskin dressed for dinner in his tuxedo, white bow tie and cummerbund, standing with a whisky tumbler in hand. 'May I?' he asked, indicating the empty chair across from Clara.

'Good evening, Mr Danskin. Of course, please take a seat.'

Danskin settled himself, crossed his legs and took a sip of his whisky. 'Have you eaten?'

'I'm awaiting my table.' Clara desperately hoped he wasn't going to offer to dine with her again. She really didn't have the energy.

'Then I won't keep you long.'

Well, that was a relief.

'What can I do for you, Mr Danskin?'

Danskin cocked an eyebrow. 'You don't know? Didn't we arrange this yesterday?'

Clara was tired and struggled to keep the irritation out of her voice. 'Arranged what?'

Danskin pursed his lips. 'To discuss whether or not you will be selling half the business to me. You said you had a meeting with Bob's accountant today and thereafter would have a better idea of its value.'

'Ah, that.' Clara finished the last of her Bee's Knees. She could have done with another one, but she thought if she ordered it would indicate to Danskin that she was in for the long haul. Besides, there'd be wine with dinner . . .

'Yes, that,' said Danskin. 'Have I done something to annoy you, Miss Vale?'

Had he? Simply by being there? Clara put down her glass on the table. 'No, of course not. I'm sorry, Mr Danskin. I've had a long, tiring day. I am going to just have a spot of supper and then an early night.' She thought of mentioning the break-in at the office but she didn't want to prolong the conversation. Besides, a man with Danskin's connections would find out about it soon enough. Instead she said: 'And yes, I do remember discussing a possible sale of the business; it had just slipped my mind for a moment. So, yes, I went to the accountant today and do have a better idea of its value. If I were to sell it to you outright, I'd be asking two thousand pounds.' Clara had not forgotten that the business was actually valued at fifteen hundred, but decided it would be wise to inflate the initial asking price to make room for negotiation. She expected Danskin would then make a lower offer.

'I see,' said Danskin, amused. 'So that's your price.'

'It's my price if I were to sell, but I still haven't decided whether I will or not.'

'Oh? And why's that?' he said sharply, the amusement suddenly gone from his voice.

'I need more time to think.'

'How much more time?' asked Danskin, leaning in across the table and lowering his voice.

Clara didn't appreciate his body language, or his tone. Annoyance bubbled again. 'As much time as I need, Mr Danskin. Now, if you don't mind, I believe my table is ready.'

Clara had no idea if it was, but she stood up anyway, indicating that their meeting was over.

Danskin stood too and pulled down on his lapels. 'All right, Miss Vale, fair enough. But may I ask if that price would include all Bob's files too?'

'I'm not sure, Mr Danskin, I would have to take legal advice on that. Would it be a deal-breaker if they were not?'

'Not necessarily,' he said, 'but then the price would go down.' He flashed a smile at her, slipping back into the easy charm of their first meeting at the office. 'But we can work out the details later. When are you going back to London?'

'I'm not sure,' she said, trying to catch the eye of the maître d'. 'I'll be here for at least another week. Possibly longer.'

'Then, Miss Vale, we have plenty of time. I'll be in touch again.' He gave a little bow, spun on his heel and headed back to the bar.

Before Clara could decide what to do next, the maître d' approached her and said her table was now ready.

'Finally,' muttered Clara.

Clara was flushed with food and wine when she retired upstairs. It had been a good meal on top of an exhausting day, and she was very much ready for bed. She opened her door, switched on the light and was just in time to see someone climbing through an open window onto the fire escape. All she saw was the back of a man. A fleeting glimpse that did little to identify him. She screamed and ran to the window as the man, in a dark evening suit, clattered his way down the outside of the building. Unless she were to clamber out and pursue him in her Charles Worth gown, there was nothing more she could do. Instead, she ran out of the room and back down the stairs – avoiding the queue of people at the lift – and reported the break-in to a shocked receptionist, who immediately got the manager on the blower.

She returned to the room, accompanied by the manager, a porter and a burly doorman, and confirmed that her things had been searched but nothing appeared to be missing. The manager offered his profuse apologies and to relocate her to another room, place a guard outside and call the police in the morning. She readily accepted.

Now she lay awake in her new room, her head clear of wine, with the covers pulled up to her chin. The window was locked from the inside. The door braced with a chair under the handle. And every creak and groan of the Victorian building jolted her nerves. Nothing had been taken, but she was convinced she knew what the intruder was looking for: the Whittaker file. Fortunately, it was still in the hotel safe.

She had not mentioned it to the manager, but there was one very clear suspect in her mind: Jack Danskin. He had been wearing a dark evening suit. He had been in the hotel earlier in the evening. He had known she was downstairs having dinner, thus leaving her room free to be searched. He knew she was looking into the Whittaker case and, she recalled, forensically going over every syllable of their last conversation, he had been asking about the files.

Chapter 14

Thursday 22nd August 1929

The next morning, after a largely sleepless night, Clara met with a police constable – the same one who had attended the office break-in. She was in the company of the hotel manager and together they went over the events of the previous evening. But once again, as nothing had been taken and no one had been injured, the policeman was reluctant to take further action.

'Isn't it enough that he *could* have attacked me? Yes, I got off lightly this time, but it might happen again. Isn't it worth investigating further?!'

'I'm sorry, Miss Vale, but he had every opportunity to attack you when you entered the room alone last night. But he didn't. It looks like you walked in on an attempted burglary.'

'Yes! The second one in twelve hours! Why aren't you taking this more seriously?'

The constable bristled. 'We are taking it seriously, Miss Vale, as seriously as the incident merits. There is as yet no indication that the two events are linked. Granted, I can see why you think they are – and between you and I, I think they might be – but until there is more evidence, we can't put any more men on this. The manager here said he will up security and call us if any further incidents occur. The locks have been changed at your uncle's office. I'm not sure what more you would like us to do, Miss Vale.'

'I would like you to investigate! I would like you to find out who is targeting me like this.'

'You would like us to do detective work.'

'Yes, I would!'

The constable nodded, sympathetically. 'I'm afraid, Miss Vale, that unless these incidents escalate to a more serious crime, our detection branch will not get involved.'

'You mean until I'm actually hurt!'

'I didn't say that, miss.'

'But that's what you meant.'

Despite her frustration that the police would not take action without further evidence, Clara had decided not to mention the Whittaker file or Danskin. Her suspicion of Danskin was simply that – a suspicion. It was not evidence. And she did not want to give over the only potential evidence she had – the file – to a police force that seemed less than enthusiastic to investigate.

So the conversation went round in circles for another ten minutes before the constable finally withdrew.

Now, with the Whittaker file wrapped in newspaper and in a shopping bag – so it did not appear to be anything important – Clara sat on the train on the way to Whitley Bay. To while away the time, she read a copy of the *Fenwick News* she'd picked up at the tea room yesterday. An editorial by the editor, Arthur Fenwick, entitled 'Let us have more talkies!' caught her eye:

I do not know why we waste time discussing whether the talkies have come to stay. Going back to the ordinary routine of silent pictures would be like taking a step back into pre-war days, they would seem so slow. Even if silent films were being made now, they would have to be high above the old standard to lure us into the cinemas. We could trust Charlie Chaplin or Buster Keaton to rise to that level – but whom beside?

I like the talkies mainly because they are exactly the kind of recreation the average business person wants at the end of a stuffy day. They are, in fact, exactly the opposite of the fare the B.B.C. think we ought to want.

The talkies I like best have the most wildly impossible

stories and situations. They are filled with America's most valuable export – the spirit of youthfulness. There is a happy holiday air right through the show. The newer talkies, too, are depending more on the stars – they will appeal on personality, as the old silent pictures did, with excellent results . . .

Like the old silent pictures did . . . Here was Arthur Fenwick speaking as though silent films were past history. And yet that's what Alice Whittaker was still showing at her picture house. How long until the public would not tolerate the 'old silent pictures' anymore? No wonder Alice and Jimmy felt they must make the transition to talkies – with the attraction of the big new all-talkie cinema, the Majestic, a small business like theirs would not survive without it.

Clara considered the Majestic for a moment and its owner – Humphrey Balshard. Was it just a coincidence that his insurance company turned down a claim that would keep his cinema's smaller rival afloat long enough for them to convert to talkies? And give them a fighting chance to stay in business? Surely there were grounds there for an appeal. But to whom could Alice appeal? Clara had no idea how the insurance business worked or how appeals could be made if a decision went against you. But she did have an idea about science. And if she could help Alice – using science – then she would.

She laid the magazine aside and took out the Whittaker file. She could find no reference that Bob had forensically examined the window that had been left open, other than to photograph it. Yes, any signs of jimmying would have been obscured by charring, but not necessarily obliterated. She would ask Alice to take her to the Tynemouth picture house so she could examine the window more closely – and perhaps, if she were able, take it back to Uncle Bob's laboratory for further examination. And then of course there was the reference to kerosene. If Bob had found traces of that, could that prove arson? Kerosene could be used for heating or lighting, so there could be a perfectly ordinary explanation for why it was there. But if not . . . well . . . she would need to check with Alice.

Clara made some notes about these lines of enquiry and then

gathered her things as the train pulled into Whitley Bay Station in a puff of smoke.

Consulting a map she had been given by the hotel concierge, and accompanied by the squall of seagulls, she walked down South Parade, a sloping street lined with bed and breakfast hotels, until she reached the seafront. There were 'no vacancy' signs in most of the windows as it was the height of the summer holidays. The cheek-by-jowl boarding houses of South Parade morphed into genteel Victorian residences and new art deco-inspired hotels, separated from the beach by a road and then a wide expanse of pavement promenade scattered with benches. Locals and visitors sat eating ice cream cones or parcels of fish 'n' chips wrapped in newspaper, while hungry dogs impatiently waited for treats, and seagulls circled, squabbling over any scraps the dogs missed.

Beyond black wrought-iron railings were cliffs overlooking an expansive beach, with St Mary's Lighthouse in the distance. Clara recognised the scene from the poster on the train. There were the red-and-white-striped beach tents, the children building sandcastles and waiting eagerly in line for donkey rides, while young men showed off their physiques as they ran into the sea. Clara looked longingly at the water. She would have loved to have had a swim wearing her new bathing suit, but she didn't feel she could mix business with pleasure and that it would not be polite to expect the grieving widow to sit around waiting while she had a quick dip.

Clara joined the pedestrian flow and walked towards a sprawling white building that looked like something out of the Arabian Nights. The white pleasure palace with its giant dome and twin turrets, topped by bronze statues of young women dancing to the clash of cymbals and tambourine, would be seen from miles out to sea. *That must be the Spanish City*, thought Clara, considering that behind its white walls would be the famed pleasure gardens, funfair and the big new Majestic Cinema.

Clara stood for a moment and considered going into the Majestic and asking to speak to the mysterious Humphrey Balshard – if he was there – but then decided against it. First things first, she needed to speak to Alice at the Paradise Picture House and tell her that she had decided to do her best to investigate her case. She checked the map again, then turned up Marine Avenue.

About halfway up the hill she came to the modest, newly decorated front of the Paradise with palm trees and grapevines painted on the pillars, and posters of Charlie Chaplin in *The Circus* pasted on the walls. A queue of people, mainly excited children carrying jam jars, waited in line to pay for their tickets at a little booth. Alice had told her that matinees were mainly filled with children who were allowed to pay for their tickets with jam jars as they came from families too poor to afford a normal ticket. 'We cash in the jars once a week with a man who sells them on to the jam and pickle factory.' She had smiled, sadly, then added: 'Jimmy always insisted we keep ticket prices as low as we could for the children. He never forgot where he came from, did our Jimmy. Unlike Balshard – he won't let any bairns in with jam jars. We don't earn much for that show, but we make up for it the rest of the week.'

Clara joined the queue of children and the smattering of adults and was soon at the front. She smiled at Alice whose face lit up as she recognised her. 'Oh, Miss Vale, you came!'

'I said I would. And I've got some ideas on how to proceed with Uncle Bob's investigation. Will you be able to take me to Tynemouth afterwards?'

Alice nodded. 'Of course. I'll meet you in the foyer. Enjoy the show!' She passed Clara a ticket.

'How much do I owe you?'

Alice looked shocked. 'Absolutely nothing! I'll see you afterwards.'

Clara, aware of the queue growing behind her, thanked Alice and went through the front doors between the two garishly painted pillars. She entered a small foyer. To the left was a flight of steps upward – she presumed to the projection room – and to her right, a small office and outside it a refreshment stall under a green-and-white-striped awning. On the walls she noticed fire buckets filled with sand and a fire axe. *Good*, she thought, *complying with fire regulations*.

Clara could hear the honky-tonk of an out-of-tune piano and she followed the other audience members through the double doors into the main auditorium. Alice had told her she and Jimmy had been slowly investing in new equipment. The projectors were still on their way, but the new sound system was already in place, and the audience would be able to hear the accompanying sound reel to *The Circus* with Chaplin singing songs even though there was no dialogue in the film. Their regular pianist was not happy with the new invention as it meant she only played while the audience were getting settled – and got half the pay for it! But for the children who could only pay with jam jars it would still be a magical experience. Clara could hear their giggles and shrieks as the usher attempted to get them all seated. He bellowed at them all to pipe down or the show wouldn't start. This was met with boos and hisses by some of the older children.

The lights were dimmed and there was a distinct smell of fresh paint mingling with the smoke of nicotine addicts. The back half of the cinema was filled with stiff wooden chairs with attached cushions; the front half was lined with wooden benches. These were filled with the chattering children, their bare knees touching side by side. The long-suffering usher took her ticket and showed her to one of the cushioned seats. They were a far cry from the plush chairs she had sat in only last week at Covent Garden when she saw *The Canary Murder Case*. But she settled down anyway, listening to the jolly piano above the hubbub of children, and waited for the show to start.

Clara watched the opening scenes of the Chaplin film with almost as much excitement as the children on the benches in front of her. She had seen the film before but it still tickled her pink. She laughed along with the children as the little tramp was mistaken for a pickpocket and chased into the big top of a circus where he unwittingly became the star performer, getting caught up in a magic act, and then later walking on a tightrope – with monkeys clinging to his head! – to escape the police. Clara wondered to herself what might be lost if this were a talkie. Chaplin's particular gift was communicating with his body and his face. Could the little tramp survive the transition to sound? Chaplin of course had a beautiful singing voice, and Clara and the audience were swooned by his sad, haunting rendition of 'Swing High Little Girl', as the hapless tramp laid eyes on the woman of his dreams. But this was a voiceover, disembodied from the actor, and better for it, in Clara's mind. But then, suddenly, the fantasy was shattered: flames started licking the circus ring floor – real flames, in full colour.

Someone shouted, 'Fire! Fire!' and then all hell broke loose. Clara, doing her best to stay calm, didn't rush straight to the door but held back to make sure the children were shepherded safely towards the exit. One little boy fell to the ground and was in danger of being trampled. Clara scooped him up and carried him out, then she returned along with the usher to help direct the rest of the evacuation. Another young man ran past them both carrying a fire bucket.

'Mrs Whittaker's calling the brigade! Get this lot out!'

'You be careful, Will!' shouted the usher as he picked up another child and passed it to one of the adult men.

'Don't worry, Alfie, I'll see if I can do owt, otherwise I'll see you outside,' said the young man. Then he ran towards the now-raging fire, hurdling overturned benches, and threw his bucket of sand onto the blaze. Clara could see that his efforts would make very little difference. She could feel the heat from the blaze searing her cheeks. And the smoke! She slapped a handkerchief over her nose and mouth and squeezed her eyes shut to ease the sting. She would not be able to stay there much longer. But she fought her fear long enough to help the terrified children to safety.

The usher – Alfie – looked at Clara over the heads of the last of them and said: 'Thanks for your help, miss, but it's time to get out.' He guided her out as over his shoulder he called to his colleague, 'Get out, Will! Leave it to the brigade!'

As she and the usher herded the last of the children out onto the street, Clara was relieved to hear the clanging of the fire brigade bell as a cheer went up from the huddled crowd. Then she saw Alice run down a side alley and decided to follow her.

Clara hurried to catch up with Alice as the woman ran towards the back of the burning building. Clara assumed they were heading towards the back door which was used as a fire escape. Alice had told her this was always left unlocked during shows, in case of emergencies like this, and if the fire had been in the projection room and spreading down the stairs into the foyer, the patrons would have been led out that way. However, as the fire was behind the screen, the safest exit was out the front door. Clara caught up with Alice as the cinema owner reached for the metal doorknob, with smoke seeping under the door.

'Don't touch it!' screamed Clara. But it was too late. Alice yelled as the heat from the metal seared into her flesh. But she held on, twisting the knob left and right.

'It's locked!' she shouted, desperately looking over her shoulder towards Clara. 'It's never locked! Could it be melted shut?'

Before Clara could answer, someone pushed past her. A fireman gripped Alice's shoulder and pulled her back. Then a second fireman steadied himself and swung an axe at the door again and again. The fireman was joined by another and another as the two women were pushed further back down the alley with shouted instructions of 'leave this to us, missus'. With the efforts of three firemen, the door finally splintered and gave in. And although their view was partially blocked, Clara and Alice were able to see the hunched body of a young man clutching two small children in his arms.

'Are they all right?' shouted Alice.

A fireman emerged from the scrum around the emergency exit. 'The bairns are all right – that brave fella saved 'em – but I'm afraid it's too late for him.'

'He's dead?' asked Alice, her voice barely above a whisper.

'Aye, missus, I'm sorry, but he is.'

Chapter 15

Newcastle upon Tyne, Friday 23rd August 1929

Clara opened the front door of Uncle Bob's house and was struck again by the shut-up smell of the place. But at least she could still breathe. She shuddered at the memory of the terrible fire at the Paradise. She had got back to her hotel yesterday evening, frustrated that she had not been able to do anything more to help Alice. She had wanted to examine the picture house for clues to the start of the fire, but the fire brigade wouldn't let her anywhere near. Then she had wanted to stay with Alice and the usher, Alfie, as the police interviewed them, but she was shooed away as surplus to requirements. She managed to catch a moment with Alice and the two women agreed to meet again the following afternoon. Alice would come through to Newcastle.

Clara had spent last night recovering at the hotel, surprised at how exhausted and shaken she was. She slept in as long as she could, but by mid-morning still had time to kill before the arranged meeting with Alice at Bob's office at two o'clock. So, she decided to visit the house. Now that she was here, she ought to open some windows to give the place an airing. She picked her way through the front drawing room, noting – once again – that every surface was covered with antiques and ornaments like a cluttered curiosity shop in a London backstreet. How on earth was she going to sort through this lot? What was she going to do with it all? She couldn't live in a house as overstuffed as this – assuming she chose to do so – but even if she decided to rent it out, it would still need to be cleared.

She managed to squeeze her way past a gramophone, piled high with magazines and record discs, to the sash window, and opened it a couple of inches. On closer inspection, the net curtains were edged with mould.

She then went to the dining room: the mahogany table was covered in stones and bones. A quick inspection revealed them to be fossils and archaeological artefacts. Now that was genuinely interesting, but the sheer volume of them was overwhelming. She wondered whether she might be able to get someone from the local museum – what was it called again, the Hancock? – to give her an assessment of some of the material. Perhaps it was worth exhibiting. And if so, they could help with the sorting and clearing . . . yes, that was a good idea. Having a plan of some kind always helped her feel better. She opened the dining room window.

Next was the library, and that was a pleasant surprise. Yes, it was crammed with books on every shelf and surface. But it was supposed to be. And there appeared to be some order. A quick perusal ascertained that the fiction was stacked alphabetically, and the non-fiction followed the Dewey classification. The librarian in Clara heartily approved. She skimmed the shelves and found her way to the 500s – the natural sciences – and her heart did a little pirouette when she saw books from Babbage to Darwin and Pasteur to Tesla. There was an entire bookcase of them, floor to ceiling. One of the books wasn't pushed in properly – she pulled it out to check if it was in the right place and saw that it was a text by Francis Galton called *Finger Prints*. The name Galton rang a bell. She was sure it had been mentioned in one of the Sherlock Holmes stories, but she couldn't recall which. A quick flick at the title page and contents revealed that it was not a misfiled fictional work but a scientific treatise by the eminent polymath Sir Francis Galton. Now this would make interesting reading!

She slipped the book into the shopping bag, alongside the Whittaker file – which was now considerably thicker with all the notes she had made yesterday. She opened the window in here too, noting that it overlooked the backyard of the house. It was a dreary yard – a mere expanse of paving with an outhouse and coal bunker – but creeping clematis and jasmine overhanging from the neighbours' garden walls suggested that it could be made into something far more appealing, if she chose to give it some attention.

She then decided to go upstairs. She had not gone up to the bedrooms when she had first come with Mr Jennings. There were five bedrooms and one bathroom, which had a commode but not a flushing toilet. That would definitely be top of her list of renovations if she were to move in. Three of the bedrooms were used as storage facilities housing more of Uncle Bob's ephemera from his travels. Clara simply opened then shut the doors. The other two bedrooms, however, were surprisingly tidy. One was clearly a guest bedroom, but the other she assumed to be Bob's bedroom due to the clothes in the wardrobe and the personal items on the dressing table. She ran her hand through the hanging jackets in the closet, releasing a miasma of mothballs mixed with stale tobacco. *These should probably go to the Salvation Army*, she thought.

She closed the wardrobe door and sat down on the bed, neatly made up with a clean candlewick bedspread. *Was this where he died?* Clara had not heard the specifics of how Bob died, other than that he'd died in his sleep, and that it was something to do with his heart. She still had to speak to his doctor. And, she chided herself, she still had to visit his grave. She was ashamed to realise that she had not even asked where her uncle was buried.

To add to her guilt, she suddenly noticed a framed photograph on the bedside table. It was of her and Uncle Bob sitting together having tea on the lawn of the Cornish holiday cottage. It was the summer of 1915, and she was wearing a white, high-collared dress with a sash around her waist. Her dark hair was in youthful ringlets, befitting a fifteen-year-old girl. Uncle Bob was wearing a white suit and a Panama hat, as if he were on the French Riviera. Neither of them was smiling as they looked at the camera, but there was an ease about them. Clara remembered that day. And she remembered the walk along the cliff top afterwards. She touched her finger to Bob's face and said out loud: 'I'm sorry, Uncle Bob. I'm sorry we didn't stay in touch. I'm sorry I stopped writing. And I'm sorry I didn't come to your funeral. I'm a shoddy niece and I didn't deserve you as my uncle. And I don't deserve to inherit all this. But I'll do my best for you now. I promise I will.'

Clara felt herself well up but bit her lip to stop the tears. She put the photograph in the shopping bag. There were other things to go through – private things – but she didn't feel ready to do so now. Instead, she decided to go downstairs to the laboratory. That's what she'd really come for anyway. She knew Bob would approve.

She scuttled down the stairs, through the kitchen and to the laboratory door. She searched for the key on the ring and found it, then pulled the light cord and went down the short flight of stairs. With more time on her hands and without Mr Jennings hovering, she perused the shelves, checking what kinds of chemicals and compounds were available, writing them down in her notebook. Then she did an inventory of the equipment and apparatus. On a desk, in the corner, were a series of notebooks where Uncle Bob had made notes on his experiments and investigations. A quick flick through ascertained what she had already deduced: her uncle had been an enthusiastic amateur. The academic level was not much above that of a clever student who had completed the first year of an undergraduate degree. Still, for a self-taught man it was very impressive.

Rather than what Clara would consider research science, Bob had focused more on criminalistics – or forensics as the Americans called it. Which of course made sense in his line of work. There were notes on the chemical make-up of soil found on the sole of a suspect's shoe; an unpleasant analysis of some vomit, which Bob had ascertained was seventy per cent alcohol; an intriguing diagram showing the angle of blood spatter across a tablecloth; and the composition of a lipstick smear on a gentleman's collar. This, Clara expected, had something to do with one of the adultery and divorce cases that Jack Danskin told her made up much of an enquiry agent's business. Each experiment or analysis was marked with a case name, and Clara wondered if they matched the files in Uncle Bob's office.

Next to the notebooks was a well-thumbed book called *A Practical Handbook for Magistrates, Police Officers and Lawyers* by Professor Hans Gross, from the University of Prague. It had originally been written in German but had been translated into English and published in Madras, India. Clara wondered if her uncle had picked it up there on his world travels. The table of contents covered subjects such as 'identifying criminals', the 'language of criminals' and 'how to deal with the press'. It explained what to do when an investigator arrived at a crime scene and how to interview the witnesses or accused. The reprint was dated 1906 and Clara expected some of the science in it to be a little out of date; nonetheless, it looked like a very useful introduction to the subject of using scientific techniques in criminal and legal investigations. It explained how to look for traces of blood, excrement; the use of weapons and ballistics; falsification of handwriting; photography and fingerprints; along with chemical analysis of minerals and plants. There was also an intriguing section on poisons and, helpfully for the case at hand, a short section on arson.

She was very tempted to settle down and read it all now, but instead decided to take it back to the hotel. She placed it, along with Bob's notebooks, into her shopping bag. Then she had a quick search through the desk drawers. On one side was a store of stationery, including some blank notebooks. She helped herself to one of those as well as some pens, pencils, an eraser, rule, compass, protractor and set square. She wasn't sure yet how she would use them, but she imagined she would want to draw some diagrams when she was finally allowed to get near the Paradise Picture House.

Then she checked the other drawer. *Hello, hello? What's this?* There was a leather case, about fourteen by ten inches, and four inches deep, with the initials RWW embossed on the front. RWW? Robert Wendell Wallace? The top of the case was fastened closed with buckles and there was a carry handle on the side. She undid the buckles, intrigued to see what was inside, and was thrilled to discover what she assumed was a fingerprinting kit. There were brushes, a set of callipers, a protractor, rule, tweezers, a magnifying glass and a couple of jars of aluminium powder, an ink pad and some waxed paper cards. There were also a few photographs of fingerprints, held in a pouch, with handwritten notations. Clara had never examined fingerprints before, but from the contents of the box she had an idea of how to go about it. There was also the book she'd found on fingerprinting upstairs, as well as the criminal investigation handbook she'd picked up down here. She buckled closed the case and placed this too in her shopping bag.

She then turned her attention to the central bench in the laboratory where she'd first seen the microscope, the charred wood sample and the note on kerosene. The note was in an open notebook and Clara was pleased to see the case name 'Whittaker' written at the top of the page. She flicked back but the file name before that was 'Armstrong', and from what she could see, it involved the examination of bullets. *Ah yes*, she thought, *I saw that file in the office*. She flicked the page to the Whittaker case and saw that Bob had been making some more notes on the Carousel fire in Tynemouth. Bob had done some calculations about the time it would take for the fire to take hold, considering the known furnishings and available accelerants at the Carousel. She grunted with approval, checking his arithmetic and his methodology. She would use a similar strategy in her approach to investigating the second fire at the Paradise. She noted too a circled note saying: *get sample of silver screen. Rate of combustion?*

Absolutely, thought Clara, *that will be essential to determine.*

Then came the note on kerosene, a petroleum distillate, with the formula $C_{12}H_{26}$–$C_{15}H_{32}$. *Yes*, she confirmed, *that's the formula for kerosene*. She then turned to the wood sample next to the microscope. It looked like it might have been the seat of a stool. She had a look through the microscope and confirmed that there appeared to be chemical scalding. She looked around the laboratory and was relieved to find what she hoped for: a test tube with a piece of wood sample in it, soaking in a liquid. She took the stopper out of the test tube and sniffed. Yes, it definitely smelt like kerosene. Clara suspected that Bob had used a soap solvent – possibly naphtha – to extract the kerosene from the wood. She took a pipette and extracted a small sample of the liquid and placed it on a microscope slide. She then slipped it under the microscope. A few minutes later she confirmed Bob's analysis: it was indeed kerosene with traces of naphtha. 'Well done, Uncle Bob,' she said out loud. The evidence before her suggested that there had been kerosene splashed on furnishings at the Carousel. She still had to check with Alice whether there was already kerosene on the premises – there or at the Paradise.

Clara's stomach grumbled. She checked her watch and saw that there was still a while before she was to meet Alice. There was time for a bite to eat. She doubted there was anything in the house, so she decided to go to a bakery to get herself a sandwich. She cleared up the bench and reset the microscope, then rinsed off the pipette and the slide. She placed Bob's current notebook in the shopping bag with the rest of her haul. Had she just managed to assemble a starter kit for a private investigator? She chuckled; it certainly looked that way!

But there's one thing missing . . . She opened the door at the back of the laboratory to reveal a photographic darkroom. She switched on the white light – noted there was a red one too – and glanced around. There was photographic developing equipment, a string with pegs strung across the back wall and . . . yes, that's what she was hoping to find . . . three cameras with a selection of lenses, flash bulbs and film spools. She selected the simplest, most portable device – a Kodak Brownie, a model she had used before to document her own work in the laboratory in Oxford – and some bulbs and spools. The shopping bag was getting quite heavy!

She shut the darkroom door behind her and was preparing to leave the laboratory when she heard the creak of a floorboard upstairs. She froze. Had she just imagined it? No, there it was again. Her mind raced. She'd left the windows open on the ground floor. Had someone sneaked in? She rushed up the stairs and locked the door, her heart racing ten to the dozen. What would she do if whoever it was tried to break in? She looked around for a weapon and found a hacksaw. She stood with it held in both hands, shaking. Then she came to her senses. *What do you think you're doing? Do you really think you'll be able to defend yourself with this if the assailant is strong enough to kick down the door? Pull yourself together, woman!*

Clara backed down the stairs, still holding the hacksaw, but no longer intent on using it. She looked around the laboratory and considered for a moment a bell jar of sulphuric acid. *Now that will do some damage . . .* However, before she committed to self-defence with acid, she noticed the window. As this was a basement laboratory it was high up on the wall, above the desk. She climbed up and peeked out. It overlooked the backyard. If she could haul herself up, she could squeeze through.

She listened and could still hear footsteps above. Then, to her horror, the handle of the door rattled. She stood on tiptoe and opened the window – which needed a bit of a push and a heave – then leapt to the floor, picked up a stool and placed it on the desk. She climbed up, precariously, then pushed her handbag and the heavy shopping bag through the window first. Then she clambered through herself, swearing as she felt her stocking tear on the window catch. But she carried on regardless and was soon sprawled in an ungainly pile on the yard flagstones.

She did not tarry. Tempted as she was to peer through the windows and see who it was who might have broken into her uncle's house, memories of the break-in at the office, and the man in her hotel room on Wednesday night, compelled her instead to run to the back gate of the yard. She yanked it open and ran down the lane and around the corner. She was just about to go into the Corner House pub at the top of St Thomas' Crescent, and ask them to telephone the police, when she saw someone coming out of the front door of her uncle's house. And then locking it. It was a woman. A perfectly respectable-looking middle-aged woman.

Suddenly Clara realised who it was. She pulled herself together and walked as calmly as she could towards her uncle's house.

'Good afternoon, madam,' she said. 'Are you, by chance, Mrs Hobson?'

The woman turned to see who was speaking to her. She gave Clara a curious but polite look. 'I am,' she said, with a strong Geordie accent. 'Can I help you, miss?'

'I hope so. I'm Miss Vale. Bob Wallace's niece.'

Chapter 16

Clara and Mrs Hobson were seated at Uncle Bob's kitchen table waiting for a kettle to boil on the wood-burning range. Clara confessed to Mrs Hobson that she had been the one to open the windows after Mrs Hobson explained that she had just been passing when she saw the open windows and was worried that Mr Jennings had been in and forgot to close them.

'He's a bit absent-minded like that, Mr Jennings is, a bit like Mr Wallace was.'

'Uncle Bob was absent-minded? I've never heard that before.'

'Oh aye, when he was focused on a case or one of his experiments, he could think of nowt else.'

Clara didn't consider that absent-minded, she considered it an admirable commitment to work, but decided not to contradict the housekeeper. She watched the woman as she got up to take the kettle off the range. She was a tall woman with a fine figure. Her honey-blonde hair was free of grey, despite being in her mid-forties, cut short and marcel-waved. Mrs Hobson appeared to be a woman who took pride in her appearance. Her clothes were well cut and on the more fashionable end of the spectrum, without giving the wearer the appearance of mutton dressed up as lamb. She was what Clara considered to be an attractive woman of middle years with, as her dreadful brother would put it, a 'bit of mileage in her yet'.

'So,' said Mrs Hobson, pouring the water into the pot and popping a cosy over it, 'have you decided to take on the house?'

Clara nodded. 'I shall certainly be taking ownership of the house, yes. I haven't decided yet whether I will live in it or rent it out.'

'Either way you'll need a housekeeper.'

'I might. I don't have a housekeeper in my flat in London. I clean it myself.'

'Oh aye? Why's that?'

'It's a small flat. And I don't earn that much money.'

Mrs Hobson looked momentarily disappointed, but then gathered herself. 'This is a big house, though, Miss Vale. D'ya think you'd be cleaning this all yourself?'

Clara looked around at the large kitchen and scullery. Her entire living room cum dining room and kitchenette of her Bloomsbury studio flat could fit in here. She shook her head. 'Probably not. Look, Mrs Hobson, I know you're hoping I'll commit to keeping you on, but I'm not in a position yet to make that decision. I'm still working things out. I don't know yet whether I'll be staying in Newcastle or going back to London and renting the place out. I need more time to decide. However, I shall certainly consider you for the job if I do decide to take on a housekeeper. My uncle seemed to think very highly of you.'

A flicker of emotion passed over the housekeeper's face as she poured them each a cup of tea. 'Did he tell you that? I didn't think you'd been much in touch these last years.'

Did Clara detect a slight barb? 'We haven't been. But he wrote me a letter and mentioned you in it.'

'Oh aye?'

'Yes. He said you were a good housekeeper and, if I needed one, I should consider taking you on. And I certainly shall.'

'Is that all he said?' Her eyes narrowed.

'What do you mean?' Clara parried, suddenly on guard.

'About me. In the letter. Did he say anything else?'

'I'm afraid that was it.'

'Oh.' With an air of huffiness, Mrs Hobson took off the cosy and poured them each a cup of tea.

Clara recognised the demeanour. Her mother would adopt it when she'd been slighted in some way and wanted her children to offer a grovelling apology. Clara would not be manipulated by her mother and she certainly wouldn't be manipulated by this woman.

She did not try to keep an edge of annoyance out of her voice. 'What are you trying to say, Mrs Hobson? What did you hope my uncle had said to me?'

Mrs Hobson put down the pot with a thud and looked directly into Clara's eyes. 'I was expecting he'd have told you about our engagement.'

Clara was glad she didn't already have a cup of tea in hand or she would have spluttered it everywhere. 'Your what?'

'Our engagement. Bob and I were engaged to be married.'

Clara was flabbergasted. She recalled what Juju Levine had told her about Mrs Hobson hoping to marry her uncle and that Bob had not been interested. That he wasn't interested in women. Still, Clara thought, she knew of men with homosexual tendencies who did get married. To keep the appearance of social respectability and in order to secure inheritances. She lived, after all, in the highly bohemian quarter of Bloomsbury where, it was said, the artistic and intellectual set lived in squares but loved in triangles. She knew of a number of married couples who had lovers of the same sex. But this was not Bloomsbury, and Uncle Bob, despite his eccentricities, was not a bohemian. No, Bob struck her as a committed bachelor. The conversations she'd had with everyone who knew him suggested nothing else. No one had mentioned a fiancée. And if he had one, why had he not mentioned that in his will?

Clara smiled, tightly. 'I'm sorry, Mrs Hobson, but this is the first I have heard of this. My uncle did not mention it in his letter to me, nor are you mentioned in his will other than as his housekeeper. I believe he left you a small bequest.'

Mrs Hobson sniffed. 'He did. Two hundred pounds. That's all.'

'I think that's rather generous, don't you? For a housekeeper.'

'For a housekeeper, aye, but I was more than that.'

Clara was losing her patience. 'I'm sorry to be so indelicate about this, but do you have any evidence of your engagement?' She looked at Mrs Hobson's hands and saw a single gold band on her ring finger. 'Did Bob give you that?'

Mrs Hobson shook her head. 'No, that's my wedding ring from my first husband. Bob was having my ring made. He was using a stone he'd dug out of a diamond mine in the Yukon when he was last there.'

Clara let out an involuntary snort. Mrs Hobson glared at her. 'You don't believe me. You think I'm lying.'

'Well, Mrs Hobson, I'm sorry, but this is the absolute first I've heard of it. Why would my uncle be leaving his entire estate to me when he was engaged to be married to you?'

Mrs Hobson stood up, placed both hands on the table and leaned forward. 'Aye, why would he? Someone's lying here, missy, and it ain't me.'

Clara stood too and adopted the same pose. 'I have absolutely no reason to lie. I arrived here on Monday, expecting to receive a small bequest. I did not expect to inherit everything. But I have. Bob chose to leave it all to me, not to you. And seeing you were merely his housekeeper, that is not surprising. There is no evidence whatsoever that the two of you were engaged, other, I'm sorry to say, than your wishful thinking. Which I was already warned against.'

'You were? By whom?'

'Someone who knew Bob Wallace better than you, it seems.'

Mrs Hobson smirked. 'Jonny Levine.'

'Actually no, it wasn't him. It was someone else.'

'His sister then. She's as mad as a hatter. They both are.'

'And you're not?'

Mrs Hobson leaned in again. 'No, missy, I'm not. I said earlier that your uncle was a bit absent-minded, but what I didn't say was that towards the end – in the last few months – he was beginning to get quite confused. So I would take what he said – and didn't say – in that letter to you with a pinch of salt. There's far more to our relationship than he told you.' She then drew back, picked up her handbag from the floor and opened it. She pulled out an envelope and threw it down on the table. 'There's my proof. Read it.'

Clara remained standing, reading the address on the envelope. It was addressed to Mrs J. Hobson at a Newcastle address.

'Open it.'

Clara did not want to be pushed around by the housekeeper, but her curiosity got the better of her. She picked up the letter and opened it.

It was dated 20th June 1929.

My dearest J,

'Jay. That's what Bob called me. My name is Jane but he always called me Jay. He was Bee. It started out as just J and B, when we were trying to keep our relationship quiet.'

'Why were you trying to keep it quiet?'

'We had our reasons. Now, read the letter please.'

Clara continued to read.

My dearest J,

I'm so sorry I forgot your birthday. I shall make it up to you. I have been forgetting a lot of things lately. I expect it's my heart. The medicine makes me tired. Perhaps we can take a drive up to Holy Island and take a walk on the beach. Perhaps we can stay at the Crown and Anchor. Remember the last time we stayed there? I shall never forget it. Let us see what the summer brings.

With greatest affection,

B

Clara laid the letter on the table between them. Her first thought was that she should analyse the handwriting and compare it to known samples of Bob's writing. She had the letter he wrote to her with the will. It certainly looked similar, but she needed to see the two letters side by side to be sure.

Mrs Hobson was looking at her expectantly, awaiting a response.

Clara cleared her throat. 'Well, assuming he did in fact write it, that says nothing of an engagement, Mrs Hobson.'

'It says he loves me.'

'It *suggests* that you and he might have been romantically involved. Although even that is far from conclusive. I admit, it certainly implies a degree of intimacy beyond that of an employer and employee, but it does not prove an engagement. I'm sorry, Mrs Hobson, that you have lost someone you admired, and it does not seem that admiration was reciprocated, but this letter was dated two days before the letter he wrote to me. The letter Mr Jennings gave me when he read the will. The letter in which you were unfortunately not mentioned in any capacity other than as a well-thought-of housekeeper. Now, if you will allow me, I'll get that letter and we can compare the two – to confirm that Bob really wrote this. And if he did, we can then discuss the contents further.'

Mrs Hobson snatched up the letter. 'You are a cruel woman, Miss Vale. Are you doing it on purpose?'

'Doing what?' asked Clara, astounded at the woman's gall.

'Deliberately trying to hurt a grieving woman.'

'No, Mrs Hobson, I am not. But if you expect me to give up the inheritance given to me by my blood relative to a woman who claims – without any substantiating evidence – that she was engaged, not married I might add, just engaged, to my uncle, then you are sorely mistaken.'

'I'm not asking you to give it up. I'm just asking you to share it. To give me some of it – let's say a few thousand pounds. It's what your uncle would have wanted.' Hobson's eyes had taken on a wild look.

Clara could not believe what she was hearing. 'If he wanted it, he would have said so. He would have written you – legally – into his will. He did not. He did, however, leave you a very generous bequest of two hundred pounds. He obviously thought you were worth that, and that I will respect. Beyond that, I bid you good day. Now,' she said, reaching out her hand, 'I ask you to give me the keys.'

'Keys?'

'To the house. And—' it suddenly occurred to her '—the keys to the office as well.'

'I do not have keys to the office.'

'Are you sure?'

'Yes, I'm sure! Are you calling me a liar twice in one day?'

'I have no idea what you are, Mrs Hobson. But I do know this is my house and you are no longer welcome in it.' The women glared at one another over the table.

'Do I have to call the police?'

The housekeeper looked like a volcano about to erupt. Clara braced herself, wondering for a moment if she were to be physically attacked.

She took a step back as Mrs Hobson reached once more into her handbag, but to Clara's relief it was only to retrieve a bunch of keys. The keys were flung onto the table, smashing into the sugar bowl, spilling the contents over the surface.

'Clean up your own bloody mess,' said Hobson, then stormed out of the kitchen.

Clara waited until she heard the front door slam shut, then took a few minutes to recover from the unpleasant encounter by finishing her cup of tea. She then cleaned up the spilt sugar, brushing it into her hand and depositing it in a bin. She was just about to wash up the cups when she had an idea. She dug into her shopping bag and pulled out the fingerprint kit, opened it and extracted the magnifying glass. Then, covering her hand with a tea towel, she picked up Jane Hobson's teacup and held it up to the light from the kitchen window. Peering through the magnifying glass she could not see anything on the cup handle, but, on the opposite side, she detected a couple of impressions where the housekeeper had used her thumb and forefinger to steady the cup.

'Bingo!'

Clara put down the cup and then retrieved two books from the shopping bag: the one on fingerprints and the handbook for investigators. She opened *Finger Prints* first, had a quick peruse, and realised it was going to be quite an in-depth read. She set it aside and opened Professor Gross's handbook. She ran her finger down the contents page and discovered that Chapter V, subsection xi on 'fingerprints' was a brief ten pages. 'That's better,' she said and settled down to read.

Chapter 17

Alice and Clara arrived at the office at the same time. If Alice had looked wan and weary the first time they'd met, she looked beyond exhaustion now: a wraith in her widow's weeds. 'Come in and have a cup of tea,' said Clara kindly and unlocked the door.

As Clara made tea Alice filled her in on what had happened in Whitley Bay after she left. Alice had spent the whole evening and most of this morning at the police station, being interviewed by the police and the fire chief, and incredibly the officials were already coalescing around the conclusion that this second fire was also due to negligence on behalf of the management.

'How can they say that?' asked Clara, incredulously.

Alice shrugged. 'It's not final yet, but I can see that's exactly what they will decide.'

'But that's ridiculous!'

'Aye, it is,' said Alice, shaking her head in despair. 'And to think a young man has actually died! Poor Will. He had no family, that lad. And we gave him a job when he had nothing. Jimmy was training him up as his assistant projectionist. And now they're blaming us for killing him instead of trying to find who really did. But can we prove it? Can we prove someone else was involved?'

Clara took out her notebook and pen. 'I don't know, Alice, but we have to try.'

Alice gave her a weary, grateful smile. 'Thank you, Miss Vale.'

'Please, call me Clara. Now, tell me what they've told you so far.'

Alice nodded. 'They think the cause of the fire was a faulty plug socket in the area behind the screen. That's dead space that we used for storage. We were busy doing up the building and had recently redecorated.' She smiled, sadly, as she remembered. 'We'd painted palm trees on the walls and grapevines up the pillars, as if we were really in a holiday paradise. Just like our name.

'We stored what was left of the paint, and the turpentine and all that, behind the screen. We were planning on moving it, but we hadn't got around to it yet. So, when the plug sparked – or so they say – the hessian covers we'd used during the decorating caught alight. Then it was made worse by the paint and all that, then finally the screen caught on fire.'

Clara nodded. She visualised the scene as she had seen it. The flames licking the projected floor of the circus ring. The paint 'and all that' certainly would have acted as an accelerant. Turpentine – a solvent – was a hydrocarbon and very flammable. She noted a chemical formula $C_{10}H_{16}$.

'What was plugged in to the socket?'

'A lamp. But we didn't switch it on that day.'

'Really?'

'Yes, we only switched it on when we were moving stuff in and out of the space. We didn't have an overhead light there, so we just put in a small desk lamp for when we needed a bit more light. It was easier than carrying a torch.'

'And when would you need more light in there?'

'Only when we were looking for something or moving things in and out. Like I said, we used it as a storage cupboard. We had extra chairs, ladders, bits and pieces of furniture and that.'

'No nitrate film?'

'No, we kept the spare films in a metal storage chest in the projection room. Just like at the Carousel. We spoke about it the other day, if you remember, about nitrate film being very flammable, so we take every precaution with it.'

'Yes, I remember. And I have something to ask you about the Carousel – which I was hoping to do yesterday – but let's finish off the Paradise first.' Clara reviewed her notes then said, 'So, apart from leaving some paint lying around you were fire safety conscious?'

'Oh yes,' said Alice, sitting up straight. 'Jimmy and me were very careful. We'd had the fire inspector in just a month before and we'd passed with flying colours. We had sand buckets and a fire escape plan and everything. Which was why I was so shocked to find the back door locked. That's always supposed to be open during shows. As a fire escape. We always unlocked it. Always.'

'You said to me yesterday that you wondered if the lock had melted shut in the fire.'

'Yes, that's what I thought. Because I knew it should have been open.'

Clara looked pointedly at Alice's bandaged hand. 'Is your hand all right?'

'Aye, it is. Don't worry about that.'

'All right. So back to the fire then. It's not very likely, the doorknob melting shut. The fire would have had to have been at blast furnace temperature for that to happen. And it hadn't had time to reach that level by the time the firemen got to Will and the children.'

Alice looked at Clara curiously. 'How do you know that?'

Clara shrugged. 'Because of what I observed. It couldn't have been longer than about fifteen minutes from the time we started evacuating the auditorium to the time the fire brigade got there. At least, that's the impression I got . . . do you think I'm wrong?'

Alice shook her head. 'No. You're right. About the timing. But I was wondering how you knew about – what did you call it – blast furnace temperature? And that the lock couldn't have melted.'

Clara shrugged again. 'I studied science.'

'Oh,' said Alice. 'That could be useful.'

Clara smiled gently. 'I hope so.'

Clara had expected more of a reaction. People were either dismissive or intrigued when she told them about her academic achievements, but Alice Whittaker obviously had more important things on her mind.

'Did the fire inspector say the door was actually locked?' asked Clara.

Alice nodded.

'From the inside or outside?'

'He couldn't tell. It had been locked with a key, not with a bolt or a padlock.'

'And where was the key kept?'

'It was usually left in the lock when we unlocked the door during shows. Then when we locked up in the evening after the final show, we would hang the key up in the office on the keyboard.'

'So why couldn't he tell that the door was locked from the inside then?'

'Because they haven't found the key yet. It wasn't in the lock, and it wasn't on the keyboard and it wasn't found in Will's pocket. I don't have it and neither does Alfie.'

'Ah,' said Clara and made a note. 'So, what do you think happened to it?'

Alice straightened up and folded her hands in front of her as if preparing for prayer. 'It was removed by whoever locked poor Will and the children in.'

'You think someone did it deliberately?'

'I do,' said Alice with conviction.

'And the police? Are they looking for that person?'

Alice shook her head and lowered her chin to her chest. 'No,' she said, without looking up. The spark of conviction from a moment ago had begun to flicker.

'But why?'

'Because – because . . .' then she looked up, with tears again brimming in her eyes '. . . they think Will did it. They – the police and the fire inspector – think that Will locked the door himself. That he'd failed to keep to the fire safety regulations, and that I had told him to do it.'

Clara was confused. 'But why would he do that? Why would you do that?'

'Exactly! There is no reason that he would. Or that I would.'

'What reason do they think you both had?'

Alice shifted in her seat. 'They think – they believe – that I told Will to lock the door on purpose to stop children sneaking in during the show without paying. They think it's what we had done for a while. That it's something Jimmy had started.'

'Why would they think that?'

'Because Jimmy had been heard in the pub one night complaining that some bairns had been doing that. But Miss Vale – Clara – I can tell you, Jimmy would *never* have locked the door. And neither would I. Alfie had been told to keep an eye on the door during the show and to collar anyone who tried to sneak in.'

'And did Alfie tell the police that?'

'Aye, he did. He's a good lad, Alfie, and he's broken-hearted about Will. They were best mates. They lived together.'

'Did Alfie say whether he saw anyone near the door?'

'He didn't see anyone. That's what he told the police and the fire inspector. But he also said he couldn't swear that the door was unlocked when the show started. So that wasn't enough to clear Will. And Will's not here anymore to defend himself. And . . .' Alice lowered her eyes, her shoulders slumping in defeat '. . . they say they have a witness. A fellow called Horace Fender who went down the alley to relieve himself. He claims that he saw Will lock the door half an hour before the show, pocket the key and walk around the front, then back inside.'

Clara was disturbed by this new information, trying to figure out how it all fitted together. 'Did you see him do that? Walking around the front? Because you would have been in the ticket booth then, wouldn't you?'

'Aye, I was. And I didn't see him. And that's what I told the police. But they either think I'm lying or that Will slipped in without me seeing him. It's a case of damned if I did and damned if I didn't!'

Clara leaned back in her chair, contemplating what she'd just heard. 'So, you're saying that the authorities think you – and then Will at your behest – were guilty of not following fire regulations and so he was responsible for his own death. And that you've lied about it to protect yourself.'

'That's right. The police told me if Will hadn't died, he'd have been arrested. And if it could be proved that I'd told him to do that, I'd be arrested too. And I still might be.'

Clara's eyes narrowed. 'Have they considered that this Horace Fender fellow might be lying?'

Alice shrugged in dismay. 'It doesn't look like it. I don't know.

I think it's that on top of a lot of things. Not least that this is the second time there has been a fire at one of our picture houses. It very much looks like negligence on our part, doesn't it?'

Clara had to admit it did. But there was no concrete evidence that it was. Clara, on the other hand, was willing to follow Bob's instincts that the woman in front of her – and her family and employees, and the poor young man who died, and the two children who nearly died – were the victims of a malicious campaign. But she still had to prove it.

'Don't worry,' she said eventually, 'we'll prove that they're wrong.'

'But how?' asked Alice, shaking her head.

'I'm not sure yet. But I have a few ideas to start with.' She checked her notes and pursed her lips. Then she tapped on the word 'lamp'.

'They think faulty wiring was the cause of the fire at the Paradise. From the lamp. Who do you think plugged in the lamp behind the screen if you didn't do it? Do you know?'

Alice shook her head. 'No. I don't.'

'Would the light have shone through the screen into the auditorium if it was on?'

'When the lights in the auditorium were down, yes. But not when they were up.'

'Would the light have been visible when the lights were just dimmed?'

'Through the screen? Yes. It would have been. We've accidentally left it on before and it shines through.'

'But it didn't this time? I can't say I recall seeing it, but then again, I wouldn't necessarily have known what I was looking at. I might have just thought it was part of the film.'

Alice stopped for a moment to think. 'I can't honestly say, Clara, I wasn't looking at the screen then either.'

'Who could have seen it? Your usher?'

'Alfie? Yes, Alfie would have seen it.'

Clara nodded. 'Thank you. And would he have switched it off if he'd seen it?'

Alice tapped her finger to her lips. 'Hmm. No. He would have asked me to do it because he couldn't leave the audience while they were getting settled.'

'How would he have alerted you if he couldn't leave the audience?'

'He would have flashed his torch at the projection box. It was our prearranged signal if he needed me for anything.'

'And he didn't flash it?'

'No.'

Clara made a note then leaned back in her chair, trying to visualise the series of events. Eventually she said: 'So that means either the light wasn't on before full darkness, or he didn't tell you that it was.'

'Why wouldn't he tell me?' Alice snapped.

'I have no idea, Alice; I'm just presenting the two logical options.'

'He would have told me,' she answered definitively, folding her arms across her chest.

Clara nodded and made a note. 'All right,' she said soothingly, not wanting to rile the already fragile Alice, 'so that means the lamp was most likely plugged in after the film started. Who could have done that?'

Alice unfolded her arms and picked at a thread on her bandage. 'I don't know.'

'It wasn't you?' Clara asked, as gently as possible.

'Of course not!'

Clara gave a comforting smile. 'I'm sorry, Alice, I'm not accusing anyone here; I'm just trying to find out what happened. So we can get to the truth.'

Alice gave a quivering sigh. 'I know, Clara, I'm sorry. I'm just a bit on edge. What else do you want to know?'

Clara held Alice's gaze for a moment, assuring herself there was a good rapport, then turned back to her notes. 'So it wasn't you. And it couldn't have been Will, because he was in the projection room, cranking the projector. So who could it have been?'

'I don't know, Clara, I really don't.'

'Alfie?'

'Possibly. But he didn't mention it.' She picked up a teaspoon and started tapping against the saucer.

'Did the fire inspector or the police ask him about it?'

'I'm not sure.'

'Could we ask him?'

The tapping stopped. Alice looked across the table at Clara. 'I suppose so. You'll have to come back with me to Whitley Bay.'

'That won't be a problem. Can we go tomorrow?'

'Yes. I've brought the children to stay with my sister in Heaton, here in Newcastle, and I'll get them settled tonight. We can go tomorrow.'

'Excellent. And I'd also like to get to Tynemouth too. I have some ideas I'd like to follow up. I've been reading my uncle's file on the Carousel fire. He had some concerns about traces of kerosene he found. His notes on this are brief, but I found more evidence in his laboratory. He noted that kerosene didn't feature in the fire inspector's report; however, Bob indicates that he found some at the fire scene. Do you know anything about that?'

Alice shook her head. 'No, he never mentioned that to me. It must have been just before he died.'

'Did you keep kerosene on the premises? Or did your brother-in-law?'

Another shake of the head. 'Not that I'm aware of. We did have turpentine though, because of the painting we'd just done, and that helped spread the fire. Like it did at the Paradise.'

Clara shook her head. 'Turpentine is fine. It's easy to tell the difference between that and kerosene – chemically, that is. The important thing is whether you specifically had kerosene.'

'No. Definitely not. That's mainly used for heating, isn't it? We had hot-water heating. Powered by a coal furnace in the basement. But that had nothing to do with the fire. The inspector didn't mention it.'

Clara nodded in agreement. 'That's right. It wasn't mentioned in the fire report. And Bob didn't pick up on it, so I reckon you're right – it had nothing to do with it. And you didn't have kerosene lamps?'

'No. We had electric lighting in the Carousel and the Paradise. No kerosene lamps.'

'All right, thank you,' said Clara, adding to her notes. 'Then that's an angle we can pursue. That and this Horace Fender fellow. We definitely need to speak to him.'

Chapter 18

It was four o'clock by the time Alice left Clara's office. After seeing her out, Clara cast a glance into the Levines' costume shop and saw both Juju and her brother busy with some customers. She tried to catch Juju's eye but didn't succeed. Instead, she went back upstairs and locked the door behind her. There was something she wanted to do.

After reading the investigators' handbook back at the house, she had figured out how to document fingerprints – first dusting them with the aluminium powder to make them visible, then photographing them. As there was a darkroom in the laboratory she had rushed down and developed the images immediately. Well, not immediately; the whole process took a good hour, as she first had to find everything she needed, but it was worth it as she now had some clear images of Jane Hobson's fingerprints. Now she needed to find some prints in the office. She didn't think the intruder had been Hobson – Juju had been clear that it was a man – but Clara did not believe the housekeeper when she said she didn't have keys. Might Hobson have let the man in? Or might Hobson have been searching for a copy of Bob's will? Fortunately, she had changed the locks, but she would be interested to find out if Hobson's fingerprints were actually here. And if not hers, whose were. Clara realised that she was acting like a child on Christmas morning, playing with her latest toy, but why not?

The doorknobs had been handled multiple times since the break-in so there was nothing useful there; however, the filing cabinet offered better options. There were a number of prints on different parts of the cabinet, including the bottom 'W' drawer. Some of them she realised would be hers, and perhaps Juju Levine's. She would need to get prints of her own and Juju's to eliminate them. Who else's might legitimately be there? Uncle Bob's? She had thought that fingerprints would fade after a few days or weeks, but not according to Professor Gross. Apparently, if not interfered with, they could remain intact for a good few years. So, she would need to eliminate Uncle Bob's too. The only place she could think of finding a match would be in the basement laboratory as the bathroom had been cleaned since his death. She'd have to go back later and see what she could find. But for now, she would dust and photograph the prints that were on the cabinet.

Half an hour later she had taken six photographs of dusted prints. Whether they belonged to the same or different hands she wouldn't know until she developed the photographs. She checked her watch. It was twenty to five. She pondered what to do next. She still needed to pop down to the Levines' shop to get Juju's prints and to tell her about her encounter with Mrs Hobson – and the latest developments with the fire investigation. By the time she'd finished there it would be getting on for dinner time (or teatime as Clara had discovered it was called in these parts). She should probably go back to the hotel for that. Would it be too late after that to return to the house, dust for Uncle Bob's prints and then develop the photographs? Did she want to be alone in the house at night?

Not really. But neither did she want to be cowed. She'd had a few scares already, but she was damned if she was going to be a Nervous Nellie about it. No, she would return to the house this evening after her meal. But she would not be unprepared. She got up, opened the cloakroom cupboard and accessed the safe. There was only one thing she wanted: the revolver. Professor Gross had a chapter on dealing with firearms and ballistics, but she already knew how to shoot. Both her parents were avid pheasant shooters and her father had an extensive gun collection. She and her sister, in the hope of improving their chances at snaffling an aristocrat, had been trained in weaponry and aristocratic country pursuits. Clara had joked that she would use her skill to see off any unwelcome aristocratic attention if it ever came her way. Her parents were not amused.

Clara picked up the weapon and weighed it in her hand. It was a .320 Webley Bulldog and designed to fit in a gentleman's jacket pocket. Would it fit into a lady's handbag? Clara gave it a try, but discovered it wouldn't unless she took out her make-up compact and purse. She would have to get herself a bigger bag. For now though, she wrapped it in a tea towel from the kitchenette and placed it, along with a box of bullets, into the erstwhile shopping bag. After that, she changed the combination on the safe, and committed it to memory.

Juju and Jonny Levine were just locking up when Clara came downstairs. Jonny was a small, bald gentleman with a neat black moustache and spectacles. He wore an immaculately cut grey three-piece suit and white shirt, but instead of a tie he sported a paisley cravat with a matching handkerchief in his pocket.

'Ah, Miss Vale, I assume? My sister has told me all about you.' He presented his hand to shake. Clara took it and shook it warmly.

'How do you do, Mr Levine. I am very pleased to meet you.'

'Please, call me Jonny.'

'Then I am Clara.'

Juju clapped her hands. 'And now we're all friends!' She looked at the shopping bag that was becoming so heavy with files, books, stationery, a fingerprinting kit, a camera, flash bulbs, a framed photograph and a revolver, that Clara had to rest it on the ground. 'Have you been shopping, Clara?'

Clara chuckled. 'In a manner of speaking. I know you're locking up, but do you mind if we go back inside for a while? I have something I'd like to do – and I have an awful lot to tell you.'

At the back of the shop, through a curtain, was a workshop area with two sewing machines, a family of dressmaker's dummies and a rainbow of fabric rolls. On the walls were sketches of theatre and pantomime costumes. Three of the dummies were wearing garish, overblown gowns.

'Cinderella's stepmother and the ugly sisters,' explained Juju. 'That's what they're doing at the Theatre Royal this Christmas. We're trying to get a head start.'

'They look, er, spectacular . . .' offered Clara, not being a frequenter of pantomime herself.

'They're hideous,' said Jonny, then smiled at Clara, 'but thank you for trying to be diplomatic. Your uncle was quite forthright himself.

He had to work very hard to bite his tongue. However, he realised that diplomacy was a useful skill to have in his business, as I'm sure you'll find out. Please, take a seat.'

Clara sat down opposite Jonny while Juju busied herself with extracting three glasses and a decanter from a cupboard. 'Port?' asked Juju. 'It's after five o'clock. We prefer it to sherry.'

'Oh, go on, why not?' said Clara, and accepted a glass. 'However, before I get too squiffy, would you mind if I took your fingerprints?'

The brother and sister were taken aback, but listened to Clara as she explained why she wanted them. They readily agreed and watched with interest as she took out an ink pad, roller and waxed paper from her uncle's fingerprinting kit, and then followed the instructions in the investigation handbook.

'I already have Jane Hobson's,' explained Clara and then went on to tell the brother and sister what had happened at the house.

'Heavens above! I cannot believe that's true!' exclaimed Juju.

Clara bristled. 'I can assure you, that's exactly what happened.'

'No, not what you've told us, my dear – I'm sure you have been scrupulously honest in your account. I cannot believe that Bob wrote that letter to her! Can you, Jonny?'

Jonny shrugged, got up and washed the ink off his fingers at a basin. 'Well, Bob didn't tell us everything about his personal life, Juju.'

'I know, but well, you know, he was homosexual . . . don't give me that look, Jonny, you know I've already told Clara that. So tell me, why would he write a letter like that?'

'Perhaps he didn't,' said Jonny.

'I was wondering the same myself,' said Clara.

'Can you confirm that it was your uncle's handwriting?' Jonny continued.

Clara shook her head. 'I was hoping to do a comparison between the letter and another sample, but Hobson snatched it away before I could. From what I recall of Bob's writing – from his letters and also in his laboratory notebooks – it certainly *looked* like the same handwriting. But I have not done a formal analysis.'

'Are you suggesting it's a forgery? That Mrs Hobson forged the letter?' asked Juju.

'It's something to seriously consider,' said Jonny.

'Yes, it is,' said Clara. 'Or she could have intercepted the letter to someone else and put it in an old envelope, addressed to her, to imply it was written to her. I can't say whether the writing on the envelope was the same as the letter. I didn't get a close enough look. And of course I don't have it anymore, or else I could have done some proper handwriting analysis.'

Jonny nodded thoughtfully. 'I wonder who it could have been written to if not Hobson? It certainly sounded like there was a degree of intimacy between them.'

Juju offered Clara a second glass of port. Clara accepted and Juju poured another for herself and her brother. After having a sip Clara said: 'A degree of intimacy, yes. But it didn't actually say "I love you". It suggested they'd spent some time together at a hotel on Holy Island. Now while that certainly implies a sexual encounter, it's quite possible they had separate rooms. They might have just been there as friends and Hobson misinterpreted it.'

Jonny laughed. 'Not very likely. Why on earth would Bob take his housekeeper on a jolly to Holy Island? I know he was fond of her, but I never got the idea they had much in common and that he'd like to spend any kind of recreational time with her – either physically or intellectually. No, I'll still plump for the forgery option.'

Clara was taking it all in. She considered what Jonny had said about Bob and Jane Hobson not having much in common. That rang true with her impression of the woman she'd just met. Perhaps she was being unfair, but the housekeeper had not struck her as an intellectual polymath like her Uncle Bob. However, there were other qualities that drew people together and, as was often said, opposites sometimes did attract. After a while she said, 'There is still the possibility that Bob was attracted to both men and women. Some people are, I believe.'

Jonny shook his head vehemently. 'Not Bob. He and I were never lovers, but I knew we were very similar like that. I have never been attracted to a woman. Not ever. And I don't think Bob was either.'

'All right,' said Clara, 'I accept that you knew him better than I did. But you are the first to admit that you didn't know everything about him. And now that he's gone, we may never know. What I would like to know though, is why Jane Hobson *believes* Bob was in love with her. Is it just her fevered imagination, or did she have genuine grounds to base it on?'

'Are you saying you will consider her claim to part of his estate?' asked Juju, sipping eagerly at her port.

'No, not that. I still contend that Bob would have made his will clear if that was the case. But it might impact on the way I treat her. I threw her out of the house because of the way she behaved towards me. That has enraged her. She might come back again. I might have to take further action against her.' Clara thought for a moment of the revolver in her shopping bag. Might she have cause to actually use it to defend herself? She hoped not. However . . . 'If she is deluded,' she continued, 'she might be dangerous. If she has genuine grounds, then perhaps she can still be reasoned with, as she is ultimately a victim in this affair. In which case I should not be too harsh with her. But there's another possibility . . .'

'What's that?' asked Jonny, swilling the last of his port around the bottom of the glass.

'That she is lying about the whole thing. That she has made it all up. That your first instinct, Jonny, is correct. That she forged the letter. If that's the case, who knows what else she might be willing to do to get her hands on Bob's estate?'

Juju's eyes were wide. 'You think she might try to do you harm?'

Clara shrugged. 'I don't want to be melodramatic about it, but I'm not going to discount that possibility. I have had a number of unsettling incidents since I arrived here. I wonder if she has been in Bob's office since he died. And if so, why? There's every possibility she may be the one who tried to get the Whittaker file. Perhaps someone paid her to do it. Or paid her to open the door for someone else to search for it. She seems awfully keen on getting her hands on some money.'

Jonny looked at Clara curiously. 'Why would someone want the Whittaker file? What's going on here, Clara, that you haven't told us?'

Clara looked from brother to sister, took a deep breath, then proceeded to tell them about her suspicions around the Whittaker case and the second fire in Whitley Bay, which neither had yet read about in the paper.

The twins stared at her, pale-faced. 'Goodness me,' said Juju. 'Poor, poor Alice. As if she doesn't have enough to worry about with the death of her husband. And now this poor young man has died too! And those children! Thank God they are all right. But it could very easily have been a triple tragedy. And you think Hobson might be involved in some way?'

Clara took a sip of her port. 'I don't know. You said it was a man who pushed you over. Perhaps Hobson just let him in. I'm only suspicious because of her seeming so desperate for money today and her anger that Bob has not left her more than two hundred pounds. But it's all pure speculation at this stage. And perhaps I am being unfair to her because she annoyed me. So I will not be making any formal accusations against her – or anyone else – unless I have proof.'

'I think that's very wise,' said Jonny, and raised his glass to her. 'And that's exactly what your uncle would have done, too.'

'I believe so,' said Clara, finishing her port and packing away her fingerprint case. She picked up the shopping bag, its strap groaning under the weight of the accumulated detection paraphernalia. Clara looked expectantly at Juju and Jonny. 'Do you perhaps have a satchel I could borrow?'

Chapter 19

A few minutes later, with her 'detection kit' transferred to the borrowed satchel, Clara left the shop as Juju and Jonny finally locked up. A green Austin 7 pulled up to the kerb with an auburn-haired gentleman at the wheel, and a boy and girl of around ten and twelve in the back. A worried-looking Andrew Ridpath got out – he was holding a newspaper.

'Miss Vale! I've just read about the dreadful fire! Are you all right?'

Clara smiled at him, grateful for his concern. 'I am, thank you, Mr Ridpath. It was a huge shock, of course, but my discomfort is nothing compared to that of the victims.'

'Quite,' said Ridpath. 'However, it says in the paper that a Miss Vale, visiting from London, helped with the evacuation. So I'm glad you are unharmed. Very glad. Look, I'm just taking the children to the North East Coast Exhibition. Would you like to accompany us? We can have a stroll around, then I'll take you back to your hotel. It's a lovely warm evening . . .'

It was a lovely warm evening, and Clara was wearing her blue summer frock and straw sun hat. She was tired, yes, but perhaps an outing like this would help her relax. She smiled at Andrew Ridpath. 'I should love to, thank you. Everyone has been talking about this exhibition, so I really ought to go.' She said goodbye to Jonny and Juju – the latter giving her a 'knowing look' – while Ridpath opened the passenger door. Clara thanked him. Back in the driving seat, he tossed his head over his shoulder and said: 'Miss Clara Vale, meet Jemima and Simon Ridpath, my niece and nephew.'

'How do you do, Miss Vale,' said the youngsters together.

'How do you do,' said Clara and smiled at the children. Clara was not always that comfortable around small children – her own nephews and nieces were something to be endured, not enjoyed – but these two were older and on first impression well behaved. The boy had his uncle's auburn hair and freckles and wore a pair of grey shorts and a buttoned-up short-sleeved blue-checked shirt. His face was flushed with excitement. The older girl had dark blonde hair, which Clara thought would probably go brown in a couple of years, worn in two plaits. She was on the cusp of puberty with a slight swelling at her chest, and her face had lost the plumpness of childhood. But her dress – a lilac flower pattern, with a pretty white lace collar – seemed like something a younger child would have worn, and a quick look at her feet indicated she was wearing flat T-bar shoes and ankle socks, rather than the pumps and stockings of an older girl. She met Clara's gaze, her eyes curious but not challenging.

Ridpath stuck his hand out of the window to indicate he was pulling out into Percy Street and carried on, parallel to the tramline until he reached the Hancock Museum, where he turned left.

'Excuse me, Miss Vale, I hope you don't mind me asking, but are you named after the village, Clara Vale?' asked young Jemima.

Clara looked over her shoulder and smiled at the girl.

'I have no idea. You are the second person to mention it to me. But before my arrival here on Monday evening I had no idea there was such a place.'

'Maybe the village is named after Miss Vale,' said Simon. 'They name villages after famous people, you know.'

'Don't be silly,' said his sister. 'Miss Vale is far too young to have a village named after her.'

'And,' said Clara, smiling back at the children, 'not at all famous.'

Simon looked vaguely disappointed; Jemima gave a shy but knowing smile.

'Why did your parents give you your name then?' challenged Simon after regrouping.

'Simon! Don't be impertinent!' chided his sister.

'Oh, that's all right,' said Clara. 'It's a very reasonable question. But the answer is: I don't know. My surname is of course Vale, so perhaps that reminded my mother of Clara Vale. She was originally from Newcastle. And of course, Clara is a perfectly ordinary girl's name.'

'I think it's a very pretty name,' said Jemima, 'don't you, Uncle Andrew?'

Ridpath grinned back at his niece. 'I do indeed,' he said, then quickly turned his attention back to the end-of-office-day traffic crawling its way out of the city centre.

For some inexplicable reason, Clara felt pleasantly flattered. She was surprised at her reaction. He hadn't said it in a flirtatious way but there was something – what was the word she was looking for? – something *nice* in the way he had said it. Clara cast a quick glance at the driver. He was handsome; not in the rakish, matinee idol way of Jack Danskin, but still manly. It had been eight years since her last romance – the one that ended in tipsy, fumbling intimacy in that Oxford flat – and she had not had the inclination to get involved with anyone since. Until now, perhaps?

Good God, girl! she chastised herself. *What are you thinking?* She'd barely met the man. He was her late uncle's accountant, lived on the other side of the country to where she did and – well – she had no idea if he was even available. He might be married, for all she knew. Clara gave herself an inward shake and put all thoughts of romance out of her mind. A few minutes later they pulled up into the car park on the Town Moor, adjacent to the newly built Exhibition Park.

The North East Coast Exhibition – which Andrew Ridpath explained was a world fair showcasing North East England's industry, commerce and culture – was in full swing. It had been opened in May by the Prince of Wales, and local dignitaries and business leaders believed this was the beginning of the great renaissance of the North East. And why shouldn't it be? The Great War had ended over a decade ago. The coal miners' strikes that had marred much of the decade had now ended – albeit with the miners having to accept lower wages. But beyond that, jobs were up, unemployment was down, and those with cash to spare were making money on the booming stock market. Clara was very impressed with the modernity of it all, in stark contrast with the backwards image she'd initially held of the city. To top it all, the sun was shining, and the first thing young Simon asked for as they entered the park – custom-built with a neoclassical pavilion and ornamental lake – was ice cream. His Uncle Andrew grinned and ruffled his hair.

'Your mam will have my guts for garters if I spoil your tea.'

'Oh please, Uncle Andrew?'

'Oh, go on then.' Andrew, as Clara was beginning to think of him, rather than Mr Ridpath, led the little group to a Mark Toney ice cream kiosk. A few minutes later they were all tucking into their delicious Italian treats. Then Simon spotted the paddleboats. Again, after a bit of good-natured arm twisting, which Clara had no doubt Uncle Andrew would succumb to, the children – who had gobbled down their ice creams – were drifting on the tranquil artificial lake. Jemima had demanded she take charge, and Andrew informed Simon that he must listen to his sister, or the boat ride would be cancelled.

Clara and Andrew took a seat on a nearby bench and watched the children. She was relieved to finally have him to herself – not for any romantic purposes, but rather because she wanted to talk about the business and update him about what had happened since she'd last seen him.

'Thanks for sending around the locksmith, by the way. That's all sorted now.'

Andrew unbuttoned his jacket and draped it over the back of the bench. Clara noticed his arms were pleasantly muscular through the linen of his pinstriped shirt. 'You're welcome. Glad he could do it at such short notice. Hope he didn't charge you an arm and a leg.'

Clara smiled. 'Just an arm and a half. I think he heard the southern accent and assumed I must be loaded.'

Andrew raised a sardonic eyebrow. 'Well, by some standards you probably are. And soon – speaking as your accountant – considerably more so.'

'I don't suppose the transfer to my brother has been sorted?'

Andrew shook his head. 'Not as far as I'm aware. But I think they're still on track for Monday. I spoke to someone at the bank today.'

'You did? Oh good. I'm glad that's still in hand. I let the library know I'll be taking some more time off.'

'Tell me about your work at the library,' he said. 'Is it a library that specialises in science?'

Clara shook her head. 'No. Just a general library. I hold a degree in Chemistry from Oxford and always hoped to get a job in science – in a laboratory – but that hasn't worked out. Did you always want to be an accountant?'

Andrew laughed, but for the first time Clara noted a tinge of something other than good humour. Bitterness? Irony?

'Not really. But my father was an accountant, and my brother still is. Jemima and Simon's father. And when I came back from the war, it was a good steady job. I took it on until something else came along. That was eleven years ago now.'

'And nothing else has come along?'

'Nothing as exciting, no.' This time his laugh was authentic.

Clara laughed too. 'So what would you have liked to have done if you had the choice?'

Andrew thought for a moment and said: 'I'm not really sure. I always enjoyed the adventure of the army, but not the war itself.' He laughed; the bitter tinge was back. 'I can't say I enjoyed shooting anyone or being shot at. But I did enjoy travelling. And I did enjoy the physical exercise. And the planning and strategy. I was a lieutenant, and helped plan some missions. So, if I could have had a civilian job like that, I would have enjoyed it. An explorer or a geographer perhaps. Something a bit more exciting than accountancy.'

'Well, there's been a bit of excitement lately, hasn't there? Walking into a burgled office the other day.'

'Oh yes, not my ordinary day on the job. But I'm glad it wasn't any more exciting.'

'Meaning?'

'I'm glad the burglar wasn't still there. And I'm glad Miss Levine wasn't hurt.'

'So am I,' said Clara, seriously, then went on to tell him that the police would not be following it up as there was no evidence that it was an actual break-in or that anything had been taken. She then went on to tell him about the subsequent break-in at her hotel room and that the police appeared to be reluctant to do much about that either.

'Good God! Do you think they're connected?'

Clara nodded. 'I do. And I think they might also have something to do with the fire at the picture house yesterday.'

Andrew turned to her, his face serious. 'What do you mean?'

'Are you aware of a case my uncle was working on about a picture house that burned down in Tynemouth?'

'The Whittaker case? Of course! This is the second fire. I hadn't made the connection until now.'

'And do you think that's just a coincidence?'

Andrew waved enthusiastically at his nephew and niece who were doing another circuit of the lake in their paddleboat. 'It would be an enormous coincidence if it were,' he finally answered.

'That's what I think too. What do you know about the case my uncle was working on?'

'Not much, other than Mrs Whittaker would pay if and when the insurance paid out. Your uncle sent in an itemised bill of expenses a few days before he died. Why do you ask?'

'Because,' said Clara, giving a slightly less enthusiastic wave to the children, 'I think that's what the burglar was looking for – both times. The drawer with the Ws in it was the one that had been searched, but that file wasn't there. I had taken it with me to the hotel to read on Wednesday night. The night there was a break-in in my room. But the file wasn't there. I'd had the foresight to put it in the hotel safe.'

'That was fortuitous. But do you have any hard evidence yet? That that's what the burglar was looking for? Other than that the "W" drawer was searched.'

Clara scowled, despite herself. 'Not yet,' she said, sharply. 'But that's the hypothesis I'm working with.'

Andrew's face softened. 'I'm sorry, Miss Vale, I didn't mean to be critical. Go on. Tell me why you think it might be the Whittaker file.'

Clara relaxed a little, but she had been stung by his suggestion that she was basing her suspicions on a tissue of evidence. And she was stung because she knew he was right. The drawer had more letters than W in it. But there was something niggling at her that she couldn't shake.

'I know it's all very tenuous,' she said, 'but I find it curiously coincidental that the day after Mrs Whittaker came to see me to ask me for help there would be a break-in at the office. And then another one at the hotel. They were clearly looking for something they thought I had in my possession.'

Andrew nodded; he seemed to be with her so far. 'And,' she continued, emboldened, 'I have read the Whittaker file and it seems to me that my uncle strongly suspected that a miscarriage of justice had occurred.' She went on to tell him about the various anomalies in the file, indicating that neither the fire department nor the insurance company had properly investigated the case. 'So,' she said, 'I am just wondering – hypothetically – whether the break-in had anything to do with that. If Uncle Bob was unearthing an official bungle – or perhaps a deliberate covering up of a crime – might there have been reason for someone to want to get the file back to stop the new owner of Wallace Enquiry Agency following up on it?'

Andrew looked impressed. 'Goodness me, Miss Vale, that is quite a hypothesis.'

'Do you think there might be something in it?'

He nodded. 'There certainly might be. But you will need strong evidence before you go public with it. What I know of the police and the fire brigade is that they don't take well to unsubstantiated accusations of incompetence.'

She pursed her lips. 'And rightly so. Yes, I would need to find actual evidence – one way or the other. Mrs Whittaker told me Bob believed it was arson and that the insurance company might have been implicated.'

'And deliberately covering it up?' Andrew looked shocked.

Clara nodded, seriously. 'Yes, I know, that's quite an accusation. However, from what I've seen of the file, Bob was thinking down the same lines. He was following a line of enquiry suggesting incompetence or a lack of due diligence – perhaps deliberate. All he's given me are some anomalies and questions. But I think they'd be worth following up, particularly now that there's been a second fire. However . . .' She looked out at the boating lake, disappointed that the children appeared to be paddling towards them.

'However . . .' prompted Andrew.

'I spoke to one of Uncle Bob's agents the other day, a man called Jack Danskin, and he suggested that Bob was becoming forgetful and confused before he died. He cast doubt that I could take what Bob had written in the file seriously.'

Andrew looked affronted. 'Jack Danskin said that?'

'He did. Do you know him?'

'Yes. He frequently appears in your uncle's accounts. But I can assure you, Miss Vale, I never saw any signs of confusion in your uncle. He was becoming increasingly weak before the end, and would often get tired, but I didn't see any mental impairment. However, I'm not a doctor.'

'Yes, that's what Juju Levine said too. And the solicitor, Jennings, never suggested there was anything amiss either.'

'Perhaps you should talk to his doctor.'

'Juju suggested the same. Do you know who it is?'

'I do. I can make introductions for you if you like.'

'Yes please,' said Clara, then pinned a pleasant smile on her face as the children, now out of the boat, scampered towards them.

Simon immediately announced that he needed to go to the lavatory. Jemima rolled her eyes. Andrew grinned and said: 'I believe there are cloakrooms in the pavilion. Would you mind waiting, Miss Vale, while I take him?'

Clara, who felt a heaviness in her own bladder, smiled at Jemima and said: 'Why don't we all go. Girls and boys?'

Ten minutes later, Clara and Jemima were waiting on the terrace outside the Grecian-style pavilion. The boys were taking longer than the girls. Clara felt compelled to engage in some chit-chat. 'So,' she said, 'do you enjoy school?'

'I do.'

'And what do you want to do when you leave?'

Jemima's eyes were fixed on her shoes. 'I don't know.'

Clara persisted. 'Might you get a job or further your education?'

Jemima shrugged. 'My father might let me work in his office – if mother doesn't need me at home.'

'Is that what you want to do? Work in an office?'

Jemima continued looking at her shoes. 'I'm not clever enough to be a teacher. And I don't want to be a nurse. So I've got to do something until I get married.'

Clara felt a wave of anger sweep over her. Here was a twelve-year-old girl who had no options before her but to tread water until she got married. 'Who said you have to get married?' she said, trying to keep her tone light.

Jemima looked up for the first time. 'Well, that's what we're supposed to do, isn't it?'

'I'm not married.'

Jemima looked embarrassed and turned away.

'What's wrong?' asked Clara.

'Nothing,' muttered Jemima.

'No, not nothing. Tell me.'

'I'm sorry, Miss Vale, I don't want to be rude.'

Clara pursed her lips. She knew exactly what was coming. But this was just a young girl. There was no malice in it. She mustn't take offence. 'You want to know why I'm not married. At my age.'

Jemima nodded.

Clara thought for a moment, then said: 'Well, because I've had other things to focus on. I went up to university. Then after that I've become a working woman. I haven't really found the need to get married.'

Jemima looked up, her large eyes curious. 'Haven't you ever been in love?'

Clara smiled at the naivete of the question. 'No. I haven't.'

'Neither has Uncle Andrew,' said Jemima.

Clara suppressed a smile. 'Well, there you go. Some people fall in love and some people don't. It's 1929, Jemima, and we women now have a right to work and to vote. Don't assume that you have to get married unless you really want to. And I very much doubt you're not clever enough to become a teacher. Do you want to be a teacher?'

Jemima looked at Clara and for the first time the older woman saw some passion in the girl's eyes. 'Oh yes, Miss Vale, I do.'

Clara nodded approvingly. 'Then don't let anyone stop you. Work hard at school. I'm sure your Uncle Andrew will help you with your homework if you ask him.'

'He's already offered.'

'And?'

Jemima shrugged and was just about to reply when suddenly Clara felt something tug at her arm. Before she knew it, her handbag had been wrenched away and a young man was running hell for leather towards the entrance to the park. Clara yelled and started chasing him. But her dress and heels didn't let her get far. As she slowed, cursing to herself, Andrew Ridpath sped past her, shouting: 'Oi, you! Stop! Thief!'

Then all pandemonium broke loose with seemingly every able-bodied male in the park joining the pursuit. Clara hurried along as best she could, and Jemima, whom Clara reckoned could easily outsprint her, very kindly tarried with her. A few minutes later, a puffing Andrew appeared, breathing heavily and clutching Clara's bag.

'Oh, you've got it!'

'Well done, Uncle Andrew!'

Andrew grimaced. 'I got the bag, but the little blighter slipped away. But I got a good look at him. Lad of about seventeen.'

Clara took the bag from Andrew and opened it.

'Is everything still there?' asked Andrew.

Clara did a quick inventory of the contents, looked up, then shook her head.

'What's he taken? Your purse?'

Clara shook her head again. 'No, the purse is still there. But my notebook's gone.'

Andrew's eyes narrowed. 'What the deuce? What was in it?'

'Various details about Uncle Bob's estate, and . . .' she felt a shiver of trepidation '. . . my notes about the Whittaker case.'

Andrew and Clara reported the robbery at the Pilgrim Street police station while the children waited in the car. The sergeant at the desk took notes but didn't seem concerned when they told him this was the third robbery, or attempted robbery, that Clara had experienced in a matter of days.

'You said nothing was taken in the first two incidents.'

'No, nothing. But the office and my hotel room were both ransacked.'

'And in this one?'

'My notebook was taken.'

The sergeant raised an eyebrow. 'A notebook, I see. Anything valuable? Money? Jewellery?'

'No.'

'And no one has been injured?'

'Again, no. But I'm sure they're connected.'

The sergeant looked at Clara, his face expressionless. 'I'm sorry, miss, but there's not much to go on here. And from what you and Mr Ridpath have told me, it wasn't the same man. The first two were adults, the second a youth. So it just appears as if you're the victim of bad luck. However, we'll keep an eye out at Exhibition Park for the young fellow and put on extra patrols. If we catch him, we'll ask him about the office and the hotel too.'

'But what about my notebook? It had important information in it. And it looks like the first burglar was looking for the same information too.'

The sergeant had by now stopped writing, as if deciding there was nothing more that needed to be added to the report. 'Do you have any evidence of this?'

Clara shook her head. 'No, I don't. However, if you were to start an investigation—'

'We will keep an eye out for the young bag snatcher.'

Clara pursed her lips. 'But I think it's bigger than that. I think it's linked to one of my uncle's cases.'

The sergeant nodded sympathetically. 'Bob Wallace. A good man. And a good detective. He also knew when to get the police involved and when not to. He gathered evidence first. With all due respect, miss, there is not enough evidence here to warrant any further investigation for now. But if something else comes up, then let us know. Thank you both for coming in.'

And with that, they were summarily dismissed.

Clara was furious, and was just about to say something when Andrew intervened and said: 'Thank you, Sergeant, for your time.' He gave Clara a warning look then flashed his eyes to the door. Clara got the message.

Outside, as they walked down the steps, he whispered: 'It's best not to antagonise him, Miss Vale. Your uncle worked hard to maintain good relations with the police. He told me once that if they got the idea that he thought they were not doing their jobs properly, or interfering with any of their cases, they would make life very difficult for him. The sergeant there said he liked Bob. Best to leave it on a good note.'

Clara stopped at the bottom of the steps, seeing the two children looking at them from the back of the car. They both looked worried.

'You're right. I realise that. And I realise too that if I'd mentioned the Whittaker case it would suggest that the investigation wasn't thorough – because if arson were suspected the police should have been involved.'

Andrew nodded. 'Yes, it would. But that would be Tynemouth police, not Newcastle. I think that falls under the Tynemouth Borough force, not Newcastle City. But still, they won't take kindly to any suggestion of police inaction or that a blind eye was turned. So my suggestion would be to take some time to gather more evidence. Or to hire someone else to do it for you. There are other private detectives in town . . .'

Clara laughed. 'Oh, that will be funny, won't it? One private detective agency hiring another one.'

Andrew smiled. 'It would. But what other choice do you have?'

Clara looked at Jemima in the back of the car. Hadn't she just told that young girl that *she* had a choice about what to do with her life? She looked up at Andrew and said: 'My other choice is to investigate this myself. I'll consider it a test run.'

'A test run?'

'Yes, to help me decide whether I'm cut out to be a detective. Didn't you say that it might take to the end of next week to sort out the bank account?'

'I did.'

'Well, then I'll give myself until then to investigate. What do you think?'

Andrew grinned, raised his hat and gave a little bow. 'I think, Miss Vale, your uncle just might have had the measure of you after all. But seriously, do be careful. And please ask if there's anything I can do to help.'

Clara smiled. 'Thank you, Mr Ridpath, I shall. And please, call me Clara.'

Andrew's eyes twinkled. 'I should be delighted to.'

Chapter 20

Back at the hotel, Clara asked the manager if she would be able to go into her old room to check for fingerprints on the window. The manager was surprised at the request, but reluctantly agreed. Perhaps he was embarrassed that the hotel's security had been brought into question, thought Clara. And that would make it difficult to deny any attempt to track down the intruder. Whatever the reason, he personally accompanied Clara to the room and brooded darkly in a corner as she got to work.

'I was not aware that you were a detective, Miss Vale,' he observed as she used her magnifying glass to hunt for prints on the outside of the window.

'No, I didn't mention it when I booked in,' she commented vaguely, not wanting to get into the nitty-gritty of her personal affairs. However, she was also trying to give off an air of professionalism, as if she searched for fingerprints on hotel windows on a regular basis.

'Aha!' she said, as she found three clear prints which, from their orientation and condition, appeared to be from the same hand. Although inside the window there were a number of prints – and she would then have to request to take prints from staff members to eliminate them – there was only one set on the outside. Clara, to the worried accompaniment of 'Please *do* be careful, Miss Vale,' climbed out of the window and onto the fire escape to better access the prints. She set to work, trying to pretend that she was not in the least bit shaken by the height of the wrought-iron platform above the streets of Newcastle below. Ten minutes later she had dusted and photographed the prints and stepped back into the hotel room, to the clear relief of the manager. 'Will you be liaising with the police about this, Miss Vale?'

'I shall if I discover there is anything worthy of liaison,' she said cryptically, rather proud of her Hercule Poirot-style retort. Then she flashed a smile at the manager. 'Thank you, Mr Jameson, for your assistance. I shall certainly let it be known among my acquaintances that the management of the Royal Central Station Hotel is most concerned about security.'

This seemed to appease the manager, who nodded his agreement. 'We certainly are that, Miss Vale!'

Clara and the manager left the room with a far more companionable air than when they first entered. 'Well, thank you again, Mr Jameson. Now if you'll excuse me, I need to dress for dinner. And I look forward to seeing what's on your fine restaurant's menu this evening.'

Diplomacy, thought Clara. *Just what Jonny Levine suggested.* As she headed off to her room, she was approached by the lift bell boy. 'Oh, Miss Vale! There you are! There's a gentleman downstairs who would like to see you.'

'Oh? Did he give his name?' asked Clara with some trepidation, not wanting to have to deal with Jack Danskin for yet another evening.

'Here's his card, miss.'

The lad handed Clara a card and she was surprised – but not displeased – to read 'Mr Andrew Ridpath, esq., Accountant.'

'Please, ask Mr Ridpath to wait for me in the cocktail lounge. I shall be down as soon as I'm dressed.'

Clara hurried to her room, hid her borrowed satchel at the back of a wardrobe and covered it with a spare blanket. Then she took her Charles Worth gown off the hanger and did her best in the shortest time possible to make herself presentable.

Andrew Ridpath was lounging in a red velvet chair, his long legs casually crossed, nibbling on what looked like the cherry from a Manhattan. He had changed from his day suit into a tuxedo. The moment he spotted Clara, he plopped the cherry back into his cocktail and jumped to his feet. 'Miss Vale! Clara! How – well, how breathtaking you look.' Then he flushed and added, 'Forgive my presumption for saying so. And forgive me presuming upon your time yet again!'

Clara smiled at him. For some reason a compliment from Andrew Ridpath didn't have the same innuendo as a compliment from Jack Danskin. 'Not at all, Mr Ridpath. Thank you. Is there something you would like to speak to me about? Has Antony been in touch?'

Andrew looked nervous. 'No, no. I'm sorry, there have been no further developments on that front. I, well, the honest truth is I just wanted to see you again. Without the children. I should have waited until tomorrow, I know, but, well . . . Will you have a drink with me? I'm having a Manhattan.'

Clara was amused at how nervous he appeared. Amused, but pleased. 'I should love a Manhattan, thank you.'

'Well, that's jolly good.' He grinned as he pulled out a chair, then summoned the waiter to bring a second Manhattan.

When the drinks arrived, he cleared his throat and said, 'After we've had a drink I was wondering if you would like to accompany me to the pictures?'

Clara's eyes opened in surprise.

He slapped his forehead. 'Oh Lord, I'm sorry, I didn't think this through, did I? Now it just seems like awful timing . . .' His voice trailed off.

It was awful timing, but Clara did not want their time together to come to an end just yet. 'Not at all. What did you want to see?'

'Well, there's a Hitchcock on at the Majestic here in Newcastle. It's his first talkie, and I've been dying to see it. And I was hoping you would come with me. But of course, I now realise that going to the pictures would probably be the last thing you would want to do. And on top of that, you're about to have dinner . . .'

Clara's ears pricked up at the mention of the Majestic. 'There's a Majestic here in Newcastle? Is it owned by the same company as the one in Whitley Bay?'

'It is,' replied Andrew, 'there are a chain of them – all called Majestic. And yes, owned by the same company.'

She looked at her watch. It was after eight. 'What time does it start?'

'Nine o'clock. It's the late show.'

Clara had been hoping to finish her dinner then go back to her uncle's house to develop the photographs of the fingerprints she'd just taken. However, she could shuffle things around.

She recalibrated her timetable and said: 'I would very much like to go to the pictures, Andrew. And don't worry, I have recovered from the ordeal yesterday. I am hungry though, so I could ask the chef to make us a sandwich to tide us over. Then we could go to the pictures and afterwards – it shouldn't be much after eleven by then, should it? – we can catch a late supper and then pop into my uncle's laboratory. I have something I need to do there. You could come with me, if you like . . .' Her voice tapered off as an endearing smile lit up Andrew's face.

'Oh, I would like that very much.'

She smiled in return and raised her glass. 'Drink up then. Chin-chin!'

'You do look beautiful tonight,' whispered Andrew as he helped her out of his car, offered her his arm and escorted her across the road to the spanking new art deco cinema. Clara was delighted by the compliment – and the company – but was a little concerned about how to handle the evening going forward. On the short drive over, Andrew told her that the owner of the Majestic was one of his brother's clients and he was sometimes given free tickets to the newest shows. Clara was peturbed to hear this and wondered how open she could now be about her suspicions relating to Balshard if Andrew's brother worked with him. Balshard, it seemed, had his fingers in many pies. She recalled that he was also a client of her uncle's solicitor, Barnaby Jennings. However, she decided to put it out of her mind for now, and just enjoy the evening.

'*Blackmail* was first made as a silent film, you know,' explained Andrew, as they approached the imposing art deco façade of the Majestic. 'Hitchcock was asked to convert it to a talkie. He had to reshoot some of the scenes, and apparently . . .' he chuckled '. . . Anny Ondra – the foreign actress in the lead role – couldn't muster a decent London accent, so they got someone else in to voice her lines. They actually shot it with the two women on set, with the voiceover off camera, while Ondra pretended to speak. I'm very interested to see how they manage it,' said Andrew.

'So am I,' said Clara, having already read mixed reviews about the picture.

As they reached the front of the queue a footman in top hat and tails ushered them in, took their coats and escorted them to their seats in the vast, luxurious auditorium. It was a far cry from the Paradise Picture House and the small, drab facilities the Whittakers had attempted to spruce up with paintings of palm trees. The Majestic had *real* palm trees in giant terracotta pots, and there was not a jam jar in sight. Nor, she hoped, would there be any flames. Clara tensed at the thought and closed her eyes, trying to keep the memories of the terrifying fire at bay.

'Are you all right?' asked Andrew, his voice fraught with concern.

Clara opened her eyes and gave him a reassuring smile. 'I am, don't worry. Shall we go in?'

She took Andrew's arm and he led her past row after row of plush velvet seats, filled with the tip-top of Newcastle society casting covetous glances at one another's jewels. There were no wooden benches. There were no children. And instead of an out-of-tune honky-tonk piano, an accomplished pianist entertained the guests with a sparkling repertoire of classical pieces on an enormous grand piano as they waited for the show to start.

Eventually it did, and after a newsreel focusing on the Great North Coast Exhibition, then a gushing speech by the Chancellor of the Exchequer telling Britons to expect unparalleled economic growth in the decade ahead, the main feature got underway. Clara and Andrew spent the next hour and twenty minutes enjoying a riveting – if clumsily voiced – flick. Clara was delighted to see that the British Museum, just around the corner from her Bloomsbury flat, was the setting for the final chase scene where the baddy was to fall to his death, and happily joined in the wholehearted applause as the final credits rolled.

'So, what did you think?' asked Andrew as he escorted her into the foyer.

'I enjoyed it very much. Quite a dilemma that policeman faced about whether to turn in his fiancée. But I would have liked to have seen a little bit more detection. How did that blackmailer find the glove in the artist's studio? What was he blackmailing the artist about? A lot was unanswered.'

'True.' Andrew nodded. 'Not one of Hitchcock's best from a plotting point of view, but very atmospheric. And a technological marvel! Who would have thought only a few years ago that we would hear actors speaking words on-screen?' He looked like a little boy on his first visit to a circus.

Clara smiled at him and listened as he waxed lyrical about the wonders of audio cinema over a light supper in the on-site restaurant – something else with which the Paradise could never have competed. But again, she put thoughts of Thursday's tragedy out of her mind as she enjoyed the food and Andrew's company. She was very tempted to say 'yes' to a sticky toffee pudding and custard after her meal, but looked at her watch and decided that they should get to Uncle Bob's laboratory while there was still something left of the night.

Chapter 21

'Have you ever been to Bob's house?' asked Clara as she unlocked the front door, carrying the satchel they'd just retrieved from the hotel.

'I haven't,' said Andrew. 'I only ever saw him in his office or when he came to mine.'

'It's a bit cluttered,' said Clara as she turned on the hall light. She indicated left and right as they walked down the hall towards the kitchen, and Andrew peered into the jam-packed drawing and dining rooms. 'I see what you mean. What are you going to do with it all?'

Clara shrugged. 'I'm not sure. Some of it, I think, might be worth donating to a museum. There's lots of interesting stuff here. But I'm not qualified to tell what has value and what doesn't. I'm thinking of asking someone from the Hancock to come and have a look.'

'That's a good idea,' said Andrew. 'But even if it doesn't have historic or cultural value, it might still be worth something financially. You could also perhaps get an auctioneer in here. I could help you with that. I've helped wrap up a few deceased estates.'

Clara stopped outside the laboratory door and turned and smiled at Andrew. 'That on top of the offer for an introduction to the doctor? And the locksmith? You've been very helpful indeed, Andrew. Do you do this for all your clients?'

Andrew took a step towards her and lowered his voice, as if there were eavesdroppers in the empty kitchen. 'Only very beautiful ones who accompany me to the pictures.'

It was a syrupy line, but Clara didn't mind. It had been a very long time since anyone had said she was beautiful. Or even just slightly pretty. 'What about the plain ones?' she asked. 'Don't they deserve your help?'

Andrew nodded. 'Of course. I help all my clients to the best of my ability. But let's just say that having you added to my client list has been an unexpected pleasure.' He lowered his head towards her and pressed his lips to hers. She felt a surge of desire and opened her mouth to receive him. Their lips and tongues began a tentative exploration as his arms wrapped around her and she pushed her body willingly against his. But then, suddenly, he pulled away and took a step back. Her arms fell to her sides.

Andrew ran an anguished hand through his auburn hair. 'I'm sorry, Clara. I don't know what came over me. I can assure you, I do *not* make a habit of taking such liberties with my clients. Or with any lady whom I have just met. I – well – you are looking so beautiful this evening, and here we are alone – but no, it's unforgivable. I am dreadfully sorry.'

Clara looked at his hang-dog expression and nearly burst out laughing. *Oh, but I want you too!* she almost said, but instead, she just nodded gently. 'That's all right, Andrew. And of course, it's not unforgivable. But you're right, we are first and foremost in a working relationship, and we have only just met. Thank you for your candour and your decency. Now, would you like to come down to the laboratory with me or would you prefer I went on my own? I can get a taxi back to the hotel.'

Andrew looked shocked. 'It's after eleven o'clock at night! Of course I shan't leave you alone. Not after that break-in at the hotel and the office.'

Clara didn't know whether to be charmed or peeved that he thought she needed looking after. She decided not to tell him about the revolver she carried in her satchel and that she could protect them both if she needed to. Instead, she said: 'Well, as long as you behave yourself then.'

'I shall absolutely behave myself. Heavens, Clara, have I made you feel unsafe? I'm so sorry, that was not my intention.'

Clara smiled. 'Of course not. I was just pulling your leg. Now, let's get to work.'

* * *

Clara carefully measured out and weighed the chemicals and compounds. Five grams of Metol, 7 grams of hydroquinone, 50 grams of sodium sulphite, 100 grams of potassium carbonate and 2.5 grams of potassium bromide, then stirred into 1,000 cubic centimetres of water. The measurements were metric, but she found the French system easier to use – and far more accurate – than measuring grains and ounces. After five minutes, with Andrew watching quietly, she diluted the solution one to three parts water into a beaker then decanted it into a glass bottle labelled *Dev Sol (Metol-$C_6H_6O_2$).*

'So that's the developing solution?' asked Andrew.

'That's right, it's called Metol-hydroquinone. Uncle Bob seems to have run out of the pre-mixed solution, but fortunately he has all the component parts so I can make some more.'

'Where did you learn to do it?'

'Oxford. It was part of my degree. Very useful too as pre-mixed developing solution is completely overpriced, but not every amateur photographer has the wherewithal to make their own.'

'I'm impressed.'

Clara smiled at the accountant. 'Don't be. It's not that difficult.'

Under the glow of a red light, she poured the contents into the developing tank, opened her camera and wound the 35mm silver bromide gelatin film around the tank spool holders. Then she clicked and buckled the tank shut.

'Right, let's leave that for five minutes.'

'Is that all it takes to print photographs?'

Clara laughed. 'No, there's more to do after that. But this is the way we develop what's called the negative from the film in the camera. After that I need to dry the negative then use that machine over there to project an enlarged image onto bromide paper. There's a couple of steps after that too, but don't worry—' she looked at her watch, it was getting late '—we should be finished before we both turn into pumpkins.'

Andrew laughed too. 'Well, at least one of us knows what we're doing, Cinderella.'

Clara smiled and turned her attention to the washing line strung across the back wall of the small studio. There were two prints pegged to it – ones Bob had not got around to removing. She unpegged them to make room for the prints she would soon be making. And then she stopped in her tracks. 'Good heavens!'

'What is it?'

'I – well – nothing. Just something private of Bob's.'

'Oh, all right,' said Andrew.

Clara stood awkwardly, holding the prints, not knowing what to do now. She didn't want to embarrass Bob – in life or death – and she didn't know how Andrew would react to the images. But it was awkward, very awkward. The first print was a candid shot of Bob lying naked on a bed, propped against a pillow, smoking and holding a book. He was smiling at whoever was holding the camera. And he looked happy, very happy. Draped over the dressing table chair were two ties, and on the floor, two sets of men's shoes, side by side. This, however, was not the photograph that had caused her to utter an exclamation.

The second shot was more artistic and appeared to have been taken by someone more familiar with photographic composition. There was light streaming in from a window over the naked back and buttocks of a man lying face down on the bed, apparently asleep. The man's body appeared younger and better toned than her uncle's. She was no judge of men's physiques, but she would guess that it was the body of someone in his thirties. Frustratingly, the man's face was turned away from the camera. All she could see was that he had darkish hair. And there was a tattoo of some kind on his right shoulder. She couldn't see what it was and would need to have a closer look with her magnifying glass.

She slipped the photographs into her satchel then turned her attention back to the developing tank. Andrew, to his credit, didn't push her to show the photographs, but his demeanour suggested he was a little hurt that she had shut him out. It couldn't be helped, thought Clara; she was not going to announce to the world that her uncle had been a homosexual if he himself had wanted to keep that part of his life private. He had died, yes, and there could be no posthumous conviction for sodomy, but she would not be the one to sully his reputation.

The next half hour was spent completing the printing process, and she tried to make up for the awkward incident by playing teacher and instructing Andrew in how to operate the enlarging projector, and then how to develop the positives through a series of baths and rinses and to finally hang them up to dry.

By the end of the process Andrew seemed more relaxed and was intrigued to see the photographs of a series of sets of fingerprints hanging on the line. 'Make sure you hang them in order,' instructed Clara, 'I need to know which prints were taken when so I can match them to locations.'

'So, whose prints are these?'

Clara went on to explain where she had taken the prints and what she was hoping to discover. 'That last one was taken from a glass tumbler in Uncle Bob's laboratory. I doubt it could be anyone other than his. But it might be. So I'll have to see if I can find more of his prints in his bedroom tomorrow. It's too late now. However, for now I'm fairly certain it is his and I can use that to eliminate prints from the filing cabinet in the office – that print over there. And those ones there are Juju and Jonny Levine's. Again, I will use them for elimination purposes. Although I don't expect Jonny's to have been on the cabinet drawer anyway. But Juju's might have been. Those ones are mine and those ones are from the housekeeper. I'll have to look at them properly with a magnifying glass and use a protractor to measure angles, but on first glance, unfortunately, they don't seem to match any on the drawer.'

'So Mrs Hobson's off the hook?'

'For breaking into the office, yes.'

'And those?' asked Andrew, pointing to the second-to-last print.

'That is from the window in my hotel room. I hope to match them to the ones on the filing cabinet. If I can, then that proves the same man broke into both the office and my room at the hotel.'

'And if there isn't a match?'

'Then that will mean there is more than one person involved, but

I think we already knew that. The boy at the exhibition is already a third party.'

'Assuming it wasn't just a coincidental bag snatching,' Andrew observed.

'Yes,' agreed Clara, 'assuming that. But it's quite a coincidence, don't you think?'

Andrew nodded. 'Yes, I do. I think the boy was hired by someone.'

'So do I,' said Clara. 'And I hope that I have the fingerprints of whoever did it here.'

Andrew looked at the prints drying on the line. 'But how can you know who they belong to? Other than the ones of Bob, Juju, Jonny and the housekeeper? Don't you have to have something to compare them to?'

'I do. I still have to work that one out. I have thought about taking them to the police to see if they have any prints on file that match. But that will only be of known criminals.' *And*, she thought, *I have to figure out how to get Jack Danskin's prints too* . . . She still thought it a bit too coincidental that the break-in occurred when *he* was at the hotel and *she* was downstairs in the dining room.

Andrew was smiling at her.

'What?'

'You know, Miss Vale, you are turning out to be a very good detective.'

She brushed away the compliment with her hand. 'Oh, I don't know about that. I'm just making it up as I go along!'

He stepped towards her and lowered his voice. 'But you have an instinct for it. Bob was right. I'm very impressed, Clara.'

She noticed the closing of distance between them. She didn't step back. 'We'll see.'

They stood for a moment, facing one another, the memory of the kiss in the kitchen still palpable between them. And then, he stepped away.

She felt a wave of disappointment.

'Are you finished here for tonight?' he asked, clearing his throat.

'I am,' she said, forcing herself to sound matter-of-fact. 'These are dry enough to take down now.'

'Then I'll take you back to your hotel.' He looked at his watch. 'It's getting late.'

'Pumpkin time?' asked Clara.

'Past pumpkin time,' he said, and smiled once again.

Chapter 22

The next morning, as arranged, Clara met Alice at the station and together they travelled through to Whitley Bay. Now they stood in front of an ironmonger's shop, its window filled with pots, pans and household paraphernalia. 'This is Gill's Ironmongers,' said Alice. 'Alfie lives in the flat upstairs – and this is where Will Spencer lived too.'

The door to the shop was locked. But there was a doorbell, which Alice rang. A few moments later a window opened in the upstairs flat and a young man put his head out and said: 'Mrs Whittaker! Come around the back, I'll let you in there. Me uncle's just shut the shop up while he pops out to the bank.'

Alice led Clara up the street, around the corner and into a back alley. A few minutes later they were being let through the gate of a courtyard, piled high with crates. Some of the crates were filled with jam jars.

'You still taking the jam jars from the bairns?' asked Alice, a slight quiver in her voice.

'Aye, Mrs Whittaker. Me Uncle Joe exchanges them. The Spanish City and the Majestic won't take the jars. But now the Paradise is gone there'll be nowhere else for the bairns to go.' Alfie paused, looking glum.

'What is it, Alfie?'

The usher sighed. 'I'd best tell you then. I'll be asking for a job at the Majestic. With the Paradise gone, I need the work. I'm sorry, missus, you know I am.'

'Aye, Alfie, I know,' said Alice. 'And I don't begrudge you the work when there's nowt else going.'

'You don't think it's disrespectful to Will? So soon after he's gone?'

'No, Alfie, I don't. You know he would want you to get on with your life.'

'I believe Will lived here with you,' said Clara. 'That he didn't have any other family.'

'Aye, that's right, miss. He was me best mate, was Will. And I shouldn't have let him go into that fire on his own. I should have saved him.'

The young man's shoulders slumped and he looked near to tears. Alice squeezed his shoulder. 'There was nowt you could have done, son. Don't blame yourself.'

'I can't help it, missus.'

'Aye, I know. I feel the same. But Miss Vale here is going to help us find out what happened. For Will's sake. Aren't you, Miss Vale?'

'I hope so,' said Clara, with the most reassuring voice she could muster.

'Thank you, miss,' said Alfie and ushered the ladies through a door. They went through the back storeroom and headed towards the stairs. 'Are you the only ironmonger's in town?' Clara asked.

'No, miss, not the only one by far.'

'I see. But is this the closest one to the Paradise?'

'It is,' said Alfie, 'that's why the bairns – the children, miss – bring their jam jars here.'

Alfie opened a door at the top of the stairs and led them into a neat little flat that smelt of lemon detergent. 'Can I get you ladies some tea?'

'Aye, please, Alfie, that'll be grand,' said Alice.

Alfie busied himself in the kitchen while Clara took out her new notebook and prepared to ask him some questions.

A few minutes later they were settled with a tea tray in front of them. While Alfie and Alice sorted the tea, Clara got down to business.

'Alfie, Mrs Whittaker tells me that sometimes the light in the space behind the screen was left on by accident. And if it was, it would shine through the screen when the lights went down. Was there any light shining through on the day of the fire?'

'You mean just as the show was about to start?'

'Yes, then. I didn't see anything, but I wasn't really looking. Did you?'

'No, miss, I didn't. If there was, I would've flashed me torch at the projection box and Mrs Whittaker would have come down and dealt with it. Cos I can't leave the audience when they're in. That's the rules. Different at the Majestic, mind, cos they've got more ushers.' He looked at Alice. 'They have four a show!'

Alice pursed her lips. 'I expect they do, Alfie. But we could only afford one of you.'

Alfie realised his faux pas and looked crestfallen. 'Oh Mrs Whittaker, I didn't mean—'

'That's all right, I know you didn't. But the fact is, we only had one usher. So if there was anything that you needed, I was the one who would have to come down to help. Isn't that right?'

'Aye, Mrs Whittaker, that's right. But there was nowt I needed you for that day. All seemed shipshape.'

Clara made a note. 'So the light wasn't on before the show, but might it have gone on during the show? Would it have shone through?'

Alfie weighed his hands, left and right. 'It might've and it might not. It would have depended on what was on the screen. Some of the darker, more dimly lit parts of the film might have showed it. But not the lighter bits. And the lamp was low down, stood on the floor, so would have only affected the bottom bit of the screen where not much was happening, if you follow my meaning.'

Clara nodded. 'I think I do. We weren't far into the film when the fire started though. Can you remember if it was a light or dark bit?'

He thought for a minute. 'It was a bright and busy bit of the film, with the tramp on the run in the circus ring, so I probably wouldn't have noticed if the light was on, no. But I did see the flames lapping the curtains. And the screen beginning to melt. And then Will rushing in with the fire bucket. I told him to leave it for the brigade. You heard me, miss, I told him . . .' His voice trailed away as his eyes filled with tears.

'Yes, I heard you,' said Clara softly.

Alice reached over and held Alfie's hand. Clara sat uncomfortably, an intruder in their shared grief.

'I'm sorry,' she said eventually. 'I'm sure this is hard, but I need to push on.'

'Aye,' he said, 'I understand. What else d'ya want to know?'

'I've got a few more questions. But to sum this one up, the lamp couldn't have been on before the film started because you would have seen it when the auditorium lights dimmed?'

'Aye, that's right.'

'But it might very well have been switched on *after* the film started, and you wouldn't have noticed because it was bright and busy on the screen and the light would have been low down and not that noticeable with everything else going on?'

'Aye, miss.'

'Right. Thank you.' Clara scribbled another note. 'So, moving on to the back door. Mrs Whittaker tells me that you were expected to keep an eye on the back door in case anyone tried to sneak in. Could you see the door from all parts of the auditorium?'

'Not all parts, no, but I'd position meself so I could. To be clear though, I couldn't see the door itself, there was a thick curtain over the entrance to keep daylight out if the door did open, but I would have seen if anyone tried to sneak through the curtain.'

'And you didn't see anyone?'

'No, miss. That's what I told the polis and the fire inspector.'

'The polis?' asked Clara.

'He means the police,' explained Alice.

'Ah, I see. Thank you.' She turned her attention back to Alfie. 'Mrs Whittaker tells me you didn't see Will unlock the back door either as he normally does before the show began. So you couldn't swear that he hadn't done it.'

Alfie gave a furtive glance at Alice, his face the picture of remorse.

'It's all right, Alfie, just tell the truth,' said Alice, encouragingly.

Alfie turned back to Clara and nodded sadly. 'That's right, I couldn't say one way or the other. If I had seen him I would've said, I swear, but I didn't. That doesn't mean he didn't, just that I didn't actually see him, if you follow my meaning. I was busy getting things ready. I wasn't watching him the whole time. I didn't need to – I knew he always did it.'

'All right, thank you,' said Clara. 'What do you think might have happened to the key?'

Alfie shrugged. 'I'm sorry, I have no idea. If it wasn't on the keyboard in the office, and it wasn't left in the door, and it wasn't in Will's pocket, then I have no idea. I told the police that too.'

Clara nodded and checked her notes. Then she looked up into Alfie's nervous eyes. 'Are you aware that someone told the police that they saw Will lock the door half an hour before the start of the show, put the key in his pocket and walk back into the front of the cinema?'

'Aye, so I've heard. Horace Fender.'

'That's right,' said Clara. 'Then tell me, both of you, what you know about him.'

Alice and Alfie looked at one another. Alfie nodded. Alice spoke first. 'He's a down-and-out. I wouldn't go as far as to call him a tramp; he's had a family in his time, and he's worked around the town on and off for years. He used to drive a milk cart. But he's a heavy drinker and has been off and on the wagon for as long as I can remember. His wife used to keep taking him back, but she's given up. When the children grew up she left him and moved away.'

'Does he live nearby?' asked Clara.

'Not since the wife left. She used to pay the rent from her own earnings. She took in laundry. After she left, he couldn't keep it up on his own. He was chucked out. As far as I know he's in and out of the Salvation Army shelter. Isn't that right, Alfie?'

'Aye, it is, Mrs Whittaker. He sometimes slept in the alley behind the Paradise. That's how he says he saw Will coming out the back door. But I don't know why the police believed him. He's blind drunk half the time. Other times me or Will – and Mr Whittaker when he was still with us – had to chase him away because he'd relieve himself in the alley or try to steal jam jars from the bairns. He'd come in here sometimes and ask me uncle to give him money for 'em.'

Clara was making notes. She wrote '*grudge?*' and circled it. 'Did you tell the police about that? That you, Will and Mr Whittaker had to chase him off sometimes.'

'Aye, I did, but it didn't make a blind bit of difference.'

'Did they explain to you, Alice, why they took his word on this?'

Alice pursed her lips. Clara could see the anger boiling. 'They said that the Sally Army folk had said he'd been sober for a few weeks. That he was trying to put his life back together. They vouched for his character. But no one was vouching for Will's character, not one bleedin' soul!'

Alfie looked near to tears. 'I did, Mrs Whittaker, I swear I did.'

Alice nodded at him. 'I know you did, lad, and so did I. But it wasn't enough. And the fact that the door was locked and it was Will's job to make sure it was open, was the thing that damned him in the end. So I was told even if Horace Fender was lying, and someone else locked the door, Will should have checked and he should have made sure no one else was able to do that, that he shouldn't have left the key in the door. And in the end, as the owner, it's my fault. I should have made sure Will did his job.'

Clara wondered what might have happened if Will had lived and this all had to go to court. She was no expert, but she reckoned that a good defence barrister would have poked holes in this Horace Fender's story and character. She checked her notes again and noted the word *jam jar*.

'Alfie, you said Fender sometimes would steal jam jars from children and bring them here to be cashed in. Do you know if he did that the morning of the fire? Or sometime soon before that?'

Alfie cocked his head; there was the sound of a door downstairs opening and closing. 'I don't, but me uncle will know. And it sounds like that's him back from the bank.'

Alfie, Clara and Alice finished up their tea, gathered their things and headed back down the stairs. They were met by a gentleman in his sixties who was introduced as Joe Gill, owner of Gill's Ironmongers, and Alfie's uncle. Alfie explained why Alice and Clara were there and that Clara wanted to ask him some questions.

Mr Gill confirmed Alfie's story about Fender sometimes cashing in jam jars. 'I'd do it for him during the week but not on a Saturday when there was a matinee. Or when there was a special showing in the school holidays. I'd think he'd nicked them from the bairns.

But on a normal weekday he might not have. And I'd not have any proof that he hadn't unless Alf told me he'd tossed him out on his ear that day.'

'Did he come around last week then? The week before the fire?'

Mr Gill screwed up his face in an exaggerated demonstration of remembering. 'Aye, aye he did. But he didn't have jam jars. Which is why I think I remember it. Because it was out of the ordinary.'

'In what way?' asked Clara.

'In that for once old Horace had money and he actually wanted to buy something.'

'And what did he buy?'

Mr Gill nodded to a tank behind him. 'A can of kerosene.'

Chapter 23

There was a queue of people outside the Salvation Army shelter waiting for their dinner. These folk, in their threadbare coats and raggedy shawls, mustn't have got the message that Clara heard last night on the newsreel: that Britons had never had it so good. Alice and Clara caught the attention of a uniformed officer – a woman who introduced herself as Major Lovelace – and asked if they could have a few minutes of her time. The major made sure the volunteers were ready for their guests and took the two ladies into a small office off the kitchen. There were only two chairs for the three of them and Clara opted to stand.

Major Lovelace recognised Alice – or at least her name – and offered her condolences about the fire and the loss of Will Spencer, and Mr Whittaker's tragic demise not long before. The formalities over, Clara took charge. 'We've been informed, Major, that a man called Horace Fender has been staying in your night shelter. Might we be able to speak with him?'

The major shook her head. 'I'm sorry, ladies, but Horace Fender is no longer here.'

'Might you be able to tell us where he is? We have a few questions for him.'

The major linked her fingers, rested them across her belly and sat back in her chair. Clara did not need Professor Gross's chapter on the 'body language of interviewees' to tell her that this was a defensive gesture. The major either had something to hide or was reluctant to give out information. As the woman was a Christian do-gooder, Clara suspected the latter.

'I'm afraid I can't do that. Mr Fender did not give us a forwarding address.'

'When was the last time you saw him?' asked Clara.

'Just over a week ago. He told me he had found alternative accommodation and that we could give his bed to someone else.'

'Is there alternative charitable accommodation in Whitley Bay?' asked Clara.

'There are no other charities providing accommodation, no, but that doesn't stop individuals from being charitable.'

'So he's living with someone?'

'I couldn't say, Miss Vale.'

'Oh, for Pete's sake, woman!' Alice suddenly burst out. 'Can you just answer the question? Me husband is dead. Me children have lost their father. I've lost me business and now a young lad has just been killed. We're trying to find out why that happened. It's doubtful the insurance company is going to pay out, and it might just be a matter of time until me and me family end up joining that queue of people out yonder. You of all people should understand that. So, can you help us?'

Both the major and Clara were taken aback by Alice's outburst. But Clara was pleased. All of this pussyfooting around didn't sit well with her nature, and now Alice had cut to the chase.

'Well, Major?' said Clara pointedly. 'If you know where Horace Fender is, please tell us. It's the least you can do since it was your defence of him that caused the police to believe his version of events at the Paradise.'

The major unlaced her fingers and leaned forward across the small desk. 'And I stand by what I said. I told the police that he had been sober for weeks. And he had been. I told them that he'd been trying to get his life back on track, and he had been. He'd been in touch with his wife, who said she would take him back if he got a steady job. He was trying to do that. Listen, Miss Vale, not everyone has the benefit of inheriting money and not having to work for a living. Horace was doing his best. And that's what I told the police.' The Salvationist fixed Clara with a steely gaze, then she turned her eyes towards Alice and softened.

'I'm sorry, Mrs Whittaker, for your loss. I cannot imagine the pain you are going through. But to be honest, I have absolutely no idea if young Will Spencer is guilty of what he has been accused. All I told the police was that Horace had been sober in the weeks before the fire, so suggestions that he might have been drunk and hence his testimony unreliable were unfounded.'

'Do you believe his testimony?' asked Alice.

'I have no reason not to.'

'Well, I have every reason not to.' Alice leaned forward, and Clara noticed a vein in her neck pulsing. 'Will would *not* have locked that door. I know him. He absolutely would not have done so. And if he had, why on God's good earth would he try to get out that way with the children if he knew it was locked? So someone's lying, and I can assure you that if Will Spencer was alive now and standing here with us, it would not be him.'

Alice's words hung in the air between them, sanctified by grief.

Eventually Clara interjected: 'Do you accept, Major, the possibility that Horace Fender was lying? You told the police that he was sober so it's not likely he had been mistaken in what he saw, but he simply, and soberly, might just not have told the truth. Would you agree?'

The major looked from woman to woman; the grief-filled stare of Alice, to the interrogative gaze of Clara. Then she let out a long sigh. 'Yes, it's possible he simply lied. But that's not what the police asked. They asked me if I thought he might have been impaired on the day of the fire. I told them that to the best of my knowledge, no, as he had been sober every night for the previous three weeks. I'm sorry, Mrs Whittaker, I did not intend to be vexatious.'

'That's all right,' said Alice, her body still taut with offence. 'So, you can tell us where to find him then.'

'I honestly can't.' The major held up her hands as Alice bristled. 'I really can't. Because I don't know where he is. And that's the truth. But I can tell you that Horace said he was getting a job and had received an advance payment that he was using to put down as a deposit on a place. And that he was hoping his wife would come back to him.'

'Did he say where the job was? Maybe we can visit him at work,' said Clara.

The major shook her head. 'He didn't. But . . . maybe . . . all right. I'll help you. I really shouldn't be doing this. We're supposed to keep these things confidential. But I do have Horace's wife's new address. She wrote to me, after she'd left him. She gave me a few shillings for the charity. She'd had enough of living with him, but she said she still loved him.'

'Thank you, that would be helpful,' said Clara, flashing a look at Alice who had not softened her demeanour. They waited for the Major to leaf through a file and find the address she was looking for. She wrote it down: *Ellie Fender, 37 Roker Street, Lemington.*

'Do you know where that is?' Clara asked Alice.

'I do. It's the west end of Newcastle. I can take you there tomorrow.'

Clara and Alice walked from the Salvation Army to the site of the burned-out Paradise Picture House.

'Did you hear what she said about Horace getting a down payment from a job?' asked Alice.

'I did,' said Clara, 'but no indication of what that job might be. And Alfie's uncle said that for once Horace had some money when he went into the shop a few days before the fire. And what did he buy? Kerosene.' Clara went on to tell Alice what she had found in her uncle's laboratory and that in his notes Bob had been querying why the fire inspection report had not mentioned kerosene at the Carousel fire in Tynemouth, when he had found evidence of kerosene at the scene. 'Bob clearly thought this was a clue that needed following up. I do too. I would really like to speak to the fire inspector who wrote that report. And to see the report on this latest fire. I'm curious to see if kerosene will be noted – or omitted – in that too. I wonder how I could get in to see him. Any idea?'

'Not really,' said Alice, 'but at least we've got the address of Horace Fender's wife. She might be able to tell us where he is. And if we can get him to tell the truth about what he really saw on Saturday, perhaps we can take it to the police.'

'Do you have the name of the policeman in charge of the case?'

'Aye, I do. It's Detective Inspector Davidson.'

Then Alice brought them to a stop. In front of them was the

blackened façade of the Paradise Picture House. Apart from the smoke residue – the stench of which still hung in the air – the front of the building appeared to have very little damage, and the hand-painted sign, with a drooping palm tree shading the cinema's name, was still intact – a sad memory of shattered dreams. Alice's chin sunk to her chest, her shoulders quivering. Clara stood quietly beside her, waiting for the emotion to pass. After a few moments, Alice raised her head and in a quiet voice said: 'Let's go in. They gave me a key.'

Alice unlocked the padlock on the heavy chain barring the front door across which was painted: *Danger! No entry*.

'Are we allowed in?' asked Clara.

Alice shrugged. 'The bank will soon start repossessing it when I can't keep up payments. But they haven't started the legal process yet. So as far as I'm concerned, it's still mine. I have every right to go in.'

As they entered the surprisingly undamaged foyer, the carpet still sodden underfoot, Clara closed her eyes to steady herself. The memory of the screams, the flames, the horror, threatened to overwhelm her, but she brought herself under control. She cast a glance at Alice, who was frozen to the spot, caught up with her own memories – not just of one fire, but two, and the tragic death of her husband in between. Clara gave her some time then said: 'Are you all right to continue?'

Alice nodded. Clara had rarely seen such bravery.

First, Alice showed her the small office where she had counted the money and stored the jam jars before the show. There was still a crate of them stacked forlornly in the corner. She then showed her the keyboard where the key to the back door was hung when it wasn't in use. Thereafter, she pointed to the stairs up to the projection room. 'I'll take you there on the way out. There are too many memories of Will – and Jimmy – there. I'll need to work me way up to it.'

Clara nodded in understanding and followed Alice as she pointed out the fire buckets – now lying on the floor – and towards the doors to the main auditorium. 'This is the way you an' Alfie led 'em out. I haven't had a chance to thank you, Clara, for what you did that day. But you went above and beyond. Thank you.'

Clara nodded in acknowledgement. Then she pushed open the

door, the wood blackened by fire and warped by water damage, and into the hall that had once been the seating area. The back of the auditorium was still relatively intact, with personal items, such as shoes and coats, strewn between broken and toppled chairs. But the front section was all but gutted, with the benches the children had crammed onto unrecognisable in the debris.

Clara reached into her satchel and took out Uncle Bob's Kodak Brownie camera. She attached a flash bulb and took a shot of the proscenium arch. She had spare bulbs in her bag, so she'd be able to take shots behind the screen area too where the fire supposedly started, and also of the back door where Will died.

An area behind where the screen would have been had clearly been the hottest part of the fire. 'Is that the storage area behind the screen where the fire started?'

'It is.'

Clara, followed by Alice, picked her way through the debris. There was very little left, but she could just about make out the remains of what might have been paint tins. 'Do you know where the lamp was and where it is now?'

'It was over there,' said Alice, pointing to the far left-hand corner. 'Plugged into the wall. But the fire inspector took it away with him. He said he'd found the remains of it lying on its side.'

'Was it still plugged into the wall?'

'There was nothing left of the cable and wiring. Just some of the metal frame that held the bulb. But you can see there where the plug socket was.' She pointed to a charred area, which Clara could not make head or tail of. If there had been a plug socket there, Clara couldn't tell. She would just have to trust Alice that it was. She then took some photographs to add to the ones Bob already had on file from the Tynemouth fire.

'I'll also need to take samples of the curtains and the screen. Or what's left of them,' said Clara, putting down the camera while the flash bulb cooled. She then reached into her satchel and took out gloves, tweezers and a pair of scissors.

Alice pointed to some charred shreds of fabric, which still had some gold fringe attached, and then up to the top of the proscenium arch where there were some scraps of screen left. 'I'll get you a ladder,' she said, and headed back to the foyer, returning soon after.

With Alice holding the ladder below, Clara climbed up with her tweezers and scissors and snipped some samples then climbed down, moved the ladder along, and repeated the process until she had a selection of samples from different parts of the curtain and screen. She had not thought to bring sample jars from the laboratory last night, but she had bought some paper bags from a fruit and vegetable stand near the train station this morning. With the samples from above bagged and labelled, she then got down on her knees to search for any remnants nearer to the floor. She surmised that if kerosene had been splashed on the screen or curtains, it was more likely to be nearer the floor than the ceiling, but there was more damage at floor level. Eventually, with Alice's help, and the use of a torch, she found some scraps among the charred remains and bagged those too.

'Right,' she said, 'I'll examine these when I get back to the laboratory. My uncle extracted kerosene from what looked like the seat of a stool at the Carousel. I can compare this to that. Now,' she said, 'let's have a look at the back door. I'm assuming it's down there.' She pointed to a narrow hallway to the right of the screen with a blackened door at the end.

'Aye, that's it,' said Alice quietly. 'That's the door they couldn't get out of. If you don't mind, I'll stay here. I can't go down there. When you're finished, let me know and I'll show you the rest of the place. Here, you might need this.' Clara took the torch she offered her and headed into the darkened hall.

Clara had been mulling a theory ever since she heard that Horace Fender had bought kerosene at Gill's Ironmongers in the days before the fire. What if Fender had come in through this unlocked door, splashed kerosene on the curtains and screen, then whipped behind the screen, switched on the lamp, and placed some fabric over the hot bulb? Or laid the lamp on its side on the floor with the hot bulb on top of the hessian splash sheets? That would account for the position in which the fire inspector had found the lamp. Or it could have fallen over in the inferno. Either way, it would have taken a while for the splash sheets to catch alight. How long? Ten minutes?

Twenty? She'd need to do an experiment to determine the time frame. But however long it took, the flames would then have spread to the curtains and the screen.

The key though, if a slow-burn electric bulb had been used rather than a naked flame, was to ascertain whether there would have been time during the newsreel, and before the main feature started rolling, to set the fire trap. She'd need to check with Alice on the timings, but what she knew of newsreels is that they were around fifteen minutes. If the lamp had been laid on its side with a sheet over it, that would also account for why the light was not seen through the screen. *Yes*, thought Clara, her heart beating faster as the hypothesis began to form, *this is a perfectly plausible explanation of the 'how'*. So, Fender, or whoever it was if it wasn't him, could have slipped in, then slipped out, during the newsreel. Then he could have taken the key that was left in the lock – Alice had admitted that Will sometimes left it in there – and locked the door behind him.

Yes! thought Clara, *that makes sense.*

From what Alfie had already told her, a curtain covered the entrance to the hallway, blocking out the light if the door opened. And there was access from behind the curtain to the area behind the proscenium arch. So, Fender needn't have come into the main auditorium at all, but could have slipped through the door, down the hall and into the behind-the-screen area without anyone seeing him. Clara examined the layout with this theory in mind and, although there was little left of the screen and curtain, she could still see where the bounds of each would have been. She took out her notebook and drew a map, making measurements with a tape measure and noting them down.

Would it have been possible for Fender to splash kerosene on the screen and curtain from the rear? If he couldn't, her theory would be implausible. Because how could he splash the kerosene in full view of the audience? She would need Alice to confirm that her drawing of the pre-fire layout was correct.

She checked to see where Alice was, but she was nowhere in sight. Clara shrugged and then headed down the short hallway to the door. There was very little left of the original door and the entrance had now been boarded up from the outside. However, Clara could still see what she assumed were hack marks from the firemen's axes on the door frame, as they desperately tried to open the door from the outside. Clara closed her eyes, imagining the horrifying last moments as Will tried, in vain, to open the door, with the two youngsters clinging to him.

She shuddered. Then she reiterated the question Alice had raised at the Salvation Army: if Will had deliberately locked the door, and knew it was locked, why on earth had he attempted to escape this way? Unless he had tried to unlock the door with a key that was in his pocket. But why then had the key not been found on his body? The whereabouts of the key, it seemed, was the real key to this case. But without that, she was left with shards of wood and strips of fabric. For now, that's what she would work with.

She took a final photograph of the hallway with the door at the end. And as the bulb flashed, she heard an unearthly scream.

Chapter 24

The screams were coming from the projection box. Clara dropped everything apart from the sturdy metal torch – which she kept as a potential weapon – and ran into the foyer and up the stairs. By the time she pushed open the door the screaming had subsided to painful sobs and anxious breathing. Alice turned towards Clara, her face ashen. She pointed a shaking hand at a man's body hanging from a rope tied to the ceiling light fixture. Clara gasped but willed herself not to overreact.

'Who is it?' she asked. 'Do you know him?'

'It's Horace Fender,' said Alice, her voice barely audible. 'I – I need some air.' She pushed past Clara and ran down the stairs, leaving Clara alone with the corpse. Clara, although horrified, was also strangely curious. She had never seen a dead person up close. And certainly not one who appeared only recently deceased. *He is dead, isn't he?* she thought, then quickly grabbed a toppled metal trunk to stand on. She thought about trying to cut him down, but she didn't have a knife. *Can I still save him?* She felt for a pulse in his neck. She couldn't feel anything, but she might have just missed it – she'd never felt for a pulse before, only having read about it in novels. So, to make doubly sure she put her ear to the man's chest to listen for a heartbeat. Silence. No, there would be no saving him. Horace Fender was dead.

He was certainly a gruesome sight. His eyes were bulging and bloodshot. His tongue swollen and lolling. Then there was a smell as his bowels had emptied at death. *Post-mortem, or just the terror of dying?* she wondered. She'd have to see if Professor Gross had anything to say about that in his handbook. If not, she would find a book on human thanatology – the study of death – at Uncle Bob's or the nearby university library. There was another smell, too, something sweet and chemical. There was something familiar about it, but Clara couldn't quite place it.

How recently had he died? It would take a professional to say, but by the warmth in his skin and the unpleasant fact that his trousers were still wet with urine she hazarded a guess that it might have been in the last hour. She remembered something she'd briefly skimmed in Gross's handbook: preserving the scene of the crime. The police would need to be called, yes, but before they were, she would gather some evidence herself.

She jumped off the trunk and ran back down the stairs. Sitting at the bottom, hunched over with her arms wrapped around her waist, was Alice. Clara stopped for a moment to speak to her. 'I know it's a huge shock, Alice, but I'm going to take some photographs and perhaps see if I can gather some other evidence.'

Alice looked up, her face harrowed. 'Won't the police do that?'

'No doubt they will, but then I'll likely be locked out of the investigation. I think Bob would have got his own evidence first, don't you?'

Alice nodded. 'Yes, he probably would.'

'All right then, I'll be back in a tick.' Clara ran back into the main auditorium and gathered her satchel of equipment.

By the time she returned Alice was standing, looking slightly more composed. 'Can I help?' she asked.

'I don't know, but come along anyway, if you've the stomach for it.'

Alice nodded. The two women walked back up the stairs. 'Do you think he killed himself?' Alice asked.

'Well, it certainly looks that way. Bit of a coincidence, though, on the day we are looking for him. Do you think he might have heard we were after him?'

'He might have. But why kill himself? If he didn't want us to find him he could have just kept out of our way.'

'Perhaps he couldn't live with himself any longer. Perhaps this is an admission of guilt,' said Clara, remembering in detective novels there would often be a suicide note found in the vicinity. 'Tell you what, Alice, while I'm taking a photograph of him, can you look around to see if there's a suicide note anywhere? But don't touch anything or move anything; we need to preserve the scene of the crime in the same way we found it.'

'All right,' said Alice and took a deep breath as they entered the room.

As Clara entered she noted the metal trunk and chastised herself for not taking her own advice. She had moved it. She should probably move it back. She put on some gloves from her satchel and repositioned the trunk into the middle of the room. Then she realised that she hadn't worn gloves when she'd first moved it. Her fingerprints would be on it. *Fingerprints . . .* if hers were on it, then she expected Fender's would be too. It was logical to assume that he had stood on the trunk himself then kicked it out of the way, accounting for it being on its side when she entered the room.

She attached a new flash bulb to the Kodak Brownie and photographed the scene. Then she took out her fingerprint kit and her magnifying glass. On examination she could see there were a number of clear prints, possibly from different people. She remembered what she'd read, about fingerprints lasting for up to a few years on certain surfaces. So, very likely, some of these would be Jimmy Whittaker's and Will's. One set would definitely be hers. One of the others would probably be Fender's. Anyone else? Alfie's? Alice's? She'd have to get prints from them both to eliminate them. Jimmy's might prove more difficult, but perhaps Alice could provide her with something that only he would have touched. She'd ask her later. And get something of Will's from Alfie.

She dusted the prints and when the flash bulb was cool replaced it and photographed the metal chest. Now she needed to get prints from Fender. This was a more difficult task than she anticipated and she had to ask Alice to help her position his hands to ink them and press them against the waxed paper. It was only when she did so that she realised the ink on his fingers would show she had interfered with the body. And if she were now to try and wash it off, that would be further interference. *Oh dear . . . what am I to do?* Well, it was no use crying over spilt milk – or in this case ink – she would just have to tell the police what she had done.

'Have you found a suicide note?' asked Clara.

'No. Nothing. Have you checked his pockets?'

'I haven't. Do you think we should?'

'What would your uncle do?'

Clara wasn't really sure. Now that she'd got it into her head that the police might accuse her of interfering with the body, she was no longer as certain that Bob would have rushed in gung-ho like this. She felt her confidence begin to ebb.

Alice noted it and said: 'Perhaps it's time to call the police.'

Clara nodded her agreement.

'So, tell me again, Miss Vale, for the record, why you felt the need to fingerprint the corpse.'

Clara and Alice were sitting in an interview room at Whitley Bay police station on the opposite side of a desk to Detective Inspector Davidson. Davidson was a man approaching retirement whose generous girth suggested he enjoyed his roast beef and Yorkshire pudding Sunday dinners a little too much.

'Because, Inspector Davidson, as I told your sergeant at the scene, I am investigating a case on behalf of my client here: Mrs Whittaker. I have recently taken over Wallace Enquiry Agency in Newcastle, and one of the open cases was to do with the fire at the Carousel Picture House in May – relating to an insurance claim. I was working on that case when I visited Mrs Whittaker on Saturday and was unfortunate enough to be caught up in the tragic events at the Paradise. As this fire seemed so similar to the previous one, it seemed natural that investigating this fire would be an extension of my existing case.'

Davidson gave her an incredulous look – as though he did not believe for a moment that she was a real detective – but then nodded for her to continue. Clara did.

'Well, today, Mrs Whittaker was showing me around the picture house when – as she has already told you – she came across the body of Mr Fender hanging from the light fitting in the projection box. As Mr Fender was one of the witnesses I had been hoping to speak to in relation to the fire, I thought it prudent to collect his fingerprints before I would no longer have access to them. And as I said to your sergeant, I did not disturb the crime scene in any way, but I do apologise about the ink. However, if the medical examiner knows it was applied post-mortem they can take that into consideration in their findings. On reflection, I should not have done it, but I realised too late. I shouldn't think, though, it would make much difference to your investigation, but best you know in advance.'

Davidson swallowed a belch, disguising it with a grunt. 'I think it's for me to decide whether or not it will make much difference to my investigation, Miss Vale, don't you?' He didn't wait for an answer but leaned forward over the desk and continued. 'So have you taken fingerprints before in your line of work?'

Clara wondered how to phrase her answer. The honest reply was: yes, she had, she'd taken some yesterday and the day before. But what Davidson was really asking, she felt, was how experienced she was in this detection malarkey. And the honest reply was: not very. But that would not garner much respect from him. So instead she replied: 'I have indeed taken fingerprints. I am a trained scientist. I hold an MSc from Oxford University. You can check with them to verify my credentials if you like.' She refrained from mentioning that her studies at the university at no point involved fingerprinting, but that was a detail he could find out for himself if he chose to dig that deep. Clara sincerely doubted he would bother.

Davidson looked summarily unimpressed. 'So they have lady scientists now, do they?'

Clara gave him a taut smile. 'They do. And lady private detectives. But I'm sure you knew that already, Inspector.'

Davidson grunted again and turned his attention to Alice. 'Why did you tell Miss Vale that she should speak to Horace Fender, Mrs Whittaker?'

Alice, Clara noted, looked bone-weary. But she raised her head and answered coldly. 'You know why. It's because Fender was the one who pointed the finger at Will. Both me and Miss Vale thought it would be good to speak to him about it.'

Clara dug her fingernails into her palms. She hoped that Alice would remember what they'd agreed to tell the police and what not to tell them. She still wanted a chance to analyse the samples she'd taken from the picture house for kerosene, so she'd asked Alice not to mention that, or what Mr Gill at the ironmonger's had told them about Fender buying some. In fact, unless they were directly asked, they'd agreed not to mention Mr Gill at all. Or the Salvation Army. They had a head start on locating Fender's wife and, if possible, Clara would like to speak to her before the police got to her. That of course might not be possible if the police already had her address on file, but then again, they might not.

Clara unclenched her fingers when it became clear Alice was not going to say anything else about Fender. But Davidson wasn't yet satisfied.

'So, Mrs Whittaker, you and Miss Vale were hoping to speak to Horace Fender. Had you managed to find him?'

'Before I found him hanging, you mean?'

'Aye, before that.'

'We hadn't, no. I was just showing Miss Vale around the building and we were going to try to find Fender after that.'

That's all true. Well done, Alice.

Davidson leaned in again, focusing all his attention on Alice. Clara had the feeling he thought she might be the weak link. 'Don't you think it's a coincidence that Horace Fender hanged himself at the same time you and Miss Vale were looking for him? And, miraculously, in the same building – the same locked building – that the two of you were in? The doctor's had a quick look and tells me Horace had been dead less than an hour before you found him. Which means, he could have been alive when you and Miss Vale entered the Paradise.'

'What are you saying, Inspector?' asked Clara sharply.

Davidson whipped his head towards her like a cobra spotting a mongoose. 'I'm saying, Miss Vale, that in my line of work, coincidences like this are suspicious. I'm saying that I find it highly improbable that you and Mrs Whittaker did not know Fender was there. I'm saying that perhaps you agreed to meet him there and then he was killed.'

'Killed?' asked Clara. 'You mean killed himself?'

'We don't know that yet. The investigation has just begun. I have not yet ruled out that someone else put the noose around his neck and hanged him.'

'Good heavens!' said Clara. 'Are you saying he was murdered?'

Davidson slammed his palm down on the desk. 'Don't play coy with me, missy. We found the gun in your satchel.'

Alice flashed a stunned look at Clara. 'A gun?'

Clara willed herself to stay calm. 'Yes, I have a gun. It was my uncle's. I have had a couple of unpleasant incidents since arriving in Newcastle, and I have taken to carrying it with me.'

'Have you applied for a certificate?'

'As I have inherited my uncle's entire estate I would assume the certificate to transfer to me.'

Davidson smirked. 'Then you would assume incorrectly, Miss Vale. You will need to reapply for a certificate in your own name. So, for all intents and purposes, you are in possession of an illegal weapon.'

'But that's ridiculous!'

'No, it's not,' said Davidson.

'W-what do you think Clara did with the gun?' asked Alice, her hands visibly shaking.

'At the moment, I think nothing. I'm just gathering evidence. But it is possible that a third party was involved in Fender's death. That the third party might have forced Fender to stand on that box – at gunpoint – and hang himself.'

'Good God! This is ludicrous!' Clara stood up. 'Are you arresting me? Do I need to call a lawyer?'

Davidson smirked again, seemingly enjoying having wrong-footed the hoity-toity lady scientist from Oxford. Then his face settled into a more professional demeanour.

'Sit down, Miss Vale.'

Clara was too agitated to sit. She glared at him.

He softened his tone. 'Please, Miss Vale, sit.'

Clara looked from him to Alice. Alice looked terrified. She sat.

'Thank you. Now, let's get some things straight. I am not accusing you, or anyone, of murder. There is – as yet – no evidence that Horace Fender died at anyone else's hand than his own. Assuming what you ladies are telling me is the truth—'

'Of course it's the truth!' snapped Clara.

Davidson raised his hand. 'Please, Miss Vale, let me finish. Assuming you are telling me the truth, neither of you ladies saw anyone else at the Paradise Picture House in the time you were there. Nor did you hear anything. If Fender was forced into killing himself, I expect it wasn't done quietly. So, for now, the evidence appears to point to him committing suicide. However, we are still left with the glaring coincidence that he did it while the two of you were looking for him.'

'What if he followed us there?' asked Alice. 'What if he wanted to speak to us and followed us inside? But then couldn't bring himself to face me? What if he killed himself out of guilt for lying about Will?'

Davidson's face softened as he turned to the grieving woman. 'That's certainly possible, Mrs Whittaker. Or perhaps he didn't lie at all. Perhaps he just felt bad about the consequences of his testimony. We will never know now. So for now, ladies, we are treating this as a suicide. However . . .' he flashed a hard stare at Clara '. . . I do not want you interfering any further with my investigation, Miss Vale. This is not a silly ladies' parlour game. So no more fingerprinting. No more guns in satchels. And I shall keep your weapon until such a time as you apply for a certificate. If you agree to these terms, I shall let you both go without further action. Do you agree?'

Clara's nails were digging into her palms. 'All right. I agree to no longer fingerprint corpses. And I agree to apply for a certificate for my gun. Now if that's all, Inspector Davidson, we would like to leave.'

Chapter 25

Newcastle upon Tyne, Sunday 25th August 1929

The next morning, a taxi dropped Clara and Alice at the top of Lemington Bank in the west end of Newcastle. Alice pointed to the valley below where the River Tyne snaked through the industrial heartland of the west of the city, then further down the valley to where the Vickers-Armstrong armaments factory belched out smog, telling her companion that that was where Bob had solved the case of the stolen ammunition. 'Your uncle was a very good detective, Clara, and by the looks of it, you're a chip off the old block.'

'I hope you're right, Alice. I've got a lot to live up to.'

Alice smiled at her. 'You're doing a grand job so far.'

The two women walked down the bank lined with Victorian-era terraced houses whose occupants serviced the various coal pits, glass works and factories in the area. This was where Horace Fender's widow lived. Speaking to her might get them into trouble with Inspector Davidson, but, Clara calculated, if he really had anything to hold them on he would have done so already. And all she had promised him was not to fingerprint any more corpses, and that she would apply for a certificate for her gun. She intended to keep both of those promises.

She had not, however, promised not to conduct any further investigations into the Paradise Picture House fire or the related death of Horace Fender. Fortunately, Davidson and his men had not sought to confiscate any of the other contents of her satchel, so she still had the photographs on her camera film and the samples from the curtain and screen.

The address they'd been given was for a narrow street just off Lemington Bank, barely wider than an alley. Washing lines were strung between the houses and a gulley in the middle of the lane looked like it might be used as an open sewer. Clara shuddered as two little girls played horseys, jumping back and forth over the gulley.

Clara and Alice knocked on a door that was soon opened by a woman with a baby on one hip and a toddler clinging to her pinny. She had curlers in her hair under a cotton headscarf.

'Aye?' she said.

'Mrs Fender?' asked Clara.

'Who's asking?'

'My name is Miss Vale and this is Mrs Whittaker. We were wondering if we could have a word with you, please?'

'Me or Mrs Fender?'

'Mrs Fender. We were told that she lives here?'

The woman's eyes narrowed suspiciously. 'Who's asking?'

'I told you, I'm Miss Vale and this is—'

Alice put her hand on Clara's arm. 'T's askin',' she said and slipped into broad Geordie.

'And who's yee?' asked the woman. After that, Clara could barely follow the back and forth, with neither woman softening her accent so the posh southern lady could keep up. The net result was the woman screaming 'Mrs Fender!' at the top of her lungs, causing the baby to join in.

Eventually an older woman, her shoulders hunched, shuffled to the door. She looked as if she'd been crying, her eyes red-rimmed.

'Mrs Fender?' asked Clara.

'Aye,' said the woman, 'I know already. If it's about Horace. The police have been and I know.'

Clara, Alice and Mrs Fender sat side by side on a narrow bed in one half of a small attic. The other half was piled high with boxes and crates. Ellie Fender lodged with another family and this was the only private space available to her.

'So, they said I was to come to Whitley Bay tomorrow, to identify the body. They'll send a car to pick me up.' The woman looked first at Alice, then at Clara. 'There's a chance it's not him. If they need me to identify him, it's because they don't know for sure.'

Alice shook her head sympathetically. 'I'm sorry, hinny, but it doesn't mean that. I've been through it meself. It's a legal thing. They know it's Horace. But the law requires the next of kin to say so. Besides, I saw him with me own eyes. And I'm sorry to say, it was definitely him.'

Ellie Fender slumped and leaned her back against the wall. 'How'd you find him?'

'He was hangin'. From the light in the projection room.'

Ellie nodded, her face frozen in grief. 'Aye. That's what the polis said. That two ladies found him. They said it was suicide. Was it?'

Clara shrugged. 'We don't know, Mrs Fender. There was no note. Was Horace the kind of man who would have left a note?'

Ellie gave a cold laugh. 'No, Miss Vale, he wasn't. Our Horace knew his letters and numbers and could write his name, but not much more than that.'

Clara nodded. 'I see. When was the last time you saw Horace?'

'Friday night just gone.'

'And what sort of mood was he in?'

Ellie closed her eyes as if to access the memory. Eventually she opened them. 'A funny one.'

'How so?' asked Clara.

'He was down. Sad maybe. But also a bit angry.'

'What about?'

'He was sad about the lad who died on Thursday.'

Alice leaned away from Ellie as if she'd been physically touched. 'You do know that it was your man who told the polis that lad was to blame for his own death, don't you?'

Ellie swallowed hard. 'That's not what he did. He didn't say the lad was to blame. He just told what he saw.'

'Which was?' asked Clara.

'Which was, that the lad – Will Spencer – locked the door and put a key in his pocket before the show started. That's what he told me.'

'And is that all he told you?' asked Clara.

'What do you mean?'

'Well, for instance, did he tell you that he had a new job and that he'd put down a deposit on a new place?'

'Aye, he did, but what's that got to do with owt? It's nothing to do with the fire.'

'Isn't it?' asked Clara.

Ellie's eyes narrowed. 'What're you getting at?'

Clara noted the change in body language and urged herself to tread carefully. Up until now Mrs Fender had been speaking freely. 'Nothing, I'm not getting at anything. I'm just trying to find out what happened on the day of the fire. We were hoping to speak to your husband, but, sadly, we have not been able to. So we were hoping he might have said something to you that could help us.'

'Help you with what?' asked Ellie.

'Help me prove Will wasn't responsible,' said Alice. 'I don't know if you're aware, but this is the second fire that's affected my business. The picture house in Tynemouth also burned down. And then my husband was killed in an accident. Not very long ago. So I was hoping, one widow to another, you could help. And that I could help you if you needed it. Because I understand what it's like to lose a man. I really do.' Tears welled in Alice's eyes and were soon mirrored in Ellie's.

Clara did not want to intrude. The two widows shared a bond she did not.

'How can you help?' asked Ellie, her voice thick with tears. 'How can you bring him back?'

'I can't do that, but maybe I can help in other ways. If I can find out the truth about what really happened the day of the fire, and clear Will's – and my family's – name, I can get the insurance to pay out. For this fire and the last one. And if they do that, I can give you something to help with expenses.'

'You're offering me money?' asked Ellie.

'Not now – I don't have any – but if I get the insurance pay-out, I can give you something then.'

Clara's eyes widened in surprise. Was Alice bribing this woman? Was it legal? Would Uncle Bob have done this? She wasn't sure, and added it to the list of things she needed to ask Jennings & Jennings in the morning. But for now, she noted, Ellie Fender seemed interested.

'Oh aye? How much?'

'I can't say how much,' said Alice. 'I don't know how much I'll get. And I've got lots of bills to pay meself. But I reckon it would be enough to cover Horace's funeral expenses.'

Ellie nodded. 'All right. That'll be a help. Because Horace will have left me nowt. I'm weeping for him now, but he could be a right bastard. I don't know if you'd heard, missus, but I'd left him. He was all right when he wasn't on the drink, and he'd stay off it a while, but every time he'd go back to it. I'd try to save up a bit, but he'd take the money. I tried hiding it, but he'd find it. And once, when he couldn't find it, and he was three sheets to the wind, he clobbered me. That's when I left him. The bairns have grown and gone. There was nowt left for me. But then a few months back he started coming round again. Like he was trying to court me. He'd stopped drinking and said he'd got a good job.'

'Did he say where?' asked Clara.

'Aye, with Balshard.'

Clara and Alice's eyes met. 'The same Balshard who owns the Majestic Cinemas?' asked Clara.

'Aye, that Balshard. But it wasn't at the picture house. He was going to be a delivery fella for the insurance office. Picking up and dropping off stuff.'

'What kind of stuff?' asked Clara.

Ellie shrugged. 'I don't know, missus, he didn't say. But he said he'd be working at the Tynemouth branch.'

Clara's eyes widened in surprise, but she didn't interrupt.

'When did he get this job?'

Ellie thought then said, 'Just before the May Day weekend.'

The weekend of the Carousel Picture House fire, thought Clara. 'Did Horace mention anything about the fire that happened in Tynemouth soon after he got the job?'

Ellie's eyes narrowed. 'No. Why would he?'

Clara noted the change in tone and backed off from that line of enquiry. For now they needed to find Horace's address. So instead she asked: 'No reason. I was just wondering. But, perhaps you can tell us if he got a place to live there too? The Salvation Army said he'd moved out because he'd got a place somewhere. Do you know where it is?'

'I don't have the address, but he said it was a flat above a shop near the Balshard office. He wanted me to come and see it, but I wouldn't. I wanted to wait to see if he was going to stay on the wagon. You can't blame me for that, can you?'

Clara shook her head. 'Of course not. I would have done the same in your situation. Tell me, did you tell the police where Horace was living?'

'They didn't ask. They didn't stay long. Just to let me know and saying they'd pick me up tomorrow.'

'Did they say when tomorrow?'

'Two o'clock, they said.'

'All right,' said Clara, her mind ticking over, reworking her proposed timetable between now and then. 'Tell me,' she continued, 'you said Horace had been sad, but also a bit angry. Do you know what about?'

Ellie closed her eyes again, no doubt remembering the last time she'd seen her estranged husband. Then she opened them. 'He said he'd been lied to.'

'By whom?'

'He didn't say. But he did say he'd been led up the garden path about summat. And that . . . well, and that he'd done summat terrible that he wished he hadn't.'

Alice flashed a look at Clara. Clara nodded at her and continued in a calm voice. 'Did he say what it was? What terrible thing he'd done?'

Ellie shook her head. 'No, no he didn't. But he did say he wanted to try and make it right, and that, well, that he needed to speak to someone about it. But if he did, he might lose his job. He didn't know what to do. I asked him to tell me what he was talking about but he wouldna. He said the less I knew the better. Because it wasn't safe to know too much.'

Alice's eyes were the size of saucers. 'Oh, Mrs Fender,' she said, clutching at Ellie's arm, 'do you think he meant about the fire at the Paradise? Do you think he was going to tell the truth about what really happened?'

Ellie shrugged. 'I don't honestly know, missus. That's all he said. And now, it's too late for him to do owt. But perhaps that's why he killed his self. He couldna see a way out of it. I think he thought that if he lost his job he would lose his last chance with me. And he's right, he probably would have. But I'd rather have him alive without a job than dead with one. Oh, missus, what am I going to do?' Her shoulders slumped and her chin fell to her chest.

Alice put her arm around her. 'I'm sorry, pet, I really am. I'll try to help ya, I will. But first we need to find out what it was Horace was trying to make right.'

'How're you going to do that?' asked Ellie.

Alice shrugged. 'I don't know. But Miss Vale here will have some ideas, won't you?'

Miss Vale just smiled sympathetically. She certainly did have some ideas, but whether any of them would help these two poor widows, she had no idea.

'I'll do my best,' she said, then rose to her feet. 'Thank you, Mrs Fender, you've been very helpful. And I'm so sorry we've intruded on your grief.'

'No, no, that's all right. I'm just grateful someone found him. Else he might have been hanging there for weeks and no one would have known. Quite a coincidence he did it when you two was there, wasn't it?'

Alice and Clara looked at each other once more.

Clara slung her satchel over her shoulder. 'Yes, Mrs Fender, it certainly was.'

Chapter 26

Monday 26th August 1929

Clara poured herself another cup of tea. She ordinarily didn't like tea without milk, but there wasn't anything in Uncle Bob's Electrolux refrigerator, which someone (Mrs Hobson?) had had the good sense to clear out and switch off after his death. She had not intended to stay at the house last night, but by the time she had finished with Ellie Fender and then talking over the case with Alice, it had been quite late. And she still hadn't tested the samples she'd gathered on Saturday! By the time she'd finished in the laboratory she was too tired to make it back to the hotel. So she had spent the night in Uncle Bob's bed.

The usual fears of being alone in a strange place were magnified by fevered dreams of Horace Fender's corpse hanging from the light fitting, while each creak, groan and murmur of the neighbour's plumbing provided a chilling soundtrack to the terror of the night. Clara wished she still had the gun, tucked under a pillow within easy reach. But the only intruders that night were the uninvited guests from Clara's imagination. Clara chastised herself; she was not one prone to exaggerated fantasies and had not felt like this since she was a child in her nursery, imagining her rocking horse turning into a fire-breathing dragon. Back then her no-nonsense nanny had told her not to be so silly and that dragons did not really exist. Clara knew that, even as a child of six. And yet, somehow they lived on in the corners of her mind. And now, to her surprise, in the corners of Uncle Bob's bedroom too.

'Don't be so silly,' she said in the voice of Nanny, and repeated the mantra until, finally, as an oak tree illuminated by a streetlamp cast tortured shadows onto the curtains, she clambered onto a chair and hung a spare bedspread over the window lintel. 'There now,' she said to herself, 'the dragon is at bay.'

She felt more like herself, more in control, as she climbed back into bed and decided that if she was going to move into the house permanently, she would buy some thicker curtains.

Down in the kitchen, after four hours' sleep, she started on her second cup of tea while contemplating the montage of photographs laid out on the large table. She had sorted the prints into three groups: the office filing cabinet, the hotel window and the picture house trunk. A fourth group consisted of labelled images of prints she could firmly identify. Paper slips were pinned to each one, identifying them as belonging to one of the following: herself, Juju, Jonny, Uncle Bob, Mrs Hobson or Horace Fender. She had not been able to get any item from Alice Whittaker that had Jimmy's prints on it, in order to eliminate them from the metal trunk in the projection room, nor those of Alfie or Will. But for now she had more than enough to work with.

Her own, Uncle Bob's and Juju Levine's prints were all found on the filing cabinet. That was to be expected. There were a further two prints that could not be identified. She moved those aside. Next she turned to the hotel. There were three sets of prints here, all three unidentified. However, with a growing sense of excitement, she realised that one of the unidentified prints from the filing cabinet was also on the window. 'Bingo!'

She took that print and, using her magnifying glass, angle projector and callipers, compared it to the three sets of prints found on the metal trunk. 'Bingo!' she said again. There was a definite match. The evidence was clear: the same person had been in the office, broken into her hotel room and been at the scene of Horace Fender's death. And that person was not Horace Fender. Horace, it seemed, had not moved the trunk he had used to stand on while he put the noose around his neck. Or at least, he had not used his hands. And had he kicked it over in the throes of death? She remembered that it was lying on its side when she first entered the room. Or had someone else – with their hands – pulled it out from under him? And had the same person forced him into the noose?

As she and Alice had discussed yesterday, it just seemed far too coincidental that Horace would kill himself while they were there without being aware that they were there. Not impossible, of course, but highly improbable, surely. What were the chances? One in a million? No, it was just too fantastical to believe that Alice and Clara had turned up at the very hour Horace decided to top himself in the projection room. And as his wet trousers showed – and the police medic seemed to confirm – he had died within an hour of Alice finding him.

Clara had spent around an hour collecting samples from the curtain and screen and then measuring and photographing the scene. So that meant he had likely arrived sometime within that hour. If that was true, then Horace – or his murderer, if that proved to be the case – had timed his death so that the women would find him. The question was begging, how did he – or the murderer – know they were there? Had they followed them? From Gill's Ironmongers? Or from the Salvation Army? Perhaps, and this caused a shudder down Clara's spine, perhaps they had been following them all day. All the way from Newcastle.

The next question was how had Horace got into the Paradise? The Whitley Bay police had searched the place and found no sign of any break-in – not even a jimmied window like in Tynemouth – so the most likely explanation was that he had come through the front door after Alice had opened it. She admitted to the police that she had not locked it after herself.

So, Horace, possibly tailed by another fellow, had followed them in. Why? To talk to them? To find out what they did or didn't know? But before he could speak to them, he was hanged. How had that happened without them hearing? If he had chosen to die, he might have done it quietly, but if he was forced to do it, as Inspector Davidson had already pointed out, why had he not called out? Clara recalled the sweet chemical whiff she'd discerned on the corpse and finally remembered what it was: chloroform. She'd used it as a solvent in the laboratory during experiments. However, she was aware that apart from the scientific use of dissolving alkaloids, it could be used as an anaesthetic. It was utilised in dentistry and some surgical procedures. And, if movies and detective fiction were to be believed, for incapacitating victims for abduction. In fact she remembered a Bulldog Drummond film where that very thing had happened.

Surely this was something that would be picked up at the post-mortem. If so, then Inspector Davidson should be open to the possibility that Horace was murdered. The question, of course, was why. Was someone trying to silence him? To prevent him from talking to Alice and Clara?

Also, if he was murdered, what happened to the assailant? Did he go into hiding and escape before the police got there? Was he watching while first Alice then Clara stumbled upon the corpse? Did he want them to find Horace's body? Was it a warning? A threat? She had evidence here that the same person who broke into her office, knocked Juju Levine off her feet, then broke into her hotel room, also touched the metal trunk Horace Fender had stood on when he was hanged. Was this man a murderer? Was he a danger to her too? Clara looked up to check that the kitchen door was locked and remembered that she had made a point of bolting the front door before she went to bed last night. However, there were always the windows ... Clara's heart started racing, and for the second time in a few hours she wished she still had her gun.

'Don't be silly,' she told herself again in the voice of Nanny, and repeated it until she felt calmer. She then picked up her pen and started compiling a summary of all the evidence she had gathered so far, including the conclusion she had come to last night in the laboratory that there was indeed kerosene on the samples she had taken from the remains of the curtain and the screen. And Uncle Bob, according to his notes, had identified kerosene at the Tynemouth picture house, which Clara confirmed when she double-checked the samples. Add to that Mr Gill's testimony from the ironmonger's shop that Horace had purchased some kerosene in the days before the fire, then, as far as Clara could tell, the evidence pointed very clearly towards Horace being the person who had started the fire at the Paradise Picture House, and possibly the Carousel Picture House too.

Horace could have slipped into the Paradise through the open rear door, splashed around some kerosene then tampered with the lamp that ignited the flames, and then slipped back out the rear door, locking it behind him. Clara's heart was racing. It all made perfect sense! If not conclusively proven, then surely there was enough here for a strong hypothesis. Enough to cast more than a shadow of doubt on Horace's damning testimony that he'd seen Will locking the door – particularly as they also had Ellie's testimony that Horace was remorseful about something. She wasn't sure what to do now. Should she suggest Alice get a lawyer? Or should she speak to the police first? She could ask Mr Jennings about that. She had already planned to speak to him today anyway, with regards to her own legal standing as an investigator.

Clara had a busy day ahead of her. The first thing she needed to do was make some telephone calls. There was no telephone in the house – something else she would need to correct if she moved in – so she would have to go to the office. She looked out of the kitchen window to see it was bucketing down with rain. Drat, she didn't have a raincoat. She would have to borrow one of Uncle Bob's.

Chapter 27

Clara was munching on a steak and kidney pie from the bakery and pie shop on the corner as she opened the office door. She had popped her head into Levine's Costumes to tell them she was there and was told by Juju she'd be up shortly. She came in out of the rain and hung up Uncle Bob's mackintosh to dry. While waiting for Juju she made some phone calls. The first was to Jennings & Jennings. Apparently, Mr Barnaby Jennings was out of town on business, but Mr Roger Jennings would be happy to see her at eleven o'clock. Next, she called Uncle Bob's doctor. Dr Malone could speak to her tomorrow, unfortunately not before.

Juju had still not appeared, so Clara turned her attention to the filing cabinet. According to the index book there was a file for Jack Danskin under D. She opened the top drawer, A–F, and riffled through until she found the Ds. But a quick search back and forth found no file for Danskin. She checked the rest of the drawer in case it had been misfiled, but no, there was no Danskin. Clara pursed her lips. This reinforced the nagging suspicion that Jack Danskin was not to be trusted. Had he taken his own file? When had he done it? Was Danskin the man who had broken in here? She already knew that he was at the hotel on the night of the break-in there. She considered the unidentified fingerprints on the cabinet and wondered if they belonged to the investigator. And if those belonged to him, what about the ones on the hotel window, and . . . and this made her shiver . . . the ones on the metal trunk from the Paradise?

'Clara, darling! How lovely to see you!'

Clara jumped, then steadied herself when she saw who it was. 'Morning, Juju. How are you?'

'Splendid! Well, not too bad for a Monday anyway. How was your weekend? Pop the kettle on and tell me all about it.' She brandished a bottle of milk. 'Your uncle used to pick up half a pint on the way into the office. He'd keep it in a bucket of cold water – and it would last him a couple of days. I think the bucket's still there . . .'

Clara went into the back room and spotted the metal pail. She lifted it up and showed Juju. 'It is.'

'Good, then keep this here. That is, if you are going to be coming into the office on a regular basis. Have you decided yet?'

'Not yet,' said Clara as she lit the little primus stove, filled the kettle and put it on to boil. 'Uncle Bob has a fancy new electric refrigerator at the house. All the mod cons! But not an indoor lavatory. What was he thinking?'

'Well, if you're not emptying your own chamber pot, perhaps it's not such an issue.'

Clara stood in the doorway to the back room while Juju took a seat at the desk. 'Eeew, now that's a thought,' said Clara. 'Nothing like an intimate knowledge of a man's toilet habits to kindle romance. It didn't seem to put Mrs Hobson off though, did it?'

'It didn't put my mother off either,' observed Juju. Then she laughed. 'Thank God for progress!'

Clara couldn't have agreed more. She of course had an indoor lavatory in her flat in Bloomsbury, and her parents' houses also had indoor ablutions. But she could remember as a child – before her mother had managed to twist her father's arm to modernise – when chamber pots and commodes were used. However, the chambermaids had dealt with it all, so it hadn't been such a burden. She remembered the stinking gulley down the middle of the alley outside Mrs Fender's house in Lemington and reminded herself that not everyone had the luxuries she was accustomed to. But she could afford it. And the last thing she wanted was a housekeeper being too intimate, particularly Mrs Hobson.

The kettle whistled and she lifted it off the stove with a tea towel.

'I've got something to show you.'

'What's that?'

'Something I found when I was developing the photographs of

the fingerprints.' Clara spooned tea leaves into the pot, gave it a stir, then gathered cups and teaspoons. She put it all on a tray and carried it into the office.

'Did you find Hobson's fingerprints on the drawer in here? Has she been snooping where she shouldn't have been?' asked Juju.

'No, not that,' said Clara, taking a seat. 'I couldn't find her fingerprints here in the office. I found some others though, but I'll tell you about that later.' She reached into her satchel and brought out a folder of photographs. There were all the pictures of the fingerprints she'd taken, but right at the back were the two shots of Bob and the sleeping man. She hadn't shown Andrew as she didn't want to besmirch Bob's reputation. However, Juju already knew he had been homosexual and it didn't lower him in her estimation.

'I found these,' said Clara, and laid them out on the desk for Juju's appraisal.

Juju leaned forward and examined the prints. 'My, my, my,' she said.

'Do you know who the man is?'

Juju shook her head. 'Can't say I do. But it's hard to tell from the back. He looks youngish – thirties or early forties at the most. His hair looks dark in this black-and-white photograph, but in real life it could be any shade from auburn to brown or black. Not a blond though, I think.'

'Yes, I agree. And he's a fit man too. Well-toned.'

Juju giggled. 'Very nice buttocks.'

'I suppose they are,' said Clara. Then, in a matter-of-fact voice: 'I'm assuming this was Bob's lover. That he took the photograph of Bob in bed, reading the book and smiling, and that Bob took this one of him when he was sleeping. This reinforces what you and Jonny told me about his romantic interests. But it doesn't entirely exclude the possibility that he could have had some interest in women too. Although the only evidence we have of that is that letter Hobson showed me. And that was not very specific either.'

'Is that a tattoo?' asked Juju. 'On his shoulder?'

'It is. Here, have a closer look.' Clara reached into her satchel and took out her magnifying glass, passing it to Juju.

Juju took it. 'Hmmm. It looks like a crescent moon set against a sun.'

Clara took the glass from her new friend and examined it herself. 'You're right, it does. Not a very high-quality tattoo. Looks amateurish. But you're right, a crescent moon on a sun. Have you seen this before?'

Juju shook her head. 'I'm afraid I haven't. But tell me, why do you want to know who it is? Bob has gone. The relationship will be over.'

Clara shrugged. 'I don't know. Perhaps it's because I feel guilty to have inherited everything without having seen him for so many years. While it seems there might have been someone here far closer to him.'

'Or it could just have been a brief affair.'

'It could have been,' said Clara, 'but Bob looks very happy here, don't you think? Even if brief, it seemed to mean something to him. Did anyone like this come to Bob's funeral?'

Juju took a sip of her tea. 'I can't say I remember anyone. There weren't too many people there. Me and Jonny. Mrs Hobson. Bob's lawyers and accountant. And his doctor. Some old clients, I think. One or two of his agents if I recall – that Danskin fella I remember was there. But no mysterious young man on his own paying his respects.'

The mention of Jack Danskin reminded Clara of the fingerprints. She went on to tell Juju everything that had happened since she had sipped port with the two costume designers on Friday evening. Fingerprinting the window at the hotel, going to the pictures with Andrew Ridpath, the work down in the laboratory that night – omitting the romantic interlude, that was private – then the trip to Whitley Bay with Alice Whittaker on Saturday.

Juju visibly paled when Clara told her about finding Horace Fender's body hanging in the projection room, her hand reaching subconsciously to her throat.

'Heavens, Clara, how horrific! For you and Alice. After all that poor woman has been through already.'

Clara agreed, then continued to tell Juju the rest of the saga of their interrogation at the police station, their visit to Fender's widow on

Sunday and then her discovery about the recurring set of fingerprints in the three locations.

Juju's voice was trembling as she asked: 'Do-do-do you think that's the murderer? That the man I saw in here last week is the same one who killed that Fender fella?'

Clara nodded. 'Very possibly, yes.'

Juju's hands started to shake. 'Then he could have killed me! I barely escaped with my life!'

Clara reached out her hands and stilled Juju's. 'Calm down. I know it's all a bit of a shock, but I don't think you were in any danger then. If he'd wanted to hurt you, he would have.'

'But he could have!'

'Yes,' said Clara soberly, wishing for the umpteenth time that she still had Uncle Bob's revolver, 'yes, he could have.'

'Are you going to go to the police with your information?'

Clara nodded. 'I am. But first I need to find out from Roger Jennings what my legal standing in all this is. I'm going to see him later this morning. Then after that Alice and I are going to Tynemouth to see if we can find out more about where Fender was living and the work he was doing – and to have a look at the ruins of the Carousel Picture House. Thereafter I might pop into the Whitley Bay police station and speak to the inspector who questioned us on Saturday. What exactly I say to him will depend, I think, on what I find out from the solicitor. I don't want to get myself into any trouble.'

'Quite right,' said Juju. 'But the sooner this scoundrel is caught the better. Do you have any idea who it might be?'

Clara nodded. 'I do. But I need some more proof. If I can confirm whose prints are in the three locations, I can give that to the police too.'

Juju leaned across the desk and lowered her voice. 'Who do you think it is?'

Clara was just about to say then stopped herself. She did not know this woman very well. Yes, she was a good friend of her uncle, but she didn't know whether Juju Levine might let the cat out of the bag too soon and inadvertently alert Jack Danskin that she was on to him. She had probably told her too much already – but there was no helping that. However, she would be more careful going forward. She smiled, tightly, and poured herself another cup of tea. 'I can't say for sure. But I will certainly tell you when I have more proof. And when I've spoken to the police.'

Juju looked disappointed. 'I understand,' she said, and pushed her cup forward for a refill. 'But perhaps you can tell me why you think Fender was murdered. If it turns out that he was. What might the motivation have been? And did the killer intend for you and Alice to find the body in the way you did?'

Clara nodded. 'All very good questions, Juju. I'm new at this detection game, but I'm not new at gathering evidence, coming up with a hypothesis and then testing theories. I'm treating this the same way as I would a scientific project.'

Juju leaned in, her heavily made-up eyes greedy for some juicy information. 'So, what is your hypothesis?'

Clara picked up her teaspoon and tapped it on the saucer. 'Well, it seems to me that someone is worried that Alice and I might be getting too close.'

'Too close to what?'

'To proving that the Carousel and Paradise fires were arson.'

Juju's eyes widened. 'And were they?'

'I think so, yes.' Clara paused a moment, contemplating what to tell Juju and what to withhold. She'd already told her about what she'd discovered in the laboratory, and the evidence gathered at the picture house. 'I think the presence of the kerosene that wasn't accounted for in the initial fire inspector's report at least warrants a reinvestigation. But no one knows that I have the ability to test for kerosene.'

'No one?' asked Juju.

'Other than you, Alice and Andrew, no.'

'How did they – whoever "they" are – know you were even investigating this?'

Clara shrugged. 'I suppose someone was watching the office. Or someone heard that Bob's heir was in town and that the files might be reopened. The Carousel was a closed case for the police, the fire department and the insurance company. But it might have been known that Bob was reinvestigating it. When he died, the case might have been closed too. But with me coming here and possibly taking over the agency – or selling it on to another investigator who might reopen the case – then whoever wanted to keep the case shut might have got the collywobbles.'

'And sent someone to steal the Whittaker file?'

'Exactly. But it was too late, as I had taken the file with me to the hotel.'

'Hence the break-in at the hotel. But you say the file wasn't there.'

'Well, it was, but in the hotel safe. I became nervous that someone might be trying to find out what I knew about the Whittaker case, so I asked the hotel manager to lock the file away when I wasn't using it. And then there was the tragic fire at the Carousel. This time someone died. I'm assuming it was mere coincidence that I happened to be there at the time, but it might not have been. And then there was the bag-snatching incident. That time they got my notebook. Anyone who reads that will know what I suspect and how far I have got in my investigation.'

'Do you have any evidence of this?' asked Juju.

Clara shook her head. 'No. As I said before, this is all purely hypothesis. The only hard evidence I have are the kerosene samples and now these fingerprints in the same location. But I need to find out who the prints belong to. And then I might find out why that person killed Fender. Although I do have some theories . . .'

'You do? Oh, jolly good! What are they?'

Clara paused again. Then reminded herself that Juju knew much of this already. And that she was friends with Alice Whittaker, who might very easily tell her all about it anyway. And Clara really did want to talk this through . . . 'Well, we know that Horace Fender bought kerosene a couple of days before the fire at the Paradise. We know he was in the vicinity of the fire close to the time it happened. That is the Paradise fire; I don't know yet about the Carousel, although it seems he'd moved to Tynemouth just before the May Day weekend. However, that's all still a bit murky. Focusing on what we do know at the Paradise – if what Alice says about Will is true – then Horace lied about seeing Will locking the door and pocketing the key. Because remember, the key was not found on Will's person or anywhere in the picture house. Although this detail never seemed to bother the authorities.

'So, my theory is that Fender was paid to set the Paradise alight (and probably the Carousel before that) and to frame the Whittakers for not adhering to fire safety standards. Fender seemed to have come into some money, enough to leave the Salvation Army and to get a place of his own. We know that he then got a job with Balshard Insurance. And Balshard are the insurers of the Paradise and the Carousel, and Humphrey Balshard owns the rival Majestic Cinemas.'

Juju's eyes widened. 'Are you saying Balshard paid Fender to start the fires?'

Clara paused and considered how to proceed. Eventually she leaned forward and said: 'This is all speculation at this point, Juju, so I'm not sure I should say any more.'

Juju leaned back with a slight air of offence. 'Who would I tell? But that's all right, Clara, if you don't trust me . . .'

'No, no, no, it's not that. You've been nothing but helpful to me and a good friend to Bob. It's just that, as I said, I'm not sure where I stand with all of this legally. I'm in at the deep end here, and I think I need to find out more about that before I proceed.'

Juju nodded, her face softening. 'Yes, I see that. But you've done marvellously well so far, Clara. You have a real knack for this line of work. Your uncle would have been proud of you.'

'Do you think so?'

'I know so,' said Juju, tears welling in her eyes. 'He was a lovely man and I miss him terribly.'

'So do I,' said Clara. 'I would have loved to have known about his detection business when he was alive. I would have loved to have talked all of this through with him.'

Juju smiled. 'Instead, you've just got me.'

Clara smiled back. 'And I'm grateful for it.'

After Juju left Clara made two more phone calls. The first was to the hotel to let them know she would be away for the rest of the day but would like to book a table for dinner. A table for two.

Then she looked up a number in Bob's telephone list. She called the operator and asked to be connected. After three rings someone answered. 'Jack Danskin here.'

'Good morning, Mr Danskin, it's Clara Vale. I wonder if you would care to join me this evening for dinner?'

Chapter 28

Roger Jennings took a drag on his cigarette and exhaled into the stuffy air of his mahogany-panelled office. 'So, Miss Vale, you say the smell you detected on Horace Fender's corpse was chloroform, but you only realised what it was last night while you were working in your uncle's laboratory?'

'Actually, it was this morning I remembered, when I was working through what I did last night. But I don't suppose the timing matters.'

'Well, it does a bit,' said Jennings. 'Inspector Davidson might wonder why you didn't mention it in the police interview on Saturday. He might wonder if you were hiding something.'

Clara gave the solicitor a startled look. 'Why on earth would he think that?'

Jennings tapped a tail of ash into an onyx ash tray on his desk. 'Well, as you are a trained research scientist, he might wonder why you didn't know immediately and tell him there and then.'

Clara cleared her throat, more from incredulity than the smoke that was settling around her. 'I'm a scientist, not a bloodhound, Mr Jennings. And besides, I'm not currently working in the field. I can't remember every single chemical at the drop of a hat. But as soon as I did, I noted it down.'

'Fair enough,' said Jennings, his fingernail scraping along the top of the cigarette. 'I'm just trying to consider what Davidson's response might be and to prepare you in advance. I wouldn't be doing my job if I didn't.'

'And that's fair enough too,' said Clara, relaxing back into her chair. 'And why I thought you might help me consider how to move forward.' She didn't add that she would have far preferred it to be his kindly father who would help her move forward, and cursed the fact that Jennings Snr was out of town. But she had to play the hand she'd been dealt. She turned her attention back to Jennings Jnr, whom she had to admit seemed to have a very astute legal mind. 'The bottom line, Mr Jennings, is that I now have a considerable amount of evidence suggesting that Fender might have set the fire that killed Will Spencer. That means his testimony – which pointed the finger of blame at Will – will surely be undermined. What do you think?'

Jennings dragged and exhaled again, careful not to blow in Clara's direction, but adding to the general fug in the closed office. 'I'm not a criminal barrister, Miss Vale, I'm a solicitor, so this isn't really my area of expertise. However, it certainly sounds like you have unearthed some interesting material that could potentially lead the case in a new direction. That, though will be for the police to decide. What isn't clear though, is Fender's motivation. Why would he do it? Do you have any idea?'

Clara nodded. 'Well, I don't have much to back this up yet, but my theory is that he was paid to set the fire – the one at the Paradise and the one in May at the Carousel.'

Jennings' eyebrows met above the bridge of his nose. 'Paid by whom?'

Clara shrugged. 'That I don't know for sure. It could be someone at Balshard – the insurance company or the cinema chain – or even Humphrey Balshard himself. And I also believe Horace Fender was killed before he could speak to me and Alice Whittaker, and that the person who did it might have done so to stop the Balshard connection from coming out. Because who has the most to lose if the Carousel case is reopened, or it's proven that Will didn't lock the door at the Paradise? Balshard Insurance, that's who. They might then have to pay up. Even if they weren't actually involved in setting the fires, they would still lose money.'

Jennings leaned forward and lowered his voice. 'That's quite a string of accusations, Miss Vale, and unless you have air-tight evidence I don't suggest you voice your suspicions outside of this room.'

'Why ever not?'

'Because, speaking as your legal representative here, you will be in danger of opening yourself up to a defamation suit. You're making a very serious allegation against a very powerful man, and Humphrey Balshard will not let that pass.'

Clara pursed her lips. She had been hoping for a bit more support from Roger Jennings and wished instead she were talking to his fussy but kindly father. But she wasn't, so she ploughed ahead, trying to get the information she needed. 'But what if the accusation is true? Shouldn't I be passing on what I know to the police?'

Jennings nodded. 'Yes, you should, when you have something more concrete. Do you have anything more tangible?'

Clara shook her head. 'I don't, no.'

'Then I suggest you delay speaking to Davidson about it until you do. You don't want the police to dismiss you out of hand, do you?'

'Of course not, no. But surely the sooner they know what I've got on Fender the better.'

Jennings stubbed his cigarette out and leaned back in his chair, his thumbs hooking into the pockets of his waistcoat. 'I agree with you, but I don't suggest you mention anything about Balshard unless you have a lot more than you have now. That's what your uncle would have done. Bob was a master of gathering evidence. By the time he finally handed over what he had to the police, the case was all but served up to them on a silver platter. Are you anywhere near that level of competence?'

Clara flushed in anger. 'Of course not! Bob was a professional detective, and I'm not.'

Jennings shrugged apologetically. 'And that, Miss Vale, is the problem here. You are taking on a very serious case involving arson and possibly murder, without any experience whatsoever.' He leaned forward, his face awash with sympathy. 'I'm not trying to be critical here, I'm just looking out for your best interests. My father would do exactly the same. And your uncle would expect nothing less of us.'

Clara's fingers were drumming the arm of her chair. 'My uncle thought enough of my potential to leave his detection business to me.'

'Potential, yes, I do not doubt it. But this is something you will need to grow into if you decide to stick with it.'

'And why wouldn't I stick with it?' snapped Clara.

Jennings let out a long sigh. 'I'm sorry, Miss Vale, we seem to be at odds here. I promise you that was not my intention. I'm just looking out for your best interests.'

'And Balshard's?'

'What do you mean?'

'Humphrey Balshard is one of your clients, isn't he? I recall your father being called back to the office on the first day we met to deal with him. Am I correct?'

Jennings raised an eyebrow. 'Indeed you are. We have been doing some conveyancing work for them. But we are just one of a number of legal firms they use.'

Clara raised an eyebrow in return. 'So, your advice to one client is not to protect another client?'

'Of course not! Listen, Miss Vale, Jennings & Jennings has a fine reputation in this town. We represent dozens of clients, big and small. I can assure you this is not the first time there has been a potential conflict between two clients we represent. We never play one off against the other. Never! If there is a genuine conflict of interest, we will pass it on to another firm – our reputation depends upon it. But this is not one of those cases. As I said, we are not criminal lawyers, but I can tell you now that I don't think you have enough to pursue a case against Balshard. And if you do, without corroborating evidence, you could be in legal trouble. That's why I'm advising you the way I am, not to protect another client. If that evidence is forthcoming, then you should go to the police with it, but not before. For your own sake, not just Balshard's.' Then his voice softened and he leaned forward. 'Please, Miss Vale, listen to what I'm telling you. If Bob were alive he would tell you the same thing.'

Clara nodded, taking it all in, allowing her breathing to steady. 'All right, point taken. I don't have enough on Balshard yet. But if I did, what would my legal standing be then? What legal protections does a private investigator or an enquiry agent have in cases like this? Am I able to question people the same way the police are?'

Jennings shook his head. 'I'm afraid not. In this country – unlike some others – you do not need a special licence to open a detection agency. As a result, you are just a private citizen with the same rights, responsibilities and prohibitions as any Joe Soap on the street. Or in this case, Josephine.' He smiled briefly at his own joke and carried on. 'So, you could very easily be arrested for trespassing on the scene of a crime – as you very nearly were yesterday, although the fact that Mrs Whittaker still owned the building would have protected you from that. But if you were to seek entry into another place in the course of your investigation, that would be trespassing. And you cannot compel any witnesses to speak to you, although they may do so willingly if they so choose. You are, though, in danger of interfering with a police investigation and withholding evidence, so I suggest you tread carefully here if you intend to continue.'

Clara stopped drumming her fingers. 'Oh, I intend to continue, all right. And I do not intend to withhold evidence. You are the one suggesting I do that, not me.'

Jennings threw up his hands and let out an exasperated sigh. 'That is not what I'm saying! I'm just saying be careful what you tell the police if you cannot substantiate it. If you cannot back up your theories then the police may not look as favourably on the other evidence you do have. They might consider you a time-waster. Bob told me many times that he had to make sure all his ducks were in a row before bringing the police into it. All I'm doing here is suggesting you do the same. Is that understood?'

Clara sighed. 'Yes, that is understood. I'm sorry, Mr Jennings, I'm just feeling my way here.'

Jennings gave a sympathetic nod. 'And I understand that, Miss Vale. I'm sorry if I haven't been more helpful.'

'No, that's not true. You have been helpful. I now know where I stand legally with all this. I'm not entirely sure what I'll do now, but at least I know the parameters within which I'm working. Thank you for your time.'

Jennings smiled at her and stood. As he showed her out of the office, Andrew Ridpath walked into the reception area, looking flustered. 'Jennings! Miss Vale! Perfect timing! You're both here. Listen, I've just had a telephone call from London from your brother Antony.' He looked Clara in the eyes, his face awash with sympathy. 'I'm afraid it's not good news. He's decided to contest the will.'

'What the deuce?' spat Jennings.

Clara just rolled her eyes.

Jennings ushered Clara and Andrew back into his office and asked his secretary to bring in a pot of coffee. 'Make it a strong one please, Mrs Armitage.'

'So what exactly did Mr Vale say?' asked Jennings, returning to his seat behind the desk. Clara returned to the seat she'd just vacated, with Andrew taking the seat next to her.

'He said to tell you, Clara – and your solicitor – that as the firstborn son, your older brother and Bob Wallace's only nephew and closest living male relative, he should be the rightful heir.'

'Well, that's just poppycock!' said Clara. 'Isn't it?' she asked Jennings.

Jennings nodded. 'It is. The law of primogeniture was abolished in 1925. So your brother is four years out of date here. Besides, the law only really applied in cases where there was no will. This is not one of those. However, Antony may contest the will on other grounds. I would need to see what they are before making a judgement on their validity. Did he give any other reasons?' he asked Andrew.

'Not directly, but he did say he is having his solicitor draw up papers, and that – and I quote – "I can't remember all the legal rigmarole but my fellow thinks I might have a case."'

Jennings made a low growling noise in his throat. 'Well, I very much doubt that if he's been advised that he's the rightful heir simply by being the closest male relative. Still, I can't dismiss it out of hand. I'll have to see what the petition says. Did he say when the papers would be arriving?'

Andrew shook his head. 'He didn't. But he was asking for your contact details. Mine were the only ones he had, passed on to him by the bank when I transferred the money to him. I asked them to do that so he could acknowledge receipt.'

'And did he? Did he acknowledge that he'd taken the money?' asked Clara, seething.

'He did,' said Andrew. 'All two hundred pounds of it.'

'The little snake!'

But a slow smile crept across Roger Jennings' face. 'Did he now? Well, well, that might prove very useful for us.'

'How?' snapped Clara. 'My wretch of a brother has taken – no, stolen – my money on top of trying to steal Uncle Bob's estate away from me. They couldn't stand each other! Antony thought Bob an eccentric fool, and Bob thought him a feckless rake. And he was right! He is a feckless rake! And now a back-stabbing one, too.'

Jennings raised his hands placatingly. 'Calm down, Miss Vale, all is not lost. Nowhere near it. Firstly, as I said, male primogeniture no longer applies in English law. Secondly, whatever other challenges to the will he may have, they have not yet been disclosed. Frankly, I can't think there could be many. Antony is not Bob's son, just a nephew. If this was your father's will and he left everything to you, then your brother – and sister for that matter – might have a case to challenge, but this is not that. Your uncle could very well have chosen to bequeath his entire estate to a donkey sanctuary, and a judge would not likely overturn it unless it could be proven that your uncle was not in his right mind when he drew up the will. That is not very likely to happen. But beyond that, if what Ridpath here says is correct, and Antony took the money offered to him for services rendered – that is to help you secure your inheritance – then that will very much go against him. Did you make it clear, Miss Vale, in your conversation with him, that the purpose of the money was so that he would write a letter declaring you competent to run your own financial affairs and hence be a fit person to receive a transfer of your uncle's bank account into your name?'

Clara thought back to her conversation with Antony. Yes, once she'd got him to focus long enough on what she was telling him – beyond that he was about to be paid two hundred pounds – that was the gist of what she had told him. She hadn't mentioned the detection agency though – she didn't want to give her brother any reason to mock her, more than he already did – so she had just mentioned the house and the bank account. 'Yes, I did. I told him I had been named in Uncle Bob's will and that I would be inheriting his estate, including the bank account. I didn't tell him about the agency though, does that matter?'

Jennings shook his head. 'I shouldn't think so, no. The important thing was at the time of the conversation he understood you were going to inherit the estate – no matter what it entailed – and that he agreed to facilitate you in that process. Is that what happened?'

Clara gave a firm nod. 'It is.'

Andrew chipped in: 'Sorry to put a damper on things – and far be it for me to tell you your business, Jennings – but neither one of us was actually in the room when Miss Vale made that phone call, were we.'

Clara gave Andrew a worried look. 'Why would that matter?'

'Because,' said Jennings, releasing a frustrated sigh, 'your brother could contest your version of events and make up whatever he wants. There was no one else listening to corroborate. Ridpath's right – that's one potential scenario, but if it comes to it, it will be Antony's reputation against yours. And from what you've told me of him, Miss Vale, he has left gambling debts across London in his wake. That will not go down well with a judge. I will certainly be mentioning that to his solicitor if and when he contacts me. However, in the meantime, it looks like your funds are still in limbo. You do not have the letter you need to convince the bank to transfer Bob's account into your name.'

Clara lowered her chin to her chest. *Oh dear. Just when I thought all my financial worries were over.* She raised her head and looked at Jennings. 'This doesn't mean, though that the estate isn't mine, does it? I still legally own the detection agency and the house? Is that correct?'

Jennings nodded. 'It is. Unless the will is overturned – which does not seem likely, to be frank, but it's an annoying complication that we will have to deal with – everything Bob left you is yours. The only issue right now is that you don't have access to Bob's capital. The bottom line, Miss Vale, is that for now you're short of cash. Ridpath here will give you a better picture of that.'

Andrew leaned towards Clara. 'Don't worry, you won't be living in penury. You still have two hundred pounds cash in the office safe, and that should go a long way. Do you think you can get your father to write the letter instead?'

Clara shook her head. 'He won't. He'll back Antony on this. I know he will. His views on inheritance are traditional.'

'And there is no one else?'

'No.'

'Then,' said Jennings, 'we'll have to take it to a judge. Ridpath, can you let the bank know what's going on? Tell them that if this is not resolved by the end of the week and Miss Vale's funds released to her, then we will take court action. That might scare them into doing something. There is nothing actually in the law preventing a woman from holding an account, it's simply convention. And as we all know, notable exceptions are sometimes made. Here is a woman who owns her own property, is thirty years old and able to vote, has an Oxford degree and has been running her own affairs for years. I think we have a good case. But it could take a while, Miss Vale, notwithstanding the added complication of your brother's spurious contestation. I expect though – at least I hope – that the mere threat of it will be enough to bend the bank trustees to our will. What say you, Ridpath?'

'I say you're bang on the money there, Jennings. Leave it to me.' He turned towards Clara. 'Miss Vale, would you care to accompany me?'

Clara pursed her lips. 'Oh yes, I shall most definitely accompany you. No offence, Mr Ridpath, I appreciate all you and Mr Jennings are doing, but I am a grown woman with a voice of my own. It's time these bankers heard from me.'

Chapter 29

In the five minutes between leaving Jennings' office in Emerson Chambers and walking down Grey Street to Lloyds Bank, Andrew tried to convince Clara that it might not be the best strategy to storm into the manager's office to demand her money. 'We are hoping for his co-operation here. We don't want to get his back up. I suggest you state the facts of your case, as Jennings did back there, and highlight that you would be happy to leave your funds with the bank if this can be resolved quickly and easily. The suggestion there would be that you would take them elsewhere if it came to the point that a judge were to declare you competent to hold an account. But do it quietly and politely.'

Clara stopped in her tracks and turned to him. 'Are you saying I shouldn't be an uppity little madam?'

He smiled down at her. 'Not at all, Clara. I think it's the Bible that says we should be as wise as serpents, but gentle as doves. I have no doubt that you can be both, if and when you choose.'

Clara, who was feeling distinctly uppity, was annoyed at what she perceived as Andrew's patronising tone; but in terms of strategy, she knew he was right. The goal here was to get her money and her financial freedom. If she had to kowtow to some overstuffed shirts in the process, then so be it. There was time to prove her worth as an independent woman another day.

Clara and Andrew entered the imposing banking hall through an enormous doorway flanked by two Corinthian columns. Andrew was recognised immediately and he and Clara were soon ushered upstairs and into the manager's office.

A slightly stooped grey-haired gentleman with spectacles greeted them. His suit, Clara noted, was impeccably cut; his collar and cuffs starched to attention. He was introduced as Mr Lansbury.

'Miss Vale, a pleasure to meet you. I worked with your father, you know. We both trained at Lloyds on Threadneedle Street. Many years ago now. How is he?'

'He is well, thank you, Mr Lansbury.'

'And does he know of your good fortune with regards to your uncle's inheritance?'

'I have not yet spoken to him about it.'

Lansbury sat back in his chair and clasped his hands in front of him. 'May I ask why?'

'Why?' said Clara. 'Because I am thirty years old, sir. I am well beyond the legal majority. I live on my own, I hold a first-class degree from Oxford, I am gainfully employed, and have financially supported myself for years. In fact, I already hold a bank account in London into which I pay my wages. I'm not sure why I didn't think of this before, but I can ask the manager there to write a letter to you.'

Lansbury nodded and pursed his lips. 'I have already spoken to your London bank manager. He tells me that since you stopped receiving the stipend from your father – for which the account was set up in the first place, with your father's authorisation – the amount of money going through your account has been very small. You are set to inherit a lot more money than that, Miss Vale. And we – and by "we" I mean me and the board – need some assurances that you are competent to manage a much larger estate. I believe your brother was to write a letter to that effect, but he is no longer willing to do so.'

'Unfortunately, that is the case. My brother has decided to contest the will.'

Lansbury's eyebrows rose. 'Has he now?'

'He has,' interjected Andrew, 'but Roger Jennings does not believe he has a leg to stand on.' He went on to explain to Lansbury what Jennings had told him about the weakness of Antony's case.

Lansbury nodded. 'Yes, it does seem like a tenuous claim, but it's an added complication. And of course, we still do not have a letter from a male relative. I'm sorry, Miss Vale, but we cannot transfer the bank account to you until we have that in hand.'

Clara bristled but remained calm. Something Lansbury had said was niggling in her mind. 'You said earlier, Mr Lansbury, that I am due to inherit a substantial estate – an estate that encompasses far more than the capital funds that are held in your bank. However, I would like to correct you on that. I am not *due* to inherit, I have inherited. It is now all mine. Isn't that correct, Mr Ridpath?'

'It is,' said Andrew.

'And my substantial estate includes property, stocks and shares and a going business. That is all above and beyond the cash accounts held in this institution. However, it is only the cash accounts that appear to be causing you concern. It is only they that you are quibbling over.'

'I am not *quibbling*, Miss Vale, I am exercising due diligence on behalf of our shareholders. And our shareholders are not – how can I put this – are not *comfortable* in the ordinary scheme of things with a woman holding an account in her own name. It's just not how things are done. It's not how we do business here, Miss Vale. It's not—'

Clara held up her hand to stop him. 'Excuse me, sir, there is no law preventing me from holding an account in my name – we both know that. And I am prepared to go to court to assert my right to do so. I may sell my house. I may sell my business. And when I do, I will have a substantial amount of cash – outside of the accounts held here. I believe there are a number of other banks in town, Mr Lansbury . . .'

Lansbury flushed. 'There are, Miss Vale, but none with such a fine reputation as this.'

'Good,' said Clara, 'then perhaps we can finally get down to business.'

Half an hour later, Andrew and Clara left the bank with an agreement to release half of the funds to her. The rest would be released after the contestation of the will was resolved. It was a reasonable compromise for both parties. Clara, however, was smarting that she could *still* not have full control of all her assets. Roger Jennings had already talked her out of ringing her brother and lambasting him on the telephone. 'Leave it to me, Miss Vale. Your brother will know which of your buttons to push, but not mine. He has no emotional leverage over me. It will come down to the law and nothing more. I am convinced the law is on your side in this case,' he had said. There it was again, the suggestion that she might get 'too emotional' about things. That as a woman, she was not trusted to hold her head. And now things had not gone entirely the way she wanted them to with the bank either. It was a partial victory, nothing more.

Andrew must have sensed her mood as they walked back up Grey Street in silence. 'Have I done something to offend you, Clara?'

Clara crossed her arms over her chest. 'Actually, you have. Now I know you were just giving me professional advice earlier about how to deal with the bank manager – and I appreciate that – but what I didn't appreciate is your assumption that I could not control my emotions without you reminding me to do so. That as a woman I am prone to hysteria.'

Andrew raised his eyebrows. 'I said nothing of the sort! I certainly didn't use the word hysteria.'

Clara pursed her lips. 'Fair enough, you didn't use that word, but I felt you implied it. And I didn't appreciate that.'

'Good heavens, Clara – Miss Vale – that's not what I meant at all. And if that's what you believe I think of you, then I'm very sad to hear it. I have nothing but respect for you. I consider you a remarkable woman. Not because you are a woman, but because of who you are, as a person. At least as much as a person can know another person in so short a time. So, I apologise. I did not mean to offend you.' He raised then lowered his hat. 'Please accept my apology.'

He sounded so sincere and genuinely concerned that he might have upset her that Clara's uppity mood began to subside. She unfolded her arms and gave a wry smile. 'Apology accepted.'

He smiled back, relieved. 'Might I ask you to lunch then? To celebrate? I thought you did marvellously in there. You were more than a match for Lansbury.'

'Thank you, I appreciate that. Unfortunately,' she said, checking her watch, 'I genuinely do have a prior appointment. However, perhaps we can do something tomorrow instead?'

He grinned. 'I would like that very much. I'll tell you what, assuming this is not too presumptuous, might you take a drive up the coast with me instead? I have a day off due to me, and, he said, looking up at the sky that was beginning to clear of the earlier rain, 'it looks like we might have some decent weather. Perhaps we could have a picnic.'

Clara thought through her day. The only thing she so far had planned for tomorrow was a meeting with Uncle Bob's doctor at nine o'clock. And that gave her an idea . . . 'Actually, Andrew, that sounds marvellous. And it could prove very helpful to me too.'

'Oh? How's that?'

Clara went on to remind him of the letter that Mrs Hobson the housekeeper showed her, implying that she and Bob were romantically involved and that there had been some kind of assignation at a hotel on Holy Island. 'Now I don't want to pry too far into my uncle's personal affairs, but if what Mrs Hobson says is true and they were romantically involved, then I think she deserves more sympathy than I have given her. So, if we are going up the coast, perhaps we could pop in there and see if anyone remembers them. Or if there are any records of their time together.'

She did not mention the complication of Bob's homosexual tendencies, nor the photograph of a possible male lover. Clara was open to the idea that Bob could have been interested in both men and women, although she suspected he wasn't. However, she needed to know for sure whether Mrs Hobson was telling the truth. 'So, what do you think? Might we take a run up to the island? I'm not sure how far it is, actually . . .'

'Further than you'd think. But we could get there in just under two hours, with a good tail wind.'

'Oh,' she said, disappointed, 'too far then.'

He shook his head. 'No, not really. It's a beautiful drive. And the car could do with a good long run. I'll need to check the tide timetable – the island gets cut off by the sea twice a day – but we could leave around ten o'clock and get there for lunch. Would that suit you?'

She smiled back at him. 'It certainly would. I have an early appointment with Bob's doctor – I want to ask him about my uncle's last months – but I'm sure we'll be finished before ten.'

'Splendid!' He grinned. 'Should I pick you up at the hotel?'

'Actually, it might be better to get me at the doctor's office. Will that be all right?'

'No bother at all.'

Chapter 30

Clara and Alice got off the train at Tynemouth railway station. There were only a few passengers on the platform, including a man in a dark blue coat who looked for a moment as though he were going to approach Clara and Alice, but at the last minute turned around and headed into the gentlemen's cloakroom. Clara wondered if she'd seen him before. There was something familiar about him. In fact, she was fairly sure he'd been on the train on Saturday, too. But she put him out of her mind and exited the station with Alice.

Although a seaside village, like Whitley Bay, Tynemouth had less of a holiday feel. Instead of excited children with buckets and spades, the genteel oak-lined streets provided shade to well-dressed ladies and gentlemen, strolling past its tea rooms, salons and boutiques. Alice led Clara past the well-to-do King's School, which offered private education to the sons of the wealthier residents of the locale – 'let's just say me and Jimmy couldn't afford to send our bairns there.' Then she ushered Clara through a small but pristinely kept park, topped and tailed by a memorial to the South African War at one end and a statue of an austere Queen Victoria at the other.

Alice then turned right into Percy Park Road announcing: 'The Carousel is just down here,' when she stopped in her tracks. Down the road, on the left, was a completely empty plot. Whatever had been there had been bulldozed to the ground. 'Dear God, what have they done?' Alice ran down the road, Clara ran after her, and a minute later they were standing in front of an expanse of rubble. 'They've destroyed it! They've bulldozed it! There's nothing left!'

'Who's done it? How could they do it without your permission?' asked Clara.

Alice had tears in her eyes but she was seething with rage. 'I don't own it anymore. The bank repossessed it. Nothing I could do without the insurance money. And the Paradise will go the same way unless we can prove it was arson.'

Clara squeezed Alice's arm. 'And we will prove it. We've already got a lot of evidence.'

'There's nothing we can get from here though, is there?'

No, there wasn't. Clara had been hoping to take samples as she had in Whitley Bay and to have a look at the window that the Whittakers said had been prised open. The window she now believed Horace Fender had used to gain access to the building to set the fire in the projection room. But there was no hope of that now.

'Well, we'll just have to focus all our attention on the Paradise then. And we might still find something at Fender's flat. Don't worry, Alice, we're still in the game.' She smiled encouragingly at Alice, who eventually gave a weak smile in return.

'You're right. Thank you, Clara. Let's not give up yet.'

'Never!' said Clara. 'Now, lead the way to Balshard Insurance.'

The women were three quarters of the way down Front Street, towards the historic priory, when Alice stopped outside a premises at the corner of Hotspur Street. 'This is Balshard Insurance.'

Clara cast a quick glance into the bay window of Balshard's, then looked up and down the adjoining streets. 'So, Horace Fender lived somewhere around here then. Above a shop. But which one?'

'Should we just go in and ask?' suggested Alice.

'Yes, let's,' said Clara. 'We can split up; you take that side and I'll take this. But let's not go into Balshard's, for now. I don't want them to know that we're here. And let's not tell anyone who we really are either. Perhaps best we say we are friends of Mrs Fender and we're here to find where her late husband lived, so she can pick up his things at a later stage.'

'Good idea,' said Alice, and crossed to the other side of the road. Fifteen minutes later the women reconvened.

'Any luck?' asked Clara.

'Aye, I've found it. The barber says he rents his flat out to Balshard's and they put staff members up there. He hadn't heard that Fender was dead but didn't seem too upset about it. In fact he looked relieved, and wondered if Balshard's would put someone better in there now.'

Clara grimaced. 'Yes, from what I've heard of him, I don't expect Horace was anyone's dream tenant. We can let Mrs Fender know the address, then perhaps she can arrange for us to have a look inside.'

'Or,' said Alice, pulling a key from her pocket, 'we can have a look in there now.'

Clara gasped. 'Where did you get that?'

Alice shrugged. 'I just asked for it. I said we'd get a few things for Mrs Fender now, then she would come and sort the place out properly in a few days. Whether she will or not I have no idea, but he didn't have to know that.'

Clara grinned. 'You're becoming a jolly good detective, Alice.'

Alice managed the flicker of a smile. 'You're not too bad yourself, Clara.'

Clara cast another quick look at the window of Balshard Insurance, and then took Alice's arm. The two women walked up the side street to the barber shop. Alice waved through the open door to the barber, now preoccupied with a client. 'This is my friend who's here to help me. I'll pop the key back with you shortly.'

The man smiled and waved. Next door to the shop was a locked door at street level. A few moments later, the two women were inside and up the stairs. Clara sniffed. The room smelt of stale cigarette smoke, sweat and something else. When they pushed open the door they could see what the something else was: a sinkful of dirty dishes, with a half-eaten plate of food beside it, turning rancid in the summer heat. Clara found a window and opened it, taking a few moments to inhale some restorative fresh air.

Then she turned to face the flat. It was just a single room with a bed and small kitchen area, with a separate bathroom and lavatory, which gave off an even more foul smell. 'No wonder the barber's not grieving his loss,' observed Clara.

'Where do we start?' asked Alice. 'And what are we looking for?'

Clara shrugged. 'I don't know. Anything, I suppose, that might link Horace to the Carousel or Paradise fires. Or dirty dealings on behalf of Balshard. Let's just see if anything jumps out at us.'

Ten minutes later, after sifting through Fender's meagre belongings, nothing had jumped out. Alice sighed. 'Well, that was a waste of time. Nothing to link him to anything other than booze and poor housekeeping.'

Clara gave her a sympathetic look. 'Don't worry. We've still got the kerosene evidence, which ties him to it. I'll pass that on to the police. Never mind, we had to try.' She felt a pressure in her bladder. She wondered if she could hold it, but wasn't sure if she could.

'I'm loath to do it in there,' she said, nodding to the bathroom, 'but I need to spend a penny. Two ticks.'

Clara held her breath and went into the bathroom, shutting the door behind her. It was as filthy as it smelt: the bath, basin and lavatory, thick with scum – or worse. She decided it was best to just squat rather than sit. She did what she needed to do, then, as she was adjusting her clothes, her shoe caught on a loose floorboard. She gave it a poke with her toe and it shifted to reveal a cavity. There was something inside. Curious, she knelt down to have a closer look, lifting the board to reveal a folded handkerchief. She extracted the hanky and weighed it in her hand. Suddenly, she had an inkling of what it could be.

'Alice!' she called out, 'Come in here! I think I've found something.'

Moments later Alice was standing in the bathroom doorway and looked down to see Clara, on her knees, holding in one hand a dirty handkerchief, and in the other a heavy key.

'Is this what I think it is?' asked Clara, her heart racing.

Alice burst into tears.

Chapter 31

Clara and Alice stood outside the offices of Balshard Insurance and readied themselves to go in. On the train ride from Newcastle to Tynemouth, Alice had told Clara as much as she knew about Humphrey Balshard. Some of it fact and some of it, she admitted, unsubstantiated gossip. He was known as the Tyneside Tycoon and had made his money in armaments during the war, then in insurance. Up until fairly recently, the cinema business had been a sideline, a hobby he'd picked up after a glorious sunshine vacation in California back in '25. Although never short of money, Balshard's businesses – first armaments, then insurance – had always been short on glamour. The holiday to California gave the Balshards a touch of stardust, so when they returned home, Balshard decided he would try to recreate some of that on his doorstep.

Now his 'little picture house hobby', as he was said to refer to it, was a chain of a dozen Majestic Cinemas across the North East of England, screening the latest Hollywood releases. With the development of the talkies and box office sales doubling in the last year, it was turning into a very lucrative business.

'He's renowned for shutting down the competition,' said Alice. 'He's tried to buy out a number of small theatres like ours, and when that's failed, well, I've heard he doesn't mind playing dirty.'

'You have proof of this?' asked Clara.

'Other than my two burned-down picture houses? No. But hopefully we can get that proof, Clara.' And as the women walked into Balshard's office, lined with framed and autographed faces of Hollywood legends, they hoped that the key they had found in

Fender's flat would literally be the key to finding the proof they needed.

'So, Mrs Whittaker,' he said, as the ladies took seats in front of his desk, 'how may I help you this fine day?'

Clara noted his Savile Row suit, amply filled by a well-fed torso, and his bald head, polished to a sheen. She nodded to Alice to take the lead.

Alice folded her gloved hands over her handbag on her lap. The key was in the handbag. 'I am not here for help, Mr Balshard. I am here to tell you that you will be hearing from my solicitor soon who will demand you pay out on my claim – on both picture houses.'

Balshard smirked. 'Since when have you had a solicitor, Mrs Whittaker?'

'I don't, yet, but Miss Vale here has offered to put me in touch with hers.'

Balshard appraised Clara. 'Miss Vale? You are Bob Wallace's niece?'

'I am.'

'I see. I'd heard you were in town.'

'You have? And who might have told you that?'

He smirked again. 'I have many people who are loyal to me, Miss Vale. Many agents and many employees.'

'And why would your "agents" – a strange choice of word – think it relevant to inform you of my movements?'

Balshard shrugged. 'Knowledge is power, Miss Vale. Now, may I ask why you think Mrs Whittaker needs a solicitor?'

'Because,' said Clara coolly, tiring of the pussyfooting, 'we have a substantial dossier of evidence that proves that Will Spencer was not responsible for the fire at the Paradise, nor was he responsible for locking the back door.'

Balshard's lip curled under his moustache. 'Do you now? And where is this dossier?'

'You'll see it in due course. We are going through the correct channels first.'

'And those are?'

'A solicitor and the police.'

Balshard laughed. 'The police have already closed the case. It's time to move on. I'm sorry, Mrs Whittaker, as I've told you before, there is unfortunately nothing more I can do for you. So I bid you ladies good day.'

Alice looked at Clara, waiting to get a cue. Eventually Clara unfurled her legs and stood up. 'Well, thank you for your time, Mr Balshard. However, I have a question before I go: did you know that your employee, Horace Fender, was found hanged in the Paradise Picture House on Saturday?'

Balshard snapped his head towards her. 'I have been informed, yes.'

Clara nodded. 'Then I assume, too, that you were informed that it was Mrs Whittaker and I who found the body.'

Balshard nodded tersely.

Clara smiled. 'Good. Then, just as a courtesy, I'm here to inform you that Wallace Enquiry Agency has formally reopened the investigation into the suspicious fires at both of Mrs Whittaker's picture houses. And as a result of Mr Fender's unfortunate death, a whole lot of evidence has now come to light – evidence that strongly suggests arson. You'll be hearing from Mrs Whittaker's solicitor very soon.'

'Get out,' growled Balshard.

'With pleasure,' said Clara.

An hour later, and Clara and Alice were sitting outside Inspector Davidson's office at the Whitley Bay police station. Clara had been in two minds about coming. She was mindful of what Roger Jennings had said about getting all her ducks in a row before presenting her evidence that might implicate a very powerful man. It was very likely, with the speed that both fires had been investigated and the cases closed, that Balshard had someone on the inside of the investigation. Whether or not that person was Davidson himself, she wasn't as sure.

Uncle Bob's file on what he'd uncovered so far on the Carousel Picture House fire suggested the fire inspector had not been very thorough in his investigation, not even mentioning the presence of kerosene at the scene. And it was the fire inspector's report that ruled the blaze accidental, not arson. She was not aware that the final report had been made on the Paradise, but neither she nor Alice expected it would be any different. Another accident would imply repeated negligence on the part of the Whittakers, which would immediately nullify Alice's insurance claim. So yes, as far as Clara could see, the fire inspector was very likely implicated.

But was Inspector Davidson? The only thing of consequence she could see was that he had taken Horace Fender's word that he'd seen Will Spencer locking the door and pocketing the key. But he had not then gone on to query the absence of that key. Was that deliberate or just an oversight? Clara did not get the impression from her dealings with Davidson so far that he was an unobservant man. He had seemed very astute at their last meeting. So, could he be trusted? And if not, what should her course of action be?

Alice had been very keen that they turn the key in. As far as she could see, it was the evidence that exonerated Will. However, Clara worried that if they handed the key over, and Davidson was indeed in Balshard's pay, it might be the last they saw of it. She had, of course, taken a photograph of the key in situ in Fender's bathroom, with Alice in the frame pointing to it, but this might not be enough if the physical evidence was to 'disappear'. So, she convinced Alice not to mention it for now. But if they couldn't trust the police, who could they trust? Who was more powerful than the police? The answer, as far as she could tell, was the courts. She decided that once she had one more piece of evidence – evidence she hoped she would get this evening – she would write up a comprehensive report, along the lines of what she would present to summarise the findings of scientific research, and give it to a judge. She would ask Roger Jennings or his father to make the introductions, and she would also ask them to take on Alice Whittaker as a legal client. If they demanded payment up front, she herself would foot the bill until the insurance payment was forthcoming. With the agreement she'd made earlier that morning with the bank manager, she now had the financial wherewithal to do that.

If it had been entirely up to her, she would not have come to see Davidson at all today. However, as Alice pointed out, Clara had evidence that suggested Fender might have been murdered, and that meant there was a killer on the loose. Might he strike again?

'You have to at least tell him about the chemical you smelt, Clara,' said Alice. 'The substance you said could knock a man unconscious. If they're not already looking for whoever killed Horace, they should be. I'm still worried about why they killed him in the Paradise when we were there. Was it to scare us away? To stop us asking any more questions? Did they think that because we are women we'd be too frightened to continue?'

'Yes,' said Clara, 'I think that might very well be what they're thinking. They're trying to scare us off.' She thought about the bag-snatching incident at Exhibition Park, the break-in to her uncle's office, then most terrifying of all, the man in her hotel room. But there was something else that had been worrying her. Up until now she had put it down to the heebie-jeebies after seeing Horace Fender's hanging corpse. But from the time she and Alice first arrived in Whitley Bay on Saturday, through their visit to Tynemouth today, she had had the feeling they were being followed.

There was that man she'd seen at the station today. She'd been thinking about it, and was almost certain it was the same man who, on Saturday, had got on the same train as them from Newcastle to Whitley Bay – and then she'd seen him on the way back again. Now, there could be a perfectly reasonable explanation for it. It was a public train and a well-frequented route. There was nothing to say this man had not, simply by coincidence, been travelling to and from Whitley Bay and Newcastle, on two separate days. And he wasn't even in the same carriage as Clara. She'd just spotted him, from a distance, on the platform on Saturday. She wasn't even sure why she'd noticed him.

Clara told all this to Alice. 'I didn't get a very good look at him, really. But I'm sure it was the same man. He had the posture of a younger man, how young I can't say. He was wearing a dark blue overcoat and charcoal-grey hat, low over his forehead, so I couldn't see his face.'

'But you think he was following us?'

'I do.'

'Then please, Clara, let's go to the police. Let's get the next train to Whitley Bay. I hear what you're saying about not giving them the key just yet, not wanting the evidence to be lost or covered up, but this man following us, and that chemical – what did you call it?'

'Chloroform.'

'Aye, that's right, the chloroform. Let's at least tell them about that.'

Clara had agreed. So here they were, waiting to speak to Detective Inspector Davidson. However, an hour later they were still waiting. Eventually, Clara flagged down a sergeant and asked if the inspector was ready to see them yet.

The man looked curiously at Alice and Clara. 'I'm sorry, ladies, didn't anyone tell you? DI Davidson has left town for a few days.'

'When did he leave?' asked Clara.

The sergeant looked at his pocket watch. 'About half an hour ago. He's off to a conference in York.'

'But he knew we were here!'

The sergeant gave a sheepish shrug. 'I'm sorry, ladies, someone should have told you. Is there something I can help you with?'

Clara looked at Alice. Alice shook her head. It was the answer Clara had wanted. 'No, thank you,' she said to the sergeant, gathering her things. 'There's nothing you can do to help.'

Chapter 32

The Royal Central Station Hotel was busy for a Monday night. A combination of summer school holidays and the North East Coast Exhibition had ensured near capacity in the six-storey hotel, with businessmen, exhibitors and out-of-town visitors buzzing in every lounge, bar and salon like bees in a hive. Clara was very glad she had booked her dinner table in advance. She had also extended her stay at the hotel. If she needed to be in Newcastle after that, she would again consider moving into Uncle Bob's house.

The way things were going, that was increasingly likely. When she returned from her trip to Tynemouth and Whitley Bay, mid-afternoon, she had picked up two telegrams from reception. The first was from Mr Rose at Bloomsbury Library in response to the telegram she had sent telling him her stay in Newcastle needed to be extended in order to wrap up her uncle's estate. He replied saying she could have a few more days but she absolutely must be back by next Monday at the latest. Clara doubted she would make that deadline, so that was very likely the end of her employment. She was surprisingly sanguine about it. She had been grateful for the work she had at the library, but the job could not be described as stimulating, not like the work she was doing now.

She lay back on her bed, fully dressed and ready for dinner, but taking a few moments to rest before the big night ahead of her. She crossed her legs at the ankles, careful not to wrinkle her clean silk stockings. *Work?* she asked herself. *Is this really work? Could this possibly be a feasible future career?* She had to admit, she had not been as excited as this since her first year at Somerville College, Oxford.

A potential new future lay before her, far different from the one her parents had envisaged for her. Speaking of her parents, she unfolded and reread the second telegram she had received this afternoon.

TONY SAYS YOU'VE TAKEN HIS INHERITANCE FROM BOB. YOU DIDN'T TELL US YOU WERE UP IN NCL. CALL US THEN COME HOME IMMEDIATELY. MOTHER.

Clara snorted. *Come home immediately? Not on your nelly!* If there was an overwhelming reason to stay up here, move into Bob's house and take over the agency, then it was this. To finally put some distance – geographically and financially – between her and her family. But there wasn't just one reason, there were a number. The last few days had been exhilarating. She felt like she was really getting the hang of this detection business. And that had been the main purpose of her taking on the Whittaker case: to test herself. Added to which she hadn't quite known how to turn down the distraught widow. But it was really Andrew's suggestion, while she was umming and ahhing about it, that had prompted her to give it a go to see whether Bob was right. Her uncle had seen her potential as a detective; it looked like he might be proved right.

Was she actually on the brink of solving her first case? She had already accumulated a lot of evidence – scientific and circumstantial – and she would be writing up her report this evening. Then in the morning she would take it to Roger Jennings and ask him to see if it was possible to set up a meeting with a judge. But first, she had one more crucial piece of evidence to gather. She uncrossed her legs, sat up, straightened her stockings and slipped into her velvet pumps. She appraised herself for a moment in front of the dressing table mirror. If it weren't too immodest to think so, she was looking smashing tonight. Her bobbed raven hair framed her carefully made-up face: kohl eyeliner, enough to highlight her dark (dare she say?) intelligent eyes, and red lipstick to accentuate her mouth, but not enough that she could be mistaken for a flapper. She ran her hands down her claret-coloured cocktail gown from breasts to hips and turned to view herself from front and back, pulling in her belly and lowering her shoulders to elongate her neck. *Is this what a detective should look like?* she asked herself.

'Well, it is tonight,' she said out loud as she slung her jewelled evening bag over her shoulder and picked up her velvet wrap.

A dance band was playing in the main ballroom with a Noël Coward soundalike crooning the lyrics of 'World Weary' into the microphone while couples foxtrotted clockwise around the room. Clara stood in the doorway between the ballroom and cocktail lounge and listened. She had heard Coward sing the song live in London when she'd accompanied Laura and Michael, her sister and brother-in-law, and Michael's supposedly eligible bachelor cousin, to the revue *This Year of Grace*. Clara had enjoyed the revue, but would have enjoyed it more without the slavering attentions of The Cousin.

When she declined to return to Laura and Michael's flat for a nightcap and asked to be dropped home in Bloomsbury instead, Laura was fuming. She telephoned the next morning, screeching like a banshee about Clara's ingratitude and rudeness. 'Word will get round, you know. There are only so many decent men these days, and if you snub your nose at perfectly respectable men like Brian, you will be taking yourself off the market.'

Clara informed her – shortly before slamming down the earpiece – that she had never been 'on the market', and had no intention of ever being so.

'Fine!' spat Laura. 'Stay a virgin for the rest of your life. See if I care!'

The call was ended before Clara could give in to the temptation of telling her snooty sister that for her information, she wasn't a virgin either!

Only once, Clara reminded herself. *You've only had intercourse once.* She thought back to the night in question all those years ago. She had been a little drunk, yes, but not drunk enough to not remember. She remembered all right. She remembered lots of panting, a little bit of pain and then, the beginnings of something rather lovely. She was just beginning to relax into the rhythm and focus on the way her body quivered and surged when, suddenly, Clive had said 'sorry, old girl, that was it'. And then she remembered the sinking disappointment before they fell asleep, in the same bed, but miles apart: she wondering whether it would have been better if she'd waited until marriage, he . . . well, she had no idea what he was wondering, until the next morning and his fumbled proposal and hasty exit when she let him off the hook. The truth was, she was as relieved to see him go as he was.

She had spent the next few weeks doing two things: one, avoiding Clive; and two, waiting for her monthly cycle. She had never been very regular and her bleeding could come anywhere between three and seven weeks. A fellow student at Somerville had loaned her well-thumbed copies of Marie Stopes' *Married Love* and *Wise Parenthood*. Judging by the titles alone, the books were not aimed at young women like Clara. Mrs Stopes was very clear in the foreword that her books were meant to give *married* women more control over their fertility and sexual relations with their husbands. However, after reading the chapters on how to ensure that women were equally pleasured by intercourse, Clara considered buying a copy and sending it, anonymously, to poor old Clive. Even though it was too late for her benefit, it might help some other woman in the future.

The disappointingly short-lived sex act aside, Clara was most concerned that she might be pregnant. It was a case of figuring out how to close the stable door once the horse had bolted, but she was relieved to find out that there were ways to reduce the chances of conception. If, Clara told herself, she got through to her next monthly bleed without being pregnant, and if, she added ruefully, she ever decided to have sex again, she now knew how to go about it.

Thankfully, her period did come, but in the eight years since she had not had the opportunity – or inclination – to put her new-found knowledge into practice. And she certainly wouldn't be putting it into practice tonight. She did need to turn up the charm enough that her partner for the evening might be led to believe she found him attractive and that she might be wooed into the sack. Seeing as he looked like the film star Ronald Colman, that shouldn't be too difficult, but flirting had never been Clara's strong point. She hoped she could pull it off. The success of her investigation depended on it.

Jack Danskin joined her on the threshold between the cocktail lounge and the ballroom holding a Bee's Knees cocktail in each hand. 'Would you like to dance, Miss Vale?'

Clara turned to him and gave him what she hoped was a warm smile. 'That would be lovely, Mr Danskin. Perhaps after dinner?'

Danskin grinned. 'Everything in its proper order, eh? Cocktails, then dinner, then dancing, then . . .' He let the words hang in the air.

Clara looked him firmly in the eyes. 'Yes, Mr Danskin. Let's do this in order.'

He offered her the cocktail. She took it and chinked glasses with him, their eyes still connected. Then he put a proprietorial arm around the small of her back and nudged her into the cocktail lounge. Against her normal instincts, she allowed herself to be guided, and they were soon seated at the same table she and Andrew had had drinks at on Friday evening.

'So,' he said, leaning back and draping one arm over the back of the chair. 'How is your decision-making coming along?'

She leaned back too, hoping to mirror his relaxed demeanour. 'Quite well, I think. I've had a very interesting week, getting to know more about Bob's business and what it will take to run it.'

'So I hear.' He gave what could only be described as a rakish grin.

'Oh?' said Clara, reminding herself to sound nonchalant. 'What have you heard?'

'This and that. That and this. For instance, I heard you had a frightful day on Saturday.' He lost the grin and gave her what she assumed was his compassionate look. 'Seriously, Miss Vale, what a terrible thing for you and Mrs Whittaker to discover.'

She too banished any sign of a smile from her face. It wasn't hard to do. 'I assume you are referring to the body of Horace Fender.'

He nodded. 'Yes, I'm referring to Fender's suicide.'

'You heard it was a suicide? And where did you hear that?'

Danskin cocked his head to the side. 'In the *Newcastle Journal*, of course. Didn't you know you've made the evening papers?'

This threw Clara. She had expected him to admit that he had heard from some of his enquiry agent sources. He had, by his own admission, worked for Balshard Insurance. She suspected he still did. However, this had wrong-footed her. She had hoped to trap him into disclosing something that he could not possibly have known unless he had been told so by Balshard or someone else involved in the investigation, or he had been following her. The man on the train could very easily have been Jack Danskin. Same build, similar age bracket. She had not even considered that Fender's death would make the papers. But why wouldn't it? Most suicides did. And as of two o'clock this afternoon, Mrs Fender would have identified his body and so the news could have been released in time for the evening edition. Clara chastised herself for making such an amateur error. She obviously wasn't as good at this detective malarkey as she had thought. However, she would not be defeated and decided to regroup. She took a sip of her cocktail to give her time to do so, then asked: 'What did it say?'

Danskin also took a sip of his drink then replied: 'Not very much. Just that the body of a man had been found hanging by two ladies in a disused picture house in Whitley Bay and that the police were calling it a suicide.'

'Did it mention who the two ladies were?'

Danskin shrugged. 'It mentioned Mrs Whittaker, the widow of the former owner of the Paradise. And it said she was accompanied by a friend, a Miss Clara Vale.'

'No mention of my profession?'

He grinned. 'Miss Vale the librarian from Bloomsbury? Or Miss Vale the science graduate from Oxford University?'

Clara paused, her glass halfway to her lips. She did not recall mentioning her employment status to Danskin. 'No, I meant my profession acting on behalf of Wallace Enquiry Agency.'

'Ah, that. No, it did not mention that you were playing detective.' He smirked. 'So how is it going? Have you decided you want to continue with this line of work, or are you prepared to sell the agency?'

'I have decided that I will see this investigation to its conclusion and then make a decision.'

'And how far are you away from that?'

She raised an eyebrow and smiled in a way that she hoped was winsome. 'I'm not entirely sure, but I'm making significant progress and will be presenting my findings to the authorities soon.'

'And which authorities are those?'

'I have connections within the judiciary who are aware of my situation.' Clara hoped her measured delivery would convince Danskin this was true. It would be true, if Roger Jennings made an introduction for her, but that, of course, had not happened yet. Danskin would not know that. Or would he? Clara decided to deflect.

'I think our table is ready. Should we go?' She raised her hand to call over the waiter, not particularly caring that it was normally the man's role to do so.

'Yes, let's,' said Danskin, homing in once more on her eyes. 'I'm famished.'

The waiter arrived and removed their glasses as Clara allowed Danskin to usher her towards the dining room.

They were just starting their dessert course when Clara managed to steer the conversation back to the Paradise investigation. Danskin had been very chatty about his life and background, as if this were an evening that was really aimed at getting to know a potential professional – or indeed, marriage – partner. He was the son of a greengrocer who had started out as a barrow boy, then moved to a stall in the Grainger Market, before buying a corner shop in Blaydon. Danskin's mother spent her time looking after six children. Jack was the third eldest. He had finished school at fourteen and instead of working in the family shop – which was already staffed by his two elder siblings – he had joined the Post Office. He had worked his way up through the ranks until he had been appointed assistant head of security in charge of investigating postal fraud. That was how he got into detection work. Then came the war. After he returned, he decided to not go back to the Post Office, and instead took up his first assignment working for an enquiry agent.

'And the rest is history.' He grinned. 'I've been doing this for over a decade now. It's time to move up the ladder.'

'And get your own agency?' asked Clara.

'Exactly that.' He leaned back and hooked his thumbs into his cummerbund – the picture of a self-satisfied man.

'Why don't you just start your own?'

He laughed. 'I've told you, I don't want to deal with the administration.'

'You can hire someone to do that.'

'I could,' he said, pursing his lips. 'But my first thought was to go into partnership. Which is why I asked you.' He leaned forward, his eyes trying to hold hers.

She cleared her throat. 'But I'm not interested in a partnership,' she said firmly, then smiled, hoping to take the edge off her words.

Danskin's eyes narrowed – just a touch – before his easy smile returned. 'That's the impression I got the last time we spoke. But as you wanted to see me again, I thought you might have changed your mind. Now that you know a bit more about what running an agency entails. How hard it can be to get the police – or anyone – to take you seriously. Especially you being a woman.'

It was Clara's turn to narrow her eyes. 'Why do you think the police are not taking me seriously?'

Danskin opened his hands, placatingly. 'Because I know the police in these parts. And I know what they would think of a lady detective – even if you are Bob Wallace's niece. Having a man as a partner would help you get around that.'

Clara could feel her anger bubbling. She tried to keep a lid on it. 'Why do I need to get around that? When they see I can do just as good a job as a man, why should it bother them that I'm a woman?'

Danskin shook his head. 'Come, come, Clara, you're not that naïve. You know how the world works. I'm telling you, taking me on as your partner is your best option to keep this business going. Assuming you will be able to hang onto the business, that is. And I could help you with that too.'

'What do you mean by that?'

Danskin let out a long sigh and leaned back in his chair, giving off the aura of a man who felt very much in control. 'I've been contacted by your brother's solicitor.'

Clara sat bolt upright. 'You've what?'

'Your brother, Antony Vale. His solicitor was given my name as someone who could testify in a court hearing about your uncle's mental competence in the months before he died.'

'I – what – when? Who the hell gave him your name?' Clara spluttered, the bubbling anger approaching boiling point.

Danskin shrugged, still appearing maddeningly calm. 'He didn't say. But he did say that your brother would make it worth my while if I were to tell the truth about your Uncle Bob. He said he has no interest in running the business himself and would be happy to sell it to me for a reasonable price, if he can inherit the rest of your uncle's estate.'

'But *I* have inherited Bob's estate,' said Clara, her voice rising and drawing the attention of other diners.

Danskin leaned forward, giving her his 'compassionate look'. 'Yes, I know. That's what I told him. However . . .' He let the words hang between them.

'What?' snapped Clara.

'However, this sort of legal wrangling can go on for months. Years, sometimes. I've been involved in these sorts of things before. And in the meantime, your life will be in limbo. On the other hand . . .' he cocked his head to one side '. . . we can make your brother's claim go away very quickly.'

'How?' asked Clara.

'By me telling him that whoever told him I thought Bob had lost his marbles was mistaken. That if I testify it will be to say that he was as sharp as a tack up to the day he died.'

Clara's breathing was becoming laboured. She worked to relax her shoulders and quell her shuddering breath. 'But that's not what you believe. You told me yourself, you thought Bob was getting confused about some things.'

Danskin nodded. 'I did. But I could say I was mistaken.'

'And why would you say that?'

'Because it would mean more to me if you and I went into business together.'

Clara shook her head, incredulously. 'But *why*?'

He smiled. 'Why not? You need an experienced hand. I can handle the likes of Detective Inspector Davidson. I am familiar with most, if not all, of Bob's open cases. You need me.'

Clara's breathing was beginning to come under control. She took a sip of wine, glad to see that her hand was steady. 'That might very well be the case, Mr Danskin, but the question is, why do you need me, if Antony is offering to sell you the business anyway?'

Danskin shrugged. 'Because that's really just a long shot, isn't it? And if I do testify against Bob, and the judge still decides in your favour, there will be bad blood between us.'

He leaned across the table and took her hand. She cringed but willed herself not to show it.

His eyes found hers again. 'And bad blood is the last thing I want between us, Clara.'

Clara smiled tightly. 'I can't say I want bad blood either, Jack. Even if we don't formally go into partnership, I'm sure we may work together informally in the future. You've already been immensely helpful to me.'

He let go of her hand, leaned back and laughed. 'Oh, Clara, you do need to work on your acting skills.'

'What do you mean?' she asked, retrieving her hand and clasping them both under the table.

He gave a patronising smile. 'You do deadpan all right, but charm is not your best suit. But that's what I like about you. I find you fascinating, Clara Vale. And now,' he said, standing and reaching out his hand, 'as promised earlier, everything in its correct order. It is now time to dance. Shall we?'

Clara stared at him, stung by his sense of entitlement. Her voice was cool and crisp as she said, 'I think not, Mr Danskin. As you have already noted yourself, charm is not my best suit. But honesty is. And honestly, I don't know if I can trust you. To dance with you or to go into business with you. So perhaps it's time to call it a night.'

Danskin lowered his voice. 'Are you sure you want to do that, Clara? We have a lot more to discuss.'

She put down her napkin and stood up. 'On the contrary, Mr Danskin, I think we've discussed enough.' She grabbed her wrap from the back of her chair and walked through the restaurant towards the cocktail lounge, aware of Danskin's eyes on her every step of the way. Through the door, she turned the corner, out of his eyeline, and approached the bar. She spoke quietly to the barman. 'Did you get them?' she asked.

'I did, miss. Just the way you told me to. Would you like them now?'

'No. I don't want anyone to see me with them. Bring them, with a bottle of champagne and two clean glasses, to my room.' She slipped a sovereign across the bar.

Chapter 33

Clara decided not to open the champagne. Firstly, she didn't yet know whether she had anything to celebrate. Secondly, because she'd already had a Bee's Knees then a glass of wine with dinner. She needed to keep a clear head. The champagne had merely been a ruse to disguise the real reason the barman had sent the waiter up to her room: to deliver the cocktail glasses she and Jack Danskin had drunk from before dinner. Clara had set the whole thing up in advance. She'd spoken to the barman and asked him to ensure the waiter who attended them wore gloves to collect the glasses – and to only touch the stems. She had taken the barman's fingerprints in the late afternoon, after she got back from Whitley Bay, so as to eliminate his prints from the mix. Any questions he might have had as to why she was doing what she was doing were soon silenced by a healthy tip – both for him and the waiter.

The cocktail glasses were wrapped in a napkin and delivered on a tray next to the champagne bucket and two clean glasses. If Jack Danskin were watching, he might wonder who it was she was entertaining in her hotel room. Well, let him wonder. If it were he who broke into her hotel room the other evening, the thought that she had a guest might deter him from trying again. And just in case it didn't, Clara had spoken to the police constable who was still on patrol outside the hotel to keep an eye on the fire escape outside her room. She had played the scared damsel in distress, to the best of her limited acting ability, and it seemed to have done the trick. The constable said he would keep an eye out for anything untoward.

Clara laid out her fingerprint kit on the dressing table and spread all the photographs of prints she had already taken out on the bed. She also placed the fingerprint card of the barman there. She had not had time to photograph it and develop it at Uncle Bob's house, but it didn't matter. The three matching prints, taken from the office, hotel and, most disturbingly, from the trunk at the Paradise, were grouped together. If Jack Danskin's prints matched, she had to face the fact that she had just had dinner with a murderer.

Using gloves, she brushed aluminium powder onto the glasses. Four sets of prints emerged: three on one glass, two on the second. She assumed that one of the sets was hers. With the aid of a magnifying glass and the enlarged photograph of her own prints, she identified which prints were hers. Thereafter she compared the other two prints to the card of the barman, and sure enough one of the sets belonged to him. The same set was on the second glass. So, that left two sets of prints, one on each glass, that belonged to Danskin. Clara compared them through the magnifying glass. After having done this so many times in the last few days, following the methods in Professor Gross's handbook, she was becoming familiar with identifying patterns in the whorls, loops and arches. It didn't take her long to confirm that the remaining prints on both glasses were indeed the same, and, by the process of elimination, had to belong to Jack Danskin.

She circled the relevant prints using her eyebrow pencil and photographed them. She would go to Uncle Bob's house in the morning to develop them. For now though, she went to the bed and selected the crop of three photographs. Again, with her magnifying glass, she compared the characteristics of the prints. And as she did so she became increasingly anxious. While the whorls looked similar, there was a marked difference in the loops and arches. She checked and rechecked, but eventually was forced to accept that Jack Danskin's prints did not match the three.

She looked up from her work and faced herself directly in the mirror. 'It's not him,' she said out loud. 'What the hell am I going to do now?'

After a few moments she went back to the bed and scanned all the photographs and prints she had. It was a growing list: her own, Mrs Hobson, Uncle Bob, Juju and Jonny Levine, Alice Whittaker, Horace

Fender, the barman, and finally Jack Danskin. She hunched over each image with her magnifying glass, and – for good measure – a torch, but finally had to accept that none of the prints matched the three. Whomever had broken into the office and searched the filing cabinet, then broken into her hotel room and finally touched the metal trunk that Horace Fender had stood on before hanging, it was not Jack Danskin.

She swept all the photos aside and threw herself onto the bed, beating the pillow in frustration and letting out a muffled howl. Eventually she calmed herself, flipped onto her back and stared at the ceiling. She had made a classic researcher's error. Undergraduates were taught, time and again, not to allow a hypothesis to take root and colour the results of an experiment. Hypotheses should be held lightly and changed as evidence challenged or disproved them, and a researcher must be prepared to follow the evidence even if it meant ultimately disproving their own theories. She would not allow herself to become disheartened. Yes, she had believed that the circumstantial evidence pointed to Jack Danskin, but the concrete evidence so far did not.

She still did not trust Danskin, and believed his association with Balshard Insurance suggested he might still be involved in the case in some way. And that his interest in becoming a partner in Wallace Enquiry Agency – or even buying it out completely – was motivated at least partly by a desire to shut down or scupper the Whittaker case. But whether she liked it or not, the prints were not his. Could he have paid an associate to commit the crimes? Someone she had not yet met? Very possibly. He could have paid the young lad to accost her in the park and someone else – an older man – to carry out the break-ins and, possibly, kill Horace Fender. But again, she had no evidence to back it up.

She did, though have evidence that Will Spencer had been falsely accused by Horace Fender, and that Horace Fender had bought kerosene, which was then used as an accelerant in the Paradise fire and that it was Fender, not Will Spencer, who had locked the back door of the cinema, with fatal consequences. And she had evidence that chloroform had been used on Fender before his death; and that he had been employed by Humphrey Balshard in some capacity. Even if there was no evidence, yet, that Balshard had ordered the fire to be lit and orchestrated the ensuing cover-up, or that he'd been involved in Fender's murder, she believed she still had enough to present to the authorities in order for Alice Whittaker's insurance claim to be reconsidered – and that was what she had been hired to do.

She got up and splashed water on her face, then cleaned off her make-up. She had earlier asked to borrow a typewriter from the hotel office. It was currently on the floor in the corner of the room. She cleared the dressing table and picked up the typewriter together with a ream of carbon paper so she could have triplicate copies – one for herself, a second for Roger Jennings whom she hoped would represent Alice Whittaker, and a third for the judge she still had to meet. Then she rang the room service bell. If she was going to write a clear and credible report, summarising her evidence so far, she needed coffee. The stronger the better.

Chapter 34

Tuesday 27th August 1929

The next morning, Clara, who had hardly had any sleep for the second night in a row, was waiting for Roger Jennings when he arrived with his secretary to open the office. The secretary asked if Miss Vale would be staying for coffee. She declined, saying she had another appointment to attend.

'I've just come to give you this,' she said, handing two envelopes to Jennings.

'What is it?' he asked.

'A summary of my findings so far in the Whittaker case. One for you, in the hope that you will take on Alice Whittaker as a client, and another to pass on to a magistrate or a judge.'

'A judge? I think you've got the wrong order here, Miss Vale. It should be the police you are handing this over to.'

Clara shook her head and told him, briefly, about what happened at the Whitley Bay police station yesterday. 'So you see, I'm concerned that Inspector Davidson is either in the pay of Balshard, or he is simply not taking me or Alice Whittaker seriously. I can't run the risk of handing the evidence to him and him ignoring it. So I thought, perhaps, if a magistrate looked at it first and gave his opinion on it, that might give me some leverage with the police. What do you think? Do you know someone we could approach with this?'

'Are you sure you won't come in, Miss Vale?'

Clara checked her watch. 'Sorry, I'm going to see Uncle Bob's doctor and he said he can squeeze me in before his surgery starts. So, can I leave this with you?'

Jennings nodded. 'Of course. I'll have a look at it. And if I think there's something in it, I can have a word with a magistrate. I can't promise he'll look at it – he might tell us to go straight to the police – but on the other hand he might not. And I take your point about not being sure about Davidson's standing on this.'

She smiled at the younger Jennings. He was much more amiable today than she'd seen him before. He must be warming to her. 'Do you think you could take on Alice Whittaker as a client? As you'll see, I think the evidence clearing her of the fire safety contravention charge is quite strong, so even if we just manage to put in another claim, it will be progress. I think, though, she'll need help with that. Could you do that?'

Jennings smiled at Clara. 'I will certainly have a look, yes. I will have to speak to my father about taking on a new client, but if the evidence is as solid as you suggest, then I don't see why not. Where are all the fingerprints and that key that you were going to give Davidson?'

'Don't worry, they're in a safe place. I'll have them to hand when needed. Perhaps you could just read through what I've written first. I reference and list each piece of evidence in there. It's not just the key and the fingerprints, there are samples from the Paradise there too. With my accompanying chemical analysis.'

Jennings looked impressed. 'I'm sure you've done a sterling job, Miss Vale. However, it might be useful if I had access to some of the physical evidence too, in due course. So I have a fuller picture of what we're working with. But it's not essential. A judge, though, will want to see it.'

Clara looked at her watch again. 'Of course, I understand. But I just don't have time now. I'm meeting the doctor this morning, then after that Mr Ridpath is taking me for a drive up the coast to Holy Island.'

'Oh yes?' said Jennings, grinning. 'Is Ridpath courting you?'

Clara shrugged, nonchalantly. 'I have no idea, Mr Jennings. You'll have to ask him.'

'I might just.' Jennings chuckled, then raised the envelope that

Clara had given him. 'But back to business. I'll give this my full attention later today. I have a few meetings myself this morning. Then let's set up a proper meeting so we can talk about how to proceed. My father will be back tomorrow, so we can take this forward then. Enjoy your trip up the coast, Clara.'

'Thank you, Mr Jennings, I expect I will.'

'So, you say you were surprised at how quickly he succumbed. Why is that?' asked Clara, sitting in front of the doctor's desk.

Dr Charles Malone, a good-looking brown-haired man in his late thirties, twirled the stem of his unlit pipe between thumb and forefinger. 'Bob was my father's patient. I inherited him, along with the practice, when my father retired. I'd met him a few times at the college library, and the occasional science lecture he attended. I knew he had been unwell, with a heart condition, but from everything Bob and my father told me, it was well under control. While his heart had to be cared for, there was nothing to suggest that death was imminent.'

'What did he actually die of?'

'Heart failure, as a result of chronic myocarditis – inflammation of the heart muscle. We must have misjudged how weak his heart muscle had become.'

'Was an autopsy conducted?' asked Clara.

Charles shook his head. 'No, no one called for one. He had been treated for a heart complaint, he died of a heart complaint – just quicker than we thought he would.'

Clara pursed her lips. 'But you said yourself, the speed of deterioration concerned you. Did you not think it suspicious?'

Charles frowned, his brown eyebrows shading his freckled face. 'Concerning, yes. Suspicious, no. It was a natural death, Miss Vale, although of course, it was still tragic. Not least for his family.' He then paused and cocked his head. 'I don't recall seeing any family members at his funeral.'

Clara caught her breath. 'No, there was no one there. I can speak only for myself, but I only heard about Bob's death after he was buried.'

Charles gave her a curious look. 'How unfortunate.'

'Very,' she said, her lips sealing in a tight line. 'But now that I'm here,' she said eventually, 'I am trying to find out as much about his life – and death – as I can. So I hope you can help me.'

'I'll do my best,' he said, tapping the empty pipe on a stainless steel ashtray. 'I was very fond of your uncle.'

'So was I,' said Clara. 'You say it was chronic myocarditis. Was it originally caused by a virus?'

'Possibly. He had had it for a few years, but he might well have caught something else that exacerbated it.'

'Was he showing symptoms of an infection before he died? High temperature?'

'Not that I'm aware, no. Just increasing fatigue in the weeks leading up to his death.'

'More than was to be expected from a man with his condition?'

'Yes, for his pre-existing heart condition, which was being treated by medication, his condition became worse than I thought it should have been.'

'Did you examine him?'

'No. I asked him to come and see me after I saw him struggling up the steps of the college library, but he declined to do so.'

'And you didn't pursue it?'

Charles gave Clara a hard stare. 'I cannot force anyone to come and see me, Miss Vale, but in case you are implying that I was derelict in my duty of care, I can assure you I was not. I began to wonder whether your uncle was taking too much medication. That might have accounted for his symptoms.'

'What was he taking?'

'My father had prescribed digitalis for his heart and barbital, to stop him from getting overanxious. It's standard. I would have prescribed the same.'

'But you thought he might have been taking too much?'

'It was a theory, yes. An overdose of barbital might have been the cause of his symptoms. When he didn't come to see me, I took it upon myself to visit his chemist, to check that he had not been getting more than was prescribed. I was assured that he was not.'

Clara leaned back in her chair and contemplated what the doctor had just told her. 'So, you suspected something might have been amiss. Enough to probe further. May I ask why? Why did you think something was amiss?'

Charles shrugged. 'Like I said, I was concerned at the speed of his deterioration. But when I mentioned it to my father, he suggested that Bob might have caught a secondary virus. Which is perfectly plausible.'

'But you have no evidence of it?'

Charles shook his head. 'None. Neither he nor his housekeeper – I questioned her about this one day when she came to pick up a new prescription for Bob – thought there was anything to be concerned about. She said he was just tired from working too hard. I asked her what dose he was taking. She confirmed it was exactly as it had been prescribed.'

Clara's eyes narrowed at the mention of Mrs Hobson. 'Might she have been lying?'

Charles was startled. 'Why on earth would she lie?'

Clara didn't quite know how to reply to that. In fact, she didn't quite know why she was even going down this line of questioning. Had her mere handful of days working as a private detective gone to her head? Was she simply being melodramatic? If she were, it would be quite out of character for her. She'd just hoped to speak to Bob's doctor in order to get a fuller picture of her uncle's life and final days. However, she had become increasingly puzzled by the conflicting accounts of those last days. On the one hand, Barnaby Jennings, Juju and Jonny Levine and Andrew Ridpath all told her that he was more tired than usual, but his mind was still as sharp as a tack. On the other, Jack Danskin and Jane Hobson both suggested that he was beginning to lose his mental faculties. And here was Bob's doctor telling her Mrs Hobson had 'no concerns'. Really? Why had she not mentioned Bob's alleged deteriorating mental state to Dr Malone? She'd been very quick to tell Clara about it. Both she and Jack Danskin. It was now clear to Clara that both Danskin and Hobson may very well have had ulterior motives in pushing the 'Bob was losing his marbles' narrative: Danskin because he hoped to muscle in on Bob's business, and Hobson because she seemed to believe that Bob would name her in his will. Might these be motives to – dare she even contemplate it? – hasten Bob's demise? To her surprise, she was contemplating it, hence her line of questioning.

Clara let out a long breath. 'I'm sorry, Dr Malone, but I have reason to suspect that Bob's death might not have been entirely accidental. And I'm wondering whether Mrs Hobson might have had a hand in it.'

Charles gasped. 'That is quite an accusation!'

Clara nodded in agreement. 'It is, and I'm mentioning it here under strict patient–doctor confidentiality. I might very well be wrong, and I hope I am, but Mrs Hobson has given me reason to be suspicious.' She went on to explain what had happened when the housekeeper came to the house. She was shocked to see Charles turning a bright shade of beetroot.

'Whatever is it, Dr Malone?'

'I – well – I am just astounded that Bob and Mrs Hobson were apparently lovers.'

Clara leaned forward. 'And why is that?'

'Because – I don't know, really. I suppose there is no reason why they shouldn't be.'

'But you seem very shocked by the suggestion. Why? Is there something you knew about my uncle? Something that was not widely known by anyone but his closest friends?'

Malone ran his finger along the inside of his collar. 'I'm not sure what you are trying to say, Miss Vale.'

'Really?' said Clara, spurred on by the doctor's curious reaction. 'It seems to me that you might know exactly what I mean. Did you know that my uncle was a homosexual, Dr Malone?'

'Absolutely not! It's illegal.'

'That may very well be the case, but did you know about it?'

'I did not.'

'Oh, but I think you did. Your reaction tells me you did.' The doctor's eyes flicked to the door. He looked like a caged animal. 'Don't worry, Dr Malone, I am already aware of it and do not think any less of him for it. We love who we love. As long as no one is hurt, I believe we should leave people with different attractions alone. The thing is, if he did have a gentleman lover, why then did Mrs Hobson claim she and he were romantic companions? That's what I'm trying to unpick here. So don't worry, I'm not about to expose Uncle Bob – or his gentleman friend – after his death. His – their – reputation is safe with me. But I am concerned in finding out whether his death was natural, or whether anyone had a hand in it.'

Charles relaxed, marginally. 'All right, I understand. But I must just clarify that I do not know who the gentleman was. Only that there was one. My father once paid an unannounced house call to Bob at home and said he saw a gentleman leaving via the back door. He was not fully dressed. Bob was embarrassed but didn't try to deny anything. He asked for my father's discretion. My father gave it.'

'But he told you?' asked Clara, trying to keep the sarcasm out of her voice.

'Yes, he did,' said Charles, clearing his throat. 'When he handed over Bob's medical files to me. He thought it might be useful to know. As his physician. In total confidence, of course.'

'Of course,' said Clara. She softened her tone. 'Well, this is very reassuring. I'm glad to see you had and still have my uncle's best interests at heart. So perhaps you can help me unpick this puzzle. Why do you think Mrs Hobson had that letter from Bob? Why did he send it to her? Do you think he might have had a gentleman and a lady lover?'

Charles shook his head firmly. 'No, I very much doubt that.'

'Then why the letter?'

'Might it have been a forgery?' asked Charles.

Clara nodded. 'It might very well have been. To try to convince me that Hobson and Bob were more than employer and employee. In fact, I'm going up to Holy Island later this morning to try to find out more. That's where she claims she and Bob had a romantic getaway. At one of the hotels. I'm going to see if I can find any evidence of it.'

Charles nodded brusquely. 'Good. Good. If she is trying a fast one, she needs to be exposed.'

'I agree,' said Clara. 'But I'd also like to know whether she might have had a hand in his death. You say there wasn't an autopsy. Might one be conducted after the fact?'

'Under certain circumstances, yes. But it would need to be ordered by a court. It's a serious matter to order an exhumation.'

'I understand that. But what might those circumstances be?'

'If evidence emerged that there might have been foul play.'

Clara pursed her lips. 'I was hoping the autopsy might reveal that evidence. An excess of barbital, for instance.'

The doctor shook his head. 'I thought that's what you were getting at. But I'm afraid you would need something to convince the police – and a judge – that there is good reason to suspect that, and that you have some evidence to back it up. And from what I've heard today, I don't think you have that yet. Do you?'

Clara shook her head. 'No, I don't. But finding out if Bob was really at Holy Island with Mrs Hobson might be a step towards that. I'll let you know what I find out.'

Charles locked eyes with her. 'Please, do that.' He then looked at his watch. 'I'm sorry, Miss Vale, my surgery is about to begin. But it has been a pleasure meeting you. I see now why Bob had so much faith in you.'

It was Clara's turn to look abashed. 'Thank you, Dr Malone. I hope his faith was not misplaced.'

Chapter 35

It was a glorious late August day, and the Northumberland sky was the brightest of blues. The few fluff balls of cloud were like reflections of the sheep on the farmers' fields on either side of the Great North Road. Andrew Ridpath's green Austin 7 purred its way through farmland north of Newcastle, past the mediaeval market town of Morpeth and then skirted the walled citadel of Alnwick, home of the dukes of Northumberland. He then turned right towards the small fishing village of Alnmouth and hugged the coast for the rest of the ride north.

Clara was delighted with the views: the vast expanse of sandy beaches, the jagged rocks and higgledy-piggledy inlets, guarded by lighthouses, marking off the miles until they could glimpse the hulking fortress of Bamburgh Castle, brooding over the bay. Andrew gave her a running commentary on all she could see, his warm, Northumbrian burr nearly lulling her to sleep. She apologised as she caught herself nodding off, telling him she hadn't slept well the last two nights. He chuckled, telling her she needn't sugar-coat that he had no future as a tour guide.

He was though an excellent host. He stopped the car and unpacked a thermos flask of tea and poured a cup for Clara. Refreshed, but hoping it wasn't too far to their destination and a lavatory, Clara climbed back in the car for the final leg of the journey. It wasn't long before Andrew, pointing to his right, said: 'And there we have it. Can you see, Clara? The Holy Island of Lindisfarne.'

Clara looked out at the flat expanse of sand with a road running through it. On the horizon she could just make out the houses of a settlement and beyond that, on a cliff, the dramatic silhouette of a castle. 'Is that where the monks lived?' she asked.

'No, that's a more recent building. Fifteen hundreds, I think. The monks lived in a monastery and priory next to the village. Henry VIII had it destroyed. There's not much of it left, just some ruins in the grounds of the island church.'

'I thought it was the Vikings who destroyed the place.'

Andrew chuckled. 'Oh, they did. On numerous occasions. But the monks kept rebuilding. It was old King Henry who finally did them in, though when he was out to suppress the Catholics. I believe they used some of the stone from the priory to build the castle.'

Andrew turned the car onto the tidal causeway, streaked with seaweed and still wet in patches from the sea that covered the road twice a day. 'I've checked the tides and the sea will start to come back in again at four o'clock. We'll need to be off the island by then or we'll be stuck here overnight. There have been cases of people mistiming the crossing and having to be rescued from their vehicles by fishermen from the island. See that little hut on stilts,' he said, pointing ahead, 'that's where people have to try to get to if they get stuck. I imagine it's a cold place to spend the night!'

'And the cars?' asked Clara.

Andrew shrugged. 'I suppose they get covered by the sea. It would be a nightmare to dry out after that,' he said, tapping the dashboard of the Austin. 'Best not to put it to the test.'

'Best not.' She smiled back at him. 'So, where is the Crown and Anchor?'

'It's on the far side of the village,' he said. 'We'll be there in five minutes.' He checked his watch. 'Just in time for a bite to eat. I've brought a picnic, but perhaps if we're going to be asking questions at the place then maybe we should act like customers first.'

Clara nodded her agreement. 'Yes, that's a good idea. But I wouldn't want your picnic to go to waste. And it is a lovely day.' She looked out at the grassy dunes as the causeway road joined the island proper. 'Should we just have something light then we can have the picnic later, after a walk? Before we have to head back home?'

He grinned. 'That sounds like a plan.'

They drove through the small village and came to a stop on the edge of a triangular-shaped green, flanked by quaint cottages and overlooked on one corner by a whitewashed double-storey building with a sign swinging over the door: *The Crown and Anchor*.

Andrew helped Clara out of the car. Customers sat on wooden tables and benches on a lawned area outside, enjoying the clement summer weather and the uninterrupted views of the priory ruins to the right, the picturesque harbour to the left and beyond that the castle. Clara and Andrew went into the dimly lit pub where a few men were propping up the bar having a lunchtime pint. A smiling landlady greeted them. They ordered two glasses of cider and a fish pie to share. Then Clara asked if she could use the lavatory.

When she emerged she saw, through the window, that Andrew had bagged them a table outside and was waiting for their order. She decided to get down to business. She had told Andrew about Mrs Hobson's claim that she and Bob had spent some time together here, but she had not told him about her concerns that Hobson might have hastened her uncle's death. Nor about his homosexuality.

Clara smiled at the landlady as the woman dried some glasses.

'Your gentleman friend's outside,' she said.

'Thank you, I see that. I'll join him in a minute. I was wondering if I might ask you something.'

'Aye?'

'Yes, you see, I'm up from London because my uncle has passed away.'

'I'm sorry to hear that, miss.'

'Thank you. We hadn't been in touch much in his last years, and that's something I regret. So I'm trying to find out more about him. Apparently, he used to love Holy Island, so I asked the gentleman outside, who was my uncle's accountant, to drive me up here to see for myself. And I see why he felt that way. It's a very beautiful place.'

The landlady beamed. 'Aye, it is, miss. I'm very lucky to live here.'

'And to work here too. He spoke very fondly of the times he stayed in your establishment. And I'm trying to find out the last time he was here. You see, he was an enthusiastic photographer, and I found a whole lot of photographs he took of the island. I'm trying to put a date on them, because I want to have them published in a book in his memory, but I have no idea when they were taken. Might you be able to check your register to see when he was last here? That might give me a date to work from.'

The landlady looked at Clara, puzzled. Clara hoped that her blatant lie was not about to be questioned. But no, the woman's face soon settled into neutrality and she nodded. 'I think I can do that. But I'll need to finish the dinner rush first. But then I'll get the register and we'll see what we can find for you, miss.'

Clara smiled, congratulating herself on her cunning improvisation. 'Thank you.'

An hour later with the cider drained and the scrumptious fish pie devoured, Clara returned to the now-quiet bar with Andrew. The landlady waved to her, indicating she and Andrew should take a seat at one of the inside tables, and then she carried over a large leather-bound book.

'We've only four rooms, and this goes back three years. But if it was before that, then I'd have to get my husband to go up into the loft to get the old registers. And he's not here at the minute.'

'Let's hope it is here, then,' said Clara, thinking that three years was a good time frame. She hadn't seen a date on Mrs Hobson's note from Bob, but she had the sense that the alleged relationship had not been going on for years and years. But she could be wrong. Both about the affair not having really existed, and the time frame.

'What was your uncle's name?' the landlady asked.

'Bob Wallace. Or Robert Wallace. Or the initials RWW.'

The landlady ran her finger down the register, page after page, as Clara and Andrew watched. Finally she said: 'Here we are, 7th August 1927. R. Wallace.'

Clara leaned over and had a look. 'Was he accompanied by anyone?'

The landlady ran her finger up and down a few entries either side. 'No, it doesn't look like it.'

Clara looked at Andrew and he nodded. 'So there you go, Clara, there's your answer.'

But Clara wasn't satisfied. 'Can you look further on. More recently? That was two years ago. He might have come again.'

The landlady looked around the bar. There were two men sitting in the corner, with their pints still half full. 'All right.' The finger continued its search until she came to 12th April 1928. Just after Easter. 'Here he is again: R. Wallace. And this time he did have someone with him.'

Clara's stomach lurched. 'Is there a name?'

'Someone called J. Smith.'

'J. Smith?' Clara remembered what Mrs Hobson – Jane Hobson – said. 'He called me Jay and I called him Bee.' But Smith. Not Hobson. It could have been an assumed name, of course.

'Did they share the same room?'

The landlady looked again. 'No. Adjoining rooms.' She looked at Clara curiously. 'Why did you say you wanted this information again?'

'To date some photographs. But it would also be useful to know if he was here with someone so I can ask them to look at the photographs too. A J. Smith, you say. Does it say whether that was a Mrs or Miss?'

The landlady cocked her head to the side and gave a half-smile. 'Neither. Just J. Smith. But I can tell you now that it wasn't a lady.'

'Oh?' said Clara, flashing a look at Andrew. 'How can you tell?'

'Because here,' said the landlady pointing to a pencilled note in the margin, 'it says "gentleman requests trouser press". That's next to J. Smith. So I think we can assume J. Smith is a gentleman. Besides, we always note if there is a lady in case of shared ablutions. See here,' she said, pointing to other entries, 'Mrs, Miss, and so on. So J. Smith and R. Wallace will both be men.'

A shadow filled the doorway. Another customer had arrived. 'I hope that's helpful, miss. I have to get on.'

Clara nodded. 'Yes, thank you. You've been an enormous help.'

The landlady closed the register and carried it to the bar where she greeted the customer. 'Af'noon, Jerry, the usual?'

Clara remained seated, her mind racing.

'So Mrs Hobson lied?' asked Andrew.

'It looks that way.'

'And she forged that letter.'

'Possibly,' said Clara, not wanting to meet his eyes.

'Possibly? She must have.'

Clara let out a sigh. Perhaps it was time to tell Andrew the truth. Not all of the truth, but some of it. Perhaps he knew already. The Levines both knew. Bob's doctor knew. Maybe others did too. 'Not necessarily,' she said, eventually. 'She could have stolen it. Or found it in Bob's things before he sent it. And she could have rewritten the envelope with her address on it. Or even used an old envelope that Bob had written to her and put the unrelated note inside. I think the important thing here is that it refers to someone called Jay, and the man on the register is a J. Smith. Of course, it might very well *not* be the man's real name. Isn't "John Smith" the classic alias of men who want to be anonymous?'

'But why would he want to remain . . .' Andrew tailed off, realisation dawning. 'You mean?'

Clara nodded. 'Yes. I've only found out recently myself. Juju Levine told me and Bob's doctor confirmed it.' She lowered her voice. 'Bob was a homosexual. But please, don't tell anyone. It didn't appear as if he was open about it in his life, so I don't think it's up to me to blab it to the world after his death.'

Andrew nodded slowly, taking it all in. 'I didn't know this, Clara. He hid it well.' He looked up. 'But I don't think any less of him for it. He was still a good man.'

'Of course he was! People get far too het up about these things,' she snapped.

'I agree,' said Andrew, placatingly. 'But let's not forget it's still illegal. So I understand why Bob kept it quiet.'

Clara, grateful that Andrew had taken it so well, softened her voice. 'Yes, so do I. Which is why I ask you to keep it to yourself.'

'Of course. But the bottom line from all of this is that it was *not* Mrs Hobson who was here with him. In fact, we don't know if anyone was *here* with him in that sense. J. Smith might very well just have been a friend. But even if *he* wasn't, *she* can no longer claim that it was she who was. And so I think that lets you off the hook – as far as any sympathy you might have had for her regarding the will is concerned. So then,' he said, looking out the window, 'that's mission accomplished. Should we go for that walk now?'

She smiled at him. 'Yes, I think we should.'

Chapter 36

The basking seals raised their heads, watching the human couple pass, wary of any encroachment. Assured that the man and woman, walking barefoot in the sand, would not trespass on their rocks, they closed their doleful eyes and continued their afternoon snooze.

'Are they dangerous?' asked Clara, never having been this close to wild seals before.

'I've not heard of any attacks, but best not get too close,' said Andrew.

A kittiwake cawed, swooping up to its nest on the cliffside below the castle. The castle, Andrew told her, was a private residence, owned by the magazine magnate Edward Hudson, who founded *Country Life* magazine. But the grounds did not extend far and Clara and Andrew were free to walk just a stone's throw away from its ramparts. They then skirted Castle Point below the mediaeval lime kilns and carried on walking around the island.

More seals greeted them, this time from the water, looking – and sounding – like big black dogs in the sea. Clara laughed. 'It looks like we're being followed!'

Andrew smiled at her and said: 'Should we stop here? If you don't mind the company?'

'You or the seals?' quipped Clara.

Andrew chuckled. 'Both.'

'Not at all,' said Clara. 'One I find entertaining, the other . . . well, let's just say I'm getting to know him.'

Andrew looked pleased and set down the picnic basket. 'How about here?'

'Perfect.'

Andrew tossed aside some dry seaweed and shells, then laid a tartan rug on the sand. Clara sat down, smoothing her blue cotton skirt over her bare legs and placing her shoes and straw hat neatly beside Andrew's. She looked out to sea as he unpacked. 'It's absolutely beautiful here. It's hard to believe it's the north of England. Today is like a day in Cornwall.'

'Cornwall? I've been there. During the war. I was based in Plymouth for a while.'

'My parents have a holiday house near Penzance. They call it a cottage, but . . .' she laughed '. . . that would be like Mr Hudson over there calling that castle a little getaway.'

'So you're from a wealthy family?'

Clara turned to him and raised a sardonic brow. 'Are you asking as an accountant or . . .' she was just about to say *suitor* but stopped herself in time '. . . or something else?'

He shrugged, unwrapping some sandwiches and laying them in their wax paper on the blanket. 'I'm sorry, that was rude of me.'

'No, no it wasn't. It was an honest question. And seeing you are now my accountant, you'll no doubt find out about my, and my family's, financial affairs soon enough. My father is a third-generation banker. The family originally made its money in the cotton mills of Lancashire before my great-grandfather, the youngest son, decided to go into banking when his older brother inherited the family business. It was my grandfather, his son, who moved from Manchester to London. And my father was born there. My mother was from the North East, as you might have heard. Middle-class family with aspirations. She moved to London when she married my father and has been climbing the social ladder ever since. Bob, her brother, stayed here. But . . .' she smiled at him '. . . you'll probably know more about that than I do.'

Andrew was listening to her with a curious look on his face.

'What?' she asked.

'Nothing. I was just wondering what you meant by "seeing you are now my accountant". Does that mean you've decided to stay, Clara?'

Clara lay back on the blanket, cupping her hands under her head and looking up at the baby-blue sky. 'Well, it is glorious here.'

'It is. Today. But Lindisfarne is not Newcastle. And neither place is always sunny. It gets wild here in the winter. And Newcastle can be bitterly cold.'

Clara turned onto her side, propping herself up on her elbow. 'Are you trying to put me off, Andrew?'

He shook his head. 'Not at all, but I do want you to go into this with eyes wide open. You said you were going to give yourself until the end of the week to see if you could make progress with the Whittaker case and to test your appetite for the detection business.'

'That's right,' said Clara. 'And it's Tuesday. Not the end of the week yet.'

'What if you haven't closed the case by then? Will you extend your trial period?'

Clara considered how much she had already achieved. Her more recent musings aside, about whether her uncle might have been helped on his way (she needed further evidence of that from Dr Malone), she contemplated the main investigation about the Paradise Picture House fire. For all intents and purposes, she felt she had already closed the Whittaker case. Alice Whittaker wanted her to prove neither she nor her husband, his brother nor their staff members had flouted fire regulations, and that she had a right to apply for an insurance pay-out. The information she had given to Roger Jennings should be sufficient to do that. She would be interested to hear what the solicitor had to say about it when she returned to Newcastle. But, and this was the complicated thing, there was now more to the investigation than the question of fire safety compliance. There was now evidence of arson that hadn't been considered before, and possibly murder to silence Horace Fender, the likely arsonist. And there were also the efforts of someone – at their own behest or at the behest of Humphrey Balshard – to try to intimidate her into shutting down the investigation, and their attempts to get their hands on whatever was in Bob's files. She thought again of the break-in to the office, the youth at the park stealing her notebook, and the break-in to her hotel room. She had been convinced that Jack Danskin was the perpetrator, but the fingerprint evidence didn't back that up.

She explained all of this to Andrew then concluded, 'So you see, this looks like it might be a longer investigation than I anticipated.'

Andrew gave a worried frown. 'And much more dangerous. If Horace Fender was murdered, that means you could be in peril too, Clara. The sooner you get the police involved in this the better.'

Clara picked up one of the sandwiches. 'I agree. But as you know, the police weren't too interested when I first went to them about the break-ins.'

Andrew nodded slowly. 'I don't think that the Newcastle police weren't interested – they did send someone around and they did put a guard outside the hotel – it's just that they didn't think there was sufficient evidence at the time to take it further. From what you tell me you've given to Jennings, that might now change.'

'I hope so,' said Clara, 'but to make sure, I've asked him to show it to a magistrate first.'

'That's wise,' agreed Andrew. 'Hopefully Jennings will have some news for you soon.'

'I hope so too,' said Clara. She took a bite of the sandwich that she was eating more to be polite than because she was hungry. Dear Andrew had gone to so much trouble. *Dear Andrew* . . . Had she really just called him that? She looked at the handsome man with the auburn stubble on his chin catching the afternoon sun. He had taken off his jacket, and just like at Exhibition Park, she noted his muscular torso under the fabric. She felt a lurch in her abdomen. Oh my, he was an attractive man . . .

Andrew must have sensed the electricity in the air because he too lay down on his side, facing Clara, their eyes – and mouths – only a couple of inches apart. Clara put down her sandwich.

'Clara, I—'

But whatever Andrew was about to say was cut off when a shaggy springer spaniel, soaking wet from a dip in the sea, bounded onto the blanket and scoffed Clara's sandwich.

'Rex! Rex! You naughty boy! Oh, I'm dreadfully sorry! He's so naughty. He's ruined your picnic!'

Two men wearing tweed, both with binoculars around their necks, ran up to them. One of them grabbed the springer by the collar and dragged him off. Andrew jumped up to speak to them while Clara sat up straight, fixing an 'oh that's all right' smile on her face. Apologies were given, with Andrew indicating all was forgiven by giving the unrepentant Rex a pat.

'Are you folks staying over tonight?'

Andrew shook his head. 'No, we'll be heading back to the mainland at about three.'

The men looked at one another and grinned. 'Sorry, sir, but it's already gone three. You and your wife must have been – er – too busy to notice.'

Clara and Andrew both looked at their watches. 'Crikey,' said Andrew, 'it's nearly ten to four! Oh Clara, I'm so sorry. I should have kept a better eye on the time.'

'It's just as much my fault as yours.'

The birdwatchers, still smiling, said sympathetically: 'Don't worry, it happens all the time. At least you didn't leave too late and get caught by the tide. You'll just have to stay over. Might we recommend the Crown and Anchor? They might have some rooms available. If not, there's the Manor House – overlooking the priory.'

'Thank you,' said Andrew, looking shamefaced. 'We'll do that.'

When the birdwatchers and their dog had moved on, Andrew turned to Clara and said: 'Golly, Clara, I really am sorry. This was not intentional, I can assure you. But we don't have a choice. We'll have to stay over. In separate rooms, of course.'

Clara gave a little smile. 'So, no Mr and Mrs Smith then?'

Andrew flushed with embarrassment. 'Goodness no!'

Pity, thought Clara, then helped him pack away the picnic.

The landlady of the Crown and Anchor was quite unjudgemental when they arrived back at the establishment like two stray kittens.

'Not to worry, these things happen. And better you found out before driving across and getting caught in the tide.' She looked at the clock behind the bar. 'It will be safe to cross again at ten o'clock tonight. Will you try again then, or will you be wanting a room for the night?'

Andrew looked at Clara and said: 'What do you think? Do you want to get back to Newcastle tonight?'

'What time will we back?'

'It'll be after midnight.'

Clara shook her head. 'No, let's wait until morning. Can we book some rooms please?'

'Aye,' said the landlady, 'will that be two rooms then?'

'Yes. Two,' said Andrew, and Clara could almost feel him blush.

Clara lay propped up in bed with the curtains open, appreciating the spectacular full moon over Holy Island. She could see the castle from her room, silhouetted against the silver orb like a scene from Camelot. It really was a magical place. She and Andrew had spent the time before dinner wandering around the ruins of the priory and the ancient graveyard of St Mary's Church to the now-familiar choral accompaniment of the Lindisfarne birds and seals. Andrew had told her as much as he knew about the island, its history as the birthplace of Christianity in England, the humble St Cuthbert and his hermitage, the monks who created the exquisite Lindisfarne Gospels, the Viking raids, and so on and so forth . . .

Clara listened with one ear. It's not that she wasn't interested, but she was distracted by the Whittaker case and all its complications. Although she believed they had made the right decision not to try to get back to Newcastle tonight, she did wish they had been able to get back in the late afternoon. She had really wanted to see what progress Jennings had made.

Instead, after telephoning her hotel in Newcastle to tell them she would be away overnight and cancelling her dinner reservation, she rang Jennings. But Jennings Jnr wasn't in. The secretary informed her that he had a late meeting and wouldn't be back until the morning. No, she didn't know if he had passed on Miss Vale's documents to a magistrate. No, sorry, he hadn't mentioned whether he had had a chance to go through them himself. But Miss Vale mustn't worry, Mr Jennings was a very thorough solicitor and he would be looking out for her legal interests. As would Mr Jennings

Snr when he returned from his trip to York. Would Miss Vale like to make an appointment to see Mr Jennings Jnr in the morning? Yes, Miss Vale would.

Clara then turned her attention to mulling over her meeting with Uncle Bob's doctor: Charles Malone. Before visiting him, she had a niggling suspicion that all may not have been right with Bob Wallace's death. But that's all it was, just a niggle. She would have been quite prepared to put it down to her exaggerated sense of suspicion that had emerged in the few days she'd been working as a private detective. Clara felt herself putting quote marks around 'private detective', because really, could she describe herself as such after such a short time? Perhaps apprentice private detective or play-acting private detective . . . No, she stopped herself, not that. This had not been a game. What she had uncovered about the Paradise Picture House fire was not make-believe. Nor were the deaths of Will Spencer and Horace Fender. She had done proper, professional work collecting that evidence. She needed to trust herself more. Because if she didn't, who would?

And because of that, she had to start trusting her instincts. Yes, she needed to get evidence to back up those instincts, like she would do with any scientific enquiry, but she would never get to that point if she didn't explore the 'what if . . .' in the first place. So, what if she was right and there was something untoward with Bob's death? Dr Malone had admitted that he too had had his suspicions about his patient's rapid decline. And he had wondered whether the barbital his father had prescribed might have had something to do with it.

But both the chemist and Mrs Hobson had said he was only getting the prescribed amount. Mrs Hobson's testimony she could discount. She didn't trust that woman one bit. Up until now, she only had her gut feeling to go on – which of course, was not very scientific – but now, thanks to the landlady of the Crown and Anchor, she knew that Hobson had been lying about her romantic getaway with Bob to Holy Island. The letter, addressed to J, was either a forgery or had been stolen with the intention of recasting the love interest to appear to be Jane Hobson. And the purpose? To convince Clara that the housekeeper had some kind of claim – moral if not legal – to Bob's estate. A woman who would go to those lengths could not be believed when she said she had only collected the prescribed medication – and no more – from the chemist.

But the chemist was more convincing. Surely someone of that professional standing would not risk his reputation by lying to a doctor, would he? A doctor with whom he was in a symbiotic professional relationship. Would there be any way of checking up on that, she wondered? She decided that she would pay the chemist a visit when she returned to Newcastle. And Mrs Hobson.

She looked out the window and saw a sliver of cloud creeping across the moon. And then, she was struck by a sudden thought, and wondered why it had never occurred to her before: was it possible that the Whittaker case, Balshard Insurance, Horace Fender's suspicious death and her uncle's death were somehow all related? Had her uncle been killed to stop him probing any further into the picture house fires and Humphrey Balshard's involvement? And had her decision to continue the investigation stirred the hornets' nest? *Yes*, she thought, *yes*. What else would explain the break-ins, the bag-snatching, Fender's death and the man who had followed her on the train? Not to mention the mysterious tip-off her brother Antony had received that Bob's mental capacity could be brought into question. If Antony could stop her inheriting the business, that would prevent her probing any further. And if that failed? She shivered, pulling the blankets over her shoulders. Had Andrew been right? Was her life also in peril?

She suddenly had a desire to talk this all over with Andrew. Yes, she had told him some of it, but not all. He did not know of her suspicions about Jane Hobson and her uncle's death. Had Hobson been paid to overdose him? She reminded herself that she had no evidence of this. But then she had an idea: Andrew had been Bob's accountant. Andrew had paid off any outstanding debts after her uncle's death. Andrew would know what had been paid to the chemist. Might that reveal how much barbital had actually been purchased?

She threw back the covers and strode to the door. She'd heard Andrew moving around in the room next door; good, he was still awake. She grabbed her cardigan to put over the oversized nightdress the landlady had loaned her, opened her door and knocked quietly on his.

Chapter 37

A surprised Andrew opened the door to Clara's knock. She bit back a giggle as she saw the state he was in. His auburn hair was sticking up at jaunty angles and his arms and legs protruded from the too-small pyjamas like those of a teenage boy who'd just had a growth spurt. The landlady's husband was obviously a considerably smaller man than Andrew. The buttons of the shirt strained across his chest and the trousers . . . well, best Clara avert her eyes from there.

'Clara! What are you doing here? Is everything all right?'

'Yes, I'm fine,' she said, in a half-whisper, pulling her cardigan closed around her, 'it's just that I want to talk to you about something.'

He looked across the small landing to the other two occupied rooms and whispered in return: 'And it couldn't wait until morning?'

'No,' said Clara quietly but firmly, and stepped into the room and closed the door behind her.

Andrew ran his hand through his hair and rearranged the angles. Then grinned, sheepishly. 'Not exactly dressed to welcome a lady.'

She chuckled, gesturing to her own unflattering garb. 'And I look like a sack of potatoes. Not to worry, fashion isn't on my mind.'

'Then what is?' he asked, indicating that she take a seat on the bed, while he sat opposite her on a dressing table stool.

She took a deep breath and then went on to tell him everything she'd been thinking about regarding her uncle's death and the Whittaker case.

His eyes grew wide. 'Are you telling me that Bob might have been murdered?'

Clara bit her lip. Then said: 'Yes, I think I am. Now, I might be completely wrong – I hope I am – and so far I have no hard evidence to back up my suspicion, but the fact that both Dr Malone and I had the same concern, completely independently of one another, rings alarm bells for me. Do you know Dr Malone personally?'

Andrew nodded, thoughtfully. 'Yes. I know him and his father quite well. Charlie and I were at school together. And with Roger Jennings too. The three of us, and a few others, all went on to serve in the Northumberland Fusiliers together. Some of them never came back. But Charlie, Roger and I did.'

'I'm very glad you all did,' said Clara.

He smiled gently, and Clara's heart skipped a little beat. But she took herself in hand and turned the conversation back to her suspicions about Bob's death. 'So, that's one of the reasons I wanted to come to Holy Island today. Yes, it was partly to do with trying to ascertain if Jane Hobson was telling the truth about being in a romantic relationship with Bob, but after meeting with Dr Malone this morning, it became clear that if Bob had been overdosing on barbital then Hobson was best placed to have been doing it. So, I needed to find out if she'd lied about Holy Island. And if she'd lied about this, then she could be lying about everything.'

Andrew leaned back, resting his elbows on the dressing table. 'So, you and Charlie think that Mrs Hobson might have been drugging Bob?'

'We think that if he had been overdosed, and he hadn't done it himself – and the doctor didn't mention that he thought that was the case – then Hobson is the most obvious suspect.'

'Why?'

'Why?' asked Clara, thinking it was obvious why, and was surprised that Andrew had asked. 'Well, because she was the one who had the most intimate access to him. She was the one who went into his house, cooked for him, did his laundry, and so forth. And she was the one who picked up his prescriptions.'

Andrew took his elbows off the dressing table and leaned forward. 'But was she the only one with intimate access to him? What about his lover? This male lover you believe he had. Who may or may not be J. Smith. Wouldn't he have been close enough to administer the drugs?'

Clara pulled up her knees under her nightdress and rested her chin on them, as she wrapped her arms around her shins. 'Now that is a very interesting thought. Yes, he would have.'

'And you have no idea who he is?'

Clara shook her head. 'I don't. I did find a photograph of the man in Bob's darkroom.'

'Oh?' said Andrew, sitting upright. 'You never told me that.'

Clara shrugged, apologetically. 'No, I didn't. I was trying to protect Bob's privacy. Even posthumously. But now you know about J. Smith in this hotel . . .' she looked at the bed, wondering if it had been in this very place '. . . then I might as well tell you.'

'So, you know what he looks like then.'

'Unfortunately not. He was lying on his stomach. Asleep.'

'Do you have the photograph here?'

'No. I don't. But I'll show you when we get back to Newcastle, if you like.'

Andrew shook his head. 'No, there's no need. You're right in respecting Bob's privacy. I have no need to know who it is. Unless . . .' he said, seriously '. . . unless the man is in some way a danger to you.' He reached out his hands and took Clara's. They were warm and enveloping. 'I couldn't bear it if anything happened to you.'

Still holding hands, Clara lowered her knees and leaned towards him until their faces were almost touching. 'That makes two of us,' she whispered.

He closed the final distance and found her willing lips.

And then, just to make sure he didn't pull away like he did the night in Uncle Bob's kitchen, Clara wrapped her arms around him and pulled him towards her. He did not object. Together, they lowered themselves onto the bed.

* * *

Clara awoke to the caw of a kittiwake. She could see the first glow of pre-dawn seeping through the cracks in the hotel room curtains and she guessed that it was around half-past five. Andrew lay silent and naked beside her, his arm gently draped across her middle. She snuggled in, enjoying the feeling of flesh on flesh and the steady rise and fall of his chest against her back. She smiled to herself, remembering their exquisite union last night, so different from her first fumbled encounter back in Oxford. Neither of them had been drunk and both were, if not experienced, at least not absolute novices. After the first throes of passion, before which Andrew still had the gentlemanly wherewithal to check that she was willing to continue – which she very much was – they had enjoyed exploring one another's bodies under the cover of darkness, giving and taking with mutual care.

Clara reminded herself that she needed to be careful if they were to continue with their sexual encounters. She remembered what Marie Stopes advised about using a Dutch cap. She would need to try and get her hands on one, although that might require some subterfuge as they were generally only given to women who could prove they were married. A visit to another town, and the purchase of a ring, might prove necessary. She was relieved to remember that it had only been a couple of days since the end of her monthly period, so her chances of conception were greatly reduced. But not entirely gone. She would, like the last time, worry until her next period. But this time, with more knowledge, she knew she would worry less.

She felt Andrew stir beside her. She turned to face him as his eyes blinked open. He looked at her, startled for a moment, then gently smiled.

'Morning,' he said sleepily. 'So, it wasn't a dream.'

'No, it wasn't,' she said, and kissed him gently on the lips. His body surged. She was tempted to respond, but then realised that it would soon be light and the hotel would be waking up. She needed to get back to her room.

'I'm sorry, Mr Smith, but I should go. Before anyone sees us.'

His face folded in disappointment, but then he pursed his lips and nodded. 'I'm sorry too, Mrs Smith, but you're right. Will I see you at breakfast?'

'Of course.' She smiled then kissed him briefly again before throwing back the covers and getting up. She found her nightdress and cardigan and pulled them on, but couldn't find her underwear.

'Have you seen my knickers?' she asked.

He chuckled. 'I'll have a look.' He turned on the bedside light and leaned over the side of the bed, revealing his naked back.

Clara gasped. On Andrew's right shoulder was a tattoo of a crescent moon on a full sun.

Andrew pulled back up and turned to face her, with a pair of silk knickers dangling over his index finger. He grinned, and asked: 'Is this what you're looking for, Mrs Smith?'

She stood stock-still.

'Well, here you go, Mrs Smith, better put them on.'

She still didn't move.

'Clara, what is it?'

'That, that tattoo. I – well – I didn't know you had it.'

'Well, why would you?'

'Have you had it long?'

'Oh, years. Don't you like tattoos? I'm sorry, there's not much I can do about it.'

'No, no, it's not that, it's . . .' But Clara didn't know how to continue. She needed some space and time to think. She needed to get away from Andrew.

'I – I'll see you later,' she said, snatching the underwear from his hand and heading for the door.

'Clara, are you sure you're all right?'

'Yes, of course,' she said, over her shoulder. Then she fixed a smile on her face. She didn't want him to think anything was wrong. She didn't know how he would react if he knew that she knew who he really was. And that he'd hidden it from her. And that he had even suggested last night that Bob's lover might have killed him . . .

'Goodbye,' she said, the smile fixed until she opened the door and closed it behind her. She looked across the landing then towards the stairwell. She could hear some movement on the stairs. She quickly opened her own door and closed it firmly behind her. Then she locked it.

'Oh, dear God,' she said, out loud, 'what am I going to do?'

Chapter 38

Newcastle upon Tyne, Wednesday 28th August 1929

Andrew helped Clara out of the car beside the Royal Central Station Hotel. 'Are you sure you're all right, Clara? You were very quiet on the way home.' Then he lowered his voice so the doorman couldn't hear. 'Look, I'm sorry I let things get out of hand last night. We should talk about it. What to do now, how to move forward. But I need to get to work now. I've got a meeting in half an hour.'

Clara forced a smile. 'Of course I'm all right. I'm just a bit tired, that's all. And don't berate yourself. I was a willing participant. Nothing got "out of hand". It was what we both wanted.' And that was true. What she didn't add was, she would not have been a willing participant if she knew that Andrew was her uncle's lover. She didn't quite know how she felt about being intimate with a man who liked both men and women, but she did know that she would not want to be intimate with someone who had deceived her. But for now, she was too fearful to bring it up.

What Andrew had said last night, about Bob's lover possibly being the person who had given him an overdose of barbital, really disturbed her. If Andrew was that man, why had he brought it up? Clara was all too willing to point the finger of blame at Mrs Hobson, so why would he try to implicate someone else? Particularly when that someone else might be him? Clara had thought about that while she bathed and readied herself for breakfast, back on Holy Island. The best she could come up with was that it might be some sort of confession. Was Andrew saying that he *had* given too much barbital to Bob?

Lying in the bathtub, Clara had considered what to do next. If she had been anywhere less remote, she might have sneaked off and got a taxi home. But she was stuck on a small island until the tide receded at ten o'clock. Even if she were to run off and hide somewhere, he would report her absence and it wouldn't take long for concerned locals to find her. She had no idea of any hiding places. And she had no idea of who to turn to for help. Apparently, there wasn't even a policeman on the island. But if there were, how could she explain her suspicions? She had just noticed the man she had sex with last night (illicitly, of course, because scandalously, they weren't married) had the same tattoo as the man she suspected – but didn't actually know – was (even more scandalously) the lover of her late uncle. She reckoned she would get short shrift.

No, just like she had done with the Whittaker case, she needed to gather more concrete evidence. Her first port of call would be Roger Jennings. Yes, it might be awkward, seeing Roger and Andrew had been school chums and were now professional associates and friends, but Roger was her solicitor and he and his father had been her uncle's solicitors too. Surely there was some kind of duty of care? Besides, she needed to find out what he thought of her Whittaker dossier.

So instead of fleeing the Crown and Anchor Hotel, as she was tempted to do, Clara had dressed and gone down to breakfast. She had pretended that everything was all right. Firstly, to the landlady who wanted to know if she had slept well (actually, madam, there had been very little sleeping involved!) and then secondly to Andrew, who – like now – seemed concerned that she was quiet and possibly regretful. She got through breakfast the best she could until it was almost time to leave.

However, there were two more things bothering her. The first: what if Andrew was dangerous? What if he suspected that Clara knew who he was and what he might have done to Bob? So, under the guise of visiting the lavatory, she had sneaked into the hotel kitchen and stolen a paring knife. It was small enough to wrap in a handkerchief and secrete in her handbag. She wasn't sure exactly how she would use it if the occasion arose, but she felt better having some kind of weapon to hand. The second thing that bothered her was the realisation that she had not, as yet, got Andrew's fingerprints. Was it possible that he was the man responsible for the two break-ins and Horace Fender's death? He did, after all, have a connection to Balshard Insurance, as he had told her that Balshard was one of his brother's clients and sometimes got free tickets for the cinema. And Andrew and his brother were in the same firm of accountants. Was Andrew acting on behalf of Humphrey Balshard?

Or was she simply being melodramatic? Even if Andrew had been her uncle's lover, it did not mean that he had anything to do with Bob's death or the Whittaker case in any way. But she needed to be sure. So, while Andrew was busy settling the bill with the landlady, Clara had opened the picnic basket and taken out one of the metal cups they had used for tea. Andrew had touched both cups, so his fingerprints would be on them. She'd placed the cup, along with the little knife she had stolen, at the bottom of her handbag.

Then she pretended to sleep most of the way home, so she didn't have to talk to him. She held her handbag tightly on her lap, with her fingers ready to slip open the catch and pull out the knife if needed. Fortunately, it hadn't been needed.

Outside the Royal Central Station Hotel Andrew looked at her curiously, his face tinged with concern – or was it disappointment? 'Would you like to have dinner with me this evening, Clara? Then we can talk about this. Or . . . if you've already had enough of me . . . perhaps not.'

By this stage, Clara just wanted to get rid of him. 'Yes, yes, let's have dinner tonight,' she said quickly. 'Will you come here to the hotel?'

He smiled at her, not hiding his relief. 'Oh yes, here at the hotel is fine. Should we say seven o'clock?'

'Seven o'clock will be perfect.' Then to alleviate his concern even more, she squeezed his forearm in what she hoped was a show of affection.

It appeared to do the trick as his shoulders relaxed and his smile softened. 'I'll see you then,' he said, raising his hat then getting back into his car.

Clara kept the smile on her face until he pulled off, then she turned and ran up the steps of the hotel. 'Good morning, Miss Vale,' said the manager as she entered the foyer. 'There's a gentleman here to see you.'

'Who is it?' asked Clara.

'Mr Danskin. He's in the smoking room. Would you like me to tell him you've arrived?'

Clara groaned inwardly. Jack Danskin was the last person she wanted to see. 'No, please don't. I'd rather not see him. Can you tell him I have telephoned to say I'll be further delayed and that I don't know when I'll be back?'

'Of course, Miss Vale,' said the manager, without a hint of censure. The customer was always right.

Clara settled down in a chair in Roger Jennings' office and accepted a cup of tea from his secretary. Barnaby Jennings popped his head in to greet her, and his amiable, warm demeanour helped calm her. She felt she was in good hands with Jennings & Jennings.

'Morning, Miss Vale!' he said cheerily. 'I believe you've been a busy bee while I was away. I'd love to hear all about it, but unfortunately I have another meeting. Roger will fill me in later.'

'I'd be grateful for your thoughts on it, when you have time,' Clara replied. 'I hope you had a good trip?'

'Splendid! Thank you. Business, unfortunately, not pleasure. A conference of senior police officers, magistrates, barristers and solicitors in York, to talk about best practice in how they all worked together.'

'In York?' asked Clara. 'Did you see Inspector Davidson from Whitley Bay police while you were there?'

'As a matter of fact I did. Have you met him?'

'I have. Did he mention me at all?'

Mr Jennings shook his head. 'Not at all. Should he have?'

'I thought he might have . . .' said Clara.

The receptionist popped her head in and said that Mr Jennings' client was waiting for him.

'If you'll excuse me, Miss Vale, I must go. I'll speak to Roger later and then perhaps you and I can schedule a meeting.'

'Thank you. I'd like that,' said Clara.

The older Jennings left as his son came into the office.

'Ah, tea! Splendid.' He eased himself into the chair opposite Clara. 'So, how was your trip to Holy Island?' He grinned. 'I hear old Ridpath managed to get the tide times mixed up.'

'Yes,' said Clara, still not sure how she was going to broach the subject of the shocking discovery she'd just made about Andrew. She decided to deflect from that for a while. 'It's a beautiful place, and the weather was perfect. But I'm very sorry I wasn't able to get back yesterday afternoon. I want to hear what progress you've made.'

Roger nodded, stirring a lump of sugar into his tea. 'Of course. Well, first things first, your brother. I have spoken to his solicitor on the telephone and he tells me they have witnesses who will testify that your uncle was mentally impaired in the weeks running up to his death and that on that basis they are challenging the will.'

Clara gave a frustrated snort. 'I know. Jack Danskin.'

Roger cocked his head in surprise. 'You know already?'

'Yes,' she said, and explained what had happened on Monday night when Danskin came to dinner. 'So, he told me that he'd been approached by Antony's solicitor. He said that someone here had contacted Antony and suggested to him that Bob had not been in his right mind before he died and that the will could be contested on those grounds. And that Jack Danskin might be prepared to testify in any legal challenge.'

'Did he say who had ratted?'

'He didn't. He said he didn't know. But my bet is that it was Danskin himself, probably in collusion with Balshard. Are you aware that Danskin works for Balshard?'

Roger nodded. 'I am. And I read your report on it all. Congratulations, Miss Vale, you have put together a very convincing case.'

Relief coursed through Clara's veins, but she didn't want to appear too desperate for his approval. She needed to come across as confident and professional, not, as she had considered earlier, merely 'play-acting' at this detection game. 'Thank you,' she said calmly. 'So, would you agree that Antony's claim could possibly be linked to all this? That Balshard is trying to get me off the case?'

'Yes, I think that is a very plausible theory. But as yet, you don't have evidence of that.'

Clara quickly hid her disappointment. 'You're right, I don't yet. But what if all this came out in a court hearing into the challenging of the will? Might Danskin be questioned on his connections to Balshard?'

Roger steepled his fingers and touched them to his lips. 'Yes, that would be one line of defence my father and I might take. However...' he paused and looked at Clara '... I'm hoping it won't come to that. At this stage, we only have two people willing to claim your uncle was mentally impaired, and neither of them has any medical background.'

'Two? Who's the second person?'

'Jane Hobson.'

'Really? Well, I can't say I'm surprised.' She then went on to tell Roger about Hobson's visit to the house, her claim that she and Bob were engaged to be married and that she was expecting to have inherited something from the will.

'Well, she did get something. Two hundred pounds,' said Roger. 'What exactly was she expecting?'

'Quite a bit more than that, it seems.'

Roger gave a disapproving tut. 'Really!'

'Quite,' continued Clara. 'She intimated that she expected a share of the main estate. That as Bob's fiancée it's what he would have wanted. She could not explain – and seemed quite shocked – when I told her that Bob had not even mentioned her in the will, other than as a housekeeper who was to get a small gift.'

'Did she provide any evidence of this engagement?'

'No. She said Bob was busy having the ring made. But she didn't say where. The only moderately convincing thing was a note that he'd written to someone called "J" which she claimed was short for Jane.' She recounted what the note said and that that was one of the reasons she had gone to Holy Island to check out her story, but that Jane Hobson's name was not on the register. 'So, I don't think J is Jane Hobson at all.'

'Whose name was it?'

'A gentleman called J. Smith.'

'A gentleman?'

'Yes.' Was this the time to mention Bob's homosexual relationship?

271

Clara was not quite sure how to do that without mentioning Andrew. And how she had come to be in a position to see him naked and to notice his tattoo. She had arrived at Jennings & Jennings with the intention to talk about that very thing, but now that she was here, she couldn't quite bring herself to do it. Not yet. 'But they had separate rooms,' she said finally.

'I see,' said Roger, in a voice that suggested he might indeed see. But to his credit, he didn't pursue it. Instead, he picked up a pen and made some notes. 'That is very useful to hear, thank you. If this does go to court, we can argue that both Hobson and Danskin have ulterior motives for trying to besmirch Bob's memory. Hobson because she was a "woman scorned" and Danskin because he wants to buy the business. I'm sure we can dig up some more evidence to discredit them if needs be. However . . .' he tapped the pen on the blotter '. . . I'm hoping this doesn't go to court.'

'Me too,' said Clara. 'What are our chances?'

'Quite good. I will talk to Antony's solicitor and tell him that we can discredit his witnesses. I'll also remind him that neither of them has any training in medicine and we'll get Bob's doctor to testify to his mental competence. And my father. And his accountant. I think a doctor, lawyer and accountant who dealt with Bob on a professional basis right up to the day he died hold more sway than a housekeeper and a private investigator.'

'A private investigator who could have been paid by Humphrey Balshard to discredit Bob's investigation, don't forget,' added Clara.

'Oh, I haven't forgotten that. But for now, I think linking the two cases – the Whittaker insurance case and the claim against Bob's estate – might be muddying the waters too much. I think we might be able to get the claim dropped without bringing Balshard into it at all.'

'Why would we want to do that?' asked Clara. 'Aren't we trying to get Balshard too?'

Roger smiled, screwed the lid onto his pen and leaned back. 'I value your enthusiasm, Miss Vale, but I think you need to take my professional advice on this. It is going to muddy the waters. Best that we leave it out.'

'All right,' said Clara, not fully convinced. 'But I assume we are still going to go after Balshard. Have you passed on my report to a magistrate?'

Roger nodded. 'I have. And the gentleman is reviewing it. He said it could take a couple of days.'

'A couple of days?' said Clara, disappointed. 'I hoped we could get going on that fairly quickly. Particularly with the evidence that Horace Fender might have been killed to keep him quiet.'

Roger shrugged noncommittally.

'What? What is it?' she asked. 'I thought you said I had made a convincing case.'

The lawyer raised his hands placatingly. 'You have. About the arson and the key. Particularly if, as you say, you have found the key. But I'm afraid the "Horace Fender might have been murdered" scenario is tenuous at best.'

'But worth looking into?'

He shrugged. 'I can't say for certain. Let's wait to hear what the magistrate says.'

'All right,' said Clara, quelling her frustration. But Roger was right. She already knew that her strongest case was the one with scientific backing – the one that proved that kerosene had been used on the fire – and the witness statements that Horace Fender had bought kerosene. That, and the key that had been found at his flat. But she did believe that Fender had been helped on his way. And she hoped that that could still be proven. Just like she believed Bob had been helped on his way too. But by whom? Perhaps she should mention it to Roger after all. No matter how embarrassing for her. Should she tell him that she had discovered Andrew was very possibly Bob's lover, and that Andrew himself had suggested that the lover would have been in a position to administer an overdose? Or would he think that too tenuous too? Clara knew the answer to that. Yes, it was tenuous. Very tenuous. She needed to get more concrete evidence. She could talk to Dr Malone about it. He already shared her suspicions. And knew about Bob's homosexuality. But was he ready to hear that his old friend, Andrew Ridpath, might be the one who had done it?

Clara hardly believed it herself. She still considered Jane Hobson to be the most likely suspect. Particularly after what Roger had just told her about her backing up Antony's claim. No, she decided, she was not yet ready to voice her thoughts about Bob's early demise. Or her shenanigans with Andrew on Holy Island.

Roger was looking at his watch, hinting her time was up. She took the hint. 'All right, thank you for your time, Mr Jennings. I assume you'll be in touch as soon as you hear anything more from the magistrate about the Whittaker case?'

'Of course. And I'll get on to Antony's solicitor again too. I'll also line up Bob's doctor in case we need him. Are you still staying at the hotel?'

'For now, yes, but I am considering moving into Bob's house. This is taking a lot longer than I expected and the bill is getting quite steep at the Royal Station. In fact, I think I'll pop around to the house now with that in mind; see if I can get the place aired out and the refrigerator switched back on so I can move in. But if you need me later, leave a message at the hotel. I'll still be there tonight, at least.'

'Righto. I'll be in touch.'

Chapter 39

Clara poured herself another cup of tea. She was sitting at Uncle Bob's kitchen table with the contents of her satchel – the evidence she had collected so far – laid out before her. She placed the tin cup from her handbag right in the middle. She had not, as yet, dusted it for fingerprints, although she had collected her fingerprint kit and camera from the hotel and had them easily to hand. However, she feared what she would find if she did. Instead, she turned to Professor Gross's criminal investigation handbook. She had already skimmed the chapter on 'Examination of Witnesses and Accused', and under the section entitled 'When the witness does not wish to speak the truth' had marked a couple of paragraphs with her pencil. She took a sip of tea and read them again.

The importance of a minute interrogatory is clearly shown in the case where a complicated plot has been laid to deceive the Investigating Officer and the falsity of the depositions must be exposed.

And this certainly is a complicated plot, thought Clara, considering that more than one person did not wish to speak the truth and had set out to deceive. Firstly, of course, there was Horace Fender – but she had proof that he had lied. Scientific proof, which was being presented to a magistrate at this very time. Secondly, there was Humphrey Balshard. The evidence against him was not scientific, but circumstantial. She strongly felt that if someone with authority – a police officer or a magistrate – were to probe further, the case against him would strengthen. Another deceiver was Jane Hobson. She had proof of that too, she thought with satisfaction, at least as it related to her supposed love affair with Bob, if not, as yet, to anything more sinister.

Then of course there was Jack Danskin. She had strongly suspected him of deceiving her, but the more she thought of it, the more she realised he had done the exact opposite. He had told her exactly what his intentions were regarding either going into partnership or buying the business. He had been thoroughly open about agreeing to testify in Antony's favour regarding Bob's mental competence. He could of course be intent on lying about that as there were plenty of other witnesses who would testify that Bob was not at all mentally impaired in his last days. But, she had to admit, as far as Danskin's dealings with her were concerned, he had not been deceitful. And as far as she suspected him of being involved in the break-ins at the office and hotel, as well as being present at Horace Fender's staged 'suicide', the scientific evidence exonerated him.

Her eyes were drawn, unwillingly, to the cup in the middle of the table. She had yet to discover whether science would exonerate Andrew. And she knew she couldn't put off that investigation much longer.

She took another sip of tea and turned to the final passage she had underlined in Professor Gross's *Handbook*.

We can in this connection learn much from the novelist [. . .] The villain will perhaps be presented to us at the outset gifted with every physical and intellectual good quality; under the mask of an honest man, he will insinuate himself into the heart of the ingenuous reader, until he finds that the author makes him speak with 'harsh' voice . . .

Well, thought Clara, Andrew certainly had insinuated himself into her heart – and possibly into Bob's too. If his crime was no more than that, then well and good. But . . . and she looked again at the cup . . . she needed to find out. She put down her own cup, pulled on some gloves and carefully picked up the metal vessel. Best she do this downstairs in the laboratory; then she could photograph the results and develop them immediately. Thereafter she would compare them to the existing photographs.

Just as she turned towards the lab door, the front doorbell rang. She considered for a moment ignoring it, but then thought it might be Roger Jennings. She had told the solicitor that she was coming to the house and he had said he would be in touch if there was any news from the magistrate. Perhaps there was! She put down the cup and headed to the door. But there on the doorstep was not Roger Jennings, but Andrew Ridpath.

Before she could act on her immediate impulse to slam and lock the door, Andrew stepped inside, speaking as he did.

'Oh Clara, thank goodness you're here! I popped into Jennings' office and the secretary said you'd left already but she thought you might possibly be here. And here you are! I'm so sorry,' he said, looking slightly dishevelled and anxious, quite different from the Andrew Ridpath she had so far come to know, 'but this can't wait until our dinner tonight.'

'I – well—' she said, 'I'm actually busy. It really will have to wait.'

'No, Clara, it won't,' he said, taking hold of her elbow and shutting the door firmly behind them. He took off his hat and put it on the banister knob at the bottom of the stairs.

Clara felt a lump of fear in her throat. What was she to do now? She considered running and locking herself in the laboratory or escaping through the kitchen door, but she wondered if she could really outrun him, and if she tried, what he would do.

Andrew ploughed on with his monologue, seemingly oblivious to her eyes flashing this way and that, seeking a way out, wishing she had the paring knife that was languishing in her handbag. She eyed the hat stand and the umbrella hanging there . . .

'You see,' said Andrew, 'I couldn't concentrate in my meeting. I kept thinking about how distant you became this morning and on the way home. It was so different to how you were with me last night. I suspected at first it was just regret for succumbing to our intimacy, but the more I thought about it, the more I've come to think it's more than that. Because, you see, the change in you was so sudden. And suddenly I realised exactly when it happened: it was when you saw my tattoo.'

Clara swallowed hard, her mind clawing to find an escape route, either physically or verbally. Might she make a run for the dining room? She could lock the door then escape through the window . . . He waited a moment and when she didn't immediately speak, he prompted her.

'It was the tattoo, wasn't it? What was it that bothered you about it?'

She dragged her eyes from the dining room door to meet his. 'It's – well – it's—' And she could think of nothing else to say other than the truth. 'It's because I've seen that tattoo before.'

His eyes narrowed, looking intently into hers. 'Where?'

'In – in – the photograph of Bob's lover. The one I told you about. He was lying naked on the bed, face down, but there was an identifying mark on his shoulder. It was your tattoo. The crescent moon on the full sun. You're Bob's lover, aren't you?'

Andrew took a step backwards and ran his hand through his hair. 'You think I'm *what*?'

Clara eyed the gap on either side of Andrew. Could she get through? But before she could make a move, he stepped towards her again. 'I can't believe you said that, Clara. Why would you think that?'

'Because of the tattoo! Obviously!'

Then, suddenly, he started to laugh. And it chilled Clara to the bone.

'I told the lads those tattoos would get us into trouble one day!'

'Lads?' she asked, confused.

'Yes, the lads I told you about. The six of us from school who joined the same unit in the war. The night before we all enlisted we went out together and got drunk. And we ended up at a Chinese tattoo parlour, getting the same tattoo. At the time it seemed like a great idea, but not so much in the morning.' He smiled at her, hoping, it seemed, for a smile back. It didn't come.

'So, there you have it,' he continued. 'There's more than just me with this tattoo. Like I told you, three of the lads are dead. But there's still me, Charlie Malone and Roger Jennings very much alive. And I can assure you, I was *not* your Uncle Bob's lover. If I were, would I have been foolish enough to go with you to Holy Island? What if the landlady had recognised me? I am *not* J. Smith. You must believe me, Clara.'

He stared intently into her eyes, all trace of humour gone. But there was no trace of malice either. Just a sincere desire to connect with her. To convince her. And with an enormous sense of relief, she realised she was convinced.

'I'm sorry, Andrew,' she said. 'But you must understand why I thought it was you.'

'Oh, I do. You were just responding to the evidence at hand.'

She nodded. 'Yes, I was. And now I need to look for other evidence and what it might mean. Because it's not just about who Bob's lover might be – either Charlie or Roger – but it's about whether one of them helped kill my uncle. Or if they didn't, if it was Jane Hobson. And if she – or they – did, why did they do it? Was it to stop him digging further into the Carousel Picture House fire? And did Humphrey Balshard put them up to it? Because that is still the theory I'm working with.' She finally rewarded him with a gentle smile. 'Will you help me, Andrew? To try to piece this all together?'

'Oh, I think that's all the piecing the two of you are going to do for now.'

Clara and Andrew looked up the stairs to the source of the voice. And there, on the first landing, with a gun trained on them both, was Roger Jennings, holding a .320 Webley Bulldog.

'That's my uncle's gun!' said Clara.

'Well observed, Miss Vale.'

'What the hell are you doing, Jennings? Put the gun away. You might hurt someone.' Andrew pushed Clara behind him.

Roger chuckled and walked slowly down the stairs, the gun still trained on the couple at the bottom. 'Don't be such a Boy Scout, Andy. Clara doesn't need your protection. Or should I rather say, your protection won't do her any good.'

'How have you got my uncle's gun?' demanded Clara. 'Did Inspector Davidson give it to you?'

Roger cocked his head to one side. 'There we have it again, those razor-sharp powers of observation and deduction. I saw it in the report you compiled too. Your uncle was good, but I have to hand it to you, Clara, you are definitely a chip off the old block. And that, unfortunately, has been your undoing. I couldn't possibly give that report to a magistrate after I saw what was in it. It's clear that it was just a matter of time until you got to the full truth.'

'The truth of what?' asked Andrew, squaring up to Roger.

'The truth that Roger was acting on behalf of Humphrey Balshard after all,' said Clara. 'My first instinct was right. You have been working to protect your biggest client against the investigation of your smaller client, my uncle. Isn't that right?'

'Correct,' said Roger, stopping on the bottom stair, which gave him a slight height advantage over Andrew. 'But it wasn't simply a matter of me protecting one client over another. That would be very foolish of me. However, Balshard has some unfortunate leverage over me, which could cause me to lose my licence – I shan't go into detail; one wouldn't want it getting out – but let's just say I couldn't afford *not* to do his bidding on this.'

Clara's eyes narrowed. 'You would even go as far as murder? Did you pay Jane Hobson to overdose my uncle on barbital? Did you pay her to kill him?'

A shadow of regret fell across Roger's face. 'No, I didn't pay her to kill him. I paid her to up his dose so that it would slow him down and tire him out. So he couldn't carry out a proper investigation. And then I paid the chemist to fudge the prescription. But the housekeeper overdid it, the stupid woman. *She* killed him, not me. And then she came up with this ridiculous story that she was his fiancée to try to get more money out of his estate. If she hadn't done that, you might not have started suspecting her. And neither would Charlie Malone.'

'Dr Malone suspects Hobson too?' asked Clara, her eyes flicking again to the umbrella on the hat stand.

'He does now. After you paid him a visit yesterday. By the way, I always suspected Charlie was a pansy. Never thought it of Bob, though. Each to their own, I suppose. But I digress. I telephoned Charlie after you left my office to ask if he would testify against your brother's contestation of the will if it came to it. He said he would. Which was a mixed bag for me. If Antony took over the business, it would get you off the case. Which was my initial plan when I anonymously tipped him off about how he could challenge the will.'

'So it wasn't Danskin then!' Clara took a tiny step back, edging towards the hat stand.

'No. He didn't call your brother. But he was the one who gave me the idea. You see, I'd heard he'd been telling people that Bob was confused before he died.'

'Why would he do that?'

Roger shrugged. 'He did a bit of work for Balshard too.'

'Was he involved in the picture house fires?' Another tiny step.

'No. He wasn't. But Balshard asked him to spread a few rumours. To undermine Bob's credibility.'

'What has any of this to do with Clara?' interjected Andrew. 'Please, Roger, let us go. This isn't who you are. I've known you all my life.'

Roger shook his head. 'No, Andy, I'm sorry, but you never really knew me at all.'

Then he turned back to Clara as she edged closer to the hat stand. He trained his gun on her. 'Stop right there. What are you planning to do? Stop a bullet with an umbrella?' He gave a cruel laugh. 'You won't give up, will you, Clara? Even if you no longer own the agency. You've come too far, and you'll want to see it to the end. In ordinary circumstances I would applaud you. But Charlie said something today that made up my mind. You have to be stopped. The sooner the better.'

'What did he say?' asked Clara, as Andrew's hand found hers and held it tight.

Roger noticed the hand-holding and smirked. But he carried on, without comment. 'Charlie asked me for a legal opinion about getting Bob's body exhumed. He said you and he had spoken about that yesterday. And I knew then that this whole thing had gone too far. Hobson I can pay off. I already have. She's left town, but you – and you,' he said, pointing the gun first at Clara and then Andrew, 'are more of a problem. But the problem ends here.'

'Yes, it does,' said Andrew as he released Clara's hand and threw himself at Roger. He knocked Roger off balance, but the solicitor still held onto the gun. The two men grappled as Clara lurched for the umbrella. But before she could reach it, the gun went off. Clara screamed as the men clutched one another until one of them fell to the floor, hand to his side.

'Andrew!' She fell to her knees beside him, his terrified eyes seeking hers.

'Get up!' barked Roger, his gun trained on her.

'He's hurt!'

'Leave him! Or I'll shoot you too.'

'You won't!'

'I bloody well will!' Roger grabbed her by the arm, dragged her up then pushed her down the hall towards the kitchen. She tried to turn to see if Andrew was all right. Roger slapped her across the face with his free hand and shoved her forward. She stumbled into the kitchen and Roger shut the door and locked it behind them.

'Right,' he said, pointing to the evidence on the table. 'Gather that lot up.'

Reluctantly, she did what she was told, hoping to buy time to think. 'What are you going to do with it?'

'Destroy it, of course. Now, put it in the stove. Then light it.'

'All right,' she said, 'but that's not all of it. There's more.'

'Where?'

'I'll tell you if you let me help Andrew.'

He raised the gun and pointed it between her eyes. 'You'll tell me now or I'll go out there and finish him off. I swear to God I will.'

Clara was shaking, but she managed to hold herself together. 'All right, it's down in the laboratory. If you wait here I'll go and get it for you.'

'Don't play me for a fool, Clara. Lead the way.'

Clara turned and walked towards the laboratory door. She reached in and pulled the light cord then led Roger down the flight of stairs.

'So what's this additional evidence?'

'More photographs. Of the fingerprints on the trunk that Horace Fender stood on when he was hanged. And I'm assuming if I took your prints, they would be a match.'

Roger snorted. 'Right again, Clara. Another unnecessary death – I swear to God I never expected any of this to go this far. I just meant to scare Fender into keeping quiet about his part of the deal.'

They stepped into the laboratory, Roger casting a dark shadow across the floor.

'That he set the fires at Balshard's behest?' asked Clara, her eyes whipping around the lab for a potential weapon.

'That's right. To get the Whittakers into trouble for flouting fire regulations. And to shut the business down. But it was never intended to kill anyone. Particularly not that lad. Everyone was supposed to get out the front door.' For a moment, Roger looked overcome with regret, and Clara wondered if she could appeal to his conscience. But then his eyes hardened.

'Stupid, stupid Horace. He was filled with remorse and wanted to confess all. I tried to talk him out of it, but he wouldn't listen. I was worried he would do something we'd all regret. And then I saw him outside the Salvation Army—'

'So it was you who followed us on the train!'

Clara's eyes fell on the hacksaw and the jar of sulphuric acid. Both just beyond reach.

Roger nodded and continued. 'When Fender saw you and Mrs Whittaker coming out from the Salvation Army, he followed you to the picture house. And I followed him. When you and Mrs Whittaker were busy in the main arena, he got inside. I collared him before he could get to you and took him up to the projection room. He was going to tell you and Mrs Whittaker everything. So in the end I didn't have a choice. I needed to keep him quiet, for Balshard's sake and mine. And it looked like you were on track to finding all that out. The scare tactics weren't enough – the bag-snatching, the break-ins, and as it turned out, not even the discovery of a hanging corpse . . .'

'The rope and the chloroform?'

He shrugged. 'I happened to have them on me.'

Clara shivered. 'What were you going to use them for?'

'I was planning on taking Fender out of action for a few days. To remove him from the scene.'

'So you did plan to kill him.' Clara's eyes continued ranging across the lab. There was a scalpel in that drawer over there . . .

Roger shook his head. 'No, no I didn't. I was going to just abduct him. To lock him up somewhere for a while. But then I realised that like you, Clara, he would never keep quiet. Even if his conscience didn't prompt him to speak, one day the drink would. He couldn't be trusted. Even though the deaths of Will Spencer and your uncle were not my fault, I was implicated in both of them. I'm the one who paid Fender on behalf of Balshard. I'm the one who paid Hobson to overdo your uncle's medicine . . .' His voice trailed off.

Clara turned to face him. He seemed to want to get everything out into the open. Which meant, she realised with a shudder, that he wouldn't let her live to tell the tale. But as long as he kept talking, it gave her more time to think of a way out of it. She swallowed hard and continued. 'So it was you who broke into the office and again at the hotel. Now that I think about it, you didn't actually break into the office, did you? You just used a spare set of keys. Just like you did to get into the house today. And the day you went to the office you had time to get there before me and Andrew. I remember, you left that meeting early, while Andrew and I wrapped up some business. The fingerprints I found on the filing cabinet drawer couldn't have been Andrew's because the villain left just a few minutes before we arrived, pushing Juju Levine to the floor. And that villain was you.'

The hard glint was back in Roger's eyes. 'It was. But this is getting tiresome. Now get that evidence for me or I'll take you upstairs and make you watch me put a bullet in your boyfriend's head.'

'All right,' said Clara, quickly, 'they're in here.' Clara pushed open the darkroom door. Roger followed her. And then, suddenly, she knew what she had to do. She grabbed a metal tray filled with Metol-hydroquinone, the developing fluid, and hurled the contents in Roger's face. He yelled, lowering his gun and wiping his face with his sleeve as the chemical seared his skin. She only had a few seconds to act. And she did. She swung back the heavy tray and smashed it across his head again and again.

Epilogue

Two weeks later

Her legs were lithe and long. The burnished orange of her bathing suit, cinched just above the knees, offset her lightly tanned arms and calves. Her thoughtful face was framed by a cloche sun hat, and if she could have seen herself she might have been reminded of the poster she had first seen on the train, advertising the holiday attractions of Whitley Bay. And today, just like on the poster, beach revellers played games or walked hand in hand, passing candy-striped tents, while children in knickerbockers, and bold young men in bathing vests, braved the cold North Sea.

Clara accepted a cup of lemonade with thanks from Jonny Levine, who was seated with his sister, Charlie Malone and Alice Whittaker on a picnic blanket. Alice watched her three children playing in the sand, her face free of the worry that Clara had grown accustomed to seeing etched into her features.

'So, explain to me what you did after you clobbered Roger Jennings,' said Jonny.

'I've already told you!' said his sister.

'I want to hear it from Clara, Juju, without your embellishment.'

'Embellishment? Heaven forbid I'd embellish anything!' said Juju, with mock offence.

Clara smiled at her new friends, enjoying being treated as 'one of the family'. 'Well, there's not much to tell, really. I whacked him a few times with the tray, to make sure he wasn't going to get up very easily, then I grabbed the gun and ran out of the laboratory. I locked him in then ran to see if I could help Andrew.'

'Oh, poor Mr Ridpath!' said Juju. 'He was so brave tackling that awful man with the gun. And to think he nearly died!'

'Yes, he did,' said Clara, seriously. 'They said at the hospital that if the ambulance had got to him just five minutes later he might not have made it. Isn't that right, Charlie?'

'It is,' said the doctor. 'Andy is very lucky to be alive.'

'And now? How's he doing?' asked Jonny.

'Much better,' said Charlie. 'I saw him yesterday and he'll be able to move to a nursing home in a few days. The operation to remove his spleen was a success, but it will still be a few weeks until he's properly on his feet.'

'And the wicked Roger?' asked Juju.

Clara rolled her eyes. 'Last I heard he's well on the road to recovery and will be transferred to a nearby prison on remand.'

'So what exactly are the charges against him?' asked Jonny.

'It's quite a list!' said Clara. 'The murder of Horace Fender. The attempted murder of me and Andrew. Conspiracy to commit arson resulting in the death of Will Spencer. Conspiracy to commit manslaughter in the death of my uncle. Then there's burglary and bribery . . . and probably more to come.'

'When is the court case?' asked Alice Whittaker, turning to join in the conversation.

'The last week in October,' said Clara. 'The Newcastle police tell me Jane Hobson was apprehended trying to get on a ferry to Amsterdam. She has spilt the beans, fully implicating Roger, who, of course, has implicated Humphrey Balshard.'

'Like rats on a ship!' Juju laughed.

Clara smiled. 'Quite. And Inspector Davidson and the fire inspector. Although, it turns out Jack Danskin was not involved – other than spreading nasty rumours about Bob. But nothing criminal as far as I've heard. And neither was poor old Barnaby Jennings, who I hear is devastated. Seems that he was completely in the dark about his son's criminal activities. And as for dear Dr Malone here, well, he is blaming himself for what happened to Bob, saying he should have acted on his suspicions earlier and raised the alarm.'

Charlie had confessed to her that he was indeed Bob's lover. That

Bob had referred to him as J – short for John Smith – to keep their liaison secret. Clara had sworn to respect their privacy and was doing her best not to divulge more than she had to in her interviews with the police. What Charlie told them was his own business. She turned to him and looked him directly in the eye. 'It's not your fault, Charlie, you have to believe that. Bob would not blame you either, of that I'm sure.'

Charlie nodded, unable to speak. Jonny gave him a comforting pat on the shoulder. 'Clara's right, Charlie, you mustn't blame yourself. And Bob would be proud of how you've helped Clara get to the bottom of the case.' Then he turned to Alice. 'What's happening with the insurance pay-out, Alice?'

The widow caught Clara's eyes and smiled. 'Well, thanks to Clara's detective work, a judge has now looked at the evidence and demanded that the insurance company reconsider their position. Balshard, who claims he knew nothing about the deaths of Fender or Bob, has agreed to the pay-out, as part of a plea deal to soften the charges against him. Although it looks like he'll still be charged with his involvement with the fires and the subsequent cover-up. So,' she said, 'leaning back on her elbows, it looks like the Paradise Picture House will open its doors again.'

'Oh, Alice!' said Juju, giving the younger woman a hug, 'I'm delighted for you!'

'Thank you.' She smiled. 'It's a huge relief. I'll also get an extra pay-out because of Jimmy's death. So I can now get his life insurance money as well as the insurance on the Carousel and the Paradise. We'll be able to buy a house here in Whitley Bay and the children can go back to their old school.'

'Will you be running the Paradise on your own?' asked Clara.

'I'll manage it on me own, but I'll be hiring help. Alfie Gill has already said he'll come back. And we can afford a couple of other ushers now too. You'll all have to come to the opening night! By then we'll have the new talkie projector from America. We'll probably open with the new Bulldog Drummond flick. Although Bulldog isn't a shadow on our own private detective: Miss Clara Vale.' Alice nodded gratefully to Clara, who smiled in return.

'Well, just tell us when and we'll be there!' gushed Juju. Then she looked at Clara. 'At least Jonny and I will. What have you decided, Clara? Will you stay up here or go back to London?'

Clara took a sip of her lemonade. 'Well, my brother's challenge to the will has been withdrawn. It seems that this whole affair has made it into the papers down south and my mother's friends have been congratulating her on her "brave daughter", and saying how proud they must be of me that I've tracked down my uncle's killer and am now a lady detective. My mother, of course, is more embarrassed than proud, but she's still enjoying the attention. So, I decided to write my parents a letter, and said that if they didn't want it to come out that Mother had pretended she was sick so she didn't have to go to her only brother's funeral, nor that they had encouraged Antony to challenge the will and do me out of my inheritance, then perhaps my father could find it in his heart to write a letter to the bank.

'So,' she continued, leaning back on her elbows and crossing her ankles, 'I am now the proud owner of Wallace Enquiry Agency, a house – and laboratory – on St Thomas' Crescent, and finally have access to all Bob's funds.' She chuckled. 'I feel like I'm starring in my very own movie.'

Juju clapped her hands in delight. 'Does that mean you'll be staying? And carrying on as a lady detective?'

Clara turned to her new friends and smiled broadly. 'Actually, Juju, I think it does.'

THE END

Historical Notes

On 31st December 1929 the Glen Cinema in Paisley, Scotland, caught fire during a matinee performance, with almost one thousand children inside. Many of the children tried to escape through back doors that should have been left open but turned out to be locked. Seventy-one children died that day and forty were injured. The ensuing investigation implicated the picture house manager, who admitted to sometimes locking the doors during the show to stop children sneaking in without paying. The subsequent enquiry found that the fire had been started by a short circuit when a metal box containing film stock was placed on top of a battery in the projection room. The tragedy was made worse by the limited number of exits, insufficient attendants and overcrowding. The manager, Charles Dorward, was put on trial for culpable homicide, but found not guilty. This was my inspiration for *The Picture House Murders*. I relocated the event to Whitley Bay, brought it forward six months and decided to not let any children die (if only we could erase tragedies like this in real life so easily).

My inspiration for a Tyneside movie mogul buying up small picture houses and theatres came from the real-life Dixon Scott, great-uncle of the Hollywood directors Ridley and Tony Scott. He was the founder of the much-loved and still operational Tyneside Cinema on Pilgrim Street, Newcastle. Dixon, however, was nothing like the wicked Humphrey Balshard, and was respected by all who knew him.

Another historical marker is the North East Coast Exhibition.

This was a world fair, opened on 14th May 1929 by the Prince of Wales and attended by over four million people by the time it closed on 26th October 1929. As I describe in the book, it was aimed at building investor confidence in the North East of England as a thriving commercial and industrial region, while celebrating its pioneering engineering heritage. The North East had suffered greatly in the years after WWI with the decline of its shipbuilding industry and a series of coal-mining strikes reaching their zenith in 1926. It was hoped that initiatives like the North East Coast Exhibition would help reinvigorate the region. And that looked like it might very well happen until events on Wall Street in New York between September and October 1929 – with the biggest sell-off of shares in US history on 29th October (Black Tuesday) – would send shockwaves around the world.

As we leave Clara and her friends on the beach in mid-September 1929, they have no idea of what is to come – but you can read about it, dear reader, in book two of the Miss Clara Vale Mysteries, *The Pantomime Murders*.

Finally, a word on the financial rights of women at the time. As noted in the book, the law of male-preference primogeniture was abolished in Britain in 1925. Prior to this an inheritance would go to the eldest, closest male relative to the deceased, even if this meant bypassing a closer female relative. Financially though, women still struggled for monetary independence, with most banks refusing to allow them to hold bank accounts in their own name without a male relative's permission, and sometimes, even then, their applications would be declined. It was only in 1975 that this practice was outlawed, and it took a further five years, until 1980, for women to be able to apply for credit on their own.

On a personal note, when I was researching this aspect of the book in February 2021, my daughter turned sixteen. I took her into Lloyds Bank on Grey Street, Newcastle, the same bank Clara deals with, and transferred an account I'd opened for her as a baby into her own name. One hundred years before that, in 1921, my great-grandmother, Mary Jane Gill, then forty-one, opened a bank account after the murder of her husband near the village of Clara Vale. She needed a letter of permission from her brother to do so.

Acknowledgements

The start of a new book and a new series, featuring a new character, is a very exciting time in an author's life. However, it goes without saying that I could not have done this on my own. The words are mine; the ideas are mine, and the long months plugging away at the keyboard or doing research are all added to my tally. But they have not been alone. Firstly, I would like to thank my dogged agent, Sara Keane, for sticking with me through a few false starts, including a detour into another book that was written but that we mutually decided not to take any further.

Many thanks to my publisher Cara Chimirri at Embla Books, who fell in love with Clara Vale when she first met her and then introduced her to her colleagues. What a delight it is to work with someone who is as interested in the period as I am – including the fashion!

Thanks to my friend and colleague at the Crime Writers' Association, Dea Parkin, who encouraged me when I was disheartened and struggling to find time to write. Thanks also to my oldest (as in longest!) writing friend, the author Gill D'Achada, whose friendship and prayers have supported me for twenty-five years – and counting.

And for longer than that (thirty years and counting!) my thanks and love go to my husband Rod, who has not let me give up when I had so many reasons to do so. For my daughter, Megan, too, who starts a new chapter of her life just as this book is being published.

In terms of research, I am indebted to Michael Chaplin and his book *Come and See: the beguiling story of the Tyneside Cinema* (New

Writing North, Newcastle upon Tyne, 2011) for his fascinating introduction to early cinema in the North East of England and how music halls and theatres were turned into moving picture houses.

And finally, to you, dear reader, for picking up this book and choosing to read it. I hope it gives you many hours of pleasure. Enjoy!

About the Author

Fiona Veitch Smith is a lover of Golden Age mysteries and historical fiction and has been shortlisted for the CWA Historical Dagger. She has worked as a journalist, a university lecturer and a communications manager, and mentors new novelists. She grew up in Northumberland, then spent her teens and twenties in South Africa. She now lives in Newcastle upon Tyne.

Visit http://www.claravalemysteries.com/ for information about the author and the world of Miss Clara Vale.